THE KIND OF WESTERN I'D LIKE TO READ

THE KIND OF WESTERN I'D LIKE TO READ

PART FOUR

A TREE OF LIFE

BUC KEENE

XULON PRESS

Xulon Press
2301 Lucien Way #415
Maitland, FL 32751
407.339.4217
www.xulonpress.com

Unless otherwise indicated, Scripture quotations taken from the
King James Version (KJV) – *public domain.*

Printed in the United States of America.

ISBN-13: 9781545600191

Hope deferred maketh the heart sick:
but when the desire cometh,
*it is **a tree of life**.*

Proverbs 13:12

Acknowledgments

I WISH TO EXPRESS MY THANKFULNESS and appreciation to the Lord for His inspiration and guidance on this project. Honestly... there were times when I was wondering where this stuff was coming from... I had no idea I was going to write some of this like I did.

And to my sweet wife Janis. (No, she is not Suzanne... but she certainly informs her!) You have stood by me through the thick and thin of our journey. Thank you Sweetheart, I love you... you're the best.

And thank you to my cousin, Barbara Yell for her preliminary work, and to Martha Ireland; thanks to you both for your patient copy-editing and input for this yarn... you ladies are grand.

Finally, I would be remiss if I didn't give an appreciative nod to a particular red horse named *"Rowdy,"* who fastidiously advised me on the likes of *"Lightfoot,"* his literary twin.

Buc

Editorial Review of Book Three:

....Peopled with an enormous cast of complex, relatable characters....

....Well-crafted, deep, funny, engaging and broad in both physical and emotional landscape. A very fun read.
Manuscript's Strengths of Book Three of the series:

- Immediate sense of time and place, and an immersion into the southwest desert landscape... in just one page. Clearly, this is an experienced craftsman.
- Voice is clear and intelligent—pages turn fast. Language is fresh: "Tye took to it like a goat to a garbage dump." "Meaner than a two-striped snake with a toothache." Dialogue is clever and character appropriate: "Why don't you just sit down and I will quit hitting your nose?" Wonderful!
- Characters are well drawn and oddly unique— *oddly* because characters in a Western almost *have* to come from Central Casting; but here, even minor characters have at least a tidbit of individuality, and that makes all the difference. The first scene with Tye and Penny, especially, is a masterpiece of meticulous characterization.
- If all writers used at least the unspoken title of "The Kind of [insert genre] I'd Like to Read," the world

of popular fiction would be a much happier place. It demonstrates an intent to tell a good story, not to just write what sells. Bravo.

- *Excerpt from Part Four* whets readers' appetites, especially since it's written in first person. Great idea to include it here AND not immediately pick up with the Colt/Suzanne/Sonny disaster.
- This is a story about people, not land squabbles or frontier gambling or trail riding—people and the complex and unique relationships among them. This is another attribute that adds to the verisimilitude.

Author's Introduction

Part Four

SOMETIMES COMING TO THE END OF A story is like saying goodbye to an old friend. It certainly feels that way with *Part Four* of this series. I am grateful for the interest folks have shown in this tale and the urging of my readers to get it done. Rarely have I had such a sense of gratification as is felt with completing part four: .... *"A Tree Of Life."* I know it took longer than it should have, but like fine wine, some aging was necessary, partly because I did not want to be rushed into bringing it to the right conclusion, and partly due to some curves life threw at me.

I found a good deal of enjoyment, after the fact, in the creation of both *"Lightfoot's and Pearl's,"* characters, never knowing either would be as delightful as they turn out to be. They are the result of doing (writing) the next thing, sorta giving them their head as it were, only to find them "stealing the show." Fun stuff.

Maybe I shouldn't admit it, but there was a lot of wandering around in this series—but on purpose. It's my own rendition of the *"Larry Bebop"* game, played on paper. What's the *"Larry Bebop"* game, you say? You're sitting around the campfire with a bunch of buddies, family members, in-laws, or outlaws; whatever the case may be, and someone starts by telling a story where Larry Bebop is put into an irretrievable situation. Think "*Indiana Jones*" here. He then passes the story to the person next to him, and that person is required to come up with some means of retrieving old Larry Bebop and then putting him into another irretrievable situation; before passing it on, etc. You can come up with some pretty innovative stuff like this. Who noticed how many times poor Colton was hit in the head before he got amnesia?

A number of folks wanted me to continue on with this saga, and I admit it was a temptation. There were a lot of different ways this yarn could spread out, and some great characters to develop, but I think I'll quit while I'm ahead, and start on something else. I will probably keep writing westerns—that 'n humor are what seem to animate me.

Finally, I hope you find a way to enjoy the smack of boots into the stirrup, and the jingle of spurs, as you swing a leg over the cantle, and slide into smooth saddle leather, even if it is only in your imagination. For those of you who have been there, you'll know what I mean. So, saddle up and hit the trail with *Part Four* of, *"The Kind of Western I'd Like to Read… "A Tree of Life."* I think you'll enjoy the ride.

Buc Keene

OTHER XULON BOOKS
by BUC KEENE

The Kind of Western I'd Like to Read
East of the Pecos
Part One

*The Kind of Western I'd Like to Read
Hope Deferred
Part Two

*The Kind of Western I'd Like to Read
Desire Realized
Part Three

*** Submitted as entrants to The Western Writers
Silver Spur Award in Best New Series Category.**

Table of Contents

Chapter One—Lightfoot 1
Chapter Two—Howard and Pearl 16
Chapter Three—Runnin' for the Rimrock 34
Chapter Four—After The Fall 52
Chapter Five—Fathers and Daughters 64
Chapter Six—Chopin' Wood 78
Chapter Seven—The Great Stampede 101
Chapter Eight—The Johnson and Carol Outfit 118
Chapter Nine—Pearl Comes Home 139
Chapter Ten—Waistman, Kemp and Runs-
    With-Horses 158
Chapter Eleven—Dodge City and Abilene 178
Chapter Twelve—The Buffalo Hunters and the
    Gambler 195
Chapter Thirteen—Kiowa Winter Camp 207
Chapter Fourteen—The Girls, The Bull,
    and the Englishman 226
Chapter Fifteen—Trailin' to Colorado 244
Chapter Sixteen—Bodalk Inago—The
    Buffalo Man 265
Chapter Seventeen—Colorado Goldfields 278
Chapter Eighteen—A Long Trail 297
Chapter Nineteen—Rendezvous 318
Chapter Twenty—South Park City 337
Chapter Twenty-One—Denver and More 359
Chapter Twenty-Two—Gun Smoke in the Rockies . 379
Chapter Twenty-Three—Desire or Disaster 398
Chapter Twenty-Four—Through it All 420
Chapter Twenty-Five—I Will Arise And Go To
    My Father. 440

Epilog 459
End Notes 463

CHAPTER ONE

Lightfoot

Staked Plains of Texas, October 1870

I'D BEEN RIDING FOR SEVERAL DAYS AND time had sorta slipped on by me; besides, it wasn't like my newly acquired "give-a-dash" was busted, it's just that the pony I was ridin' was looking sideways back at me and I could tell he was wondering on whether or not to dump my sorry carcass and go find some grass, and that made me smile. It felt like that smile might'a cracked my face 'cause there hadn't been much to smile about for a while, but the horse never paid that no mind—he just snorted and stretched his neck to get me to let up on the reins some.

"What's your problem?" I said, "you think filling your belly is the only thing that matters?"

The horse didn't answer, but I could tell what he was thinking and that got me to thinking too. I hadn't eaten either, and my stomach was tryin' to get my attention by rubbing against my backbone like a dead chinaberry tree branch on the side of a house. So I started thinking about food, and of course bacon and eggs came to mind, and I could almost smell 'em. I'd left in quite a hurry and the way I had been feeling then crowded out any thoughts of food, as well as a lot of other things for that matter, but it's funny how eatin' will catch up to you eventually. I was sure hankerin' for some bacon and eggs.

I loosened my grip on the reins and let my horse drift off to the left towards a line of green a mile or so away. I figured maybe he smelled water, and since I wasn't really going anywheres in particular that direction seemed as good as any other, who knows—maybe I might scare up a jackrabbit or something.

Some folks think this here Llano Estacado is a barren desert or high plains devoid of life, but it isn't. There's snakes, and lizards, and horned toads, a few miscellaneous birds, the occasional scrawny road runner or jackrabbit, along with scruffy coyotes, and flea-bit wolves, to chase 'em. There's still thousands of buffalo out here, too, but they'll soon be done for by the buffalo hunters at the cockeyed rate they're shootin' 'em. I reckon there's still elk, and antelope, and an occasional white-tail, or two, hanging round in some of the bottoms, but you gotta be quieter than this clod-hopping nag I was ridin' if you're going to sneak up on one of them. Of course, this is a favorite haunt of the Comanche as well, it's no wonder they're so danged mean, what with a menu like that and all.

Some call this country the "Staked Plains," and I'm not sure why. I'd heard maybe it had to do with how the Spanish, or somebody, had tried to cross it and drove down stakes to mark the way to see how far they had come and maybe to find their way back, but I don't know if there's any truth to that or not. Personally, I suspect it got its name from the streaks of color in the cliffs and hills here 'bouts, but it seems to me they'd a called it the "Streaked Plains" then, not the "Staked Plains." Anyway, if it was up to me, they could call it the 'roof of hell,' cause that's what ridin' across it was like.

The horse picked his way down through a cut-bank to a jumble of brush and willows that were making a gallant effort to look a little green and fast losing the battle. He then broke out into an old buffalo wallow that was several yards across and all grown up with prairie grass. From the green of it, water must have been somewhere nearby. The red horse near jerked the reins from my hand as he buried his nose in the grass. I let go, grabbed my empty canteen, swung a leg over the saddle horn and slid down.

I'd no sooner hit the ground than my pony lifted his head, still chewing grass around the bit, and started for the other side of the wallow with the bridle reins tangled around his ears and hung up in his mane.

"Now hold on hoss, you ain't fixin' to leave me a foot out here are ya?"

I hadn't had the horse to long, and had not even come up with a handle for him yet, so I wasn't real certain if I could catch him, should he get off to rambling ways. The last thing I needed was to be left a foot out in this "no-man's land." I hurried after him, but he stopped after pressing through some buffalo berry brush, to shove his muzzle into a small pool of water. He sucked it dry faster than the piddling little creek could fill it. He'd snort and blow through his nostrils and lift his dripping mug until another mouthful or two would flow in, and then suck that up too. I watched him until he finally had enough and turned back to the wallow and cropping grass.

It weren't much of a creek, but this late in October it was a wonder it was running at all. Green scum ribboned the edges of the flow and some had dried on the exposed creek bed, while most of the mud from the streambed was cracked and dry from the hot sun. I walked over to the edge and found a smooth-running place and stooped to fill my canteen, then took a long pull of the tepid water. I'd tasted better—a lot better, and some worse. The bitter bite of alkali wasn't too bad, though there was a heavy taste of moss—or something like it. At least it was wet and there were no dried skeletons of dead critters around so I figured it wasn't poison.

I looked at the horse contentedly grazing, and he was still on his feet, so I took a couple more swallows of the water, shutting off my nose like you do so's you can't taste, and had a good drink. Well—had a drink anyway, then listened to my stomach gurgle and growl as it renewed its efforts on my backbone.

I refilled the canteen and started off up the little stream to see what was for supper, thinking, if the Injuns could hunt and gather, so could I. Right then and there I decided against becoming a member of the local redskin band though, all I could come up with was a couple of little leaf walnuts and a handful of buffalo berries, the last of which I spit out as soon as I put 'em in my mouth, once they turned to tasting like soap. They reminded me of the girl I'd fed a couple to a few years back, and since I didn't want to think about her, I chucked the rest of them into the brush and went looking for a rabbit or prairie chicken, anything with a little meat on its bones.

All I saw was a few little birds flitting about in the bushes and cheeping at me. I knew it was way past nesting season so there'd be no eggs, but I'd heard the Injuns would eat birds and remembered somewhere in the Bible it said something about a sparrow being sold for a farthing—whatever that was, and although I'd never thought about it before, what would they be buying sparrows for, if it wasn't to eat 'em. I began to look at the little brown birds in a new light. After several unsuccessful attempts to bean one of the little critters with a rock, I gave up in frustrations.

"Who wants to eat a dad-burned tweety-bird anyway," I grumbled, and continued making my way on up the creek bed, my stomach a growling. I looked at the westering sun and thought, ma would be putting supper on the table about now. The idea of her cooking set "Mr. Stomach" to complaining in more earnest, but it was no use, I for sure was never going to stick my feet under that table again.

I suppose I would-a gone hungry for another night if I hadn't near stepped on that rattler. It struck, but surprising myself, I was even quicker and all's it got was a mouthful of dirt before I smashed its head with a rock and stood watching the twisting, writhing body until it lay still.

I hesitated. They say, "necessity is the mother of invention," but I'd never eaten rattler before. I'd heard it tasted like chicken, Pops uses to say that. He was the grizzled old ranch hand that'd been on the place since before I was even born, and he always sounded like he knew what he was talkin' about—he wouldn't steer me wrong, and I like chicken. I picked up the snake, pulled my belt knife, and lopped off its head, then carried it back down to the spot where I'd left the horse.

The red horse lifted his head when he saw me and chuckled in his throat, then went back to cropping grass.

"Wha'd ya think, I'd done gone off and left ya?" I said. He just kept right on eating—like a horse—and I figured, *that figures.* I skinned out the rattler, cleaned the carcass, and cut the meat into several long pieces, then washed them well in the creek. Finding some dry mesquite and a bunch of dead leaves, I soon had a little fire kindled, and then sat around waiting impatiently while the meat broiled on green willow sticks that I had stuck in the ground around the coals. I guess it was more black than golden-brown when I finally had them cooked to my satisfaction—I wanted to be sure it was done, since you can't be too careful cooking up snake. I decided to think of it as chicken instead, you know, so it would be more appetizing, and then took a skinny piece of *"chicken"* and gingerly bit it off the willow stick. It was hot and tasted mostly like… well… like burnt chicken with too much mesquite smoke on it. The next thing I knew, there was no more *"skinny chicken"* left and my stomach was happy.

I stomped out the rest of the fire, splashed some water on the ashes, then walked over to where the red horse was chomping grass and I was just about to grab hold of the bridle, when he head-shied and lunged away from me a few steps.

"What's the matter with you, you jackassed, merry-go-'round dropout? Come here!"

The horse dipped his nose to the grass snuffling while I walked over. Once again, he moved off, trotting to the opposite side of the wallow.

"You jughead," I said, "I was just going to take that bridle off so you wouldn't have to be eatin' around the bit, but have it your way." I walked back to the stream looking for a shady spot and thinking about cooling off.

"I wonder if there's a hole in this stream big enough to get wet in?" I said it out loud and the horse nickered back at me. "You never mind, I ain't talkin' to you," I called back. I decided to explore up the creek a little farther since the country seemed a little flatter off that direction, and I suppose I traveled a half mile or so up the creek bottom before I found what I was looking for. As it turned out, I found a whole lot more than what I was looking for as well.

First of all, I found a nice pool of water, mostly covered with green scum. It was backed up behind a man-made rock and mud dam that was two to three feet high, with a stone-lined spillway on one side. Someone had planted a couple of chinaberry trees near what had once been a little log cabin, but now lay in a charred and weathering ruin with wild mistletoe and morning glory vines running over it. A few scraggly fruit trees struggled for life, the dry irrigation ditches at their base a mute testimony to their hardiness. I was delighted to find a few red and yellow apples hanging from some live branches on a couple of the trees. Hurrying over, I picked a big red one, rubbed it on the front of my shirt and bit into it.

"Lord that's good," I said, enjoying the taste with no thought of a prayer, while the cool juice from the crunchy fruit ran down my throat. I had forgotten just how good an apple could be.

I walked around what had been the yard of the homestead and read the mute testimony of what had happened here. "I'll bet the Comanche found them and that was all she took. Too bad... they had a nice little start here." Walking around to the upstream side of the place, I found just beyond the stunted fruit trees what had been a garden area, and nestled down in the grass was a whole patch of both watermelons and muskmelons. A tiny trickle of water still ran a course beside the vines before it eventually ran off and dried up in the sunbaked earth. Some of the melons appeared lush and ripe.

I hauled out my belt knife and hacked off the vine from a big, long watermelon and packed it over to a grassy spot in the shade of the chinaberry. I sat down and sliced it open. Now I like watermelon, and I particularly like it on a hot, and dry dusty day like this one. In fact, I can't think of anything more satisfying than a cold, red, juicy slice of melon on the best of days, let alone today. It felt like the ultimate reward for trekking, Lord knows how long, across that ol' Llano, and when I popped open that melon and carved out that juicy red heart, I practically foundered in the sweetness of it all. Something revived in me a little, and I decided maybe there were some things left worth living for after all, even if people were no dashed good.

"Watermelon's good," I sighed, "it won't let you down." I scoffed then at my own cynicism; I'd been reduced to looking to watermelon for the meaning of life. 'Course I had thought at one time there was a whole lot more than this, but I'll be hornswoggled if I was going to let any of that stuff intrude now. This was just too good.... too sweet. I squelched the rising ache in my gizzard and concentrated on the sparkling pink drops of watermelon juice running down my arm and dripping from my elbow.

After a while I stood to my feet and eyed a clear spot of water out in the middle of the pond. Shucking my clothes, I pushed aside the green scum and waded out to float and rinse off the sticky watermelon juice. The water was cool and refreshing and I soaked for over an hour, just back-floating and squirting little geysers of water up in the air through my teeth and watching 'em splash back down. I was probably a little colder than I wanted to be when I finally sloshed to shore and stared down with some embarrassment at the fancy tooled leather gun belt with its silver studded holster and the pearl handled Colt. The matching silver concho belt, hat band and fancy silver spurs on my new black boots piled next to the black jeans and shirt, were a reminder of the anticipated impression I'd vainly hoped to make. I felt my ears burn and the sinking in my gut for the thousandth time, before I could shut it down and get back to recalling the merits of water-melon. Watermelon and a cool swimming hole… and red apples. Red apples and diamondback chicken. I scoffed again and turned to put on my duds.

I was just cinching up the gun belt 'round my waist when I heard a noise behind me, and being a might jumpy, I whirled in a flash to face the unknown, my gun in hand. From the brush downstream, my saddle horse appeared and walked over to rub his forehead against my shoulder.

"Huh!" I scolded, "so now you want to make up, do you?" I turned my back on him and walked a few feet away to stand with arms folded. The horse came over and stood behind me and when I made no response, he pushed me with his nose, making me lose my balance.

"No!" I said, still refusing to turn to him. I walked another five steps away before stopping to see what he would do. The gelding walked over, nickered low in his throat as if to say he was sorry, and rested his chin on my shoulder.

"Okay, if you promise to never do that again, I'll forgive you." I reached up and patted him on the nose.

"Looky here at what I found," I said, and led him over to the remains of the big melon I'd cut the heart out of. The horse stuck his nose into the rind and sniffed it a few times and then began to eat the rest of the melon, rind and all.

"You know, you're not such a bad fella when you wanna be, what'll I call you? I can't keep callin' you 'horse,' why half the broomtails in Texas are liable to show up. What about Lightfoot, you think that'd be alright? You got those white socks on your feet, and I reckon that name would suit ya. You like that?" The horse nickered again and kept right on crunching watermelon rind. I patted his neck and began to reconsider; "Maybe chow hound would be better, wha-da-ya think?" He didn't answer, probably because he, too, understood the merits of watermelon.

I got to looking around and decided this place wasn't half bad, maybe I'd just camp out here for a few days and enjoy the melons. I went ahead and pulled the saddle off ol' Lightfoot and then, having second thoughts on the contrariness of some nags, I took a piece of rope from my saddle bags and fashioned a set of rude hobbles around the sorrel's front feet. You'd a thought I'd ax murdered his mother from the look he gave me. Snorting his displeasure loudly, he moved off to the other side of the yard, lifted his tale and broke wind in my general direction, then calmly proceeded to crop grass and ignore me altogether.

I took the insult in stride, thinking a horse with an attitude was the least of my problems, but then that got me to skirting around those other problems like a kid with knee pants in a patch of poison oak. All that stuff I'd left behind me, and I doubted anyone was ridin' up my back trail and haulin' it all along with 'em, but still, a fella in my position couldn't be too careful, you never can tell when someone or something will jump out at 'cha and booger up your whole day. Right now, I figured maybe I didn't have no problems after all, 'cept where my next meal was coming from. There was a little gold left in my saddle bags, but you can't eat that, and there sure wasn't no general stores around, so I might just as well get busy and set some rabbit snares. Rabbit tastes like chicken too, 'cept with jackrabbit, it's more like chicken that's been swimming in sagebrush tea.

It was too bad I didn't have a little salt. A little salt, and maybe pepper too, but I'd lit a shuck in such an all fired hurry there was a lot of things that got left behind, most of which I was well shut of, or so I keep tellin' myself... still—I wished I had some salt. "First chance I get, I'm gonna get me some and keep it in my saddle bags; pepper too," I said.

I'd been living the good life for about three days when it began to cloud up in the west and a stiff breeze came up. I figured it was gonna blow some and started looking around to see what kind of cover I might find. I wasn't too keen on getting caught out in a West Texas hail storm, and from the look of what was brewing on the horizon, that was just what was coming my way. The scrubby little trees and brush along the stream didn't offer much in the way of protection and so it looked like my best bet was the two chinaberry trees in the old homesteader's yard. I headed for the nearer tree, dragging my saddle along with me, and wondered why I pictured the homesteader as an old man. Funny how we form impression, I thought briefly as I hunkered down on the lea side of the tree and tried to juggle the saddle over my noggin without smashing my hat. Just because this homestead was old, didn't mean the homesteader was. Chances were he never had time to get old.

I looked over at Lightfoot and called to the red horse. "If you don't want your sorry carcass pounded into a puddin', you better get it under that other tree pronto." The horse just lifted his head, pricked his ears towards me and then went back to chewin' grass with his tail to the wind.

The sky grew darker and then you could hear it coming. It was roaring towards me like a stampeding herd of loco buffalo, and when I peeked around the tree trunk, I saw a dirty, gray wall of clouds and dust pushing tumbleweeds and flying debris ahead of it. It was stretched from earth to sky and was heading straight for me.

I pulled my neckerchief up over my face to where just only my eyes could see out and reached to adjust the saddle over my head once more, then closing my eyes I braced myself. Something bumped against the saddle, nearly knocking it from its perch, and I popped my eyes open to see Lightfoot, he apparently had second thoughts about the storm. The fool horse was under my tree and was actually trying to get his head in under the saddle with me.

"What's the matter with you, change your mind?"

The horse nickered and then gave a short squeal as the first, walnut sized, and I mean big walnuts, not those piddling little leaf ones, smacked him on his rump, and then the storm closed in around us. I shut my eyes as the wind and dust swirled around and the hail stones pelted down. The tree blocked the worst of it but branches and leaves were falling and crashed around and enough ice got through to pummel Lightfoot pretty good, if his squealing and dancing around was any indication. All I got was some smashed fingers until I finally had enough sense to let go of the saddle skirts and get 'em back in underneath. Course when I let go, the saddle did smash my hat some, and that was a dashed shame.

Most of the dust and dirt had passed, being swept along ahead of the storm, and now just the roar of the frigid wind and crash of hail engulfed us. I opened my eyes and got the shock of my life—well—maybe, the second or third most shock of my life anyway. I was staring through the shroud of hail and rain at the hazy figure of an Indian hiding under the other chinaberry tree.

For a minute there, I thought I was a goner and letting the saddle drop I jerked my six gun and held it on the savage. I was about to plug 'im when I realized that the Indian wasn't paying any attention to me at all. He was so busy trying to hold his horse still and crawl underneath it and the chinaberry to escape the hail, that he either didn't know, or didn't care that I was even there. About that time a hailstone managed to free-fall through the battered canopy of my chinaberry tree and struck me on the end of my nose. I let out a yowl, dropped my gun in my lap and scrambled to haul my saddle back up into place. I looked over at the Injun who had managed to get his horse calmed down enough to huddle underneath it again, and I'll be hornswaggled if it didn't look like he was grinning at me. He hollered something in Injun at me over the roar of the storm, and I got the distinct impression it was a rather snide remark. I had a sudden impulse to pick up my shootin' iron and teach him some manners, but then I saw him get beaned on one of his big ears that was stuck out too far from under his horse, and when he screeched and jumped up to smack the underside of his pony, well, that set the horse to dancin' around again and the redskin to scrambling for cover once more.

When he was finally crouched under the nervous animal, he looked daggers at me and rubbed his ear. It seemed to glow redder than the rest of him by at least twice as much, and I met his gaze with the biggest, toothiest grin I could muster, just to show my appreciation for his clowning around.

"Bet that smarts," I hollered.

The Indian made some sort of rude gesture in evident contempt, and then just sat there studying me, his hands fingering a bow laying on the ground at his feet. He had the dress and scalp lock of a Comanche, and looked to be around my own age. It was obvious he held no fear of me or my weapons.

Well, I don't know how long that storm lasted with us both just sitting there sizing each other up, but it must have been close to half an hour before the hail finally let up and the worst of the storm moved on east, leaving behind a steady drizzle. It was cold and uncomfortable, and I needed to find a bush pretty badly, so was lookin' around, fixin' to regain my feet, when I glanced back over to the other chinaberry tree. The Indian was gone. I don't know how he did it, one moment he was there and the next he was gone, vanished, disappeared into thin air— well actually, the air wasn't all that thin, in fact it was actually kinda thick with all that rain and mist and ground fog creepin' up and settling in.

I felt my scalp prickle… you know… like it does when you hear things go bump in the night and you know no one's there? The storm had neutralized us for a brief spate of time, but we were still mortal enemies, and I knew the Comanche would be looking to count coup on me any second. Even now he was probably sneaking up behind my chinaberry or drawing his bow from the cover of the buffalo brush to pin an arrow in my brisket. My weapons were just too good a prize for him to ignore and it had me speculating on which way to dodge.

Lightfoot nickered then, and when I looked at him, I saw his ears pricked forwards, he was staring off to the east. An answering whinny came from the brush and scrub downstream, and then I glimpsed the retreating form of the Comanche as he rode away, following the path of the storm.

"That's about the queerest deal I've run into in a while," I mused, "wonder why he never made his play?" Of course, I was glad he hadn't, but I was thinking it was probably time for me to move on anyway, I'd about wore out my welcome around here and besides, between me and the horse, the melons and apples were about all gone.

I was studying the funny looking long shadow the setting sun was casting, off 'ol Lightfoot and me out onto the prairie in front of us as we trotted along, and amused by the long, spindly legs of the shadow horse, and the disproportionately tall shadow rider, that was me. I was sorta absently wondering silly things like; "what if that shadow were to suddenly break away from the horse and me and go galloping off across the range without us?" It was the kinda thing my older brother used to say, but then he'd add that, *"You would die, 'cause you can't live without your shadow."* He'd say stuff like that, and of course that got me to thinking about him, and thinking about him got me to thinking about her and—well, I just didn't want to spend so much as a "tinker's darn," visiting either thought, so I said to the horse, "Lightfoot, can't you come up with something more interesting for me to occupy my attention with than your goofy shadow?"

Lightfoot said nothing, but I could tell he knew I was staring at that point on the top of his head between his ears, for they began to alternately twitch back and forth and I could just imagine what he was thinking.

Why doesn't this tub a lard lose some weight? Or maybe, *how about trading places and I ride you for awhile and you loan me your spurs while you're at it?* The sense of humor of this nag amazes me. Imagine me letting him use my spurs, that's near as bad as messing with a fellers hat.

Suddenly the sorrel's ears pricked up and he lifted his head and whinnied, and from down in a low coulee, some fifty yards away, came an answering whinny. I looked down to see a wagon and a couple of horses sitting next to a bunch of scrub oak. It looked like a back wheel was busted, and there was a big man and a kid standing there lookin' at it and then at me 'n Lightfoot. I eared back the hammer on the .44 when I saw the fat man haul a lever action out of the wagon and point it in my general direction.

"Rest easy, mister, I'm friendly," I called and nudged Lightfoot in the ribs. The horse grunted and then started down the slope towards them.

CHAPTER TWO

Howard and Pearl

Somewhere on the Llano Estacado, Fall 1870

THE FELLER LOOKED TO BE ABOUT FIFTY or so and gave me a surly scowl, then set the rifle back on the seat of the wagon after I holstered the Colt. He then turned to the kid and growled, "I told you to pile up those rocks under that axle, do I have to tan your hide again?"

I looked at the kid and was surprised to see the sullenest child I think I've ever seen. The kid was probably around ten or eleven and couldn't have weighed more'n seventy—maybe eighty pounds soakin' wet. He was dressed in shabby, old overalls, a shirt full of holes and wore shoes a couple a sizes too big. It was a cinch the old man hadn't gone bust buying clothes for the young'un. The face was dirty and the hair longish and looked like it had been hacked off with a butcher knife. As the kid bent to wrestle a rock that I'd a had trouble with under the wagon, I noticed his eyes. Talk about no expression, they were about the deadest, flattest-looking pair of eyes I'd ever seen. He looked as if he could care less if school kept or not.

The old man just stood there mean mouthing his kid and never once lifted a finger to help. He then turned to me and spit a stream of tobacco juice in my general direction. He reminded me of a couple of old buffalo hunters I'd run into a few years back, and I couldn't help wondering what rock this country was hatching these fellers out from under.

"Don't 'cha think that boulder a might big for your boy there, mister, why don't 'cha give him a hand?" I offered this as a friendly suggestion, but then some folks just don't take kindly to suggestions, no matter how harmless they are offered.

"Why don't you drag your sorry ass off'n that hoss and give my girl here a hand yourself, if you're so all-fired set on playin' the 'Good Samaritan.' I'm goin' yonder and get a pole to pry this box of kindlin' up in the air." With that, he picked up an ax and stalked off towards a line of post oak fifty yards away.

I slid down from the saddle and went over to peer closer at the kid. For a moment, I had my doubts, but when she looked up at me, I saw a quick flicker of light in what were bigger than usual eyes, in a rounder than usual face, then she turned back to wrestling with the boulder.

"Here, let me roll that rock, you can go bring a bunch of those flatter stones over."

The girl rocked back on her knees to sit on her heels and stare after the grizzled old man. "Your pa's as surly as an old bear with a sore toe, is he always this grouchy?

"T'aint my pa," she said.

I looked after him in surprise, "Then who is he?" I said, looking back at the girl.

"He's Howard Raphael and he won me in a poker game from my real pa." she said with no more feeling than if she were asking me to pass the butter.

"A poker game? Why in the world would he want a young'un like…?" Then I stopped. I had been thinking she would have been just one more mouth to feed and it didn't make sense, but the girl had fixed her gaze on my face that said something like, *"What do you think, numbskull?"*

And I must have recoiled in shock, for she turned red in the face and walked over to grab another flat rock.

What in the world is wrong with people? She was no more than a kid. Shoot, as near as I could tell, she hadn't even gotten out of her girlhood and made a good start on womanhood. I started a slow burn on Howard Raphael.

"You got a name kid?" I asked, and the anger I was feeling towards Raphael must have come through in my voice, for she jerked her head up with the first sign of emotion I'd seen in her and looked fearfully in the direction the old man had taken.

"Pearl... but he don't like me talkin' to no one."

"Well Pearl, how old are you?"

"I'm old enough," she said with a grunt and near dropped the flat rock on my toes.

"You can't be more'n ten or eleven," I said, "and that ain't *old enough*."

"Go tell him that and see if it don't earn you a knuckle sandwich," she said bitterly, then with a glance over her shoulder, added "I'll be thirteen in a couple of months."

Now I ain't one to meddle in other folk's business, and in fact, seems as though, try as I might, to mind my own p's and q's, trouble has a way of sneaking up on me when I least expect it. Now here it was again, staring me in the face like a specter through the window on a dark night. I sure didn't want or need no adolescent girl tagging along with me, but this whole thing was beginning to smell like buttermilk gone bad, and was starting to stick in my craw, so unless Howard Raphael told a whole lot different kind of a story than Pearly here, meddling was just what was going to happen... probably to his hurt.

I waited until 'ol Howard came puffing back up to the wagon, dragging a trimmed-up pole with one hand and carrying the ax in the other, then I said, "You know Mr. Lincoln put an end to slavery, don't you?"

18

Howard just looked at me like I'd fallen out of a well, and then growled at Pearl to get ready to haul the busted wheel off when he and *"the Samaritan here,"* levered the wagon up.

Raphael jammed the pole under the axle and threw the bulk of his considerable weight onto the end of the pole. For a moment, he sorta teeter-tottered out there, looking like a cross between a catfish flopping on the bank and a one-armed possum hanging from a sycamore. He turned angry eyes on me and then bellered at me like a mad bull, "Stop pickin' yer nose and lend me a hand before this thing catapults me into the next county," an idea that held considerable appeal for me, as I am sure it did for Pearl.

Reluctantly I went over and hauled down on the pole with him until we got the wagon jacked up with both of us sitting on the end of the pole down on the ground. Pearly wrestled the broken wheel from the axle and was struggling with the spare wheel to lift it up on the spindle, while 'ol Howard continually hollered and berated the poor kid for her clumsiness.

Well, I could see that the wagon wheel was way more than the girl was going to be able to handle, and the more she fumbled with it the more Raphael hollered, and the more he hollered, the more she fumbled around, so when he took to cussing her, I decided to get up and lend her a hand. It was a cinch she wasn't going to be able to do it by herself. My sudden departure however, had unexpected, if not delightful consequences, for I had no sooner jumped up from my spot on the pole when the law of gravity took over, the wagon came down, and the springy, green pole with Howard Raphael, went up. Quite rapidly, as a matter of fact, with the latter desperately clawing at the former while astraddle it. He wasn't actually launched into the next county, it was more like a fat toad clinging to a swamp reed in a high wind. The fresh-cut, green pole, vibrated rapidly up and down in the crotch of the wildly flailing old man, and for a moment there, I thought he may have created a new register on the musical scale, what with the staccato screaming he was decorating the atmosphere with. It even set off a pack of coyotes howling in outraged protest, the next hill over. I was certain he was doing a close, two-part harmony, although how he did this with only one set of vocal cords is something medical science might want to look into. It sorta reminded me of the noise a kid makes while riding a wagon down a bumpy hill—only deeper.

The pole finally vibrated off the pile of rocks and dumped the old man onto the ground. He rolled off and curled up like a slug with salt poured on it. He was still moaning, although without the vibrato now. I liked the vibrato better, it had a much more cultivated sound. Apparently, so did the coyotes for they had toned down their responses while Howard tried to catch his breath.

Pearly clapped a hand over her mouth and stifled a laugh-out-loud she'd started during all the ruckus, and then disappeared from sight to the other side of the wagon. I had no such compunctions however and had myself a good laugh at his misfortune, thinking it couldn't have happened to a more deserving fella. I made a mental note to give thanks for the Lord's sense of justice the next time I prayed… if I ever did again. His sense of justice, for the most part, was still a real bafflement to me.

"What the hell did you get off that pole for?" Raphael snarled, "it must have been obvious to even a lunkhead like you that I couldn't hold it up all by myself."

"Hey," I said, "I was only tryin' to help the kid out… thought you had it."

"You dumb brush-popper… " he cursed and got slowly to his feet to stand straddle legged and bent over at the waist, his hands on his knees and breathing hard… "I ought a nut you—see how you like it."

"Aw heck," I said. "I been on broncs that gave me a pounding worse than that, most of us Texas boys have. You're gonna have to toughen up a little if you're going to ride the rough string out here." I gave him my biggest toothy grin, still tryin' to get the picture of him being catapulted off into a cactus patch verses his pole vibration stunt out of my mind, and trying to decide which was better.

"Where's that good-for-nothing kid?" Howard hollered.

Pearly came slowly around the wagon and he told her to haul up some more flat rocks to stick under the axle, and was using language no little kid should have to hear. He then went over to fish out a jug from under the wagon seat and settled down on a rock while holding the front of his overalls out away from his crotch. He took a pull from the jug and proceeded to bark orders at the girl as she hurried to collect a pile of the required stones.

We tried it again then, and he had the girl pile the stones up under the axle while the two of us held the wagon bed up until it was high enough to slip the wheel on. It was short work after that, and once the nut was tightened down, 'ol Raphael didn't even bother to lift the wagon and take the jack out, he just hollered to his team and the big draft horses jerked the wagon off of the pile of stones and they were ready to roll.

"Get on the wagon," he said to the girl. Pearly stood there hesitating, looking back and forth from Raphael to me, and I was fidgeting 'cause I really didn't want to be saddled with no girl and yet there were some things about this whole business that just didn't set well. I decided I'd string along with them for a few miles and see what was up. I looked at the girl and nodded my head towards the wagon and that same dead look came back into her eyes as she climbed to a seat by the old man. He clucked to the team and they bounced the wagon on up out of the wash and onto the high plain.

It was near dark when Howard Raphael edged his team through a notch in the prairie and rode the brake of the wagon down a buffalo trail to a shallow valley below. A line of green marked a sometimes creek that was so cluttered with wild grape, buffalo berry, and wild plum, it was doubtful there was any water at all.

I set Lightfoot to follow and listened to the old man cussing the creek for having no water and wondered if I should stuff cotton in my horse's ears, fearing he might take up some of the grungy old teamster's ways, but since I didn't have no cotton and since I figured he might as well get used to it if he was going to be traipsing around in the west anyway, I gave up the whole thing as a bad idea. 'Sides, it wasn't my business to be fetching my horse up with Sunday School learning anyhow. I figured he was already near grown and probably had a pretty good collection of bad habits already dug in. It did rankle my hide some, however, that Pearly had to jounce along on the wagon seat next to the old buzzard and put up with his vile tongue.

The wagon came to a stop in a patch of grass partially shaded by a big old cottonwood and I swung down from the saddle and made my way to the stream bed. When I peered through the brush, all I could see was damp ground, and, having discovered the source of Howard's irritation, I stood back up and walked over to where the old man was slamming things around in the back of the wagon.

Raphael tossed out an iron spider for the campfire and the ax and then climbed down from the wagon and glowered at me like it was my fault the creek wasn't creeking. "Gonna be another dad-blamed dry camp, why can't there be water where there's supposed to be water?" he groused.

"There's water here," I said with a mild grin, enjoying his rankle.

"Sayin' it don't make it so, numb-nuts," the old man said and spat another stream of tobacco juice at my boots. I jumped back and was thinking if folks was gonna keep on doing that, maybe next time I should get brown boots, 'stead of black ones.

"You got a shovel in there?" I said with a nod towards the back of the wagon.

Howard snorted in disgust and made some comment that might have led one to believe he was contemplating the fertilizer business if they didn't know better. He then turned to the wagon, dug around a minute, pulled out a short D-handled shovel and tossed it at me.

"Don't know what you think you're gonna do with that," he said. "You'd be far better off rustlin' up some far-wood." I just grinned at him, picked up the shovel and turned toward the brushy creek bottom.

Raphael was hollering for Pearl to bring up some camp-wood, but the girl had disappeared into the bushes the minute the wagon had stopped and had not been seen since. He continued to slam things about setting up camp and muttered dire threats of what he was going to do to her, once she came back.

I whacked out a space in the brush of the creek bed and cleared a spot to dig a hole. About ten inches down, water began to well up and I worked to widen and deepen my little puddle. When it settled, we'd have water enough for camp, but then I decided to make another sump further down the creek bed in order to water the stock.

Raphael glanced at me as I walked past, and shook his head, then bent to strike a match to his fire. "Pearl, where the blazes are you?" he called then continued his mean mouthing of the child.

I had just started hacking out another spot in the stream bed when I heard Pearl hiss me.

"Psst!" she said, "Where's Howard?"

"Pearl, are you hiding?" I stopped to lean on the shovel and peer through the brush to where the girl was squatted down, looking like a rabbit in a briar patch.

"Yes," she whispered back, "not so loud."

"How come?"

"I want you to take me with you."

"Take you with me, how am I supposed to do that?"

"I don't know," she said in frustration. "You're the grown-up, can't you just shoot him or something'?"

"Huh," I chuckled, "now why didn't I think of that?"

"I mean it," she said. "I hate his guts. If you don't take me away, I'm going to chop him in his sleep."

"Chop him?" I said in surprise. "What do you mean, chop him?"

"I'm going to take his ax and chop him when he's asleep."

"Pearly," I said, "you sure you wanna do that?" I couldn't help smiling at her big-eyed, sober intent. Clearly, she had no idea what such an act would entail. "It's not quite the same as loping off a chicken's head, ya know."

"I could do it," she said. She stood cautiously and peered past me towards the wagon. "I've chopped chickens before, can't be that much different to chop a man."

"Huh, choppin' chicken's heads off don't send you to hell like choppin' a man's head off would.

The girl paused and stared at me, her mouth dropping open and a frightened look in her eyes. "Hell?" she said. "Do you think I'd go to hell?"

"That's usually what happens if you murder someone," I said cynically and, feeling a little awkward with the idea, turned back to my digging.

Pearl squatted down and watched me dig for a minute while thinking it over, then with a nervous look back towards camp she said, "What if I don't kill 'im, just chop off his leg or something, would I go to hell then?"

"Well no…" I paused in my digging, "not unless he bled to death, then you would."

I could see her resolve weakening and added, "'course he might be able to get you if he's still alive."

Pearl seemed to shrink, her shoulders drooped in dejection and her chin dropped to her chest. "What shall I do?" she said. "Why can't you just take me?"

I guess there are times in a fella's life when he has to do the very thing he just plain doesn't want to do, and this was one of them. I sure didn't need no kid, especially an adolescent girl, tethered to me. There was no telling how long it would be before I reached a settlement or someplace to leave her, and it was a cinch I couldn't take her back to where I came from. I most certainly would have to head for someplace to leave her if I did what I knew I should do, and that fit into my plans about like a size fourteen boot in a size ten overshoe.

"Pearl," I said, "You pick up an armload of those sticks and head back to camp. I won't let him hurt you anymore and we'll see, maybe we can figure out a way for you to go with me."

I kept digging as the girl slowly picked up some sticks and then drug a dead branch back towards the camp. I could hear the old man chewing on her for taking off like that and she said something back I didn't quite catch, but there was just enough sass in the tone of her voice to haul ol' Raphael up short as a high-tied bronc side-stepping and wall-eyed, 'cause he never said nothing back.

About that time, I hit water and got to business digging out a tank in the mud for the horses. When that chore was finished, I walked back into camp and leaned the shovel up against the wagon wheel. Pearly was on her knees, cutting up a couple of taters with their jackets on, and Howard looked up with a butcher knife in his hand from the bacon he was slicing and said, "Well?"

I shrugged and said, "You got a bucket and a dipper?"

"Don't tell me you found water? What are you some kind a danged Injun or sumthin?" He nodded towards a

25

dipper hanging by a water barrel on the side of the wagon, then said, "There's a bucket on the tail gate."

I retrieved the indicated pail and walked to my first seep and knelt to carefully dip the cool, clear water off the top. The puddle had settled out pretty well, enabling me to get a bucket full which I carried over and set on the ground near where the cooking was going on.

"Well lookee here, fresh water. Girl, you get a move on and brew us up a pot of coffee." Turning to eye me skeptically, Raphael said, "How'd you manage that?"

I shrugged and said, "It's an old trick I learned from the Apache once when I was an unwilling guest of theirs."

"Huh?" he said and looked after me perplexed. I walked over to catch the trailing reins of my saddle horse and led him to my newly constructed watering hole.

"C'mon Lightfoot, we'll leave him to puzzle that one out."

I led the red horse up to the waterhole I'd dug and saw it was still riled some. I just stood there waiting for my pony to shove his mug in and start drinking, and I'll be danged if he didn't just stand there looking at it too.

"What you waitin' for?" I said, "c'mon—drink up." I pulled his head down with a short yank on the reins, but he just jerked back and shook his head rattling the bridle, then stood there. I could a swore he was waiting for that water to clear up too, probably so he could admire his reflection while he was drinking.

"C'mon." I said, "I ain't got all day—you ain't had a decent drink since we left this morning. You mean to try and tell me you are too persnickity to drink this water? If you are, you ain't never going to survive the Texas Panhandle."

About that time there was a ruckus behind us and I turned to see one of Raphael's big blacks clopping through the brush in our direction. He came up to edge past Lightfoot, shoved his muzzle into the tank, and near sucked it dry with one great drought of water. Lightfoot snorted in disgust, pinned his ears back and made a fast lunge at the workhorse, tryin' to nip his neck, but the big black just squealed, tossed his head, and nipped Lightfoot right back, then held his ground waiting for the tank to fill again.

To my amazement, Lightfoot took several quick back-steps while the bridle reins burned through my hands, and turning, the horse trotted out of the brush with head and tail held high. He was the very picture of injured dignity and haughty pride, then he met the other draft horse coming in to join his teammate. My red hoss whirled his hindquarters and aimed a harmless left-footed kick at the unsuspecting draft animal. The big horse broke into a short, lumbering trot, to elude the quarrelsome saddle horse and then moseyed on up to join his buddy at the "good enough" water hole.

My grin faded and sobered up as I was reminded of another horse I'd had, a big gray that carried on like he could a been Lightfoot's twin, and another pang of remembrance struck deep and set quivering like an arrow in the oak door of my past before I could get it slammed shut again. For just the tiniest moment, I wondered what might have become of that other horse.

I followed Lightfoot out and found him cropping grass back of the wagon. The old man and the kid were still puttering about getting supper ready when I walked over to the horse, retrieved my makeshift hobbles from the saddlebags, and put them around his front feet. I then proceeded to remove the saddle and bridle and drape them over a bush, ignoring all the while the flattened ears and uncooperative stance of my jug-headed mount.

"Well, ain't you the one to get your back up in a snit?" I chided. "Serves you right. If you weren't so highfalutin snooty, you could a had your belly full of that water, but no—you fooled around and let those clumsy plow horses beat 'cha out of it." I swatted him on the butt with my hat and sent him crow-hopping a few steps off into the bushes, then I walked back to the fire.

"If you ain't got nothing better to do," Raphael growled, "you can try fillin' that water barrel on the wagon. Then maybe I might just let 'cha have a bite of my supper."

"Sure thing, old timer," I quipped, and winking at the kid, I picked up the pail, dumped the rest of the water into a pan beside her, and headed back to my first seep. I had just gotten comfortable down on one knee and was dipping a couple dippers full of water into the bucket when Lightfoot hopped over beside me and without so much as an, "excuse me please," shoved his muzzle into my seep and sucked it dry. Amazed, I watched the horse lift his head and stare blankly straight ahead until the water welled back up again and then dropped his dripping mug back into my water hole to drain it dry a second time. When he raised his head this time, he turned to eye my half-full pail of water, bumped me once and then turned to shuffle back out of there.

"Well, if that ain't the darnedest thing," I said and turned back to stare at the water slowly rising back up in the hole.

Later we sat around the fire, that is, the kid and I did, and watched as Raphael doled out two measly pieces of bacon and a few half-cooked-half-burned taters onto two tin plates and adding a couple of dry biscuits, he hands them to Pearly and me. He then proceeds to eat the rest of the food directly from the fry pan with his fingers, sopping up the leftover bacon grease with a couple more dry biscuits.

"What they call ya when they ain't mad at cha?" Howard asked around a mouth full of food.

I stopped chewing and stared at him, my mouth hanging open like the trap door of a pair of red flannels hanging on a clothesline. I hadn't thought about that. I sure wasn't going to tell him my real name and hadn't even considered what handle to use.

"What's the matter, numb-nuts, don't you know your own name?"

I swallowed hard and said, "Course I do and it sure as heck ain't that." I cast about for some idea for a name to use and saw some rocks on the cliff face opposite the stream bed catching the last of the sun's rays. Cliff, Stoney, Rocky, none of these seemed to suit me, and then my eyes fell on the ax chopped into a chunk of wood.

"Well?" Raphael said, looking expectantly.

Pearly was watching too and since I was not particularly fond of the moniker he'd been calling me, I said, "Woody—you can call me Woody."

"Woody? I suppose that's short for Woodrow. You got a last name?"

"Woody's enough," I said, letting my annoyance creep into my voice at this blatant breech of range etiquette.

"Well, Woody's enough, where might you be headed off to, come daylight?"

"Reckon I'll be headin' for the nearest settlement," I said.

"What you plannin' to do there?" he said.

"Oh, probably get me a little better traveling outfit and take care of some unfinished business. How about you, where you going?"

Raphael said, "That ain't none of your damn business." He got up, pulled the jug from under the wagon seat and filled his coffee cup before heading for the bushes. "You get to bed," he snapped at Pearl before he disappeared into the dark.

Pearl heaved a big sigh and I saw that dead look come into her eyes again. She made her way to the back of the wagon, and I said, "Pearl, get your blankets and spread them out here by the fire, you're sleeping out here tonight."

The girl stopped, a flicker of hope coming into her eyes, and looked questioningly at me. "Hurry," I said, "and bring anything else you may be wanting to take along. Hide it inside your blankets."

Pearl was rummaging around in the back of the wagon when the old man came back, buckling up his overalls. He poured another cup full of whiskey. It was plain he was already pretty well schnockered, for he nearly stumbled into the fire when he tried to sit back down. The noise had stopped inside the wagon and I watched silently as a roll of blankets dropped noiselessly to the ground. Pearl's white face gleamed for an instant from round the back, and I gave a slow shake of my head, as ol Howard drained the last of his cup and said with a slurred voice, "Ain't sha going to get shaum shleep?"

I nodded and said, "Yeah, in a minute," then watched him stagger to the front of the wagon and clumsily work his way up onto the wheel and tumble into the front of it.

"Where'sha at, girl?" he mumbled. I heard a crash as he fell over something. Pearl gave a little scream and jumped out the back, then crouched down listening but not moving. All was silent until presently the old man's snoring could be heard. Apparently, he lay where he'd fallen and was fast asleep.

Pearly picked up her bedroll and hurried over next to me. I motioned for her to be quiet and walked over to catch Lightfoot and cinch my rigging on. Digging in my saddlebags for a pencil, I found a scrap of paper and scribbled a short note:

> To whom it may concern: Be it known that the girl, known as Pearl, a minor of no blood relationship to one, Howard Raphael, in whose company she has been kept against her will, is voluntarily requesting that the cowboy known as Woody assist her in getting to the nearest settlement. Raphael's claim to have "won her in a poker game

from her father," is invalid as no one can own another person according to the Emancipation Act of Mr. Lincoln. A sum of one hundred dollars has been extended to Mr. Raphael in consideration of expenses incurred for her keep. Should Mr. Raphael wish to contest his claim, he should see the sheriff at the nearest settlement, where charges of indecent liberties and rape of a minor will be filed by Pearl.

I read the note to Pearl and had her sign it. Counting out five twenty-dollar gold pieces, I set these and the note on the wagon seat under a rock to keep it from blowing away, and left.

Mounting up, I kicked a boot free of the stirrup and gave the kid a hand up behind me, where she straddled my saddlebags with her bedroll tucked in between us, and then I nudged Lightfoot with the spurs. Riding towards the two work-horses, I herded them ahead of us along the buffalo trail that followed the dry stream bed and rode out of camp.

"Wow, that was easy," Pearl said. "You didn't have to shoot him and I didn't even have to chop him."

I chuckled at the kid's simple observation. "You sound like you're sorry 'bout that. You want me to take you back so you can?"

"Naw—too much work. He'll get his one of these days, let's just get out of here."

We rode a couple hours in the pale light of a finger-nail moon and a gazillion stars, following the creek bed most of the way, and pushing the draft horses along ahead of us at an easy trot. The trail eventually wound up through a thirty-foot-high cut-bank and came out on a wide grassy prairie. I goosed Lightfoot with the spurs and charged the work horses, sending them lumbering off across the plain in a slow gallop, then swung the red horse towards the east and rode on, my head nodding. The kid was already asleep against my back.

Her sleeping like that made me think of another girl I'd carried that way—an Indian girl I had taken back to the Kiowa. I mused a bit on how long ago that was? Must have been four, going on five years now. I wondered what had become of her. Probably married to some Kiowa buck with two or three papooses of her own. "She was sure pretty for an Indian gal," I said it out loud to the horse, then added, "but nowhere near as pretty as..." I stopped myself right there. None of that had anything to do with the here and now. My talking out loud must have disturbed the kid, for she mumbled, "What?" against my back.

I just said, "Never mind—you go on back to sleep."

Fort Griffin lay somewhere to the east and I was skirting the cap-rock of the Llano Estacado on its southern rim. Somewhere to the north, was a vast hidden canyon full of Indians and they were someone I wished to avoid. Lightfoot just snorted and pulled at the reins as if to say, "Forget it!" Ignoring him, I wondered if I could find the Palo Duro Canyon. The whole of the Llano Estacado was infested with the Comanche, Kiowa and Kiowa-Apache, or at least those that had refused to stay up in the Nations, which was most of them, and I had heard the army was soon to mount a campaign to force these Indians back to the reservation. I figured they were going to have a hard time rooting them out of those formidable canyons, if I was any judge, and I had only seen a little of it. Actually, it would not be a bad place to hole up for a while if a feller kept an eye peeled, had a decent outfit and could get shut of the kid.

These and other thoughts strolled through my mind like a family of coons through a corn field, while I rode along, half asleep, for another hour. Finally, I dozed and Lightfoot eventually came to a stop and started to graze.

I jerked awake and elbowed Pearl to get down and then followed her to the ground. The sky was just pinking up on the horizon and, figuring we put enough country between us an ol' Raphael, I stripped my bedroll from behind the saddle, loosened the cinch, and told Pearly to roll out her blankets and get some more sleep.

The girl wandered over behind a bush for a few minutes while I hobbled Lightfoot and then came stumbling back, blinking like an owl without saying anything. She spread her blankets and crawled into them and soon was fast asleep. I wasn't entirely sure she even woke up... least wise, not all the way. I unrolled my soogan, pulled off my boots, stuck my six-gun under the coat I was using for a pillow, took one look at the back trail, and then laid down and stacked a pile of zees of my own.

CHAPTER THREE

Runnin' for the Rimrock

Palo Duro Canyon, Fall 1870.

I AWOKE WITH PEARLY YELLING, "WOODY! Woody!" I heard it as, "would he, would he," and wondered who she was yelling at, and would he what?

I sat up in my blankets and was staring over the edge into the bottom of a canyon some hundred feet or more below, and not six feet from where I'd spread my bed. Lightfoot had stopped in the dark and commenced to grazing just nigh of the rimrock edge, and I had stepped down just a few feet short of a nasty fall. I was pondering on that, for it reminded me of another, near-mishap I'd had down in the badlands of old Mexico one dark and stormy night. I was saved that time too, by the good sense of the cowpony I was riding. Looking up in front of me, I could see the windswept grass of the prairie, moving off to the horizon likes waves on the ocean, while directly in front of me was this nearly invisible rent in the earth that moved off to the right for another hundred yards before it came to a point, then doubled back on the opposite side, some fifty yards distant from where I sat. It continued to widen off to the west. Here was a spot that was practically hidden from sight at a distance, due to the grass that grew right up to the edge of the declivity. It would not appear at all until one was almost on top of it. I wondered what was that fool girl screaming about and turned to see?

"Woody! Woody! Look!" Pearl screamed again, and at that moment a bullet spanged off a rock next to me and went whining off into the canyon. I grabbed my .44 and rolled sideways onto my belly to look up and see the girl on her knees with her blankets tumbled about her, pointing towards our back trail.

I did not at all expect to see what I saw. Old Howard Raphael was up on one knee on his wagon seat, his team hitched all up, and he was drawing a bead on my towhead. I snapped a shot back at him, even though the distance was too great for my hand gun, and then yelled at Pearl, "Get down!" Those crazy work-horses had made their way back to his camp in the dark, something they'd never do if you wanted 'em to, and the trail in that damp creek bottom must have read like the shadow of a tall Injun on a snowy day. I mentally berated myself for not having traveled farther through the waving buffalo grass last night, since we'd left a pretty plain trail. 'Course I might a rode off into this crazy canyon if I had.

A puff of smoke from the old coot's rifle was simultaneous with a bullet that kicked up dirt a few yards from Lightfoot. The report followed, Pearl screamed, and I jumped up and raced barefoot for my saddle horse and the rifle in its scabbard. The horse was crow-hopping skittishly away at all the commotion, when a second bullet mowed the stems off the grass next to him like an angry bee. That old buzzard was trying to shoot my pony.

"Whoa!" I hollered at Lightfoot and managed to catch my lunging mount and reach down to jerk the hobbles loose. A quick glance at Raphael, revealed that he had dropped back onto the wagon seat and was whipping his team into a gallop in our direction. I hauled the cinch tight while Pearl came running towards us, and had just enough time to mount and yank her up behind me, before he got into pistol range. Drumming my bare heels into the horse's sides, we raced off at a right angle to the hidden chasm until I reached the end of it and then dodged Lightfoot back to the left, making it appear that I was riding in a zigzag pattern to avoid his gunfire. When I reached a point opposite the racing wagon again, I snapped a pistol shot in his direction, then spun the horse to race straight away.

Raphael was hollering and cursing behind us, while slinging lead with one-handed shots of the rifle. He did not see the yawning gap of the canyon until his team shied violently at the very edge and then veered hard to the left at a ninety-degree angle. I reined in and turned the horse to watch, while Pearl's mouth gaped near as wide as my own. The momentum of the wagon caused it to whiplash, then snap the tongue with a loud pop when the front axle was jerked sideways. Fortunately for the workhorses, the single trees tore loose from the undercarriage as they galloped, pitching and bucking, to safety. Howard Raphael and his wagon were not so fortunate. With a throaty roar of terror, he and the whole contraption plunged over the precipice, until his cry was cut short and just the clatter of the breaking-up wagon, rattling through dirt and rocks was heard, followed by a few more tumbling rocks... then all was silent.

"Jeepers," Pearly said. "That was so cool."

I nudged Lightfoot back, riding around the yawning rent, to get our stuff, and said to the girl. "Cool? What do you mean cool? Do you think he looked cold?"

"No, but it was just so right, I mean, he really deserved that, it came about so neat-like, no muss, no fuss... it was cool."

I just grinned and shook my head. The ideas kids come up with these days, I sure didn't see anything cool about it, if anything, it was hot... hot lead flying, hot horses running, and hot blood pumping at fever pitch. It was anything but cool, but Pearl wasn't asking me what I thought.

"I think God sent him crashing' over that cliff for the bad things he's done to me."

"You do, huh? You think God's like that?"

"Sure," she said. "He's angry with the wicked every day."

"Who told you that?"

"My mom," she said simply.

We had ridden back around the canyon rim and pulled up to where our bedrolls and my boots lay. I pushed Pearly off and got down to put my boots on, thinking about what she'd said. I wasn't too sure about God meting out justice to the wicked every day. I'd met a lot of wicked folks and most of them seemed to just go on about their wicked ways with no intervention from God at all. Maybe old Howard was just plain too intent on catching us to pay attention to where he was going. On the other hand, I knew of a lot of good folks that bad stuff had happened to, and I was wondering if God was to blame for that as well. Maybe they were bad and nobody knew it but them and God, but that idea did not set too well with me either. Mostly because some bad stuff had happened to me that I figured I didn't deserve, and I was not sure I wanted to start sifting through the piles of good and bad stuff in my back yard to figure it out. Truth be told, there probably was some wicked stuff there that I was plenty willing to over-look and figured God should too, since mostly I tried to be a pretty decent feller... well, except for that one thing. But I was skirting around that wider than the edge of the rimrock I'd just stepped over to and was looking down in. That's when Pearly left off gathering her things together and came over beside me to stare down at the wreckage.

"Whoa," she said, "He's scattered stuff from here to breakfast."

Nonplussed, I nodded in agreement. I left-off philoso-phizing and began a study on whether or not I could find a way down to try to recover some of Raphael's things. I needed an outfit and if I could get the horses down into the canyon, we could travel a whole lot more comfortably.

"Pearly, see if you can catch up that team," I said, nodding to where the harness horses were grazing. "We got to find a way off the cap and get down there and recover some of that stuff."

"You go, I'll wait here 'til you get back."

I looked up from tying my bedroll behind the saddle and studied the girl. She seemed distant, sobered, even scared a little and I said, "What's the matter Pearl?"

She glanced up, wide eyed, from under a lowered brow, her chin resting on her brisket and it reminded me something of a lizard looking out from under a rock.

"I don't want to look at no dead man's guts!"

Her answer startled me. "Dead man's guts?" I said. "Why would you have to see his guts?"

"He went over the cliff and his 'bowels burst asunder'," she said with certainty.

I was astounded. "Where did you come up with that idea?" I asked.

With a knowing look, she said, "When Judas hanged himself and the rope broke, he went over the cliff and his bowels burst asunder, that means he spilled out his guts." Pearl finished her declaration with an exaggerated shake of her head and shrug of her shoulders as if to say I should know these things.

"Well Pearly, you can't stay here, some Injun is liable to get ya. You come along with me and if ol' Raphael's guts are strewn all over, you won't have to look at 'em."

I was grinning at Lightfoot's ears as we rode along the rimrock looking for a way down. I said to the horse, "She was ready to chop off his head yesterday and today she doesn't want to look at his guts." Lightfoot bobbed his head up and down a couple of times, pretending he understood the vagaries of twelve-year-old girls, but I knew he was just as befuddled as I was.

Pearl was up on one of the draft horses and I was leading the other and we had been riding the cap for a mile or so, when we finally found a steep cut with a well-traveled buffalo trail that wound down a stair-step embankment to the valley floor below. I nudged Lightfoot when he hesitated on the brink and with a snort loud enough to flush a couple of chickadees, he started down.

Leaning far back on the sorrel's haunches, I yelled to Pearly to do the same, while the horses slid and stumbled for the first twenty feet or so on the steepest part. Finally, the track leveled out to a more gradual decline and we traversed the stair-step hillside.

"Who made all these trails on the side of this hill?" Pearl called.

Indeed, it did look like someone had meticulously carved the whole hillside with flat, lateral pathways, two to three feet wide, and at the same intervals up and down.

"I don't know, probably God," I said.

"God? Why'd He do that?"

About the only thing, I could figure that might have done this kind of carving was water, so I said, "It happened during the flood."

"The flood, what flood?"

"Noah's flood, you know—Noah and the ark. Look you can see how these ridges were made as the water went down."

"Wow," she said. "Then this whole canyon was full of water at one time."

"Yep," I said. We finished our descent and reached the valley floor, then turned our mounts back up the canyon towards the wreck. I was looking at the terrain and wondering what it must have been like with all that water and the fountains of the deep breaking up. All around me was silent testimony of the violent upheaval that had taken place here. How could anyone deny that the flood had happened? It was the wickedness of man that had brought God's judgment upon the Earth and caused all this. I guess God can judge the wicked. Maybe Pearl in her child-like thinking was right about what happened to Howard Raphael afterall. It was enough to give me pause, maybe someday I would study on what might befall those who had done me wrong, but not right now. I had an outfit to gather.

It was not a pretty sight. We rode up to the wreck to find stuff scattered down a rocky scree and jumbled in a pile at the base of the cliff. Raphael's body was about half way down the slope, lying face down with his head out of sight. It had lodged between two large boulders. If his guts had spilled out, they were not visible.

"Come here Pearl," I said.

The girl was hanging back, her eyes big in her pale face.

"No!" she said.

"It's alright, you can't see any guts, come on over here. I want you to see that he is dead, once and for all."

The girl came slowly up the scree, crawling over and around the rocks.

"Where's his head?" she said.

"Stuck down between those two rocks. His neck is broken, he will trouble you no more."

Pearl stared at him for a long while and finally tentatively pushed his leg with her foot. "He's really dead ain't he?"

I nodded. "You go ahead and climb up there and bring down that ax and shovel, I will pile some rocks on top of ol' Howard here and leave 'im lay right where he landed."

While Pearl busied herself collecting the tools and camp gear, I went through Raphael's pockets and found the letter and gold coins I'd left earlier. These I stuffed into my pocket and proceeded to roll stones and pile them up over his corpse. Saying a brief prayer for his soul seemed more a formal obligation than anything else and I wondered if it did any good anyways, since God and I weren't talking much these days. I felt pretty certain He wasn't exactly listening to me, but I went ahead and mumbled something about the green pastures, then turned and walked off the slope with serious doubts that Howard Raphael was enjoying any such thing where he was at.

Two days later, we were making our way east along the canyon floor. I was looking for an exit in the rimrock that would allow the two-wheeled cart I had cobbled together to go through. I had found the back axle intact with a broken wheel and was able to replace both back wheels with the front ones. Using boards from the wrecked wagon, I built a crude box affair and had Pearly sitting amongst the gear we'd picked up, guiding the team along behind me and Lightfoot. It was slow going but I was in no hurry. Eventually, we would find our way out and I'd take Pearl to Fort Griffin and find some place to leave her.

The canyon seemed to be widening and if anything, the walls were getting higher and farther apart. I was enjoying the wild beauty of the place and thinking I might come back and hole up in one of the many side canyons, as there was plenty of game and buffalo, to say nothing of wild cattle. If I could find one with a good spring, I might just drop off the face of the earth for awhile.

"I'll grow a beard and become a hermit," I told Lightfoot. My cayuse had nothing to say about that, but I could tell he didn't think that was a very good idea. Pearl however hollered up a loud, "What?" I just told her, "Never mind, I wasn't talkin' to you."

The valley floor was more than a mile across and covered in grass that nearly reached my stirrups, then it opened up into an even wider valley with the east and west canyon walls farther apart. Through the center, a line of trees marked a stream course and we rode in that direction

"Looks like a creek over yonder," I called to the girl.

Pearly shaded her eyes against the afternoon sun and said, "Good, no dry camp tonight."

We'd gimped by the last couple of days with water for the stock from springs we'd found along the way, but there never seemed to be any available when it had come to stopping time.

It took about an hour to bump the cart across the valley floor to the banks of a wide creek that was flowing in a south-easterly direction. Here was a stream that would lead us out of the rimrock and to Fort Griffin if I didn't miss my guess.

"We'll camp over under those trees on the other side," I told Pearly. She gave me a quick smile and a nod of consent.

"How'd you like a fish-fry tonight?" I asked.

Pearl said, "I love catfish and corn dodgers."

"Corn dodgers? You know how to make corn dodgers?"

"Sure, there's cornmeal, I can make 'em."

"Okay," I said. "You make 'em and I'll go catch us some fish."

I was hacking off a limber willow pole and trimming off the leaves when I happened to look back across the valley the way we came and felt my heart jump into my throat.

"Pearly," I hissed in a hushed voice. "Don't light that fire."

Crouching low behind the brush of the stream, I hurried to where the girl could see me and signaled for silence with a finger to my lips, then motioned for her to come. Pearl looked questioningly at me and hurried over.

"What's wrong?" she said.

"Indians," I said and pointed out across the plain.

A half mile away, a large band of Indians was moving up the valley with several warriors out in front, followed by women and children, travois and dogs. Behind came a large horse herd and more braves. A number of young riders were racing their ponies back and forth along the column and appeared to be teens engaged in some sort of game, like keep-away or tag. They would race about tagging one another with coup sticks while attempting to avoid being tagged.

I glanced quickly at our horses, but they were out of sight of the band of Indians, contentedly grazing, and since the breeze was blowing down the valley, there was no imminent danger of our horses being discovered, or of them discovering the passing herd.

"What are those redskins doing?" Pearl said as she watched the youth race madly about.

I was watching the lead rider, nervous as to what he might do once they crossed our cart track.

"Playing tag," I said.

One of the lead riders stopped his horse and studied the ground about where our cart would have passed through the grass and turned to stare in our direction, when the press of the playing riders swept around and past him, trampling over our trail. The chief, for so I supposed him to be, kicked his pony forward and began to yell and shake his lance and shield at the offending youngsters, and then continued on up the valley floor to the north.

"Whew!" I breathed. "For a minute there, I thought he was going to pick up our trail."

"Who?" Pearl said.

"That lead Indian, probably their head chief. Didn't you see him looking this way?"

"No, are they dangerous?"

"As a baby rattlesnake... most likely Comanche."

"What would they do to us?" Pearl asked, peering nervously at the passing band.

"You don't want to know. When you say your prayers tonight, be sure to thank the Lord they didn't see us."

43

I decided to move camp downstream away from the Indians' direction of travel and finally settled on a hidden glade just at twilight. Pearl set to work fixing the corn dodgers while I went fishing, and soon I had four nice catfish cleaned and ready for the fry pan. We risked a small fire with bone-dry mesquite, just long enough to cook our food, then doused it and ate in the gathering starlight.

"Woody," Pearl said, "Where you from?"

"Texas."

"What part?"

"South of here."

"You got any kin?" she asked.

"Yeah, why you wanna know?"

"No reason, just wondering. I got no brothers or sisters and my ma died four years back, when I was eight. Since then it was just me and pa. He took to drinking after ma died and it changed him."

"I'm sorry to hear that, Pearly," I said, thinking some of my own folks. "Do you miss them?"

"Not my pa so much, but my ma, yeah, I miss her a lot."

"I can understand that, must be hard losing your ma when you're a kid." I didn't say it, but I thought it's hard losing your ma when you're grownup too.

"Is your ma alive?" she asked.

I shifted uncomfortably before the twelve-year-old's question, then said, "Yes!"

"Is she nice?"

I was surprised at that question. I had never considered my mother in any other light. "Of course she is," I said somewhat evasively and wishing to change the subject.

"Can I go stay with her?"

"What? What did you say?"

"You've got to take me somewhere. Take me to stay with your ma. Is your pa good?"

I was flabbergasted. There was no way I was going to take her back there. Funny, I thought, that she should ask if my pa was good. Not nice, but good. I guess after having a pa that was neither nice nor good, that was of paramount importance to her.

"My pa is good," I said slowly, remembering my pa's unswerving loyalty and integrity, "but I can't take you there."

"Why not?" she said.

"Because I ain't going there. I'll take you to Fort Griffin and put you on a stagecoach to someplace else."

"I got no place else to go—I want to go to your house."

"I told you, I ain't going there." She was beginning to chafe my hide.

"Then put me on the stagecoach to your ma's. Would she want me? I can work."

The frightened look in her eyes touched a numb spot in me and slowly massaged a little feeling back into my *"give-a-hoot."* I began to think that it might be possible to send Pearly to mom and dad, just as long as she didn't know who I really was, and Id' be long gone from Griffin by the time she ever got there to tell them.

With a big sigh, I said, "Yeah, ma 'll want you— so will pa."

"Can I go then? You can write a note and let them know they can have me—can I?"

I huffed and scratched a tickle on the top of my head, then let it bump back against the trunk of the big cotton-wood I was sitting under and stared up at the stars. Those same stars that looked down on the home place where I'd viewed them so often. Stars that also looked down on a log cabin on a perfect little hill, far away, and, oh no! Stars that looked down on a little white cottage surrounded by a picket fence down by the creek.

Unknowingly, an unbelievable and unheralded sad-ness swept over me like an earth-to-sky storm sweeping across the plains. It rolled me along before it in a relent-less grip of regret, that left me helpless to steer a course away from its heart-rending power. With eyes closed, I struggled like some wild thing in a trap, while memories surged through the chinks of the walls I'd put up to stop them. With a low groan, I felt the onslaught obliterating me. It dissolved all sense of purpose, worth and desire, erasing my very personhood, until it was as if I were nothing, a big numb zero sitting under that tree.

"Woody! Woody, what's wrong?" Pearly was up on her knees beside me, shaking me. "What's wrong with you?" she said again.

I straitened up and shrugged off her hands, pulling away from her. "Pearl, shut-up and go to sleep!" It was harsh and came out a little meaner than I had intended for it to, but right now I just didn't care. I got up, picked up my bedroll and went off into the brush to bed down and try to sleep.

The next morning, we ate a few cold corn dodgers while getting ready to go and I saw that Pearly had the same dead look in her eyes that I'd noticed when I first came upon her and ol' Raphael. I scoffed to myself. For the first time, I understood where that look came from, and I was willing to bet dollars to doughnuts, the look was mirrored in my own eyes.

Nothing was said as I hitched the team while she loaded stuff into the cart. When I went over to saddle Lightfoot, he turned a little prickly on me... probably because of the way I jerked him around bridling him and slamming the saddle down hard on his back. Anyway, he swelled up like a blood-eyed horned toad when I hauled on the cinch and I probably threw my knee into his belly a little harder than necessary too, 'cause he broke wind and crow-hopped away, dragging me with him since I still had a hold of the cinch strap.

"Hold still, you jug-headed son-of-a-flea-bit, sway-backed, milk-horse," I snarled. I took another pull on the cinch and tucked the end around the ring, then flopped the stirrup off the horn and let it bang him in the ribs.

Lightfoot stood straddle-legged with his ears laid back flat, and the look in his eyes about matched mine as I stepped up on him. We just sat there a moment and then I said, "Well?"

Pearly was watching and I was expecting one of Lightfoot's usual smart alack remarks like; "That's a deep subject," or, "A well's a hole in the ground," or maybe, "It's wet too, once you get into it." Something like that, but I no way expected him to bog his head and turn his belly up to the sun, like he did. He commenced to broncin' all over the place, and I lasted for three or four jumps; maybe five if you count the one where he bucked me clean up into the air and I was lucky enough to fall right back down on top my saddle again. Anyway, on the next jump, I was launched upward, turned over twice about treetop level, once on the way up, and again on the way back down, and then made the startling discovery of just how hard the deceptively soft looking grass in a creek bottom can be.

After that three things happened about the same time. Lightfoot went to calmly cropping grass, Pearly did a laugh-out-loud, and I, trying to suck air back into my pancaked lungs, writhed around like an angleworm on a hot rock.

I slowly got to one knee, found a stray cubic foot of oxygen and watched Pearly wipe her eyes and look for something to blow her nose on. Lightfoot stood looking back at me while chewing a mouthful of grass around the bit with his ears pricked forward. He had a look that said, "I always like startin' the day with a little rough housin'—it's good for the circulation."

I went over and climbed on him again, dispensed with saying, *"Well,"* this time, and rode him up out of the creek bottom to follow it downstream.

The stream we followed eventually flowed from the canyon and two days later it led us to what I guessed was the Clear Fork River. Here I headed downstream, figuring that Fort Griffin was somewhere in that direction. Pearly hadn't said much as we camped and even less as we traveled, and I didn't see much need for conversation either since every time I looked at her mopping around it reminded me of why I was mopping around. Lightfoot on the other hand, was the only one who had managed to retain his sense of humor and I figured his cutting up, by snorting at bees and blasting them off the honeybush mesquite we passed, or jumping sideways whenever a tweety bird flew up sudden like, was just his way of trying to get a rise out of me, so for the most part I ignored his coltish pranks.

Eventually, we came to a wide flat, backed by a mesa that supported several stone buildings and a number of wooden structures. The United States Flag flew prominently from a pole in front of the largest of the buildings on the mesa and the whole compound looked down on the sprawling flat below.

This, I assumed, was Fort Griffin, although I saw no fortification other than its strategic location up the mesa. What was even more curious to me was the fifteen to twenty Indian teepees pitched to one side of the flat and near several rudely constructed sod and mud huts with a spattering of wood buildings, situated on both sides of a wide street that made up a town of sorts.

"What are these Indians doing here with these white folks?" I said to Lightfoot's ears, but he didn't know and what's more he didn't care.

"Do you think they are dangerous?" Pearl said.

Apparently, her greater concern for danger had gotten the better of her self-imposed silence of the past few days. Even if I had told her to shut up, she knew as well as I did that I didn't mean permanently. Course it had been kinda nice, the peace and quiet and all, but to expect an adolescent girl to not babble like a brook in a rain forest for more'n three or four minutes is quite a reach, even for me. It may have seriously impaired her female development. I'm thinking temperament here now, not the other way.

"I doubt it," I scoffed. It was highly unlikely that the Indians had pitched a war camp in the very shadow of Fort Griffin.

"I don't wanna see no Indians," she said. "Promise me you're not going to leave me with no Indians."

I turned to look back at the anxious girl and studied her face for a minute. "Pearly," I said, and my voice softened a little bit, "I won't be sending you off to live with no Indians."

I saw a grizzled old fellow with a bushy black beard chopping wood in front of one of the sod huts, and asked him if there was a stage depot in town. He stopped his chopping, wiped his brow with a dirty bandana and leaned on his ax. Shifting his chew into one cheek, he spat a stream of tobacco juice in my general direction and pointed up the street.

"Faller Griffin Avenue here to the end and you'll find it at the Occidental, that's at the foot of Gov'ment Hill," he said. "Hit's next to the telegraph office, which is next to the post office." He wiped his mouth on his sleeve and went back to chewin' and choppin'.

We rode to the end of the street and stopped in front of a vertical log structure with a sign that read Occidental Hotel. On one side was the post office and on the other the telegraph office from which a wire was strung on poles that led up the hill to the fort. A high board fence surrounded a compound in back which contained a wagon yard and livery stable. I directed Pearl to follow me as we rode through the gate and stopped in front of that establishment.

I howdied a young man who came out to meet us and asked him, "You got some place we can put up our cart for a couple of days?"

"You can leave it over there along the fence," he said, pointing to the spot. "Do you want me to grain your horses?"

Lightfoot looked expectantly back at me as I was stepping down, so I nodded to the man and handed him my reins. "I reckon. You got any place where me and the kid here can get a bite to eat?"

"There's a dining room next to the bar in the Occidental," he said with a nod towards a back door with a sign over it. "I'll need a buck each for these horses, in advance. How long you stayin?"

"Don't know yet, here's three buck for now," I said and handed him the money.

Pearl followed me into the hotel in wide-eyed wonder. You'd a thought she was in the Palace Hotel in Saint Louie the way she was gaping at everything. I led the way into the dining room and we sat down at a table next to a window that looked out onto the street.

Pearl was staring out the window at a tall Indian who was leaning up against the building across the street, when the waiter came over.

"Is that Indian a murdering heathen savage?" she blurted out

The portly fellow in sleeve garters bent his bald head and stooped to peer out the window in the direction she was pointing.

"Nope," he said. "More like a murdered heathen savage."

"A what?" Pearly said and turned from the window to stare at the man.

"He's a Tonkawa. 'Bout twenty years ago, all his tribe except for maybe a hundred of 'em, got wiped out by the Comanche and Kiowa. Now they stay here in the protection of the Fort and scout for the army. That's Grayhawk, one of the best trackers they got. Now what'll you have?"

I ordered steak and home fries and told Pearl she could order anything she wanted. She ordered up something called a Denver Omelet, which looked pretty interesting to me; scrambled eggs with chopped up ham, green peppers, onions, and cheese. It was served with hot buttermilk biscuits, sweet cream butter, and strawberry jam, along with a tall glass of milk. I had coffee and it was the best meal I'd eaten since... well, in a powerful long time. I allowed as how it sure beat diamondback chicken.

The breakfast was fifty cents a plate, but that was probably because Griffin was so far from anywhere else and they had to cart all the stuff in. I checked at the hotel desk and learned that there was a stage that came through once a week from Abilene, Kansas to points south, but anyone wishing to get to the Pecos would have to route clear down through San Antonio and catch the westbound coach that runs the military route. I was all too familiar with that ride, and didn't wish that on my worst enemy. Well... maybe, but never mind that. By the time I pinned notes to Pearly for all the different connections she'd need to make, she'd look like a walkin' bulletin board.

CHAPTER FOUR

After The Fall

Crossed Sabers Ranch, Fall 1870

BECKY SABER STARED THROUGH TEAR-filled eyes as the shadowy outline of her older brother mounted the sorrel and rode away, not looking back. Her pleading question hanging in the air, still unanswered. With sobs wracking her body, she turned grief stricken, back to the horror of Sonny and Suzanne, lying dead on the porch of the little cottage. She could hear shouting and people running and when she emerged from the brush of the pathway, she could see Lance and Rusty kneeling over the inert forms of Sonny and Suzanne. Tommy was hollering and running up the fence line towards her folks and the Kluesmans, who were all hurrying towards the gruesome scene.

Becky stumbled through the little gate and collapsed on her knees in the grass, sobbing bitterly at the sight of her dead brother and Suzanne, who lay beneath his body, blood running from her nose.

"It was Colt," she said. "Colt is alive and he shot them. Why would he do such a thing?"

Her father thundered up in a dead run with Gunner Kluesman close behind. Jessica and Mabel followed with

Tommy babbling, "Somebody shot and killed Sonny and Miss Kluesman."

Grant paused to take one look and then rushed to kneel by his fallen son and lifted his lifeless body, while Gunner gently pulled Suzanne's unmoving body from under him, to stare at her blood-soaked blouse.

"My Gawd, no!" the big blacksmith cried, and lifting his stricken daughter in his arms, he stumbled down the steps towards Mabel who stood weeping openly in the yard.

Jessica rushed past them to Grant's side and knelt to stare at the still, white face of her son. Rusty and Lance stepped back, their hats in their hands, and silently watched as the rancher laid Sonny back on the porch and began to unbutton his shirt.

Gunner sat down on the grass holding Suzanne on his lap, while tears streamed unashamedly down his cheeks. Mabel was on her knees, gently wiping blood from her daughter's pale face and crying openly, when suddenly, she gripped her husband's arm and said, "Gunner!" Suzanne's mother had seen a flicker of movement in her daughter's eyelids.

The big German stopped his weeping and bent his head to listen at his daughter's breast, a glimmer of hope coming into his eyes. He could hear a heartbeat.

A low moan emitted from Suzanne's lips as her eyes fluttered open, the blue of them registering confusion. With an unsteady hand, she reached to push the handkerchief Mabel was wiping her face with away from her sore nose.

"What happened?" she managed to whisper.

"She's alive," her father shouted.

The stunned crowd on the porch turned to stare at the Kluesmans, and saw Suzanne groggily sitting up in her father's lap.

Grant turned back to his son. "That's strange," he said, "There is no exit wound." He'd rolled Sonny over onto his side and was looking at the back of his shirt. All he could see was a little blood on the back of his head and shirt collar. He rolled Sonny back and continued to unbutton the front of his shirt, opening it.

"Well would you look at this," he gasped.

Jessica peered over her husband's shoulder as Becky and Tommy pressed in close behind and the two cowboys stepped over to stare down. Lying on Sonny's bare chest was the heavy brass medallion of the Comanche, Bodalk Inago—the snake man, and lodged in the center of the silver snake embossment, deeply embedded, was the .44 slug from Colton's gun. The medallion had stopped the bullet.

"Good Lord," Grant cried. "The medallion Colt gave him, saved Sonny's life." He pushed the medallion aside and bent to listen at his son's chest. Grant rose up from Sonny's bruised torso and then to everyone's amazement, doubled up both fists and hammered them down hard on Sonny's chest. Sonny convulsed and then lay still. Grant hammered him again and then bent to listen. He lifted his head with a grim smile and said, "I got a heartbeat." He began a rhythmic pumping of his son's chest until Sonny uttered a low moan and whimpered, "Stop it."

"Sonny's alive," he choked out. Everyone began to laugh and cry at once. "They are both alive," the rancher said, "It's a miracle, thank you, Jesus!"

"Daddy," Becky sniffed, "It was Colt…Colt shot Sonny."

"Well he didn't kill him," her father replied. "Thank God, he didn't kill him." Then he looked at his youngest daughter and added, "Are you sure?"

"Yes," she said, "I saw him—it was Colt, all dressed in black."

"Where is he now?" Jessica said.

"He rode off down the creek on a red horse," Becky said.

Grant turned to Rusty and Lance. "You boys get your horses and trail him. Be careful, but bring him back."

Suzanne, bewildered, rose to her feet, her folks helping her up. "What's going on?" she said. "What's wrong with Sonny?"

The tall cowboy lay panting on the porch as the Kluesmans walked back to those gathered around him. He moaned and reached a weak hand to where his father was lightly slapping his cheeks, drawing the blood back into his pale face. "Quit," he said, and then struggled to rise on one elbow. With another groan, he clasped a hand to his bruised chest and lay back down with a thud. "I feel like a herd of buffalo's been dancing on my brisket."

"Do you know what happened?" Grant asked his son.

"No—yes—I don't know. Somebody was in the bushes... oh, my God, it was Colt—Colt's alive! Mom, Dad, Colt's alive and"—he paused, his voice losing its intensity— "and he shot me."

"I saw him too," Suzanne said in a low, trembling voice.

"How come I'm not dead? Lord, my chest hurts." He sat up and gingerly felt about his chest and rib cage, and then his fingers touched the medallion.

"That saved your life," Grant gave a cynical scoff. "Colt's gift to you has kept him from killing you, but that doesn't erase the fact that he tried. What I can't figure out is why he would try."

"He saw Sonny kissing me," Suzanne said sadly. "Just before the gun blazed I saw him over Sonny's shoulder, then all went black."

"Yeah, I jumped in front of you," Sonny said. "At first, I didn't recognize him, but he must have been watching us... the first time I really get to kiss you and wouldn't you know it, he'd be here to see it." He shook his head in sorrow while Suzanne looked sick and turned away.

"Your head must have snapped back with the impact of the bullet and hit Suzie in the face, knocking her unconscious," Gunner said. He reached a hand to Suzanne's face and turned it to peer at her swollen nose. It was bruised and distended and was beginning to discolor. It was plain she had taken a painful blow.

"Can you stand?" Sonny's mother asked him. "We better get you up to the house and send for the doctor."

"I'll try," Sonny said. With gritted teeth, he labored painfully to his feet.

"You sit here on the step," his father said, "I'll get the buggy."

"Both of you sit and rest," Gunner put in, "Grant, I'll go with you and bring my rig down. I want to get Suzanne back to town."

Suzanne and Sonny sat dejectedly, side by side, neither of them speaking as they watched their parents hurry off to the house. Tommy was down by the creek investigating Colton's disappearance, and Becky had walked out to meet Lance and Rusty who were riding their horses down the lane from the barnyard. They saw them stop to speak briefly with Grant Saber before they rode on towards the girl.

"Sonny," Suzanne whispered, "Colton's alive."

"Yeah, he's alive and he's a murderer." He spoke with something akin to awe and disbelief in his voice. "He's back from the dead to become a murderer." He shook his head sadly.

"He is no murderer," Suzanne turned on the cowboy. "Colt is no murderer."

"He ain't, huh?" Sonny said slowly. "What do you call this bullet in my medallion then?"

"It's my fault," Suzanne said, incrimination in her voice. "I knew he was alive. In my spirit, I knew it. I should never have let you talk me into believing otherwise."

"Good Lord, Suzanne, you can't possibly blame me. It's been so long, you know we both thought Colt was dead and I have grown to love you so. You made me love you."

56

"I made you love me?" Suzanne was incredulous. "How did I do that?"

"It was just you... who you are," he answered. "I hurt to the very depths of my being for you—for your loss. You were so devastated, so vulnerable, so hopelessly lost, and so precious. My own sense of loss at his death seemed pale by comparison—even to the point of being unimportant. Don't you know how that drew me to you?"

"No," she sighed.

"Well, it did, it still does. You were giving up on life and I couldn't let that happen and my coming alongside you like that—what did you think, that I'd not end up loving you? Colt is not the only one who can feel deeply about things you know."

Suzanne was at a loss. As she listened to Sonny, she got the uneasy feeling that he was somehow blaming her for all this. It was as if she was somehow responsible for how others felt, particularly in regards to her, and she was perplexed. She had no control over such things.

"I'm sorry, Sonny, I know it must have seemed like I was taking you for granted much of the time, and I am truly grateful that you were there for me, but now..." her voice trailed off into silence.

Sonny shifted uncomfortably with a low groan, his hand going to his chest. He recognized the signs in the girl and for a moment he thought she would clasp her arms about her knees again as in the days of her deep melancholy.

"What do we do now?" he asked.

Suzanne turned and looked at him and then got to her feet. Her father was bringing his buggy down the lane towards them.

"You can do what you want," she said. "I am going to go find Colt."

Sonny sat the fidgeting stallion and stared north across the rolling sand hills. Grass and scrub brush fought for toe-holds in the low-lying areas and tracks of cattle, deer and antelope crisscrossed the buffalo trails everywhere. The trail he had been following was several days old, and led to the edge of a sand dune that rose ten feet in front of him, and there it disappeared, the whispering sands from the steadily blowing breeze having long since covered the tracks.

He pushed his hat back and ran a thumb across his sweaty brow and swallowed hard against the ache in his breastbone. "Looks like he was headin' north by northeast, I sure hope he steers clear of the Injuns," he said to Tornado. "If he thinks he has trouble now..." Sonny let the remark go unfinished, pulled his hat back down over his brow, tugged on the lead rope of his pack mule, and spurred the big grulla up the dune, holding a steady course for the other side.

An hour later he rode out of the blow-sand and headed down a long grassy slope towards a line of cottonwood and willows. It marked the course of Little Sandy Creek, and he was hoping to pick up the tracks of his brother's horse in the cover of the trees, if the cattle and critters hadn't completely wiped them out. Colt would have to go to water sooner or later. "Too bad I didn't get a look at the horse he was riding," Sonny said to his mount. "Becky said it was a red horse with white socks and a blaze face. Shouldn't be too hard to spot."

Sonny had ridden out against his mother's protests, five days after the tragic incident at the little cottage where Colton's bullet had struck him down. It was truly miraculous that the condemned medallion of the Comanche Snake Man, the one his mother had so disapproved of, had stopped the .44 slug. But not, however, without inflicting a good deal of discomfort to Sonny's breastbone. His whole chest had turned an angry purple and was still an ugly shade of blue-black. It hurt if he made any sudden movements or took a deep breath, and a sneeze was devastating. In fact, most all his bodily functions were an ordeal. But the trail was getting cold, and Sonny had to find his hot-headed brother and set the record straight. So he saddled up Tornado, loaded a couple of pannier boxes full of grub and gear onto old Hank, their cantankerous mule, and headed out before daylight. Besides, he wanted to know what in the world had happened to Colt, and where he had been for the past two and a half years.

Sonny's thoughts went to the blonde schoolteacher. He had not seen Suzanne since the attack and had made no effort to look her up before he left the ranch. He supposed she was still at Wade's Landing and making plans for some sort of search of her own, for she had certainly been determined about it when last they talked. She had not even looked back after leaving him in a forlorn heap on the porch. "So much for true love," he said bitterly. "Why didn't I just let well enough alone and stick to waddin' pools?"

Sonny pulled up at the edge of the trees. He smelled smoke and became instantly wary of possible Indian trouble. It wasn't until the wind carried the sound of bleating sheep to his ears, along with the occasional barking of a dog, that he relaxed his vigilance and kneed the dark horse forward. Riding through the brush, he eventually came out into a grassy little glen and nearly trampled his horse over a bunch of sheep nibbling at the grass of the place.

Hank broke out in a raucous braying when he spied the sheep, voicing his obvious alarm at the unfamiliar sight of the wooly creatures. The sheep scattered as one, and Sonny was reminded of a flight of birds in the way they fled. A sheepherder's wagon was parked next to the stream under a big cottonwood and a couple of draft horses were hobbled on the grass across the brook. A short, wiry man with white whiskers, was busy fixing a meal over a campfire and dropped the lid he'd been holding with a stick into place on a Dutch oven. Cautiously he stood up to face the rider. Sonny saw the man's eyes dart to where a rifle stood, leaning up against the wagon wheel, but then he relaxed when Sonny spoke.

"Howdy, name's Sonny Saber and I ride for my Pa, of the Crossed Saber's outfit. Mind if I step down for a bit?"

"Help yourself," the man said. "'Bout got these biscuits done, if you'd care to join me, your company would be welcome."

"Don't mind if I do," Sonny said. "I got grub along, you needin' anything?"

"Nope, got biscuits and honey, and this pot of whistle berries is about done, grab a plate and make yourself to home."

"Think I'll take you up on that, you say there's honey?"

The man nodded and began spooning beans onto a tin plate. Sonny swung down from the saddle and loosened the cinch, he then snapped a length of lead rope to Tornado bridle and tied him and Hank off to some willows. Hank had calmed down some and both animals went to grazing as the cowboy walked to the fire. He accepted the plate of beans and watched patiently as the shepherd lifted the lid again and snatched out a couple of golden brown biscuits. He reset the lid in a clatter with one hand while, with the other, he deftly dropped a biscuit on Sonny's plate, and then one on his own.

"Help yourself to that coffee pot," the man said, then began dishing up a second plate of beans. Sonny squatted on his heels and setting his plate on a flat rock, he poured a cup of the steaming black liquid and took a sip. Balancing the plate on one knee, he began to eat and study the herder. The man was swarthy and dark complected from long hours in the sun, but had clear, gray eyes that spoke of an honest forthrightness and determination, Sonny figured he'd have to have if he was going to survive as a sheep man in cattle country.

Sonny's attitude towards sheep was no different than the rest of the cowboys he knew. Sheep were smelly, stupid creatures that gnawed the grass down to the roots and ruined the range, but he drew the line at the wanton slaughter and destruction some cowboys inflicted on the unfortunate shepherds and their flocks.

"Name's Sam Bass," the man said. "I suppose you be wonderin' where I'm headin' with all these woolies here?"

Sonny shrugged. "Ain't really none of my business, long as you keep 'em pointed west and across the Pecos. You'll be off Crossed Saber range then."

"I hear tell there's sheep range opening up down near Fort Stockton, and I'm headin' this bunch down that-a-way. They are irrigating the range out of Comanche Springs and there's good ground to be had. I thought I'd stake me out some before I send for the wife and kids back in Missouri."

Sonny nodded his head and accepted a pint jar of wild honey the man held out. "Ain't seen nothin' of a feller ridin' through here lately on a red horse, have you?"

"Nope." Bass said. "Been following this stream course west for the past few days, but you're the first person I've seen since I left Dallas. There's talk of a railroad being pushed through, and I met a mess of Russian immigrants while there. They were camped along the river, waiting to hear from the army as to when construction was to start, and were plumb happy to see these sheep. I made a pretty good run of it too, sold every yearling lamb I could spare. Seems them Russkies favor lamb, they paid top dollar for 'em."

Sonny looked at the open-faced shepherd and said dryly, "You might wanna be careful who you noise that about to, not everybody's on the up and up in these parts."

"Oh!" The man's face turned pale. "I see what you mean. You just seemed like an honest feller 'n I figured you could be trusted."

"Yeah, well, not everybody is, so keep that in mind."

Sam watched honey spool from the glob on his spoon to run down onto the halved biscuits on his plate and nodded contemplatively. After a moment he said, "You don't like sheep."

"Nope," Sonny said.

"Don't suppose I could change your mind about that either, could I?"

"Nope," Sonny said again.

"They ain't so bad," Bass said, "there's good money in 'em."

"Huh," Sonny scoffed but made no further comment.

"They lamb twice a year, you can shear 'em twice a year, and lamb chops are delicious."

"If you like that sorta thing," Sonny said cryptically and glanced towards his horse and mule. He had better things to do than jaw with this sheep man about sheep.

"Okay, who's the fella on the red horse?"

"My brother."

"What cha lookin' for him for?"

"Attempted murder."

"Murder? Who'd he try to kill?"

"Me," Sonny said. He rose to his feet and stepped to where he could place his empty plate and cup in a dish bucket on the tailgate of the wagon, while Sam Bass stared open-mouthed after him.

"You? Don't look like he succeeded... how come?"

Sonny stepped to the side of his horse and tightened the cinch, then untied him and the mule and swung astride with a painful grimace. Turning his mount to face the sheepherder, he said, "He found me kissin' his sweet-heart. Thanks for the grub and if you keep to this stream, she flows into the Pecos a few miles farther down. You'll have to swim those lint-bag lawnmowers[1] to the other side and then you'll be off our range. Take care." He touched the brim of his hat and rode on out of the camp, scattering sheep from his path as he rode. He left Sam Bass with unanswered questions written all over his face.

CHAPTER FIVE

Fathers and Daughters

Wade's Landing, Texas, Fall 1870.

SUZANNE STEPPED INTO THE SHERIFF'S office and looked nervously at the big man behind the desk. "Good morning, Mr. Anderson, I wonder if I might ask a favor of you?"

Clay Anderson's face became animated with delight when he looked up to see the young schoolteacher standing before him. At a glance, he took in her bruised features and the slight bend to her cute little nose. Quickly he leaped to his feet, sending the chair he had been sitting in, scooting back against the wall.

"Yes ma'am," he said, always eager to help her in any way he could.

Suzanne held out a brown tin-type photograph to the sheriff. "Can you make up a wanted poster from this?" she asked.

Sheriff Anderson took the photo and studied it slowly. "This is Colt Saber," he said.

"Yes," Suzanne sighed. "I need to find him and I don't know what else to try."

"Are you swearing out a warrant for his arrest?"

"Oh, my no! I just need to talk to him... to find out where he is."

"He shot you, didn't he?" There was a hint of accusation in the big Swede's voice.

"No," Suzanne shook her head sadly.

"Well, he shot his brother. I believe he's wanted by the law."

"He didn't mean to do that."

Sheriff Anderson's mouth compressed into a thin, tight line and he shook his head. "How can you know that?"

"I know," Suzanne replied, "and if I can find him, I'll prove it."

Clay Anderson studied the picture for a moment and said, "You want this poster to indicate criminal charges?"

"Oh no! No criminal charges. The family is not pressing any charges, we just have to find him."

"So, it's a missing persons poster you need then?"

"Yes, can you do that?"

Anderson set the photograph on his desk and scratched his head. "I suppose. It won't get much circulation without a reward."

"I am prepared to offer two hundred and fifty dollars... is that enough?"

The sheriff grimaced and said, "Five hundred or a thousand would be better. Do you have that kind of money?"

"No," Suzanne shook her head.

"Without a substantial reward, it's not likely the poster will get much circulation. Even the law won't pay it any mind unless it says he's wanted for something."

Tears began to well up in Suzanne's eyes and her lips trembled. "You mean no one will see it?" she asked.

Clay felt Suzanne's grief and took a step around his desk towards her, then paused when she moved back a step. Feeling the sadness of her plight as well as his own at her obvious avoidance, he said, "Perhaps we could say he is wanted for questioning in an armed assault case."

"Wouldn't that be just as dangerous? What if someone shoots him?"

"Well," the sheriff said, "it wouldn't be a dead or alive poster. That way, with a good reward it should garner some attention and get folks looking."

"You mean bounty hunters, don't you?" Suzanne looked worried.

Clay Anderson had a guilty look about him, but said, "Not necessarily, there will be a lot of folks looking. We'll get them up in stores, post offices, stage and train depots—a lot of places where folks congregate. Someone's bound to see him somewhere."

Suzanne got a hopeful look in her eyes, the first she had since she entered the office. "I do hope so, can you get started on the poster right away? I will see how much money I can raise for the reward."

"I got a couple hundred dollars set aside for a rainy day, you can have that," he said.

Suzanne realized that Clay Anderson's generous offer sprang from the sincere affection he held for her, even knowing that Colt's return could only further remove her from any chance of some future relationship between them, but she also knew that accepting it would be wrong. As much as she liked the big sheriff, now that she knew Colt was alive, as the focus of her affection, Clay and all others, had faded into obscurity. She must find Colt and make him understand.

"Thank you, Clay," she said softly. "That is sweet of you to offer, but I could never deprive you of your hard-earned money."

"I'd be honored for you to have it, if it would help."

"I know you would, but no. You've worked far too long and hard saving that money, and this is not your rainy day, it's mine. You keep it for yours."

Red faced, Clay Anderson shuffled awkwardly from one foot to the other, then set the hat he had been holding on his desk. He started to ask where she intended to get the money, then thought better of it and said instead, "Let me know as soon as you get the funds, I'll need to put the amount on the reward poster."

"I will sheriff, just as soon as I can arrange the finances." Suzanne noted a shadow pass over Anderson's face when she assumed a more formal manner and called him by his title. She abruptly turned towards the door and, bidding him "goodbye," she stepped out into the street with a tumult of emotions running through her. She hated to disappoint Clay, he had been such a good friend, had even championed her by coming to her rescue in the Claude Bollinger affair, and she knew he was probably in love with her, in his own way. Still, it would never do for her to trade on his affections. "Oh Lord," Suzanne prayed, "help me." She must write to Kathreen and tell her what happened. Perhaps she would know what to do.

Dear Kathreen:

I am at a loss to tell you of all that has occurred since we last corresponded, but feel I must write and let you know what has happened. Perhaps you may offer me some fresh insight, for I am at my wits end as to what to do and am desperately despairing as I compose this letter. After you left last summer, I missed you terribly and I am sure it comes as no surprise that Sonny renewed his suit of me.

When I learned of your dumping him into the river, I was conflicted over his attentions, for I was certain your actions spoke louder than words. Oh, how I wish I had listened to my heart and left Sonny to you. As it was, after some time had passed and it became apparent, at least to me, that Sonny's regard for me was genuine, I became convinced that he did love me. I know it was shallow of me to allow his displacement of you, and accept that place in his affections, but the truth is, I was convinced Sonny and you were finished after that last episode between the two of you at the river. Did you know, he even got upset with me and went off to see Margarita?

Anyway, I found myself the reluctant recipient of his suit, and quite despairing of life itself. So much had happened since Colton's disappearance, it seemed that Sonny, and everyone, and even God Himself, was indicating I needed to accept the fact of Colt's death and move on. Even my own body seemed to be telling me that… that my chance of becoming a bride and of motherhood, was passing me by. I must be honest, that scared me a bit.

So, one Saturday, when we had been invited out to the Sabers for a barbeque, Sonny and I had a falling out over Clay Anderson taking me to the harvest party dance at the DeYoungs' while he was away to St. Gaul delivering cattle to the army. I brought up his taking Margarita out and we had a few words. They were civil enough, I suppose, but when he walked away to the barn, my mother came over and told me to go talk to him and get things settled between us. I had been feeling pretty low, not wanting to lose his friendship, and yes, his romantic attentions too, so listening to my head and having deadened my heart, I went to the barn. We talked some, and when Sonny suddenly opened his hand to me and said he was releasing all claims on me, I panicked and said I'd be his girl.

Kathreen, I don't know who was more surprised, him or me, but before I knew it, he scooped me up in his arms and went dancing out in front of everybody, announcing that I was his girl. That made everyone happy and I guess it made me happy too, at least it settled that question for me. I had to resign myself to Colt's death and it was requisite that the great love I bore for him must die, too.

I had not even really come to terms with that before Sonny whisked me off to a little cottage he'd built down by the creek. After showing me the inside, we had just stepped out onto the porch, when Sonny unexpectedly pulled me into his arms and kissed me. I guess I did expect that kiss... should have figured it was coming, at least, and was thinking the right thing to do was to kiss him back and return his embrace. After all, if I was going to be his girl... it's strange the thoughts one can have on the spur of the moment, especially when we are posing, to use the term you coined. It was then that it happened. Only seconds before Sonny's face blocked my view and his lips touched mine, when we were already in close embrace, I saw someone standing in the brush over towards the creek.

It was Colt. I'm heartbroken to have to tell you this, and I keep asking myself, Why! Why! Why now, at the very moment of Sonny's— of our first kiss, would this happen?

There was a terrible shout and I saw Colt rush from the brush, crying out in a voice of despair like the very damned, "No! No!" Startled, we broke apart and I cried out, "Colton, no," for I saw him drawing his gun, just before Sonny jumped in front of me. There was a loud report and then all of a sudden, all went blank.

It breaks my heart to tell you this, but Colt shot Sonny in the chest.

I came to with a splitting headache and a bloody nose, not knowing what had happened. Everybody was there, and when my dad picked me up, Sonny was left lying on the porch with his father working over him.

We all thought he was dead, but do you remember that heavy medallion Sonny used to wear around his neck under his shirt? It was that snake-man thing Colton had taken from the Comanche and given to him. Apparently, the bullet from Colt's gun hit that, but did not penetrate, and the impact so stunned Sonny that he was slammed backwards, unconscious, and that caused his head to snap back and hit me in the face with enough force to bloody my nose, and knock me unconscious. You should have seen the blood, it was all over the porch

where we were lying when they found us.
I guess they thought we were both dead
at first, but after I came to my senses, and
Mr. Saber got Sonny's heart going again by
beating on his son's chest, they all stood
around in bewilderment at what had happened. I guess Sonny and I were pretty
confused too, it all happened so fast and
Colt was nowhere to be found. Becky had
gone to the creek and saw him ride away
and the dear girl was still crying her heart
out when she told her father and mother.

You should see that medallion, it is really
bent up and Sonny is very badly bruised,
and I can tell you I wouldn't win any beauty
prize myself. My nose is swollen and may
even be broken and both my eyes are black.

Kate, I suppose it serves me right, I had
no business letting those false ideas betray
my heart. I knew Colt was alive... all that
long, lonely time, I knew it. What can I do?
Colt is gone again and no one knows where.
We don't even know where he has been for
the past two and a half years. I am sure he
believes he killed us, what with the blood
and all, and will never be back here again,
so I am going to find him.

I spoke with Sheriff Anderson about putting out a reward poster, but I only have
two hundred and fifty dollars to offer. Sheriff
Anderson said that's not enough, that it
should be at least five hundred, or better yet,
a thousand, if I hope to attract anybody's

attention. I do not have that kind of money, and do not know where I can get it, unless from Sonny. He may still have some of his wild-horse money left, but it seems very awkward to ask him for that kind of help now. Besides, he has gone off on his own in search of Colton, and I do not know when he will be back. I shudder to think of what might happen when those two meet up.

I am desperately undone, but somehow rejoicing in the knowledge that Colt is alive and that he had come back to me. Now I find him lost to me again and fear the worse… that he is no longer running to me, but away from me and the memory of us, just as fast and far as he can. I must go and find him and make him understand.

Please forgive me in the matter of Sonny, and if you know of anybody in Saint Louis that might have knowledge of Colt, will you please let me know?

Sadly, Suzanne.

Kathreen McClusky folded the letter, replaced it in the envelope, and then tapped it thoughtfully against her chin. For a moment, she mulled its contents over in her mind and then, with a slight scoff and a shake of her head, she jumped to her feet and hurried off to find her father.

Scranton McClusky looked up from the papers he was working over on the big walnut desk in his study when his daughter burst into the room. One glance at the determined look on her face, and he knew she was up to something, what, he didn't know, but figured he was about to find out.

"Daddy," Kathreen began, "I've got to go back to Texas."

"You what?" he said.

"I've got to go back to Texas, and I need two thousand dollars," his daughter said.

"Two thousand dollars, what for?"

Kathreen handed her father Suzanne's letter. He took it, eying his fiery redheaded daughter skeptically. Opening the letter, he scanned its contents and then burst out with a loud, "What?" He looked briefly up at his daughter, the confusion plain on his face, then reread the letter, this time more slowly.

"It says here she needs one thousand dollars, how come you want two?"

"A thousand for the reward, and a thousand for expenses for us to go find him."

Kathreen stood patiently, her lower lip caught between her teeth watching her father. Finally, Scranton gave a big sigh, tossed the letter on his desk and pushed the wire rim glasses from the bridge of his nose to his forehead.

"Two thousand dollars?" he said disbelievingly. "You want me to give you two thousand dollars so that this… this Suzanne can try to find that boy?"

"He's not some boy, Daddy. It's Colt, Colton Saber, the fellow who rescued me and brought me back from New Orleans."

As she spoke, Kathreen crossed quickly to her father's chair and clasped his arm with both hands, causing the swivel chair he was sitting in to turn Scranton away from his desk, and left him staring up into the compelling, green eyes of his daughter. Why was it he could never say no to his little girl… now a big girl…no, a fully-grown woman, with those persuasive eyes? Yet, she still had a lot of the little girl left in her. Despite her ordeal in New Orleans a few years back, she had proven to be amazingly resilient after the affair at the Arabian Nights and that scoundrel LaRoush. He'd attributed much of this to the two trips she had made to Texas and her new-found friends out west. He was sure her newly found interest in religion had also played a stabilizing role for her as well, and it was not because he was ungrateful, but two thousand bucks... just to help her friend find this Colton with the mark of Cain on him?

"Princess," McClusky said, patting the back of his daughter's hand. "Just how much of this affair pertains to you, and what makes you think it's your business anyway?"

"Don't you know, Daddy? For the past two and a half years, Colton has been missing and it nearly killed Suzanne Kluesman, for she's loved him so. Now he has reappeared and then disappeared again in this terrible misfortune. Can't you see how undone she must be? What if it were me, wouldn't you expect my bosom friend to come to my aid?"

Scranton McClusky squirmed uncomfortably under his daughter's imploring grip and the logic of her argument. Suzanne Kluesman had been a welcome and frequent visitor in his home, and he knew a bond closer than sisters existed between her and his daughter since their common ordeal with that wretched LaRoush. Still, he could not see what Kathreen's running off to Texas was going to accomplish, other than perhaps get out those wanted posters.

"Maybe we could wire her the money, Princess, but I don't see what good you can do her, especially if she is going off to look for Colton."

"I will go with her," Kathreen stated emphatically. "We will find them together."

"Them," her father said. "Who else is missing?"

"Sonny," Kathreen said awkwardly.

"Sonny, you mean the older brother is missing?"

74

"Yes, he is out looking for him too, and Suzanne and I need to be there, who knows what those two will do when they meet up again."

"Wasn't this Sonny writing to you awhile back?"

"Yes," Kathreen said defensively.

"Um-huh," Scranton said, nodding his head. "I thought so. Listen, Princess, are you sure you know what you're doing? Just how many times do you think your heart can be broken?"

Kathreen let go of her father's arm and blinked back a tear. Looking away, she said, "I've got to go with her... I've got to go too, even if it is to play second fiddle..." she swallowed hard..." I've got to go."

McClusky stood to his feet and clasped an arm about his daughter's shoulder. "Alright, Princess, we will see what we can do."

———

"Just how do you expect to find him?" Gunner Kluesman was looking angrily across the table at Suzanne, who was busily compiling a list of things to do before she left. He had been arguing with her about the foolhardiness of her traveling off across the country in search of Colton Saber.

"I don't know," Suzanne said, "but as soon as Kathreen gets here, we are going."

"In what? Do you think for one minute I am going to allow you two young ladies to go traipsing off across Texas? Why the Indians or the Comancheros would have you before the week was out."

"We are going to disguise ourselves as boys, drifting cowpokers looking for work, or something," Suzanne said simply.

"What? Absolutely not! It would never work, you'd have to cut off all your long hair, and neither of you would ever hide your... yourselves in a pair of bib-overalls anyway. I utterly forbid it."

"Well, we could take the stage then, go from town to town and keep asking until we find somebody who has seen him." Suzanne was determined to go.

Gunner could see that there was no easy way of talking her out of this, and he knew he was fighting a losing fight anyway. The stubborn streak that was her German heritage was not going to give in to him, and even if he did manage to convince her of the foolhardiness of this venture, sooner or later she must follow her heart. He also knew the recrimination she was going through for not following it in the first place. She had insisted Colt was alive all along, while everyone else had said he was dead and urged her to move on. Gunner's mood softened, and he turned to where Suzanne had stepped to stare out the parlor window.

"You are faced with choices that grow more pressing with each day that passes," Gunner said, "and that is to follow your heart. You must follow the one you love, how I do not know, but I do know that your story.... Colt's story, even Sonny and Kathreen's story are still being written and not yet finished. I don't know what adventures, pleasures, unhappiness or peril wait for you on this trip, but I know you have to go, that you will not be complete until you do. I know you did not ask for this, that this is not your choice, you would have preferred that Colt had come home one day earlier, that Sonny had never given you that kiss, that Colt had never shot him. But that's not the way of it. This thing has come to you and if you are to live the romance, then you have only one choice. The road lies open before you and you must take it. If traveling it means bobbed off hair and bib-overalls, then so it must be. The only thing I ask is that you wait until winter is over. This will give you some time for your reward poster to circulate and a chance for someone to see him and respond. This way you'll have some idea where to start looking."

———

Dear Kathreen, I trust this letter reaches you in time, for I must urge you to delay your trip West until springtime. Although it nearly kills me to wait, my father has prevailed upon me to not start this search in winter, and I have reluctantly agreed. Mostly because it will give my reward posters time to circulate and work for us. I want to thank you and Mr. McClusky for going assurance on the reward. I have ordered the posters from Sheriff Anderson. Please inform your father that I will pay him back just as soon as possible, once the reward is collected. In the meantime, let us pray that someone will respond with useable information on Colt's whereabouts. Could you keep an eye on the papers in Saint Louis? Perhaps something will turn up in them. You have my heartfelt gratitude for your friendship and help in this matter and again let me offer you my humblest apology for my part of what happened between me and Sonny.

Yours truly, Suzanne Kluesman.

CHAPTER SIX

Chopin' Wood

Fort Griffin, Texas, November 1870.

I STEPPED OUT OF THE STAGE OFFICE AND was scratchin' the back of my head, with Pearl close on my heels. Her self-imposed silence had vanished like a meatball in an Italian cow camp, and she was babbling away a mile a minute, as soon as the door closed behind her.

"What did he mean, I can't travel by myself?" she said.

"He said you're too young to ride the stage all that way alone."

"Then you'll just have to go with me," she asserted.

It never ceases to amaze me how females, no matter what their size, just assume they can boss a fella around like some old mother hen with a passel of chicks. When I chose not to dignify her remarks with the answer that I would dearly have loved to give her, since I knew it would have no more effect than spittin' in the ocean, I just locked my jaw and kept walkin' towards the wagon yard, Pearl trotting to catch up, as I lengthened my stride.

"Where we going? You can take me to your ma's, can't you?"

"I'm going to get Lightfoot and you are going to go up to that room I rented, and take yourself a much-needed bath," I growled.

"You need a bath too, Woody. I wasn't going to say anything, but you smell like a tarpaulin off a gut wagon."

I stopped to stare back at this upstart kid and saw a look of defiance staring me back. "Dash it all, Pearly, if you ain't as contrary as a lop-eared ol' jenny. Any more sass out of you, and I am liable to turn you over to the Tonkawa. Now go take that bath."

Sullenly she turned back to the hotel and mumbled, "Don't know why you won't take me."

I watched her go and hid a smile, then sniffed my armpits and spent the next couple of minutes trying to blink the water out of my eyes and get my breath back. The kid was right, but a tarpaulin off a gut wagon? Where's she come up with this stuff? Not that she was far wrong, maybe a good bath would help some.

I rode Lightfoot up the hill the fellow had called Government Hill, probably because there was a government post on top, and pulled him up in front of the building with a flag pole. The horse snorted his disgust when I slapped the reins around the hitching rack and hurried for the door. There was a raw wind blowing and my pony turned tail to it and then reminded me to hurry up, he had a warm stall and a pile of oats to get back too.

An orderly showed me into the office of a Lieutenant Colonel S. B. Hayman, post commander, and I saw a large, middle-aged man with graying, mutton-chop whiskers framing a too-red pair of cheeks, indicating a fondness for whiskey. He was seated in a creaking wooden swivel chair. The Lt. Col. looked dubiously over wire-framed spectacles perched on the end of his nose, and asked, "What can I do for you?"

I said, "My name is Woody... Woodrow..." I almost said my last name since I'd forgotten to come up with a pretend last name for Woody. I quickly cast about for a suitable end-name and spying the potbellied stove in the corner that was keeping the chill at bay, I blurted out, "Stove... Stover. Woodrow Stover, and I got this kid I need to get back to the Pecos. You got any soldiers that might be heading that way? She needs an escort."

The Lt. Col. was looking skeptically at me. "How come you don't take her yourself?"

It was an awkward question for me, so without saying too much, I briefly explained how I was, driftin' over to the cattle crossing on the Red, in hopes of pickin' up a cattle drive headin' for Abilene or Dodge City, and I needed to get the kid to some folks who would take her in back on the Pecos.

"Who is this kid?" the Lt. Col. asked, "You say she's a she?"

"Yeah, 'bout twelve to thirteen or so. I came across her and an old man up on the Llano. She claimed her Pa lost her to this old codger in a poker game down in Kentucky and she'd been travelin' with him ever since."

"Good God," Hayman said, and jumped up to lean forward with his hands on his desk. "You mean her Pa gambled her away? What kind of crazies do we have out here?"

I smiled grimly and nodded my head. "'Bout every kind there is, I reckon."

"Is this kid alright? I suppose he..." the Lt. Col. broke off from stating the obvious.

Again, I nodded a silent affirmation, then said, "She's okay I guess, she's got a lot of sand and is dead set on going to these folks on the Pecos. She claims her Ma died and she's got no other kin but her drunkard father, and she'll run away before she goes back to him."

"What happened to the jasper who won her at poker?"

"He met with a fortuitous accident when chasing us, after I took the girl away from him one night while he was drunk."

"Fortuitous, huh? What happened?"

"He failed to see a gap in the caprock up on the high plain and run his wagon off a cliff into the Palo Duro."

"Huh," the Lieutenant Colonel said. "Sounds like divine retribution to me."

"Yep, it killed him, said his name was Howard Raphael. He won't be troublin' no youngsters anymore."

"How come you don't take her?"

I thought I detected a note of sarcasm in his voice, and pretending I was uninterested I said, "I've already been saddled with her for far too long, and life on the open range is no place for a kid. She ought to be in school and learning womanly ways, not runnin' around with me in boy's clothes, taking up with spittin', profane language and such."

Well, I guess I made my case, because the Lt. Col. said he did have a Sargent who was being reassigned to Fort Stockton in a couple of weeks and he could provide escort for Pearl. I was some relieved to hear this, but wondered aloud what I could do, hanging around for two more weeks, when my pony was itchin' for the Red. Actually, he wasn't, but I like folks to think my cow horse is a real go-getter, it might inspire him to greater levels of accomplishment.

"Sometimes the Army hires civilians for wood-cutting detail, you ever handle an ax?"

"Yeah, but I don't like it... can't do that from the back of my horse too well."

The Lt. Col. gave me a pathetic look and shook his head. "You cowboy types are all alike. Did it ever occur to you that there is a whole lot more to life than forking some flea-bit bronc or yanking the neck off some poor scrawny cow with a short rope?"

"Nope, not anymore it doesn't. How much does this wood-peckin' job pay?"

"Five bucks a day, you have to sign up. Go see Sargent O'Flarety out at the front desk."

I told him I'd give it a go for a couple of weeks until it was time to put Pearly on the stage and then I was headin' out of here. He nodded with something akin to resignation, as though he had failed to talk sense into one more cowpoke, then turned back to the papers on his desk.

By the time I'd signed Sargent O'Flarety's wood chopping roster, and stepped off the porch to my saddle horse, I could see ol' Lightfoot was less than enchanted with me for my treatment of dumb animals... him in particular. I took that as an admission on his part to the fact, and when he laid his ears back flat and tried to paw me once with a hind foot while I was catching the stirrup to mount, it left no doubt in my mind of it. Once I was up on the hurricane deck, the silly bronc got his back all humped up, and then tried to claim it was that way 'cause I'd left him short tied out in an arctic blue norther. He kept it humped up that way too, all the way back down Government Hill just to prove his point. I chided him on being one of those Tennessee bred nags and told him a real cowpony actually enjoyed these little Texas breezes. Lightfoot just snorted snowflakes in disgust, his frosty breath whipped away by the rising wind, then he broke for the livery barn in the worst, bone-jarring trot I ever felt him use.

Pearly let out a screech loud enough to crack paint, when I pushed the door to my hotel room open. Thinking I had got the wrong room, I paused to take a second look at the room number, but nope, I had the right room. She scrunched down as best she could in one of those trundle-out bathtubs that she had sitting in the middle of the room near the heating stove, and stared angrily back at me with just her head poking out of the soap bubbles.

"Woody," she said. "Don't you think to knock before you enter a lady's boudoir?"

I stood there dumbfounded, having forgotten that I had sent the kid to her bath, and was still puzzling over the boudoir word, with my mouth open wide enough to catch flies. I suppose I'd a caught on faster 'n molasses in January too, since, in less awkward moments, I knew what that Frenchy word meant, but I was plumb horn-swaggled at finding this suds-be-draped girl soaking in a tub in the middle of my room. My face redder than the hubs of Hades, I mumbled out an apology and stumbled back through the door into the hallway and pulled it to. I was somewhat amazed at this turn of events. Pearly was no lady yet, but she was well on her way, and wasn't exactly the kid I thought she was either.

I made my way down to the front desk and asked the clerk why they didn't have a bathroom, but he just looked at me like I had two heads, and then asked me where I thought I was?

"Hey," I said, "I know where I am. I just didn't expect to find no naked female sittin' in a tub of water in the middle of my room."

With the patient endurance one reserves for small children, the desk clerk explained that the Occidental could provide a trundle bath tub and hot water at a guest's request, but had no spare rooms for bathing. The rest of the affair was none of his business and then he reminded me that I owed him for one bath.

"Well, make it for two and bring up some more hot water," I said.

"When?" he asked.

I just shrugged my shoulders, my hands outstretched, and shook my head. He should'a known there was no tellin' that. I left him muttering under his breath, and headed for the mercantile store that we had passed on the way in.

83

Conrad and Rath's General Merchandise Store was a picket and mud structure built with two rows of logs in vertical alignment about a foot apart, with the intervening space filled with brush, reeds, grass, mud or any other thing that might have come in handy. These walls were plastered over and painted white. The entire building was fronted with a wide porch. I learned from the clerk who waited on me that goods were freighted in from Dodge City, Kansas when they could get them. It looked pretty well stocked to me, but then again, I had been looking at ol' Raphael's two-wheel cart for the past couple of weeks. The clerk was a pretty gal, about my own age as near as I could figure, and said her name was Miss Elizabeth, though I didn't ask. She spoke with one of those Scottish Highlander accents that was a joy to listen to, and she was pretty easy on the eyes as well, although I didn't really pay that no never mind.

She helped me pick out some girl's clothes and personals, giving me a skeptical look when I told her I didn't know Pearlie's size.

"Ya say she's a lass ah twelve or thirteen?" the lady said.

I nodded my head and she said for me to take the garments that she put into a bag and thrust into my hands, "back to the lassie and then send her down once she has finished her bath and she'd fix her up with the rest of what she needed."

I nodded again, somewhat embarrassed that I hadn't paid more attention to Pearlie's size and all. I paid for the stuff along with a change of clothes and some sturdy work boots for wood chopping, and headed back for the Occidental with the packages under my arms. I ignored the clerk behind the desk, and he ignored me, his pointy head stuck in a week-old newspaper.

"Pearly, are you decent?" I asked and rapped a knuckle on the door.

"Just a minute," Pearl said.

I heard the water slosh, then patiently waited while I figure the girl was drying herself off with the towel.

"I hate to put these smelly clothes back on," she called.

"I bought you some new duds," I said through the door. "If you come here, I will hand them through to you."

There was a squeal of delight and the wet slap of her bare feet on the floor, then the door opened a crack and she stuck her hand out. I handed her the package, and with a "thanks," Pearly snatched the parcel and slammed the door shut. For the next few minutes I listened to her delighted giggles while she rustled through the tissues and packages like a family of mice doing a fandango in a crepe paper factory. Finally, the door popped open and she said, "You may come in now."

Well I never expected the sight that met my eyes. There was this pretty little gal, all done up in a frilly dress, a ribbon in her hair, and smelling like grandma's sweet-pea patch. With her eyes sparkling, she looked up at me expectantly.

"Who are you?" I kidded, "and what have you done with Pearl?"

"I am Pearl," she said, then pirouetted with a flourish.

"Naw, naw! Pearl's some freckle faced kid I left in here. Wha'd you do with her?"

"Woody, it's me, you big ninny. Don't you know anything?"

"Well, I know when I left, there was a dirty faced kid in a tub full of water, and now I find a little fairy princess... what was in that water, some kind of magical pixie dust?"

"Just soap and water, you big simpleton, it's me, Pearl, I was here all the time."

"You mean to tell me you was hidin' in there like that all this time? Why if I'd a known that I woulda..."

"You would have what?" she prompted, a sudden coyness creeping into her voice. Not being unfamiliar with feminine wiles, I marveled at how quickly the feminine mystic took over in this young girl seeking affirmation of her beauty.

"Why, I… I might'a been on my best behavior," I said bowing low as if to royalty.

"Oh, don't be silly, you couldn't help yourself, not with all your troubles and stuff."

I chuckled and gave her a big grin, wondering how she knew I had troubles.

"There's a lady by the name of Miss Elizabeth, who said for you to come and see her and she would fix you up with all you need for traveling to the Pecos." I saw delight in Pearl's eyes and she rushed up to me, but stopped just short of a hug.

"Tarp off"n a gut wagon?" I said.

She nodded in embarrassment and stepped back a few more steps.

"I'm sorry, I wouldn't want to get my new clothes mussed up."

"You go see Miss Elizabeth," I said, "I'll take care of the tarp."

Fort Griffin was just getting a good toe-hold on its reputation as the roughest boarder town in the west, and I could see why. I counted no less than seven saloons, with the "Deney Saloon" at one end of Griffin Avenue, to the "Bee Line" at the other. There were numerous gambling houses as well, and along River Street were at least five "Cribs," where the ladies of the night plied their trade.

Two of the cattle drive trails passed through here as well, the Chisholm and the Western, on their way to Dodge City. It had been my intent to connect with one of the cattle drives up at the crossing on the Red, once Pearl was off on the stage, but since the cattle drives passed through here anyway, I figured I might just as well wait right here and chop wood for the Army. It would beat camping out in a tent for the winter up there.

Griffin, or "The Flat," as the town was called, was fast becoming a center for the growing buffalo hide trade as well, and as a result there were more and more hunters arriving, most who would have made the likes of Buff Waistman and Sylvester Kemp, the two seedy hunters I'd encountered at Big Springs a few years back look like choir boys by comparison. I was returning a captured Kiowa girl to her people, at the time.

I was some concerned about going off during the day to chop wood and leaving Pearl to fend for herself. This tough town was no place to be leaving an adolescent girl alone in the hotel, so I decided to go see if Miss Elizabeth over at Conrad and Rath's might have any ideas. I found the shop clerk in close conversation with another clerk, a young fellow near her age. They were in the dry goods section away from the others in close conversation when I spotted them, and when she saw me approaching with obvious intent, she quickly said, "I got 'a go, Henry," and turned to walk towards me.

Hank lit out of there like he'd been caught stealing chickens and I would 'a bet the two of them had been discussing more than the price of dress goods, if I'm any judge.

"Am I interrupting anything important?" I asked as Miss Elizabeth approached.

"No... ah, Mr. Stover, in' it?'

I gave her a sly smile and nodded my head like some old, all-seeing sage while looking over her shoulder at the retreating form of Hank. The pretty young clerk drew herself up, patted her hair in place, even though it wasn't out of place, and regained her composure despite a very red face.

"Wha kin ah do fer ya, Mr. Stover?"

"I need to find a place for Pearl for a few days while I'm working," I said.

"Workin' at what?" she said.

"I'll be riding out in the morning on wood cutting detail for the Army."

"Ow long will ya be gone?"

"Most all day, I suspect, any chance you could keep an eye on the kid?"

Miss Elizabeth looked thoughtful. "Ow long is a few days?"

"Just until I can send her off on the stage... two weeks at the most."

"She kin stay with me then," she said.

When I told Pearl my plan, she was delighted. She and Miss Elizabeth had hit it off pretty well when the store clerk had helped out with her clothes and girly things. So now I was relieved of the responsibility and worrying after the kid while working.

On the Clearfork of the Brazos at the end of town, I had to goose Lightfoot with my spurs a couple of times to get him to step off the bank and into the shallow waters of the ford. I guess he figured the water was too cold to go wading, but finally he joined the wood wagons and the others, and we rode out just as the sun was topping the horizon to the east. A grove of oak, elm and cotton-wood, about five miles distant from town, was the chosen wood lot of the day. Most of the big timber along the river and closer in, had been felled for saw logs to feed the steam powered sawmill along-side the creek. This mill had supplied much of the green lumber with which the town and the fort had been built. When the lumber dried, it twisted and warped, cracking in the hot sun, and gave everything, the post buildings in particular, a rather shabby, dilapidated look. This led to more needed repairs, often made with green lumber from the mill again, and the whole process would just repeat itself. I guess it gave the soldier boys something to do beside chase Indians, but to listen to them tell of it, they were not too pleased with the task. I listened to the grumbling of a couple troopers riding nearby.

"If we hadn't 'a whacked all the trees down around the flat, we wouldn't have to be ridin' so dad blame far for stove wood," a young private said.

Sargent O'Flarety twisted in his saddle and spoke back over his shoulder to the two recruits. "To date, we have fallen one thousand and twenty-five oak, elm, and cottonwood for that mill, with more n' eighty-three thousand linear board feet of lumber cut."

The Private looked at his riding mate and shook his head. "That's a lot of wood cuttin'."

His friend was batting his head around like a prairie dog sitting under the nest tree of a redtail hawk. "Ain't we in danger of Indian attack, riding this far from the fort?"

The first fellow said, "There's always that chance. Shoot, a bunch of Kiowa attacked the mail coach just yesterday up on Mountain Pass within a mile of the Picket Station. They hit 'em in that steep section with the cliff-like sides just this side of Abercrombie Pass."

The other soldier, apparently a new recruit, seemed even more anxious. "Didn't the mail coach come in yesterday?"

"Yeah," his friend replied. "The six-man patrol from Phantom Hill ran the red-sticks off and the coach rumbled on through."

These two Privates, along with three others and the Sargent, made up the patrol escorting the wood cutting party from the fort.

The rest of the wood cutters were a motley crew of mostly older men down on their luck and, I figured, looking to make a little beer money. Me, I was along just to keep busy so I wouldn't drop dead of boredom and wouldn't have to be thinking about... well, stuff.

We reached the grove of trees and everyone piled out of the wagons or dismounted and tied their horses to the bushes. I pulled a ten-foot picket rope from my saddle bags and snapped it to Lightfoot's halter, which I had left on under the bridle so my horse could crop grass while I chopped wood. It was plain to me he had the better end of the deal, but he snorted me one anyway, when I tied him off to a clump of willows. He wanted to know how come I didn't take the bridle off so he could eat better, and I could see I had to do all the thinking around here. If the Kiowa or Comanche show up, I don't intend to have to bridle my horse before I skedaddle. Talk about horse sense, with Lightfoot its way overrated, and I told him so. He did his usual rebuff: ignoring me, then insolently turning away and bumping me with his rump in the process. He then walked to the end of the picket and stuck his mug into the grass.

The Sargent put me to work felling the trees, and the others to sawing up logs and rounds using sawhorses and bucksaws. He instructed me to pick out the dead and dying trees first as they would be the driest, and when I told him I knew that already, he just scowled and told me, "Get to it."

The bite of the ax, when it sunk into the dry wood of a tall dead elm, sent a quiver vibrating up the trunk. I watched the top whip back and forth and warily stepped back. The fool thing was in danger of snapping off. It was a widow maker in the making, and since I had no widow to make, and didn't figure I would have, I took another hefty lick at the thing with the ax, finding myself a little bit peeved because of it. There was a loud crack and I jumped back just before a ten-foot length of the top pile drives into the ground where I had been standing. I shook my head and looked up at what was left of the swaying top, then let my gaze wander on up through the naked limbs of the forest canopy, past some nasty looking clouds that probably carried snow, to a patch of blue heaven and raised my eyebrows at Him.

"You tryin' to kill me?" I said accusingly. I pushed the tree top aside and finished whacking the rest of the elm down.

By noon, I was aching like a busted tooth in a candy store, and was glad for the lunch break. My hands were sporting pretty good blisters too, and I gave myself a good mental scolding for not having bought a pair of work gloves when I had the chance. I'd have to find some bacon grease and rub into 'em when I got back to town. I walked over to where there was a cook fire burning near the wood's edge and poured myself a cup of coffee and noted the grizzled old cook with a face full of stubby gray whiskers and a couple of snaggle teeth, giving me the eye.

"You ready to put the nose-bag on?" he said.

I nodded and accepted the plate of beef and beans he handed me and grabbed a couple of biscuits as well, then found an un-split round of oak and sat down. The food was good; I had worked up quite an appetite and was doing my best to put it all away when ol' snaggle tooth came over.

"Those sojer boys over there near drank up two pots o' coffee. They be keeping me busy grinding coffee beans all morning. I don't know why they don't get off'n their dead bobtails and do somethin' useful 'round here."

"You don't consider their presence here a deterrent to the Injuns?" I said around a spoonful of beans.

The old man looked unimpressed and shook his head. "Not much, there's only six of 'em. If the heathen show up, we'll be pretty much on our own."

"Well, we must have fifteen or twenty extra guns here in the whole bunch of us."

He snorted in disgust, "Yeah, and I doubt that there's more'n five or six of 'em can even shoot or brought a gun along."

Well, that surprised me some and I got to looking around at the men scattered about. I couldn't see a single one wearing a side arm and only saw two or three rifles leaning up against the wood wagons. My eyes fell on my gunbelt looped around the saddle horn. I had taken it off to work, and now all of a sudden, I was feeling uneasy, like I was in church without my pants on. As soon as I finished these Pecos strawberries, I was going to go put it back on.

I was holding out my coffee cup to the old man, who said his name was Strawberry Jensen... probably 'cause of the beans... for a refill, when he said a bad word and nearly poured hot coffee on my hand.

I jerked my cup back and turned to see over my shoulder, what he was staring at. I saw two Injun braves in full war paint, mounted on ponies, ki-yi-in' and shaking their lances in the air towards our camp.

Like a cat falling into a toilet hole, the whole camp came to life. Plates and cups hit the ground, and the six soldiers rushed to mount their horses and charge off to where the Indians were riding about. I hurried over to Lightfoot and strapped on my gunbelt, with a strong sense of misgiving. Something didn't seem right about the whole affair.

I watched as the two warriors turned to flee from the approaching soldiers, who spurred after them. Untying Lightfoot's lead, I unsnapped it and stepping into the saddle, I coiled the rope while watching with interest the chase out on the prairie. The rest of the camp was on full alert, while those with guns took up positions, finding what cover they could. More than half of them had no guns at all, but old Strawberry Jensen was yelling at them to hitch up the teams to the wagons, and grab up long sticks that would look like they had guns to the Indians.

I was worried that this was some trick of the Indians to lure us into a trap, and began to look warily behind us, back into the woods. All of a sudden there came blood curdling war cries back out on the range, and I whirled about to see a large band of the savages riding furiously toward the six troopers.

Sargent O'Flarety and his men nearly turned their mounts inside out getting them turned around and headed back to us. They were riding for their lives with forty or fifty Kiowa and Comanche doing their best to stop them. Trouble was, the whole bunch was heading our way.

"You men line up in front of the wagons," Strawberry Jensen yelled. "Hold up your sticks and shake them at the Injuns and yell like a bear trap had a-holt of your privates."

In confusion, the wood cutters lined up, then began to follow Jensen's example, who was hollering and shaking his rifle like it was tryin' to sprout wings and fly off without him. I rode to a position behind the line of men and unholstered my .44, as the fast approaching soldiers thundered towards camp with the redskins close on their heels.

"When they come within range, you men with guns fire 'n' don't shoot the sojer boys," Jensen called. "The rest o' you keep shakin' your sticks."

I never saw the beat of it. Once the Indians were in range we began firing, while the troopers raced into camp, quit their saddles and unlimbered their own weapons. The first volley broke up the charge and sent the Indians into full retreat, back to where they drew up out of range and began yelling war cries and shaking their weapons at us. The wood cutters responded with their sticks, yelling and making cat-calls back that near put the Injuns to shame. I punched out the empties and thumbed fresh cartridges into my smoking six-gun. For a minute there, I thought we were in some kind of "bad-mouth your worst enemy Texas finals." Finally, the Indians turned and with a few sporadic gestures by the more dedicated of the band, they rode off out of sight. I turned, looking mildly surprised at the motley crowd of celebrating old codgers. You'd a thought they'd just won the Revolutionary War single handed, or something, the way they were carrying on.

I rode over to where Sargent O'Flarety was com-
mending Jensen for his quick thinking and rallying
of the men.

"Where'd you come up with that idea?" O'Flarety said.

Larn't it from you sojer boys," Jensen said and reached
in his hip pocket for his plug.

"From us?" the Sargent said in surprise. "I don't
understand."

Jensen took a chew off his plug of tobacco. "Shore,
just last July one of your Lieutenants was bringing up
about forty new recruits to Griffin from Fort Concho when
they were jumped by a band of Injuns. They were camped
at the foot of a bluff, not far from the Mountain Pass Picket
Station, and since the men were recruits, they only had
six or seven of the old breech load rifles among them. A
Private John Carlton was in charge and when the war
whoops attacked, trying to steal the horses and mules,
he passed out the guns and told the rest to grab up sticks
the size of rifles. The men with the real guns fired while
the others jumped up shaking their sticks and the Injuns
thought they were out gunned and took off, just like these
redskins did here." Jensen finished his declaration with a
snaggle-toothed grin in obvious relish, then punctuated
his final remarks with a stream of tobacco juice at the
Sargent's boots.

Sargent O'Flarety jumped back, "Well I'll be dawged,"
he said. "Private John Carlton? I know him. Who'd a
thought that rascal had enough moxie to pull that off?"

"Page outta your own book, Sarge, page outta your
own book."

I was plumb tuckered by the time I pulled Lightfoot
up in front of the big stone and timber home where Miss
Elizabeth Boyle kept house for her father. When I knocked
on the door, Miss Elizabeth answered and led me into a
big parlor where an elderly gentleman was asleep in a

rocking chair in front of a cheery fire that crackled on the hearth of a huge stone fireplace.

"Papa," Miss Elizabeth said, "This is Mr. Stover, Pearl's guardian."

The old man opened his eyes suddenly and held out a hand of greeting. "Hoot man, an wha brung ye to the God-forsaken likes o' the Flat?"

I grinned with enjoyment at the old man's talk, although it was mighty hard to understand. He had me listening as attentive as a robin at a night-crawler's funeral.

"Ere ye a Presbyterian, then?" the old man challenged.

"No sir, Baptist... I was raised Baptist," I said with a smile.

"Harrumph, one of those water dowsers are ye? Well, never mind that, me lassie here's a Presbyterian. Always has been, 'n' always will be. I dinna bring her all the way from Dalray in Ayrshire, Scotland to see her matched up with no water-dunked Baptist."

"No Papa," Miss. Elizabeth put in, "Mr. Stover has come to collect Pearl, he ha-n't come a'courtin'."

"He's not?" The old man said. "What's the matter with him, has he not got eyes in his 'ead? That's the trouble with Baptists, they dunna know a good thin when they see one."

I looked up at Miss Elizabeth and gave her a huge grin. She blushed red and nervously smoothed the front of her skirts with both hands, then mumbled, "I better go find Pearl.

"Ayrshire, Scotland," I said. "Isn't that where those milch cows come from?"

"Nay, nay, Ayrshire county's wool, man, wool. Hoot, dunna ya know anythin'? Dalray is a wool manufacturing town, man, the confounded cows be damned."

I watched in amused silence while he filled a large-bowled Churchwarden pipe[1] with tobacco, then fumbled in the pockets of his robe for a match. Seeing a nearby candle, I grabbed it and held the flame to his pipe, taking care not to catch the large bushy walrus mustache under his prominent nose, on fire. I could just imagine what his opinion of Baptists would be then. He clutched my hand with both his to steady the flame, and perhaps to avert such a conflagration as well, then sucked furiously at the flame until the Churchwarden was puffing good. Then he let out a yell and pushed my hand away after the candle dripped hot wax onto his leg.

"Augh! I suppose ye think ye have to set fire to me so's ye kin baptize me proper then, is thet it?"

"Sorry sir I didn't mean to...."

At that moment, Pearl and Miss Elizabeth came back into the room.

"Woody," Pearl said. "I see you met Grampa Boyle, isn't he wonderful?"

I was surprised to see the old man's demeanor change so rapidly. He held out an arm to Pearl and said, "Come 'ere lass," then pulled her to the side of his chair while she draped an arm about his shoulders.

"Grampa Boyle has been telling me all about Scotland. Did you know it's across the Atlantic Ocean and it has real castles with real kings and queens and princesses and such? Just like in the storybooks."

"I 'ave a corned beef just aboot done Mr. Stover," Miss Elizabeth put in. "Would ye kear to sup with us?"

I looked at my sore hands and soiled work clothes and shook my head. "I just come to collect Pearl. Perhaps some other time when I am more suitably attired."

I thought, *listen to me talk.* What I meant was better dressed, but there was something about this lady, and this house, and maybe the fact that these folks were from Scotland... across the Atlantic, that had me using forty dollar words. I was probably trying to make 'em think I was more'n a five-dollar-a-day cowpoke, who was chopping wood instead of punching cows. I mumbled on, "I'm afraid I wouldn't be very good company this evening. You ready Pearl?"

"Well, then, do let Pearl stay, she's spent all afternoon helping me prepare the meal. We have plenty of room and it would be much better for me lookin' after her here, if she were close at hand."

"You wanna do that?" I asked the girl.

"Yes," Pearly said. "I'll stay for now."

I bid the old man good evening and was replied with another, "Harrumph!" There were some more derogatory remarks aimed at Baptists in general and me in particular, but I was being hurried to the door by Miss Elizabeth and didn't quite make it all out.

"Good night Mr. Stover," Miss Elizabeth said when we reached the door. Opening it she ushered me out onto the stoop. "Never mind Papa, he's got a good heart."

"I hope so, for your sake," I replied. "I think Hank Smith's a Baptist."

She gave a little gasp and shut the door quicker'n a jackrabbit on Valentine's Day. I chuckled to myself and walked off the porch to my waiting cowpony. I had no more idea of Hank Smith being a Baptist than I did of what the future held in store.

A week later I was stretched low over the neck of my red horse, racing for the Clear Fork of the Brazos, and trying to reach the Flat before a dozen or more Indians used me for a pin-cushion.

Lightfoot and I had been riding along minding our own business, just talkin' about the weather and such, and he was letting me know his opinions on the whole horse-and-rider thing. It was spitting snow a little, and I'll admit we could see the vapor of our breath some, but I had just casually reminded him of the benefit of having me up there keeping the snow off his back, when this band of Kiowa or Comanche, they was too far off to be sure, came busting out of a draw and spotted me and the sorrel. The redskins started in with their signature howling and came for us as swift as the wind, so I reminded Lightfoot that if he didn't want to become some Indian pony, all painted up like a hootchy-kootchy gal, he'd better put wings to his hoofies and get us out of there.

I was on my way back from wood cutting and was trailing the rest of the wood cutting party after a rather necessary call of nature had caused me to fall behind. This was good and bad. Good, because as scared as I was now, Lightfoot probably would not have been content to have me astride, and bad, because it left me easy prey for the hostiles.

I think it unfair that in a horse race such as this one, the Indians have the advantage of riding

bareback and stripped down of all unnecessary clothing. If I knew who to talk too about this I would, but not right now. Arrows were starting to whiz past me and rain down all around. My only hope was that they would not want to shoot a good red horse like Lightfoot.

I could see there was no way I was going to make it to the crossing before they caught me, so instead, I rode a bee-line straight for the river. The good news was that I was going to beat them there, the bad was the river ran some fifty feet below the bank I was charging toward.

I doubt Lightfoot knew this, otherwise he may have decided on becoming a hootchy-kootchy horse after all. At any rate, we hit the edge and went sailing off the bluff like some giant Pegasus without the wings. I quit the saddle and went free falling after my horse and for one quick second, I saw this look in his eye that said, *"You got to be kiddin' me."* We hit the ice-cold water with a cannon ball splash big enough to stop the river flowing down stream for about a minute or two. I think I was sitting on the muddy river-bottom for a few seconds with no water around me at all before it all rushed back in, colder than a dead witch on the back side of the moon.

Lightfoot lunged to his feet and scrambled to the opposite shore with water streaming off him and my saddle. He hollered some unkind words at me and then lit out for town like the very Devil himself was after him.

I was left bobbing like a cork in four or five feet of water with everything I got stinging like a thousand spankings. Arrows were raining down on me from the bluff above where the Kiowa-Comanche band had all unhorsed and were engaged in some friendly archery competition with me as their bulls-eye. I kicked for the opposite shore and felt for the gun at my hip. Luckily it was still in the holster and probably accounted for the nasty bruise I felt there. Drawing my .44, I held it out of the water long enough to clear the barrel and then snapped off six shots in succession, motivating the would-be Robin Hoods to withdraw for cover, effectively ending the archery shoot.

Stumbling up the bank while reloading, I watched for the Indians on the opposite side, but none put in an appearance before I reached the cover of the brush and trees. Shaking with cold and wet to the bone, I dog trotted towards town, the trundle tub at the Occidental a welcoming thought on my mind. Lightfoot and I would no doubt have this little escapade to chew over, provided he made it back to the wagon yard and wasn't being decked out in hootchy-kootchy paint instead.

"Pearl," I said, as Sargent Compton loaded her valise into the boot of the mail coach. "When you get to Wade's Landing, go directly to the post office and tell the Post Mistress you need to go out to the Crossed Sabers Ranch. The Crossed Sabers... you got it?"

"Yes," she said in a subdued voice. "Who do I ask for?"

"Just tell the lady you need to go to the Crossed Sabers, she'll do the rest... and Pearl...there's no need to mention my name. I'd just as soon no one knew where I was."

"Really, how come?"

"Never mind, it doesn't matter, just promise me you'll keep that highly developed chatterbox of yours shut. Will you?"

"They're going to ask me how come I'm there, what did you think?"

"You can tell them whatever you want, just not about me. Tell 'em about ol' Howard, that's as good a story as any. The rest you can make up as long as you leave me out of it. You promise?"

"Okay," she said, "but they're going to wonder how come I'm there."

"Just tell them somebody told you they are good, God-fearing people who care when bad things happen to young girls, and know how to help out."

"Alright," she said unconvincingly. "Goodbye Woody, I hope to see you again someday."

Pearl stepped up on the step of the coach and then turned and hugged my neck, then said, "Thanks, I'll always love you." She turned and fled into the coach.

"Funny she should say she loved me," I mused out loud. Adolescent girls can get some strange notions sometimes. I had no illusions about Pearly keeping her big mouth shut. That would last about as long as a June bug in a hen house, and it wouldn't take the folks long to figure out who Pearl's reluctant rescuer was. It was time for me to be moving on.

CHAPTER SEVEN

The Great Stampede

Texas Midlands, Fall 1870.

SONNY INCHED FORWARD ON HIS BELLY through a thicket of buffalo berry, his rifle on half-cock, and peered through the tangle of brush. About forty yards distant he spotted them and raised his rifle. He peered along the sight until it settled on the head of a young jake, then squeezed the trigger and saw the wild turkey's head explode in a burst of feathers. The big bird thumped and thrashed about while the rest of the flock fled in a flurry of thudding wings. After pausing until the turkey lay still, he warily got to his feet and walked over to pick up the bird. "You'll make a welcome change to my larder," he said. He walked back to the camp site where Tornado and Hank were picketed and spent the next hour dressing and spitting the young tom over the coals of a small fire.

It had been a day since he had left Sam Bass, the sheep man, and he had traveled steadily east towards the Sweetwater country. Somehow, he had a hunch that Colt might be retracing the trail he had followed when he had taken the Indian girl, Seeaugway, back to the Kiowa. He traveled with both reluctance and determination to find his brother. What would he do when he found him? Sit down and make him understand that Suzanne was all Colt's and that he was only an afterthought? Not likely. Did he even want to? Yeah, this was something he had to do. Fools rush in... and he had been a fool to think that he could replace Colton in the heart of the blacksmith's daughter. It was up to him to find Colt and bring him back to Suzanne... then he would ride on.

The country he rode through was rich in game, plentiful with antelope, deer, wild turkey and buffalo. Sometimes he encountered herds of the shaggy beasts that stretched for miles to the horizon. At times, he would endeavor to ride around them, but most often he chose to push on through, scattering the grazing animals as he passed. These beasts had been an impediment when he'd ridden with Goodnight's cattle drives up to New Mexico Territory and Colorado, although the herds had been nowhere near as vast as these. It took constant vigilance on the part of the cowboys to keep the buffalo from mixing with the longhorns and fights would break out between the cattle and their distant cousins.

Sonny had passed the night with a belly full of roast turkey, and now sat Tornado on a slight rise, studying a herd of bison in front of him that seemed to have no end.

"Son-of-a-gun, Tornado, there just ain't no help for it but to ride on through the brutes. Let's go." He spurred the stallion down the slope and gave a hard tug on the rope of the reluctant Hank. The buffalo eyed the intruders suspiciously and moved out of their way as the horse and rider and pack mule made their way amongst them. Sonny found the flies were almost unendurable, even at this time of year. He pulled his neckerchief up over his face, and the brim of his hat low over his eyes and put the grulla into a steady trot.

The sun was high overhead by the time he reached the farther edges of the buffalo and his nervousness began to subside some. It was an uncanny feeling, being surrounded by these animals, for some of the bulls were immense. If they should suddenly decide to run, he'd be in a heap of trouble.

An hour later he had left the great herd behind and Sonny was musing on the vastness of the prairie and feeling not a little insignificant out here. His eyes studied the horizon and he realized he could actually detect the slight curvature of the earth.

"You know Tornado, if Columbus had ridden out here, he would a known the earth was round. Look at that. I wonder if he saw that at sea? They say you can see the same thing on the ocean." Tornado just snatched a bite of buffalo grass as they rode on.

The monotony of the prairie and the methodical pace soon had Sonny's head nodding. He felt sleepy. A worrisome bit of branch and a couple of inconveniently placed rocks under his bedroll had interfered with his rest the night before and now he was fighting sleep. He was still several miles from Big Springs and had been holding the stallion to the east, relying mostly on his shadow that swung around in front of him as the afternoon sun dipped towards the western horizon. It was his hope to make Big Springs before dark and hang out there a couple of days as there should be travelers passing through this favorite waterhole on the converging trails. Here he might glean some information on his brother.

Sonny was no stranger to sleeping in the saddle. Long days and nights on the trail drives made most cowboys adept at snatching a little extra sleep when mounted, while a sort of sixth sense seemed to keep watch and instantly snap them back awake at the first hint of the unusual. He was no different, and then for a moment, he rode wondering what it was that had awakened him. Tornado had quickened his pace slightly and there seemed to be the faint rumble of thunder behind them in the west. At that point, Hank cut loose with an anxious braying and ran up against the stallion, causing the big horse to break into a lope.

"What's with you critters?" Sonny said. "That thunder's miles off." He listened again. The thunder seemed to be a little louder but still he felt no alarm. Thunder storms were not unusual on the range and often you could see them miles away, dumping a wall of water with nary a drop coming anywhere near you. He turned in the saddle to see the sun edging to a clear horizon with no storm in sight. Wherever the storm was, it was not in view.

Suddenly he noticed a tremor in the buffalo grass they rode through. There was no wind to speak of, yet the grass seemed to be trembling, not like it waved when the wind blew but like it was shaking. It was unreal, almost as if some strange trembling of the ground were happening. Birds begin rising from the grass and winging away, and the horse and mule became increasingly restless.

"Ah, I know what this is," Sonny said, "this must be one of those earthquakes I've heard tell of." With that realization came a sense of wonder and excitement, for he had never been in one before. He felt no real threat, for there was nothing out here to fall on him, and short of the ground opening up and swallowing them, he perceived no real danger. On the contrary, he began to look about curiously at the new phenomenon with relish. He tried to pull in his mount for a better look, he didn't want to go galloping full speed across the prairie and fall into some rent in the ground should it open up, but the big horse would have none of it, if anything, Tornado broke into a full gallop and began veering off to the north. The funny thing was, Hank was running alongside the stallion, matching him stride for stride with no urging whatever. Sonny knew that the animals could sense things often overlooked by humans, and so, trusting to their instincts, he gave the horse his head and settled to the ride.

The thunder was louder now, but something was wrong. This sound did not ebb and fade and roll like any thunder he'd ever heard before. Instead, it seemed to increase in volume with each beat of his horses' hooves and Sonny had the strange and disquieting feeling that he should know what this sound was, that he had heard this before, or something like it. In near panic, he looked back and just as it dawned on him that this was the sound of stampeding cattle, he saw a line of buffalo pouring over a distant hill behind him. They were in full flight, stretching out across the horizon as far as he could see, and headed right for him.

Cold fear gripped his heart, leaning low over Tornado's neck he yelled to the horse, "Run!" and then began an earnest prayer for their escape. He had heard of people caught in these deadly stampedes. Sometimes, for no apparent reason, these herds would run, maybe just the sudden flight of a bird or perhaps in a futile attempt to escape the tormenting flies, and folks who were unlucky enough to get caught, usually wound up just a grease spot. Sonny had been immensely foolish to ride so close to this gigantic herd.

While driving cattle, Sonny had ridden many times to try to head the leaders of stampedes. He had even seen the end result of a rider who had gone down in such a crush and it wasn't a pretty sight, but even the largest cattle herds he'd trailed had an edge to them. They were nothing like this, and on a good cowpony you could usually out ride or work to the edge of the bunch, but as good as Tornado was, and as scared as Hank was, the tall cowboy did not hold out much hope of reaching safe ground before the massive herd overtook them.

They rode like the wind, but in the end the big stallion and the game little mule were slowly overtaken and swallowed up in the thundering, mindless, rush of plunging buffalo, running heedless of the rider and his animals.

Tornado was whistling in anger and Hank squealed in fright as they ran on. The horse that had been king of the wild began to bite at the buffalo that hindered his efforts to escape to the left, and Hank ceased braying and laid his big ears back to bite them too. Sonny, sure they would go down any second, kicked his feet free of the stirrups in desperation. If his horse fell, he would attempt to jump to the back of one of the crazed bison. He'd ridden some rough stuff, but never a buffalo, and knew this line of thinking was insane, but in the press of preservation he was prepared to try anything.

Tornado picked on the wrong bull to bite. A huge buffalo bull, his hump parallel with the cowboy's knees, having received a painful bite that nearly tore off one ear, wavered a step and began a wicked hooking of his curved horn into the heaving flanks of the plunging horse. Tornado screamed in pain, his gait faltering, and Sonny saw the bull's horn tear into the stomach of his mount just behind the cinch. Immediately, he drew his pistol and shot the buffalo, point blank, between the eyes. Instantly, the bull pitched forward onto its nose, its momentum carrying it headfirst in a rapid, tumbling somersault. As the buffalo came bowling over, its flailing hind legs caught and swept Sonny from the saddle, carrying the rider with it in a tumbling, tangle of legs, over and over. Sonny, with the fear of the eternal, wrapped his legs and arms as best he could around the underbelly of the rolling creature and held on for dear life.

The press of the on-rushing herd carried the dying bull for two more somersaults until the big animal skidded to a stop in an upright position over a slight depression in the prairie floor, its human cargo trapped beneath its heavy bulk. At first, the buffalo following immediately behind the big bull veered aside, trying to avoid the downed animal, while others tried to jump over the bull's carcass, but the pressure of the stampede soon had the buffalo trampling the dead animal. Only its massive bulk kept Sonny from certain death.

Nearly suffocating, Sonny struggled for breath in the dust and rancid coat of the dead bull. Quickly, he drew his legs and arms under the animal's body, only half aware of the marvel that a depression in this particular spot enabled him to do so. He felt the solid thud as hoof after hoof impacted the sodden body of his unlikely refuge. It seemed like an eternity passed as he lay there choking and gasping for breath in the dirt and the pungent smell of manure. At some point, there was the cracking of bones and he could feel the carcass shifting over him and splaying out, but still it provided the buffer he needed to spare him from the deadly hooves of the on-rushing buffalo. Eventually, the paunch ruptured and the stomach contents flowed out and around him. The smell of blood, hair, hide and guts clogged his nostrils and the din was horrible. He had a brief thought for Tornado and Hank, despairing that they were suffering a similar fate, when a plunging hoof struck him in the side of the head and all went black.

He was floating in a suffocating blackness… drowning in a bottomless sea of stench and filth, and holding his breath to keep from breathing in the foul-smelling water, until at last he could hold his breath no longer and was forced to pull a little air into his tortured lungs. To his surprise, he found he could breathe a little under water as long as he took small, shallow breaths. He thought he must swim to the surface, but an oppressive heaviness seemed to hold him inert. Something was worrying his left leg. He could feel it being pulled, then shaken vigorously and it seemed to be the only part of his body that could move, and that not of itself. Confused and dazed, Sonny fought to regain consciousness and make sense of where he was and what was happening.

In the wake of the stampeding buffalo, a coyote trotted in a zigzag pattern from the corner of a nearby hill. Wary and watchful, with tongue lolling out the side of its mouth, the young male kept a watchful eye out for the wolves that were soon to come, and then made its way up to the pulverized mass of a large buffalo bull. The scent of blood and flesh was strong and the coyote paused to lick its slathering jowls before it approached. This was a feast too good to pass up. Sidling up to the carcass, the coyote licked at the edge of the mutilated corpse, then took a bite of flesh. Quickly it began to gorge on the meat, swallowing great chunks down before a pack of its cousins showed up and ran him off the kill. Suddenly the coyote's teeth bit into a hard chunk of leather and there was a quick reaction that pulled the morsel from its jaws. Surely this animal was dead, but if not, so much the better. The coyote liked nothing better than to crush the last spark of life from its victim. Intrigued, the coyote pounced on the protuberance again, grabbing the leather thing in its jaws, and began a vigorous shaking and tugging in an effort to yank it free from the rest of the carcass. What was this thing? It seemed to have a life of its own. Something about it reminded him of the hated two-leggeds. In earnest, he renewed his efforts to separate it from the bull.

Suddenly there was a horrendous yell and a portion of the carcass erupted, sending hide, hair, and bloody flesh flying through the air. Startled, the coyote's jaws dropped, and then it tumbled backwards with a frightened yelp. It had been chewing on the boot of one of the two-leggeds who had sneakily hidden itself inside the dead buffalo. Now it was sitting up and yelling at him, nearly scaring him out of two year's growth. In confused haste, the coyote turned tail and bolted away some fifty yards, spurred on by the wild yelling of the two-legged as it sat in the middle of his dinner. The coyote stopped to look back as the man-thing made a series of coyote calls in mockery, then it turned in disgust and trotted off. If the two-legged wanted the buffalo that bad, he could have it. There was plenty more such carcasses scattered over the plain in the wake of the great stampede.

Two Dogs had been trailing the white-eyes on the dark horse for the past hour. He was sure the Tejano was the same one that had escaped from Snake-Who-Talks' camp the time the fire mulo had raced through their midst. It was later reported that the rider with the dark stallion, captured from where the grass was sweet, had been the one responsible for that chieftain's death, for he had hurled the enchanted snake to wrap itself about Snake-Who-Talks' neck. His must be powerful medicine to have bested the young chieftain in such a manner. Although Two Dogs had disdained Snake-Who-Talks for his disrespect of the elders and the old ways, and knew he had gotten what was his due. Still, to count coupe on his killer and kill this enemy of the people, or better yet capture him, would be a real boon to Two Dogs' status as war chief in the council circle.

Riding on a vision quest, near the vast herds of the shaggy tasiwoo, Two Dogs had been searching for a place to connect with the old ones. It had been his hope to see one of the great, white, enchanted bulls, when he came across the shod tracks of the horse and mule. Seeing the shod hoof prints, and then once having the Tejano in view, the Comanche war chief sought the cover of the paralleling hills and kept his distance. The tall rider seemed to be oblivious of his presence and Two Dogs was careful to not look directly at his foe, lest the spirits should cause the white man to feel his eyes upon him. Most of the white-eyes did not know such things, but the tall rider may be an exception, his medicine being as strong as it was. There was talk amongst the younger braves who had followed Snake-Who-Talks, that the tall rider was one who lived in the Weeping Lodge and had been among those who had caused the angry fire bees to attack and thwart their surprise raid. It was even rumored that he was brother to the Kwihani Killer, but Two Dogs knew that could not be true, he had witnessed those two intruders' death in the fire of the lodge when the singing stone spoke. Two Dogs was woefully aware of his own ignorance in the important matters of the spirit realm and knew that if he was to ever achieve the wisdom necessary to lead his band against the invading hordes of white-eyes, he must find direction from the old ones. He would do well to look for a sign if he was to be successful in capturing this tall Tejano.

But something was wrong. The tall white-eyes seemed to be slumped in his saddle, riding heedless of his whereabouts. Was he ill? Two Dogs suspected a trick. Surely one possessed with the strong medicine of snake-people would not ride so carelessly. Perhaps he did know of the Chieftain's presence and was only behaving like pretender possum. Two Dogs halted his pony behind a bush and studied his quarry.

"Ha, I do believe the Tejano is asleep. This is good, I will ride ahead and take him by surprise." Two Dogs rode behind the cover of a nearby hill at a brisk trot and cut around the sleeping cowboy, to pull up his pony behind a clump of chaparral and wait. Eventually he saw the horse, rider and mule approaching, but at that point the Comanche chief heard the distant rumbling and nervously wheeled his pony about. He knew what this was, this was the tasiwoo on the run. Two Dogs drummed his heels into his pony's flanks and raced away to the north where a high hill would protect him from the rushing buffalo. By the time he had gained this vantage point, he could see the white man racing with his horse and mule to escape the path of the onrushing tidal wave of bison. "The Tejano is stupid to ride through the tasiwoo, he must learn the hard way the foolishness of meddling with the medicine of the buffalo." Even as he spoke these words, Two Dogs knew he was about to see the white-eyes swallowed up by the impending stampede and felt some misgiving at losing the opportunity to count coup on this important enemy. With a mixed sense of amazement and justice served, the Indian Chief saw the wild stallion the cowboy rode bite a massive bull's ear, the ensuing goring of the horse, and its rider's dispatch of the magnificent bull. When he witnessed the crash of the huge buffalo sweep the luckless rider from the saddle, and his disappearance into the boiling dust, lost under the pounding of a thousand relentless hooves, he began to seriously doubt the extent of the tall one's power. Perhaps he was not in possession of such great medicine after all.

Two Dogs sat his horse and waited until the stampede passed. He never ceased to be amazed at the power of these animals when they ran. This would serve the people well for in the wake of such a stampede there would be much meat to gather. Soon he would ride to summon the Badger Clan to the feast, but first he must ride down and see if anything of the white-eyes was left. Perhaps he might find one of the fire sticks or the small pistola of the Tejano. He would be able to weave a fine story in the telling of this incident at the council fire. He turned to face the sun and spread his arms, holding aloft his hide shield and lance, then offered a prayer of thanksgiving to the spirits who provided such bounty for his band. When next he looked down from the hill, he was surprised to see brother coyote approaching the large pulverized carcass of the massive bull that had unseated the white-eyes and swept him to his doom. Already the meat-eaters were hurrying to the carnage.

The coyote began tearing at the dead animal while Two Dogs paused on the hill long enough to secure an arrow to his bow. He would ride down and dispatch this mischief-maker of the plains, it would be one less to despoil the meat for his people. When he turned again to look down, it was with amusement that he saw brother coyote jerking and tugging at something on the far side of the tasiwoo's carcass. Funny this trickster worrying with some obstinate hunk of hide when all the mass of fresh meat lay before him for the taking. The chieftain was about to drum his heels into his pony's side, when suddenly there was a loud cry and he saw a large portion of the buffalo's hide erupt into the air and the white-eyes sit up with arms waving at the offending coyote. Brother coyote was sent scurrying off several yards before he stopped to stare back at the strange spectacle. The chief could scarcely restrain a smile at the trick the spirits had played on the trickster, but then the enormity of what he had witnessed struck him. What medicine was this that the white-man who had been swallowed up in the buffalo stampede should now reemerge, like one born anew, from the carcass of one of the greatest of these brute beasts. The man stood erect to his feet, spoke something insulting to brother coyote who looked back at him sullenly and then trotted off. He was unhurt. Mesmerized, the war chief saw him walk off to retrieve his pistola and head piece. Such medicine had never been seen or heard of amongst any of the people. This buffalo man wielded unusual power now, not only that of the snake, but now of tasiwoo as well. He had easily fooled brother coyote. The chief's scalp lock prickled, he must ride silently away lest the spirits warn the white-eyes of his presence.

"Stupid coyote," Sonny said. He watched the varmint trot out of sight behind a swell in the grass. "Chewin' on my boot when it had all this fresh kill."

Sonny was a mess. His clothing was intact, although it reeked with the blood, manure and offal from the dead bull. His only injury seemed to be the rising goose egg on the side of his head. Gingerly he felt of the spot, then climbed from the remains of the big buffalo and got shakily to his feet. A wave of dizziness passed over him and for a moment he thought he would fall, but after a few deep breaths of cool air, his sight cleared and he felt steadier. His gaze swept the horizon as far as he could see. The prairie grass was trampled, while here and there the carcasses of dead buffalo, many of them the young, the old, and the feeble, dotted the range. The coyotes and wolves would feast well for the next few weeks. Already the vultures, crows and ravens were winging their way through the sky.

He turned to look at the flattened carcass before him. This had been his salvation and it was a marvel to see. What had once been a magnificent, powerful brute of a beast, now more closely resembled a ten-inch-thick, pulverized carpet of hide, hair, bones and meat. It was hard to believe that this had been what had saved him. Truly it was miraculous. So many things had had to come into play; the unlikely landing on the somersaulting bull's belly, the way he had been covered in the depression of the prairie, and the sheer magnitude of the bull itself. The way the sinew and bone and hide and muscle had endured the relentless pounding of the trampling herd. Even his location in the stampede. Tornado and Hank had obviously gained ground towards the northern edge in their headlong flight to get away, effectively reducing the number of animals that did trample over Sonny and his buffalo buffer. With a thankful heart, Sonny walked back the way they had come, found his gun where he'd dropped it, and what was left of his hat that protruded from a prairie dog hole. He pulled it out and found it stretched in an impossible cone shape from where a heavy hoof had plugged it into the open hole. To add insult to injury, his hat was filled with fresh buffalo manure, rocks, and dirt. Ruefully, he dumped the contents, he would need his head covered out here on the prairie, but not before he found some water and washed things up a bit.

He saw nothing of his horse or mule. That was a good sign, hopefully they had managed to escape the stampede. Making his way to the edge of a nearby hill, he looked for sign. He was at a place on the northern edge of where the stampeding buffalo had passed, and here he looked for the shod hoof prints of his animals. The ground at the edge showed nothing but the prints of the fleeing buffalo and he walked on, hoping against hope that somehow his animals had escaped. If he was set a foot out here, then his situation was indeed desperate. Even if he did find Tornado alive, he feared for the big grulla's life. The puncture wound in his gut was a grave injury.

Rounding a bend of the hill, Sonny saw a young heifer buffalo up on her front legs, her back legs useless on the ground. The animal's back was obviously broken. She gave a pathetic bawl as he came into view, struggled to get away briefly, then stood looking at him nervously. Mercifully, Sonny drew his sixgun and put a bullet between her eyes. The heifer dropped like a rock, thrashed about for a moment and lay still. He drew his belt knife and probed for her heart, then made a quick cut and watched as the animal's life blood pumped out to soak into the ground.

"Funny how the ground that nurtured the life of this critter, should now receive back its life," Sonny said. His thoughts were turned to how the Indians in their beliefs found this to be significant, and he was reminded of something he'd heard a preacher say about the blood, how that the life was in the blood, and that when the earth opened up to receive the blood of the dying, the death was atoned for, that it was God's way of allowing for the death of his creatures. Of course, there was that whole bit about when Cain killed Abel. God said his blood was crying to him from the ground. Obviously, God saw the death of Abel differently than that of an animal. There was another strange aspect that the preacher had spoken of too, regarding the sacrificial altar where sin was atoned for. The priests were to poor out the blood onto the ground, but at times they were to throw it against the stones of the altar. Apparently, blood going into the ground corrected the wrong of sin, but blood on stone spoke of the judgment of sin. The obvious thing to Sonny was that blood soaked into the ground went out of sight, but blood spilled on rock was in plain view. Somehow it all seemed to make sense in a mystic sort of way. How many times had he tracked a wounded animal during the hunt and searched for the blood trail? It was the blood, visible on the rock or that had not yet soaked into the ground, that led him to the final doom of the animal… its judgment.

Quickly skinning back enough of the hide to reveal the best cuts, Sonny removed the back-straps of the young buffalo and taking them, along with the heifer's tongue, he headed east in the direction of Big Springs. If he was stranded out here, at least he would have meat.

For the next hour Sonny trudged in the hot sun while flies and gnats swarmed about him, his clothes drying and stiffening on his body. A line of willows off to his right promised a stream course, and he made his way in that direction. Eventually he reached it and was relieved to find a shallow brook chattering over stones. Dropping his burdens, he plunged his aching head into a cool pool of water and drank his fill. Sitting up, he pulled off his boots, struggled out of his clothes and sat down in the stream to wash the stench of the dead buffalo from his tired body.

Later Sonny was laboring over a campfire, trying to get it started. The matches in his shirt pocket had been soaked when the buffalo's stomach had ruptured and although they were now dry, they refused to light. He had fashioned a temporary bow from a willow stick and the rawhide thong that tied his gun holster down, and was now sawing away with a dry stick and a block of wood salvaged from a dead stump. Another chunk of dry wood was used for his drilling block and he patiently sawed the swivel stick, with dried moss and leaf duff at the ready. He had started fire like this before as a kid, but had forgotten what a chore it was. Finally, a tendril of smoke wafted up from the drill block and he prodded some of the dry tinder to the spot and gently blew on it, but the ember turned gray and went out. Clad only in his long-johns, still wet from their washing, with the rest of his clothes spread over the bushes to dry, Sonny's teeth chattered as he renewed his efforts.

"If the Indians can do this, so can I," he said.

The next time the smoke threaded up, he ran the drill a little longer, and this time his gentle puffs ignited the thistledown and leaf duff, coaxing up a blaze. With a sense of triumph, he saw the tinder ignite and burst into flame. Sonny applied small sticks and grass, then wood to the little fire, grateful for its warmth, then sat back on his heels. "Fire, the stuff of men," he said with a satisfied grin. He chuckled at the imaginary image of Tornado, down on his knees, trying to start a fire.

Sonny had just popped the last medallion of back strap into his mouth and was checking the strips of meat he had hung by the fire to dry on a makeshift willow rack, when a sudden thudding of hooves caused him to spring erect with his gun drawn. Into the circle of firelight walked Hank, and close behind was Tornado, the stallion, driving the reluctant mule.

"Well thank God," Sonny said. "Look at you two. Hank, looks like you dern near lost my pack. Can't have been very good, slipped around like that. And look at you Tornado, still herding him along?" The mule's pack had shifted drastically to one side, causing him to lumber unsteadily in a side-long gait.

Tornado snorted loudly and bobbed his head up and down as the cowboy came around to catch his bridle and examine the hole in his side. Streaked with dried blood, a loop of gut about the size of a little green apple pooched out of a fly-blown hole. Sonny studied the wound where the buffalo's horn had caught the big horse just behind the cinch strap. Leading his horse to a spot near the fire, Sonny tied him off and began to unsaddle him. Hank began a disgruntled chuckling and waited his turn.

"Never mind, Hank, we've got to take care of the big fella here. You just be glad no buffalo bull sent a horn on an exploratory trip into your gizzard."

Two days later, Sonny dropped an arm load of wood next to his fire pit at his camp in the cottonwoods. He figured this was probably the feeder stream that drained into Big Springs. He would have much preferred to have camped there, in order to question any passersby about Colt, but his horse's condition demanded he rest the animal until the wound healed. Sonny had pushed the loop of gut back in and performed rude surgery with the aid of a needle and thread and the wound was healing nicely.

The horse and mule were standing nose to tail, switching flies from each other's face, when Tornado flattened his ears and side stepped into Hank, bumping the mule awake. The big horse tried to avoid his rider as Sonny's approached to scrutinize the wound.

"Easy son," Sonny soothed. I ain't gonna hurt ya, I just want to check your side."

Sonny had tied up the horse's hind leg to his nose in order to doctor him, and the big stallion was still a little reluctant whenever his rider approached with his concoction of medicine. A smear of "Balm of Gilead" willow bark ointment attended the wound and he gave a satisfied grunt at the horse's progress. "A few more days, big fella, and we will head out of here for the Springs."

CHAPTER EIGHT

The Johnson and Carol Outfit

The Flat, February 1871

IT HAD BEEN A BLEAK AND COLD DECEMBER, one that matched the cold December in my heart. Ever since Pearl had left, it had been days of cutting wood and nights huddled around the stove in a little shack I had rented behind the livery, nights of restlessness and worry, until fatigue and sleep pushed out the ghosts... the memories that seemed to be always banging at the door, along with the wind. I took my meals at the hotel and waited anxiously for a cow outfit to come through. I was certain Pearly had long since reached Wade's Landing, and was worried that news of my whereabouts was probably already in front of those I didn't want it in front of. If it hadn't been for the weather I would have struck out for the Red long before this. Trouble was, most honest cow-outfits wouldn't be traveling until spring, so the chance of landing a job with one was pretty slim and the crossing on the Red would be no place to spend the winter.

Around the middle of February, I rode in with the wood-cutting detail and spotted a large herd of cattle bedded down along the river on the opposite side of the

Flat. Neck reigning Lightfoot from our place in the line, I rode towards the chuck wagon of the camp.

I stopped my horse next to the wagon and watched an old gent with a dirty apron tied around his waist wrestle an arm load of fire wood out of a tarpaulin hanging beneath it. I stifled a grin when my horse snorted loudly and champed at the bit, startling the scrawny fella, who bumped his head on the bottom of the wagon,

"Son-of-a-sea-biscuit-eaten-sea-biscuit-eater," the cook cried. He rubbed his balding head ruefully while turning accusing eyes on me. "What the blazes you doing sneakin' up on a feller like that?" he growled. "Hain't you got no horse sense?"

"Sorry," I said with a grin. "Is the trail-boss here about?" Only a fool argues with a skunk, a mule, or a cook, and since I figured the feller was in no mood for palaver after bonkin' his head like that, I got right to the point.

"No," the cook said. "Dash it all, that hurt."

He was still scrubbing his shiny scalp with stubby fingers, so I hooked a knee around my saddle horn and settled back to wait until he finished coaxing out the goose egg that was rising on his noggin. Lightfoot shook his head, rattling the bridle, and I caught him eyeing the bunch of saddle horses in a near-by, roped off corral. I figured he was sizing 'em up to see which ones he'd have to whup to get his share of the grub.

The scrawny cook finally stopped nursing his goose egg, and turned a menacing eye on me. "What cha' want him for?"

"Lookin' for work," I said.

"Well, he's in town throwin' dice, and probably will be for most of the night. You might as well step down and get yourself some coffee." He stooped to regather his scattered firewood and nodded toward a large pot simmering on the edge of the campfire.

"You ridin' the grub line?"

"Naw," I said. I dallied Lightfoot's reins around a bush and grabbed a tin cup, then walked over to the fire. "Done some droving and was lookin' to sign on for Dodge City."

"Well, we're headin' for Dodge with these slab-sided beeves. I reckon John Wesley will want to talk to you."

"Ain't he a preacher?" I said.

"Hardly, couldn't be farther from it. His pa is, I guess, and he named him that. His last name's Hardin and he is a hell-raising kid that thinks he's a hand with a gun. He has a 'leave me alone and let me go to hell by my own trail' attitude. Huh, he's scarcely dry behind the ears."

"What's a kid like that doing headin' up an outfit like this?"

"Aw, he's cousin to the owners, Jake Johnson and Columbus Carol, and they put him in charge, probably to get him out of Gonzales before the Texas law nabbed him. He killed a colored freed man, a darky by the name of Bob King, after King tried to cut a beef cow from the herd. Bob claimed the cow was his and Hardin pistol whipped 'im. The kid and most of his kin, too, are pro-south and don't hold too much with northern sympathizers. You're not one are ya?"

"Nope, folks around the Pecos didn't get involved much, interferin' with things that weren't botherin' 'em none." I wondered why this Hardin was still trying to fight the war.

"Well, anyway he's a bad actor, goes around bragging that he's killed four men. I think the first one was when he was fifteen, he stabbed another boy over some stupid argument. Funny thing about that, you'd think his pa, being a circuit riding preacher, would have frowned on that, but if stories are to be believed, it seems the old man spent more time hiding out the boy from the authorities than worrying about his actions. Hardin's galled just about everybody in the outfit, including his cousin, James, another ne'er-do-well who thinks he's a fast gun too, but he's not near as mean as John Wesley. The two don't seem to care about nothing, and are a pair to draw to if you're looking for trouble."

I didn't say anything, but I thought plenty. Shooting people was one thing, going around bragging about it was another.

Squatting on my heels, I nursed a cup of coffee, enjoying its warmth through my work gloves, and studied the outfit. I counted five riders circling a herd that was spread out on the grass along the river. A Mexican lad, working as a wrangler, was rigging more rope on pickets to give the horse herd better graze, and I saw Lightfoot watching with interest. There were two more riders coming towards camp from the river bottom and dragging up dry driftwood for the fire. They pulled up next to the wagon and swung down to retrieve their ropes, while the cook began to grouse at them for stirring up the dust.

"Dad-gum it, Schnoz, you're getting dirt in my beans."

"Oops, sorry," the rider with the big nose said, "I thought you had the lid on 'em."

The other fellow was coiling his rope and looking me over with a critical eye. He appeared to be near my size and age, perhaps a year or two younger, and wore two six-guns slung low on both hips. Sizing me up, his eyes settled on the pearl handled .44 and with a sneer he asked, "Who's the new buscadero?"

I ignored the remark, stood to my feet, dropped my cup into the dish bucket, and without saying a word, picked up the bucksaw leaning against the wagon wheel and walked over to the log he had just drug up and began sawing off a hunk of firewood.

The cook and Schnoz took a few steps away from us, looking warily at each other and Two Guns assumed a threatening posture in front of me. "What's the matter pistolero, cat got your tongue?"

I thought, wouldn't you know, this puffed-up toad had to be the young tough the cook spoke about. The last thing I needed was to get off on the wrong foot with this outfit, and since a closed mouth gathers no boots, I bit back the brilliantly, blistering, retort forming on the back of my tongue, swallowed hard, and just kept on sawing.

"Aw, look at that, the gunny is nothing but a wood-cutting, camp flunky." The rider turned to the others as he made the remark, then turned back to look at me with a derisive laugh before he stepped into his saddle. "When you finish sawin' the log, flunky, you can pack up a couple buckets of water for the sourdough here." With that, he rode back towards the river, cackling like a hen that just laid a triple yolker. My ears were burning as I watched him go, but a slow smile was forming at the corners of my mouth as I imagined what he'd find to chortle about if I suddenly threw this bucksaw and wrapped it around his neck.

"Don't let him gall you none," the cook said. "That's Hardin's cousin, Jim Clements and he's studying hard to become a half-wit. He's doing his best to keep up with the boss's bad-boy reputation. The two of them have been competing for that honor ever since we started the gather of this herd of cows in South Texas. If you ask me, this whole bunch of beeves was probably gathered by moonlight from both sides of the border." The cook scratched the stubble on his chin, then added, "Course you never heard that from me, but it wouldn't take much of a brand inspector to see most of these critters have made recent acquaintance with a running iron. You might want to think twice about joining this outfit."

I sawed off another hunk of wood and then began stacking the rounds in a pile near the wagon. I was doing some serious thinking on what the cook had said about signing on. I sure didn't need to be matching fast-draws with those two, but it was time for me to be heading for parts unknown. Perhaps hiding out in such a nefarious outfit might be just the right ticket for covering my tracks.

"Name's Hickney, Tom Hickney, though they've hung the handle of Hiccup, or just plain Hic on me." The cook stuck out his hand, and I set down my armload of wood and reached out to shake his gnarly palm. I was wondering if I should continue my masquerade as Woody Stover, but when Hic saw my hesitancy, he said, "Never mind, half the outfit's on the dodge and sportin' some made-up moniker or another. I'll just call you Pecos if that's alright."

It was well after dark by the time Hardin rode in and he seemed somewhat flushed and agitated. I found him to be of slight build with dark hair and a hardness about his eyes that belied his youthfulness. He barely had a word for me as he filled a plate with beans, but did say if I wanted a job riding drag, it paid thirty dollars and found, per month, and to be ready to leave before daylight. He wolfed down the beans and gulped a cup of coffee, cussin' Hic for it burning his mouth. He then swung into the saddle and rode off towards the herd, glancing back over his shoulder toward the Flat.

Hardin had no more than left camp when a U.S. Army patrol rode in looking for him. They said they were following a man that had ridden this way, who had just gunned down three Mexicans in an argument over a three-card Monte game at one of the gaming parlors in town. They were looking to arrest him for the murders.

Jim Clements jumped up before anyone else could say anything, and told the soldiers, "We haven't seen anyone ride by, we were minding our own business and you'd do well to mind yours and get back to shootin' Injuns and stop botherin' honest folk."

The Sargent and his men looked us over for a few minutes, and then his eyes fell on me. I could see it was Sargent O'Flarety.

"That you Stover?" he said. "What you doing with this cow outfit?"

I shrugged, "Just signed on for a sight-seeing trip up the Western Trail."

"So, had enough of wood choppin' huh? You haven't seen anybody ridin' this-a-way from town, have ya"?"

It was plain to me O'Flarety wasn't putting a whole lot of stock in the word of these South Texas cowboys. The air was heavy with tension as the soldiers and the cowhands waited for the new hand's answer. I could see Clements looking daggers at me.

"Well Sarge," I said, "the only feller I've seen ridin' 'round here in the last half hour or so, beside yourselves, was the boss of the outfit, and he just rode out to check on the herd."

O'Flarety tucked his lower lip under his upper in a tight, thin line, then clenched his jaw and nodded his head slowly. He looked us all over once again, reminding me of a chicken hawk roosting on the post of a chicken pen. "Okay," he said, "if you see a feller ride in with twin holsters sewn into the inside of his vest, cross-draw fashion like, let us know." The Sargent wheeled his horse about and spurred back towards town, the other soldiers following.

Clements' eyes followed the soldiers until they disappeared into the darkness, then turned an accusing eye on me. "You damn near gave us away, flunky, what ya think you're doing?"

A peculiar sense of amusement came over me as I watched Clements strutting his stuff in front of the watching hands. It was obvious that he had missed what was so plain to the others.

"Why nothin'." I said in my most laconic drawl. "I just told the Sargent the plain, God's truth. Didn't your momma teach you that?"

"You leave my momma out of it," Clements bristled, "you calling me a liar?"

It was plain that Jimmy Clements was losing traction and spoiling for a fight, and I thought I might as well 'beard the lion in his den,' but on the other hand he was the boss's kin, and I needed this job. Still, there was no sense in pussy-footing around because sooner or later it would come to it.

"Let me ask you a question," I said. "What do you call a person who tells a lie?"

"Ha!" Clements said derisively. "I call 'em a no good, low-down, four-flushin', liar." He turned to the others seeking their approval, then turned back to state belligerently to me, "And I back it up with my guns." With that statement, his hands crossed in front of him, hovering near the handles of his pistols.

"Well, that's too bad, guess you're going to have to shoot yourself then."

"What?" Clements seemed to lose some of his cockiness.

"You just stood up there and told a bald-faced lie to them soldier boys in front of every last man of us, and by your own definition called yourself a liar."

Cousin Clements was bogged down deeper than a short-legged jackass in a long-legged mud hole, while the other hands began to snicker and laugh.

"Aw hell, it ain't no lie to tell some damned blue belly a tale to throw 'em off the trail."

"Come here, Cousin Jimmy," I said. "It's alright to call you that, isn't it? I want to show you something."

I walked past where he was standing in the firelight to stop by one of the logs drug up near the chuck wagon, then drew my belt knife with him watching intently as I made a slash on the log.

"Now it's apparent to me, you reckon yourself a hand with a gun, what with your fancy, cross-draw rigging and all, so I figured you'd appreciate a little stunt I learned as a kid."

Clements was bewildered and the other cowboys were watching with interest, as I strode back past him to the other side of the circle of light.

"Are you watching?" I said.

When I reached the other side, I whirled and threw my knife at the hash mark, palmed my six-shooter and drilled a hole into the mark a split second before the knife buried its point into that self-same hole.

I was calmly ejecting the spent cartridge and replacing it with a fresh one, as a low murmur swept through the watching cowboys. Jim Clements walked over to squat on his heels and stare at my knife.

"Well I'll be damned," he said. He stood up, walked to where his horse was tied, mounted up, and rode off towards the herd.

The cowboys all gathered around to have a look, and I must admit. I was feeling some proud, and a lot lucky too, 'cause I hadn't practiced that little stunt for some time. Hic withdrew my knife and handed it to me.

"That should break him of suckin' eggs, but it won't," he said. "I'd keep a sharp eye on my back trail, were I you."

"That's probably good advice," I said, holstering the gun,

"How come you did that?" Hic said. "Showin' off like that, most guys would of shot him."

"You're right, but a wink's as good as a nod to a blind mule." Just figured I should give him a chance to know what he's up against, and Hardin too, in case they get any ideas. 'Sides a little showin' off might stop a lot of blood lettin', if you know what I mean."

"I know what cha mean and with most folks I'd agree it was a savvy call, but with these two..." He shook his head, "You may still have it to do."

I went into town the next morning to pick up my gear, pay the last of my rent, and get my final pay from the pay-master up on Government Hill, and then I decided to stop

126

by the mercantile to pick up a few items, and got hauled up short as a milk cow tied in the barn with her calf being sold to the neighbor. Staring back at me from a wanted poster tacked to a bulletin board by the door was a picture of me. It was an old picture taken a couple years back, and I'd put on some weight and a whole lot more worry lines to my mug, but it was me alright. Somebody wanted me bad enough to post a one-thousand-dollar reward for information as to my whereabouts. I glanced this way and that, and then snatched the poster down, folded it in half and stuck it inside my shirt. I needed to study it at a more convenient time.

Inside, I ran into Miss Elizabeth and she seemed just as embarrassed to see me as the last time we'd met. Ever since the night I didn't stay to dinner, things had been a bit awkward between us, and I couldn't tell if she was pleased or not that I hadn't come a courtin'. Since Pearl left, we'd barely let more'n a, 'how'd you do' and a 'just fine' pass between us. But since I was clearing out, I thought I should at least thank her for helping me with Pearl, and wish her and Hank well.

"Miss Elizabeth, I'll be headin up the trail soon, and I just wanted to thank you for your thoughtfulness regarding Pearly."

"So, you be leavin' us then, Mr. Stover?" she said.

"Yes ma'am, joining that cow-outfit across the river."

"It was my pleasure to help out young Pearl. I trust she reached her destination alright."

"Far's I know," I said, not wishing to let her know that I had no idea whether Pearl had or not.

Miss Elizabeth looked me steadily in the eye and said, "Woodrow, I hope you find what it is you are looking for," and then with a knowing nod of her head, she added, "and please be careful."

Now that last, had me worrying like a four-year-old on a knot in his shoe lace. Did she know about the wanted poster? I thought for a moment to ask her, but then decided I shouldn't. Best to let things lie as they might.

"Thanks, Miss Beth, and my best to you and Hank. Don't wait too long on tellin' your father about him, and... I have no idea whether Hank is a Baptist or not," I said with a sheepish grin.

"I know that," Miss Elizabeth said, "but he is." She looked nervously towards the back of the store.

"Don't worry, your pa will come around. From what I can tell, Henry's a good man. You two be happy. Goodbye." I slapped my hat back on my head, grabbed my packages and turned to the door.

"Woody, please be careful," she said again, and I saw a look of concern in her eyes as the door clicked shut behind me. I wondered again if she knew of the poster I had kyped off the front bulletin board.

Once across the river I pulled up Lightfoot and took another look at the poster. A thousand dollars was being offered for information as to my whereabouts and it was a missing persons poster, not your usual Wanted: Dead or Alive one. That had me breathing a little easier, but I had no illusions about this. The reward was enough to garner the attention of most anyone, especially those who made their living as bounty hunters. I would need to be on the lookout. The poster went on to say I was wanted in connection with a shooting in Wade's Landing, Texas and that the Sheriff of that town should be contacted. I wondered if that four-flushing Wiggins was still sheriffin' there. Another question that was worrying me was, how many of these posters were out there? That's when I made the decision to grow the beard and long hair.

Life on the trail was not new to me, I had spent a few days droving with Charley Goodnight and Oliver Loving, and often pushed cattle for my dad, but that had been nothing compared to this outfit. Trailing beeves in winter was a whole lot different than in the summer time. What we lacked in heat and dust was more'n made up for in cold, wind, rain, and mud. Half the time the rain was sleet or snow, and trying to sleep in weather like that, rolled up in blankets with a tarp underneath and around you, made for some uncomfortable nights to say the least. The chiggers of summer were absent in January, but the dad-blamed fleas were ever present year around. Half the time I felt I was the designated community picnic grounds for every flea in Texas. The only relief any of us had was when we dressed down to our birthday suits and stood shivering in our slickers, while holding our steaming clothes on sticks over Hic's cook fire until the pesky vermin was smoked out.

Most of the hands were decent enough, but John Wesley and Jim Clements were perched on everybody's last nerve. For the first few days out of the flat, Hardin kept to himself and seemed to spend a lot of time glancing over his shoulder, but once we had some distance behind us and no more blue-legs showed up, he seemed to settle down to reveal, to me at least, his true personality. He carried twin pistols in holsters sewn into the front of his vest and spent a lot of time jerking them and pointing the guns at whomever might be standing by. He seemed to particularly like goading his cousin, Clements, with this little stunt, always catching him off guard, and when Jimmy would react, too late, drawing his own guns, John Wesley would purse his lips and make a pow sound, then laugh at his kin's befuddlement. Clements was not above trying the same stunt on Hardin, but that seemed to inflame the young trail-boss, and a couple of times, I thought Hardin was going to drill him. It was plain to me, the young tough had a hair-temper to go with his hair-triggers, and a big mouth that looked a whole lot better when it was closed.

I minded my own business and did my best to stay out of their way, but one stormy night, I had just ridden in from a restless herd with the cold wind and sleet blowing down the back of my neck. Hardin had been sipping from a bottle he kept, and began to brag about his experience with the three Mexicans at Fort Griffin. He had just jerked both pistols in another of his fast-draw poses and said, "These two little jewels sure put the fear of God in those greasers. They claimed I cheated, and then the three of them pulled knives on me. I reckoned they was fixin' to do a little carvin' on my hide. You should of seen their eyes bug out when I snatched these beauties out. I told them never to bring a knife to a gun fight and then shot 'em in the guts before any of them could so much as toss a single toad sticker."

I probably should have just kept on rolling out my blankets and tucking the tarp around them, but listening to this kid bragging about sending those three Mexicans to their eternal reward without any regard for what he'd done, struck me as calloused beyond belief. I knew what sort of thoughts could dog a man after shooting someone and it is no small thing. Perhaps I scoffed a little too loudly because the next thing I know, ol' J.W. is challenging me.

"What's your problem fella, something stuck in your craw?"

I knew I should just shut up and crawl into my soogan, but before I could help it, I heard myself sayin', "Yeah bud, there is. Do you think you can just go around any old time you want and indiscriminately kill folks?"

"Hell yeah," Hardin flared, "if they cross me I can." He stopped twirling the guns and settled both of them on my brisket and I felt myself go cold.

"What's going to happen when somebody comes along who's just a little bit faster and plugs you?" I said.

"I'll worry about that when the time comes. You wanna try me?"

His question prompted a riot of feelings inside my head. Strangely, I found that fear of dying was not one of them, in fact I had the ridiculous notion that I would be doing the world a great service to palm my six-shooter and eliminate this pimple on society's butt. Not for one moment did I think I couldn't beat him, even if I was staring down the bores of both his cannons. He was just too cock-sure of himself, but then I remembered what it was like to take someone's life and I sure didn't want to wrestle with those demons, especially for killing someone as annoying as Hardin.

"Hardin," I said, my voice flat and tinged with ice, "You're going to stand before Jesus and explain to Him, not me, for your senseless murders. You know it, your pa knows it, and every last one of us here knows it. Now I could draw my gun and shoot your lights out, even if you do have the drop on me, and frankly, I don't give a hoot in hell if you do get a shot or two in me, 'cause I don't have a dern thing to live for anyway. But sure as God made little green apples, I will kill you, then we can both stand before Him and give an account, and I will be sure to tell Him what an arrogant ass you are."

I waited then, with every eye on the two of us. I saw Hardin's eyes turn to slits and pure hatred was shining there. I swear I could see his thumbs going white on the hammers of his two guns and in that instant my hand flashed to my hip and my pistol was in my palm, the hammer in full cock. But I didn't shoot, for at the last moment, Hardin's eyes wavered and faltered and he looked toward the noise of a rider in fast gallop coming hard from the herd. The distant roar of cattle on their feet in full stampede before the storm had reached all our ears.

"To hell with you," John Wesley hollered. He holstered his guns and shouted, "To your horses, boys, we got us a stampede." He sprang for his mount and thundered out of camp, the rest of us following behind.

We let the cows run before the storm until they finally played out and then spent the rest of the time heading back to where we started from, picking up strays along the way. I do not know how many cattle we lost that night, but it was quite a few. Two days later, we were finally on the trail again. Hardin was certainly not a skilled trail-boss and didn't seem to want to spend much time recovering cattle that were not his in the first place.

What was the most surprising to me was that after the stampede, Hardin seemed to bear no rancor towards me at all. It was as if the incident between us had never happened. But I wasn't fooled. The look I had seen in his eyes was one of deadly intent. I was convinced that John Wesley Hardin was a cold-blooded killer and that once that glint came into his eye, no appeal would change that. I studied on it some, not so much on Hardin's disregard for life, but the revealed aspect of my own disregard. I was some surprised and yet not, to realize that there was a part of me that no longer cared if school kept or not. It all seemed so pointless. Money, job, position, family... love? All the things everybody is scrambling for, what was the point? It all seemed slated for disappointment and dissolution and even if you did manage to scrap to the top of the heap, in the end you die and it all gets left behind. I had been riding along, living from day to day, giving attention to where my next meal was coming from and maybe that of my horse, but the incident with Hardin had brought to the forefront of my consciousness, the fact that I could have easily been killed, that I knew it when facing him, and that I just plain didn't care. Some call that a death wish, I guess, and looking at it now in the cold light of day, I have to admit that this was about what it amounts to. I don't care. All the things that had made life seem so worth the living before, now just seemed like so much fluff. Hardin's bullet could have mercifully put me out of my misery. I almost wished it had. And that stuff I had said to Hardin about us standing before the Lord. Did I really believe that myself? I used to, with all my heart, but now I was not so sure. Had my morality, or lack of it, started to dictate my theology? This kind of thinking was making me feel about as awkward as a stork in hip boots. Maybe I should just press on and find out what 's on up the trail; there is a lot of country to see in the West, and that seems like as good a reason as any for keeping body and soul together. Yeah, I'll do that and leave the philosophizing to the theologians and experts.

From my place on the drag, I watched a wicked longhorn bull make a run at Hector Morales as he passed too close to the herd with the remuda. For some reason the huge bull, with obvious signs of Spanish fighting blood in his veins, had an immense dislike for mounted riders, which may have dated back to a time spent in the ring— probably a result of harassment by the picadors. Morales, the young Mexican wrangler, was nearly unseated and his horse given a painful jab before the youth could spur away from the crazed animal.

Hardin had taken a liking to the bull, probably due to a compatibility with rebellion. He had given orders that no one was to shoot the animal, shooting being a sentiment harbored by the rest of the hands, and so we continued to put up with the rouge beast. I was told that half of the outfit had been the object of the bull's attacks at one time or another, so I watched the bull standing defiantly to the side while the other cattle filed past. He was swinging his head from side to side with quick movements in watchful pose for any other mounted men, his tail held high in an arc, and was the picture of belligerence and defiance, pawing the ground.

At that moment, Ben Martin rode up and pulled rein, to sit his horse beside me.

"That piss-ant needs to be taken down a notch or two," he said.

I smiled and slowly nodded. Martin and I had become good friends, and I found the likable Arkansan, from Fort Smith, to be easygoing and companionable.

"You best at headin' or heelin'?" I asked.

He grinned, "can do both, but probably best at heelin', why, what cha got in mind?"

"Good, shake out a loop and let's go fix his little red wagon."

"The boss don't want 'im killed," Ben said.

"I know, we're just going to teach him some manners, come on."

I took down my rope and spurred towards the bull who was staring after the last of the passing drag. By the time he turned to see me and Martin bearing down on him, he had no chance to react before it was too late. My rope settled around his wide horns and Ben's swung expertly to catch both hind feet and soon we had the big bull stretched out on the ground, obscured from the rest of the outfit by the cloud of dust that followed the herd.

"Now that we got 'im, what we going to do with 'im," Martin asked.

I smiled grimly at him. "You got a saw?"

"Jeepers, you gonna cut him with a saw?" Ben said, "why not a knife."

"Not his nuts you ninny, his horns."

"Oh," Martin said. "Good idea... no, no saw."

"Well, he's just too dad-blamed cocky with this massive rack, they're going to have to come off. Hog tie him while I go find a rock."

"A rock! Geez, Pecos, are you crazy? Whatcha going to do with a rock?"

"Just get 'im trussed up, I'll show you."

I walked around in the churned up ground the cattle had left, until I found a slab of rock with a sharp edge and packed it back to the trussed-up bull. Dropping it by the animal's head, I said, "See if you can work that rock in under his horn while I find another."

I continued searching for a second rock, one slightly smaller but still with a sharp edge and good weight. When I found one to my liking, I brought it back, and had Martin sit on El Toro's head. To Ben's amazement, I began to hammer on the horn, striking it between the rocks, while the animal bellowed in anger and pain. Eventually, the outer horn shell broke loose, leaving the inner live shell, which quickly separated under the relentless pounding. Once the horn was off, I bashed the stubby end left, pounding it back until it was flattened and then had Ben help me roll him over, where I repeated the operation. By the time we were through, most of the fight was out of the bull, and when we let him up, he took off for the herd, like a scalded dog, barreling into the rear of the drag and knocking critters out of his way, until he was lost somewhere in the middle of the gather.

The Spanish bull was not seen by anyone for over a week and finally the boss began to question us as to where he might be. Martin and I kept our own council on that, and then one night at chuck, Hardin came grousing into camp on a rampage. He demanding to know, what the hell had happened to his bull. It seems he had seen it and its horns were gone, they were now all funny like and shriveled up with just two, four inch stubs sticking out the side of its head, "lookin' like some damned toadstools or mushrooms."

Everyone was ignorant of course, as to what might have happened, and when Martin wondered if it might have caught some sort of strange disease, John Wesley quit his rant and went to worrying that the whole herd might get infected. At any rate, he had us break camp in the middle of the night and head up the trail, as if we might be able to outrun it or something.

It was one of the strangest looking sights I ever saw, that big bull with goofy looking mushrooms sticking out each side of his head, but he never again bothered any horse and rider and wouldn't let Martin or me get within a country mile of him.

When we reached the crossing at the Red, it was near dark and Hardin had us water and bed the herd down on the Texas side of the river. It was a crossing long used by the Indians who followed the buffalo, and it was eventually marked out as a trail drive crossing by a man named Legit. Most of the herds bound for Kansas crossed here and it was the jumping off place into Indian Territory. What lay ahead of us was, for the most part, unknown. Raiding war parties from the tribes of the nations were frequent against the cattle drives and often cattle were demanded as payment to pass. If cattle were not given, the band of Indians would ride away, only to return in the dark of night, stampede the herd and take as many cows as they could in the resulting chaos. John Wesley was about to learn this first hand.

Early the next morning, we were pushing the gather across the shallows, being careful of attending holes of quicksand, and were busy keeping the herd strung out on a narrow gravelly bottom, when a band of Kiowa appeared on the north shore of the river. The Indians waited until the last of the stragglers climbed up the bank and then closed in around those of us riding drag. Harding had been keeping a wary eye on the warriors, and came riding, hell-bent-for-leather, followed by Clements and a couple other hands, when he saw the Kiowa close in.

Martin and I had turned to face the redskins when Hardin charged in and pulled his pony up, showering the standing Indian mounts with gravel. He had both six-guns pulled and was shouting at the stolid Redmen who calmly sat their ponies and waited.

"What the hell do you heathen want?" Hardin demanded. He held both guns at the ready, muzzles pointing slightly upward.

When the noise calmed some, one of the band, a brave of about thirty with two eagle feathers in his scalp, kneed his paint horse forward a few steps and held up a hand.

"Woha'te, give woha'te." The Indian then held up both hands, palms outwards and fingers outstretched. He did this twice, then pointed at the back of the herd. It was plain to me and should have been plain to John Wesley that these Indians were asking for a toll of twenty cattle.

"We don't got no wohate," Hardin shouted, "You get your red tails out of here before I ventilate 'em."

The brave gave Hardin a tolerant look and proceeded to explain by sign language that the Paw... the buffalo, had been taken by the white-eyes and now it was only fair that they give up some of the cattle to feed their starving women and children.

"What's he jabbering' about?" Hardin was disgusted. "I can't read all this gesturing and gibberish. Any of you boys read sign?"

I edged Lightfoot up a couple of steps and said, "He says the white-man took away all the buffalo and he wants twenty cows to feed his hungry women and children."

Hardin's temper reached the boiling point. His face got red and he looked like a dog I saw once trying to pass a peach pit.

"Twenty cows? Why you thievin' Red-stick, the only thing I'll give you is hot lead," and upon that declaration, John Wesley Hardin began an indiscriminate firing at the band of Indians. Jim Clements drew his two guns and did the same. Before they could wheel their horses about and race away, several of the Indians and their ponies were hit, one or two of them seriously, including the brave who had been the spokesperson.

"Twenty beeves, they must think I'm dumb as a box of rocks. I should a killed every last one of 'em."

"There's probably going to be hell to pay for the ones you did shoot," I said.

Hardin got that glint in his eye and said, "Pecos, or whatever your name is, neither you, and for sure, no damn Redskin, is going to tell me how to run this outfit. If you don't like the way I do things around here, you can just haul your freight."

Nature gave us all something to fall back on, and sooner or later we all land flat on it. I figured for John Wesley it was about to be sooner.

The next night an unseen band of Indians stampeded the herd. A little after midnight the squall of a mountain lion was heard, first on the flank side and then on the opposite side. I was ridin clockwise to the bunch when a galloping Indian rode past dragging a cougar skin. The herd came to their feet as one animal and bolted to the west, away from the scent of the predator. I fired an ineffective shot at the fleeing Indian and then turned to race after the herd.

By the time the herd was turned and milling, the rest of the riders were exhausted and some of them were missing. That night we lost over fifty head to the Redskins and two good horses had to be shot because of broken legs. John Wesley looked like the hind-end of bad luck, but no one was going to tell him how to run the outfit, especially me or the dashed Indians.

CHAPTER NINE

Pearl Comes Home

Wade's Landing, West Texas, December 1870.

WHEN THE STAGE ROLLED INTO WADE'S
Landing at last, the girl called Pearl stepped down and
turned to the driver.

"Where is the Post Office?" she said.

The driver nodded towards the building where he had
stopped the coach. There was a faded sign that read,
Munson's Store & Mercantile. He struggled with the ropes
that secured the luggage on top of the coach, and said,
"In there, girly."

"Thank you for delivering me safely to my destination,"
Pearl said, "although that was a horrendous ride."

The driver shrugged and said, "Next time, take
the train."

"There is no train that comes here," Pearl replied in
exasperation. "Just give me my bag please."

The driver secured her carpet bag from the pile of other
luggage and dropped it at her feet in a poof of dust. Pearl
turned an appraising eye on him as he climbed down with
a mailbag, and was about to say something more about
his treatment of her luggage, but then thought better of it.
She followed him through the door, and on into the store.
Setting her valise by the door, she quietly waited until the

stage driver completed his business with the matronly lady in the postal cubical. She then gave a mock curtsey and an insincere smile when the driver tipped his hat and jauntily passed her on his way out the door.

"Bull whacker," Pearl said under her breath as she watched the man return to the seat of the coach. Then he was gone and Pearl felt a mix of apprehension and relief. Relieved that the dreadful stage ride was over and apprehension on what would come next. Would the folks at the Crossed Sabers take her in?

"Young lady," the Post Mistress said, "Can I help you?"

Pearl broke from her reverie of the journey just completed and looked at the kindly lady with the wire-rim glasses perched on the end of her nose.

"Yes, ma'am, I need to know where the Crossed Sabers Farm is," Pearl said.

Mrs. Munson gave an approving smile of the young girl's manners and wondered that a girl of such tender age should be traveling alone in the West.

"The Crossed Sabers Ranch is about ten miles on the road south of town," she said. "Have you business there?"

"Yes, ma'am, I hope so. Do you know if anyone will be traveling that way soon?"

Mrs. Munson frowned. "There's almost always someone from the ranch picking up the mail when they come in, but that is usually on Saturday. This is only Wednesday. I don't know if anyone is in town today, or not."

"Might there be any other way to get there?" Pearl asked nervously.

"You can rent a horse at the livery or walk. Can you ride?"

"I know how to ride," Pearl said. "What would that cost?"

"I am unsure," Mrs. Munson said, "maybe fifty cents a day. Don't you think it would be better to wait until someone drove in?" Mrs. Munson suspected the young girl was penniless, or nearly so.

Pearl sighed, "I have urgent business at the ranch. Is the place hard to find?"

"No, dearie, just follow the road south and you'll eventually get there, but I'd advise against it... for two reasons."

"And what are they?"

"One, the country is no place for a young girl alone. The Comanche and Apache still roam up and down this river valley, and two," the post mistress stepped to the window and pulled the curtain aside to look out, "it's about to storm."

"Um, well, thank you, ma'am, I will check at the livery." She opened the door and stepped out onto the porch into a rising, cold wind.

Pearl was beginning to wish she'd spent her last dollar on a horse. The valise she carried was getting heavier by the minute and although the storm had not yet broken, it looked like rain, or even snow, could start falling any time soon. She had a sweater in the valise, and spying a clump of mesquite a few yards off the road, she decided to step into its shelter and put the sweater on. It would lighten her load some and keep her warmer too. She removed her outer coat and knelt to open her bag when the sudden snort of a horse right behind her caused her to jerk erect and whirl about.

Seated on a spotted pony, was an Indian warrior looking intently at her.

———

Malo Cactus, the half-breed Comanche had been riding north, returning to his people in the canyon called Palo Duro, when he spied the young white maiden walking along the road. This had amazed him. Could the white-eyes be so foolish as to allow their children to wander around alone in the wilderness with a storm coming?

Surely not, this must be some sort of trick. Perhaps she was bait to trap him, for he knew the Texicans were intent on stopping the trade of captives between the 'People' and the Mexican Comancheros. He, in fact, had been returning from just such a trade, and was now enjoying the warm footwear he had gotten along with a fine copper kettle in exchange for a small Apache child taken in a recent raid. He had been glad to be rid of the little girl for she had cried the whole way to the Rio Grandè. A Comanche girl would never have been such a crybaby.

But now, this maiden. He looked this way and that. Were the accursed Texas Rangers hiding just out of sight to take him captive? He decided to follow her for a while, but keep out of sight and ride parallel to the road she walked, to see what might happen. If she were alone, this would be too good to be true. She would make a fine trade with the fat Mexican trader, Diaz, whom he had left just two days earlier. He could take the girl and ride back to the Rio and intercept the Comanchero on his way back from Del Nortè. If he succeeded in her capture, she should be worth far more than the white-man's boots and cooper kettle that he got for the Apache maid. If the girl was comely enough, he might just keep her for the winter and then trade her. He could use a nice warm girl to share his blankets when the wind whistled around the teepee.

Soundlessly he followed the young girl for more than a mile, keeping constant vigilance on his back trail. There was no sign of others about. Malo Cactus began to think she was indeed alone. Perhaps she was another one of the throw-away white-eyes with the vaca head, otherwise she would have to be crazy to be out here alone like this. One other time he had found just such a gringo throw-away, a fine, strong, young man lying naked in the bushes. He had traded for a horse, a blue shirt with the brass buttons, and a rifle that time. This maid, although young, would make a good trade as well.

It was somewhat confusing to the breed why the enemies of his people would throw away their young like they did. The People would never do that. They knew that those of their young, afflicted with the vaca head, possessed special spirits and they were treated with honor, for they often had the insight of the old ones. Even those who did not were easily trained with a little beating, to do menial chores about the village. No, the People would never throw such a one as this away. Now the maiden had stopped behind a large mesquite clump, and was taking off her clothes. Malo Cactus was convinced she was crazy, it was much too cold to be removing garments in this wind. Quietly he kneed his pony toward the maiden who heedless of his presence, was squatted down and digging through her bag. Then his horse snorted.

———

Pearl let out a piercing scream, her worst fear realized. Before her was a blood-thirsty savage and his appearance galvanized her into instant action. In panic, she started jumping up and down in one place, all the while screaming at the top of her voice. She was certain she would be murdered at any second, but the Indian only sat his horse looking mildly amused and not a little puzzled.

Pearl soon realized that her crazy antics were confusing the wild Indian, and then the thought occurred to her that if she were to act crazy, maybe the Indian would just ride away, not wanting anything to do with her.

Letting loose a cry of maniacal laughter, induced largely by the fear she was feeling, Pearl hooked a finger into the throat of her blouse, made a horrified expression and continued to dance about in greater frenzy. She rolled her eyes up into her head and began to foam at the mouth, remembering a rabid dog she'd once seen, and hoped the Indian would be put off, fearing rabies.

Suddenly she stopped, glared at the warrior and making a hissing sound like an old tom cat, she curled her fingers into claws and slashed out toward the startled Indian with clawing motions.

Malo Cactus had lost all doubt, this was indeed one of the crazy ones. No wonder she had been thrown away, even his horse was shying backward nervously. He gripped his war club; a solid rap on her noggin would put an end to this foolishness.

Pearl saw the Indian reaching for the war club at his side and, shrieking as loud as she could, she tore the bonnet from her hair and flung it violently at the Indian pony's face. Then, as the startled animal shied rapidly back, she rushed heedlessly toward the horse with claw-like fingers extended, snarling viciously, and hit the animal in the shoulder with all her might. Malo Cactus, in an effort to keep his seat on the plunging animal, dropped his war club and made a desperate grab for his pony's mane just as the crazed white-girl slammed into his mount. The panicked animal lost footing and was propelled over onto its side, falling with its rider, and pinning Malo Cactus's leg under it. The crazy white girl landed on top of them and for one terrible moment, Pearl was face to face with the fallen breed, his eyes opened wide in bewilderment, staring up at her from his position at the bottom of the pile. Pearl uttered another, halfhearted hiss into his face, but it quickly turned into a scream of fright as the Indian's pony began to scramble to its feet again.

The brave's arm was before her, clutching the pony's mane, while his left leg was still encircling the pony. At the moment the horse lunged to its feet, Pearl sunk her teeth into the Indian's arm and bit him, while grappling for a hold on the horse herself. Her bite broke his grip and the Indian, yowling in pain, let go of the horse's mane. At the same time, Pearl unwittingly kneed the Indian painfully in the groin as she scrambled astride his horse. Flung aside like a dirty garment, the Indian groaned in agony and crumpled to the ground while the crazy little maiden took his place on the horse. In abject dismay, Malo Cactus watched the throw-away white girl gallop up the road and out of sight, leaving him afoot in the gathering storm.

————

Tommy Saber had spent the past hour hauling wood from the stack along the fence to add to the pile on the back porch. It was his job to replenish the pile of stove wood, and he had just loaded the last stick into the wheelbarrow of his final load, glad to be done with the "dumb job," when he heard a clatter of hooves coming down the driveway in a dead run. He rounded the side of the house just in time to see an Indian pony flying towards him, covered with lather, an obvious run-away. On its back was a girl hanging on for dear life.

Tommy jumped in front of the galloping horse, threw up his arms and shouted, "Whoa!" His actions caused the Indian pony to shy violently to one side, but barely break stride. However, the movement was just enough to break the hold of the girl on its back, and she was propelled forward as her mount sidestepped out from under her. Flying off the horse, she hit her would-be rescuer full in his open arms, and sent the two of them bowling over backwards to skid to a stop on the grass. The girl ended up on top of Tommy, the daylights scared out of both of them. For a moment they lay there, the wind knocked out of them, and then, as if on cue, the two youngsters both began to cry. Tommy because of the road-rash on his back and because of the scare he had just had of an attacking Comanche that suddenly became just a "dumb ol' girl," and the girl because… well, because she was a girl, and maybe because getting dumped off a wild mustang could have hurt her as well. Finally, the girl, still crying, pushed

145

herself to a sitting position and looked down at the boy she was sitting on and tried to smile through her tears.

"Well," she sniffed, "here I am. I've come to help out." The girl made a couple more, halfhearted sobs and struggled to catch her breath. Tommy had already stopped crying and was wondering why this stupid girl was still sitting on him.

"Get off me," he said angrily. "You darn near broke me in two."

By this time, Jessica Saber had come from her kitchen and Grant Saber, Tommy's father, was striding up from the machine shed. The folks stopped in amazement to see the young girl sitting on their son, and the two of them arguing heatedly. There was a strange Indian pony with feathers and paint standing foam-flecked and trembling up against the corral.

"What's going on here?" Grant roared. "You kids pipe down."

At Grant Saber's authoritative command, the two youngsters quieted down. "That's better," Grant said. Jessica lent a hand to the girl and helped her arise from off their son.

"Now who are you?"

"My name is Pearl," the girl replied, looking scared, "and I have come to help out, and I have just been scared to death by a wild, murdering, heathen savage, and I took his horse by acting crazy. When he fell off, I jumped on and rode like the very devil himself was after me, until I got here and what's-his-name there, jumped in front of me and made me fall off on top of him. It's a good thing too, or I might have been hurt, although it did knock the wind out of me, but I suppose I might forgive him that because he did cushion my fall."

"Geez-Louise, Jessica," Grant said, and gave his wife a pleading look that said, "Can't you shut her up some way?"

"Is this the Crossed Sabers? I hope so, I've been traveling for weeks to get here, and when I got to town the lady said you wouldn't be coming in to town until Saturday and this is only Wednesday, and I have been trying to get here for so long that I couldn't wait for Saturday. I didn't want to spend the last dollar Woody gave me to rent a horse, so I decided to walk here and then it got so cold that I stopped and took off my coat to put the sweater on that was in my bag, and so I didn't see that murdering savage until he had snuck up practically on top of me and scared me nearly to death..."

"Now slow down, dear," Jessica interrupted. "This is the Crossed Sabers Ranch. Why were you trying to get here?"

For the first time since her bombastic arrival, Pearl showed a reluctance to answer. "Well... I have come to help out. I need to stay here because I heard you folks were good people, and I need someplace good to stay. I am a good worker."

"We don't need no workers who go around jumping on kids," Tommy said, picking himself up off the ground and looking aggravated.

Grant was scratching his head and his wife looked at her husband in confusion. "Where are your folks?" the rancher asked.

"Momma's dead and Poppa's a drunk," Pearl stated simply. "He's somewhere back in Illinois and sold me for drink."

"Sold you for drink?" Jessica was shocked. "What on earth are you talking about, child?"

"Drink and poker." Pearl stated positively with a nod of her head. "He lost me to Howard Raphael a little over a year ago."

"Good heavens, child," Jessica said. "Are you saying your father gambled you off in a card game?"

"Yes, me for three jugs of whiskey."

"Well, what's your pa's name?" Grant prodded with another look at his wife, "and who is this Howard Raphael and where is he?"

"Pa's named Toby, Toby Harmon, and Howard Raphael is the smelly old man who won me in the poker game. He took me to Texas in his wagon after promising we would marry once we got to a big enough town, but we never did. He took me to wife anyway, although I thought I was way too young. Besides, he was much too old for me, he probably would have been dead before I was twenty... if he wasn't dead already."

"Pearl," Jessica said in alarm, "how old are you?" Once again, her eyes sought those of her husband.

"I turn thirteen this month," the girl said pertly.

"I'm already thirteen," Tommy said with a superior air. "What did you have to do as his wife?"

"Tommy," Grant said. "I want you to go catch that Indian pony, rub him down and turn him into the corral with the other horses."

"Aw Pa," Tommy said, "I want to hear the rest of Pearl's story."

"Never mind that, go do as you're told." The rancher watched his son leave and then turned to the girl. "What happened to this Raphael, and who told you we were good people?"

Pearl said, "Howard Raphael drove his wagon over a cliff and died in the wreck. I figured he'd burst his bowls asunder, but Woody showed me he'd just broke his neck... there were no guts lying about. Woody told me to come here."

"Who is Woody?" Grant said.

Suddenly Pearl got this guilty look on her face. "I can't say," she said.

"Why not, dear?" Jessica asked.

"I promised not to," Pearl replied.

"But he told you we were good people and for you to come here?" the rancher's wife asked. Pearl nodded her head.

Looking around, Jessica said, "Where are your things? Surely he didn't send you off with just the clothes on your back. Haven't you got a coat?"

"I left my coat and bag back where that blood-thirsty savage was. I had no time to stop and get them."

Grant turned towards the bunk house, "Better take her into the house, this storm is about to bust loose. I'll go get Lance and Rusty to ride back up the road and see if they can find her things and that pesky redskin."

Jessica Saber led the way into the kitchen with Pearl following. She stopped to pick up a few sticks of wood from the pile on the porch, and was astounded to be pushed aside by the girl, who took the sticks from her hands, eager to help.

"Let me do that," Pearl said.

Jessica shook her head in amazement. "Good heavens, girl, you just got here. Why don't you come in and have a seat at the table, the wood can wait?"

"It's alright, missus. I can still bring in the wood." She followed the rancher's wife into the kitchen, her eyes darting to the wood box by the stove. Walking over, Pearl dropped the sticks into the box and then turned her backside to the warmth of the cook stove and held out her hands to it. "I don't mind helping out, ma'am, I've carried and chopped wood since I was four years old."

"Four years old?" Jessica seemed surprised.

"Yes, ma'am, I can chop wood, hoe taters, carry water, slop hogs and even milk a cow."

"How are you at keeping house?"

"Just fine; I can sweep and dust and mop, and wash clothes, and make beds, and do dishes, and empty chamber pots, though I don't like to, and I can clean lamp chimneys, and pour in the oil, and haul out the ashes from the stove and dump them down the toilet hole. I can iron and fold and put away clothes. . . all that sort of thing."

"Can you cook?"

"Oh, yes, ma'am, I'm good in the kitchen. I can peel spuds and churn butter and make biscuits but my specialty is corn dodgers. Corn dodgers and catfish. Woody liked my corn dodgers and catfish."

Jessica finished pouring boiling water into a china teapot and set the lid back on. "Tell me more about this Woody," she said.

Pearl suddenly went quiet and that same look of guilt came into her eyes.

"Pearl," Jessica said, "What is wrong? Did this Woody mistreat you somehow?"

"Oh, no, ma'am, nothing like that. He rode up like one of those knights in shining armor and made ol' Howard give me up... well, took me away at least. He rescued me. He said since the war, no one could own somebody else, that President Lincoln had said that. That's what that war was all about, you know."

"Yes," the rancher's wife nodded with a smile. "So, why this reluctance to tell me who he is? Has he got a last name?"

Pearl nodded in affirmation and watched Jessica pour a stream of tea into two pretty china tea cups.

"Well?"

"It was Stover, do you have any oatmeal cookies?"

"Yes, Pearl, see that cookie jar on the table in front of you? Where was this Woody Stover from?"

Pearl removed the lid and peered inside the jar. Taking a couple cookies, she immediately dunked one of them into her tea cup and then took a bite before answering.

"West Texas," she said around a mouthful. Pearl suddenly paused in her enjoyment of the treat and looked up at the older woman. "Do we have to ask the blessing over tea and cookies?"

Jessica got a twinkle in her eye. She was beginning to warm to this precocious girl who she saw as an interesting mix of child and young lady. It was a symptom she recognized altogether too well, having raised two teenage daughters already. In fact, where was Becky anyway? Her sixteen-year-old daughter had yet to put in an appearance and meet the new girl.

"Do you want to?" she asked.

"Maybe we should," Pearl said. "I don't think we can ever be too thankful to the Lord."

"I don't either," Jessica said. "Would you like to do the honors?"

Pearl nodded, set her cookie down on a saucer, and then quietly, reverently, folded her hands and began to pray.

"Dear Lord, we are thankful for thy bounty and these gifts we are about to receive. Bless this food to the use of our bodies, bless this house and these good people. Bless the missionaries and all who do the work of the gospel, and bless the President and the Nation, and bless Woody and keep him safe until we can marry, in Jesus name... amen."

She finished her prayer and looked up to see the rancher's wife staring at her with another look of amazement.

"Pearl," Jessica said. "How old is this Woody?"

Pearl took a bite of cookie. "Oh, he's old, probably twenty or thirty, but he's not anywhere near as old as Howard Raphael. Howard was like somebody's Grampa. He snored, and if you'll pardon my saying so ma'am, he farted a lot, too."

Jessica's eyebrows shot up and she gave the girl a censuring look. "I will overlook that this time, but remember that kind of talk is not lady-like and is frowned upon in my home."

"Oh, excuse me, ma'am, I will be sure to remember that."

"Pearl, one other thing to always remember. Men do not like crudeness and vulgarities in women."

Pearl nodded and slowly munched her cookie.

Jessica went on. "Do you plan to marry this Woody?"

"Yes," Pearl said matter of factually, "when I am a couple of years older."

"You'd only be fifteen then. Are you sure you want to marry that young?"

"Well, I couldn't expect him to wait forever, could I? I'd need to marry up with him before he found someone else."

"How do you know he doesn't already have someone else?"

"Oh no, he doesn't. I don't think he even likes women. Whenever I tried to talk to him about that, or even his family, he just told me to 'dummy up', but I'll change his mind about all that stuff."

At that moment, Becky came down the stairs and walked into the kitchen to find her mother talking with the strange young girl.

"Who's this?" Becky said.

"Becky, this is Pearl. Pearl, meet my youngest daughter, Becky."

Pearl jumped to her feet and gave a polite curtsey. "Pleased to meet cha," she said. "I've never had an older sister before, we shall have a grand time."

Becky lifted inquiring eyes to her mother. "What is she talking about and where did she come from?"

Jessica started to explain about their new guest but Pearl interrupted.

"I just traveled many weary miles, all the way from Fort Griffin, to Fort Concho, to San Antonio, and then on the military road to Fort Stockton, and then finally by way of the stage to Wade's Landing, and I've come to work for my keep."

Rebecca Saber looked at her mother in confusion and Jessica gave her daughter a reassuring smile. "We are still sorting it all out, honey. Seems like somebody named Woody Stover sent her here and she has quite a story to tell. Can you take her upstairs and make her comfortable in your room? You can fix up Gwen's bed for her."

Pearl had already finished her tea and was peering from the kitchen into the parlor. "Oh, you have a piano, I have never seen one except in church when I was little before momma died. May I go look at it?"

Jessica Saber nodded and Becky slowly followed the younger girl into the parlor. Pearl was chattering away about how nice everything was and in its own place, when suddenly she stopped. She had just picked up a framed, family portrait from off the piano and was staring intently at the people pictured there. Slowly she turned to the other girl and blurted out, "What's Woody doing in this picture?"

"Momma," Becky called, "you'd better come in here.

––––––

Sundays were a mixed blessing for Suzanne. As the winter days dragged by, she found it harder and harder to wait for spring to come when she could begin her pursuit of Colton. For some inexplicable reason, Sunday seemed to be the hardest day of all to drag herself out of bed and get ready for church. Perhaps it was because seeing the Saber family there without Colt or Sonny provoked such strong memories for her. But she went because folks were counting on her and she never ceased to be surprised that once she was there, once the music and worship, the prayers and the spoken word was heard, she would always come away with new hope. Even seeing Colton's mom and dad and Becky and Tommy drew her to them in their shared loss. So it was that on that particular Sunday, as she looked up from her place at the piano to see the Saber family filing in, she had no idea the strange young girl with them was about to change her life.

When the service was over, Jessica Saber made her way down the aisle to where Suzanne sat. She was ushering the new girl ahead of her, and stopped before the blonde piano player to say, "Suzanne, I want you to meet Pearl Harmon. Pearl, this is Suzanne Kluesman, the lady I've been telling you about."

Pearl gave a shy smile and held out her hand. "Pleased to meet cha'," she said, and gave a slight curtsey.

Suzanne took her hand and smiled sweetly. "And I you. Did you enjoy the service?"

"Oh yes, especially your piano playing. Do you think I could learn to play like that?"

Suzanne gave Jessica Saber a questioning look while answering the girl. "I am sure you could."

"I can see you are far lovelier than I, and with such piano playing, it is no wonder Woody was in love with you. I must learn to play as well."

"Woody—who's Woody?" Suzanne said.

Jessica told Pearl to wait in the wagon and she would be along directly, then turned to the questioning schoolteacher.

"Pearl has identified a picture of Colton as someone named Woody, who rescued her and sent her to us. Someone she last saw in Fort Griffin about a month ago."

Suzanne's heart lurched in her breast. This was the first news she had had since his disappearance last fall, and although a missing-person poster had been circulated, not one shred of evidence had been reported as to his whereabouts until now. She must speak with this child.

Jessica Saber said, "I am sure you will wish to speak with Pearl, so would you and your folks like to come out to the ranch for dinner today?"

Suzanne quickly replied in the affirmative and went in search of her parents.

Pearl said, "He said his name was Woody, but I think he just made that up when ol' Howard asked him what his name was; he took too long to answer. His real name is Colt then? I like that better."

"Yes," Suzanne said with a sigh. She was sitting on the piano bench and the youngster, Pearl, was standing beside her. Both were gazing at the family photo of the Sabers, while the finishing touches were being put on the Sunday dinner in the kitchen. A low murmur of voices between her mother and Mrs. Saber could be heard in that direction, and she knew the rancher's wife was filling Mable Kluesman in on the amazing story her young protégé had told.

"He sure is a good-looking cowboy," Pearl said. "Are you sure you are still engaged?"

Suzanne was startled by the question. She had never considered it otherwise, but now that it was brought to mind, it would be certain Colt would have no such idea, given that he now thought her dead.

"Of course we are," she said, somewhat nettled, "Why wouldn't we be?"

"I don't know. Isn't there some sort of rule that if you don't marry within a certain amount of time the engagement period expires?"

Suzanne looked pensive, "No, not unless one or the other of you has died."

Pearl seemed surprised. "Then how come he left you?"

Her face blanched suddenly white and a wave of guilt and shame swept over the young schoolteacher at the question. This was a question that haunted her day and night, and now here it was again, the answer being demanded by this strange adolescent girl, a girl on whom Colton had obviously left his mark, as well.

With a gasp, Suzanne buried her face in her hands and sat trembling before her young inquisitor. Finally, she lifted a crimson face and smiled faintly at Pearl. "Honey, whatever you do, never let anyone talk you out of what you know to be true in your heart."

"Well then, I probably shouldn't tell you this, but I know I am going to merry Colt so I guess that makes us rivals."

Suzanne sniffed, gave a knowing nod of her head, and then with a smile, said, "We best find him first, don't you think? Now tell me what you know about him; where was he, what was he doing, how did he look, was he well... did he ever say anything about me?"

Pearl took a seat on the bench beside the anxious young woman and, placing her hands together in her lap, said, "I know he is smart and funny and rides a horse really well. He talks to his horse all the time. . . calls him Lightfoot, and the way the two of them carry on, it almost makes you feel like you're not even there. He was cutting wood for the army at Ft. Griffin and renting a shack behind the livery stable, and was waiting to catch a cattle drive coming through for Dodge City. I think he really preferred the cowboy life to wood cutting. He was in good health and looked like a knight in shining armor to me. He wouldn't speak about his family much, said he would never be coming back here, and never mentioned that the Sabers were actually his kin. I never heard him talk about you except for that one night in his sleep when we were out on the trail. He'd had a bad night of it, and must have been dreaming of you, for I heard him cry out in his sleep, *'Oh Suzanne!'* I never questioned him about it because he had told me to shut up earlier, so I did... for three days, until we reached The Flat, and by that time I had forgotten about it 'til now, I did wonder who Suzanne was though. I last saw him at The Flat when he put me on the stagecoach to come here and that's when I told him I loved him."

Suzanne patted the younger girl's knee, "I love him too, sweetheart, more than life itself, and I certainly understand your loving him. He does that to a lot of girls without even trying. I am going to find him and when I do, if he still doesn't want me, then I'll put in a good word for you."

At that point they were called to the dinner table. Pearl stood up and with a serious look on her face said, "The first thing either of us have to do, is get that horse, Lightfoot, away from him. Otherwise he is never going to pay any attention to either one of us."

CHAPTER TEN

Waistman, Kemp and Runs-With-Horses

Big Springs, Texas, Late Fall 1870

WHEN SONNY SABER RODE INTO BIG Springs he could see that another party was already camped some distance away on the other side of the lake. Riding Tornado in that direction, his sense of smell was soon overpowered with the putrid stench of rancid buffalo hides, and he made a quick decision to camp up-wind of the two scruffy characters he saw lazing about a large campfire. They were passing a jug back and forth between them and looking his outfit over with a critical eye.

"Hyer," one of them called, "Where ya bound fer in such an almighty hurry? Whyn't you get down and set a spell and give us the latest news?"

Sonny reined in the stallion and sat studying the two for a moment before replying. Both of them seemed to be pretty badly used up, and looked like they'd been fired in a furnace. He couldn't quite put his finger on it because they were covered with dirt and grime of obvious duration, yet they had a singed, almost blackened look, judging by appearances, and the booze wasn't helping anything either.

"You two fellers haven't seen a cowpoke riding through in the last week or so, have ya? He's mounted on a flashy red horse with white socks and a blaze face."

The second fellow spoke up then; he seemed a bit surlier than the first, perhaps it was just that he wasn't as deep in his cups as the other fellow, but he said with a note of contempt in his voice, "Who wants to know?"

The first fellow burst out laughing at his companion's remarks as though it was the funniest thing he had ever heard and said, "Good one, Sly," and then whopped him on the back with a big ham-handed slap that caused Sly to nearly drop the jug.

"Dammit, Buff, you near made me drop the moon."

"Oh, don't lose any of that Kickapoo joy juice," he said with another boisterous laugh, then grabbed the jug from the fellow called Sly and took a pull at it.

Sonny gave a disgusted snort and tapped his heels into Tornado's sides. It was a cinch he wasn't going to learn anything intelligent from these two. What was it, "He who carries on a conversation with a drunk, makes two idiots."

"Hey, don't leave," the one called Buff said. "We just rolled in from the killin' grounds with this load of hides and are headed to the Colorado. Who'd you say you was lookin' fer?"

Sonny pulled up and looked back. "Rider on a sorrel horse," he said tersely.

"You're the first white man we seen in more'n a month. Nothin' else 'ceptin' poison mean Injuns out here," Buff said. The other fellow muttered something under his breath, shot Sonny a contemptuous look and took the jug from his partner.

"Keep an eye out then," Sonny said dryly and rode on.

He rode to the opposite side of the lake and pulled up near the remains of a small teepee frame to make camp. Soon he had a fire blazing and then slipped away to search for a prairie chicken for his supper. He found a spot where there seemed to be an abundance of crickets and snuck through the covering reeds of the lake shore until he spied a flock of the birds chasing the bugs. Selecting a fat cock, he drew a bead on its head with his rifle and pulled the trigger. The sage cock was decapitated and left flopping about on the grass while the rest of the flock flew out of sight in a flurry of wings.

By the time darkness fell, he had finished the meal and camp chores and was relaxing by the fire, looking absently at the skeleton poles of the little teepee. "I wonder if that's where Colton and Willow stayed," he said. His thoughts turned to his brother and the dusky Indian princess and all that had happened since the time Colt took her back to her people. Sadly, he shook his head and looked up at the stars mantling the evening sky. "Why Lord?" He waited, as though the answer might come on the rising breeze, but only the rustle of the reeds along the lake and the steady twinkle of the stars was all that he discerned.

Sonny came awake and sat bolt upright in his blankets, trying to figure out what it was that had awakened him. The night was silent, even the sounds normally heard were absent. Then he realized that his horse and mule were unusually quiet. Throwing off his blankets, he pulled on his boots, picked up his rifle and got up to investigate. Moving to the picket area, he saw that the animals were missing. Perhaps it was the sound of them being led away that had awakened him. Both Tornado and Hank were usually wary of strangers. Had Indians snuck in and taken his horse and mule? Both the picket posts that he had driven down earlier were in place, so it was pretty certain they hadn't pulled lose their tethers. Listening intently, Sonny thought he heard the soft foot-falls of his horse and mule moving off around the lake and he set out to follow in that direction.

Had Indians stolen his mount and pack animal, and were they now headed for the buffalo hunter's camp to rustle their stock as well? Sonny didn't know, but proceeded at a fast walk to catch up. Whatever was going on, his would be an extra and necessary gun to spoil the redskins' mischief.

―――――

Runs-With-Horses watched from the cover of tall reeds around the big spring his people called Mobeetie, the Sweetwater, while the two white buffalo hunters passed the jug of fire-water back and forth. He thought it strange that they posted no guard to watch their horses for even the large work animals were a prize to the People. What they lacked in speed, they more than made up for in size and could provide much feasting at the encampment circle of the Kiowa.

Runs-With-Horses, in his twentieth autumn, was renowned amongst the various bands on the plains as a skilled horse thief. His fleetness of foot had enabled him to capture many ponies, both from the neighboring bands of Indians, but even more so, from the white-eyes who were uncommonly careless about tending their horses. He had captured so many that it was thought by this time he should be a wealthy and important chieftain in the council circle of Santana's band, but Runs-With-Horses had no care for such things. To him, the exhilaration of the chase and capture, particularly of the ponies of the hated white man, was reward enough; that, and the prestige he gained each time he rode into the encampment with a new prize. Of particular delight was the attention earned from the young maidens of the camp, and the envy of the other warriors. Usually he would give the stolen pony away to someone, and after a few days of enjoying the company of one or another of the young maids, and spending time eating at her father's fire, he would set out again on another conquest.

"Good," he said. "The white-eyes will sleep the fire-water sleep this night, their ponies will soon be mine." He settled down amongst the reeds to wait for darkness, keeping a watchful eye on the hunters' camp. This theft would be of double satisfaction, for he would count coup on men who were wanton killers of the *paw*. Not only would he take their horses, he would leave them stranded afoot with their stinking wagon of hides. He smiled to himself and made a mental note of the terrain, mapping the most silent route to take once it got dark.

His thoughts were interrupted by loud talking in the hunters' camp. Rising up cautiously to peer through the grass, he was surprised to see a third rider mounted on a magnificent stallion and leading a loaded pack mule. He had stopped and was exchanging words with the old hunters. With a start, Runs-With-Horses realized that this was the Buffalo Man, and the powerful dark stallion was none other than the legendary "Thunder Horse" of the Sweetgrass range. A horse he had dreamed of catching since his youth, the very one that had first led him to develop his skill as a horse talker. When the stallion had been taken from the wild more than a year ago, he had been filled with anger and bitterness at the white-eyes who had preempted his capture of the powerful stallion. It had been small compensation that the Thunder Horse had been taken by the Buffalo Man, for he had set his heart on having this mighty animal. Even if the Buffalo Man had used the powerful spirit medicine the Comanche claimed he had to take the Thunder Horse, the young brave was convinced he contained enough cunning of his own, that he would have eventually caught the horse himself, had not the Tejanos interfered.

Runs-With-Horses was skeptical of the story the Comanche were circulating about the Buffalo Man and his medicine. He was supposedly responsible for a young Comanche chieftain's unusual death by a flying serpent, one that the Buffalo Man had caused to fly from the ground and encircle the chief's neck when he was attacking the Tejano and his two younger companions on top of the Kiowa's Perfect Hill, a sacred place of spirit council between the people and the old ones. He knew of the Perfect Hill and had even been part of the purging of the white-eyes' structures at White Bear's orders after the Kwihnai Killer had built his wickiup there. But as to the rest of the tale, and the Buffalo Man's part in it, he had his doubts.

He was also skeptical of the relationship some claimed between the Buffalo Man and the Kwihnai Killer, that they were brothers, and that the Kwihnai Killer was friend to the Son of the Great Spirit. Kicking Bird, a lesser chief of the Kiowa, made this medicine talk after the entire band had been unsuccessful at pinning the Kwihnai Killer to the ground in the arrow flights test that left a cross sign where he had lain untouched, as a silent testimony of his medicine.

But an important war chief of the Comanche's Badger Clan, one Two Dogs, a renowned seer, had witnessed firsthand the Buffalo Man trampled in a mighty stampede of *paw,* only to rise again unscathed and unhurt from out of the mangled remains of a huge bull. In possession of the animal's power and strength, he had rebuked brother coyote in the scruffy dog's own language after it had chewed on his foot, causing that heckler to flee in humiliation and disgrace. Two Dogs had been trailing the Buffalo Man at the time, intent on his capture to bring this enemy of the Comanche to the elders for judgment, but after witnessing the awesome power of his medicine, he quickly rode away lest the spirits should whisper on a breeze to the Buffalo Man and he be discovered and set upon by serpents.

It had only been fifteen suns since this had happened, but already the story had spread throughout the plains tribes. The Buffalo Man had been riding the Thunder Horse at the time he was swallowed in the stampede. The Thunder Horse had been gored by the huge bull, but now, here was the Thunder Horse alive and well, and this rider had to be the Buffalo Man. Runs-With-Horses was elated, before him was a prize of notable proportion. Not only would he steal the Thunder Horse, but he would count coup on the Buffalo Man and once again prove the People's medicine was stronger than that of one of the invading white men's most powerful shaman.

Through narrowed eyes, the young warrior watched as the Buffalo Man rode out of the hide hunters' camp and went around to the other side of the lake. He stealthily changed positions for now his focus was on the capture of the Thunder Horse. He would take the mulo as well, for he must not leave the Buffalo Man anything to ride, and mulos were good eating. But first he must disguise his scent. Taking a roundabout route, he made his way towards the buffalo hunters' camp, keeping out of sight of the two careless men passing the jug. Coming up to where their big horses were grazing, he cautiously located a recent pile of horse manure. While the curious draft animals looked on, he proceeded to fill a buckskin bag he'd slung over one shoulder with the fresh dropping, before quietly slipping away.

Runs-With-Horses had just reached the opposite side of the spring and was slipping through the grass when a shot rang out. He thought he had been discovered and flattened himself to the ground. Was the Buffalo Man shooting at him? Then he heard the flapping wings of the prairie hens and, holding as motionless as though carved in stone, he listened as footsteps passed him in the grass, went over to retrieve a flopping sage hen and then faded off in the direction of the lower end of the lake. Over the next hour, he slowly worked his way to a spot downwind of the Buffalo Man's camp, keeping the breeze from the lake blowing the smoke of the white-eye's fire in his face, and then waited.

The moon was moving to the western horizon when Runs-With-Horses sat up and stretched his cramped muscles. The Buffalo Man was rolled in his blankets and he could hear his gentle snoring. It was time, and his heart beat slightly faster as he anticipated the capture of the coveted Thunder Horse. Swiftly he stripped off his buckskin jerkin and reached into the sack of horse manure. He took a liberal amount of the stuff and began to cover his upper body, leaving no bare skin uncovered. He even smeared manure in his hair and scalp lock and face. Masking his scent with the horse scent would allow him to approach the white-eye's horse without alarming the animals. Picking up his buckskin bag, he shook out the remaining horse turds and stuffed his shirt into it, then slung it across his back, and quietly began his approach to where the big stallion was grazing.

Tornado jerked up his head and stared into the darkness at the low chuffing sound. A figure was moving towards him in the dark and the scent was peculiar, but spoke of one of the draft horses he had seen earlier. He gave an answering nicker in his throat and moved a few steps toward the figure in the dark. With ears pricked forward, he waited for the stranger to approach. The mule, Hank, moved up beside the stallion and the two waited as Runs-With-Horses walked directly up to the stallion while making the low guttural noises in his throat. When the Indian was close enough to the horse to breath in his face, Tornado tossed his head a couple of times, but, fascinated at the breath of this strange man, the horse stretched his neck and reached out his muzzle with nostrils distended to inhale the wind the man was blowing into his nose. The big grulla liked what the man was doing. He felt a kinship and something moved through him that spoke to the wildness and freedom he had once known. He did not mind when the man bent and took the lead line loose from the picket post and coiled it about his shoulder before turning to the mule.

Hank was momentarily alarmed when the man smelling of horse manure reached out to him. He had just started to bray when fingers quickly pinched his muzzle and the man's breath began to blow softly into his nostrils. It tickled and the mule quieted down, allowing the strange smelling man to unfasten the picket and lead him away with the horse.

———

Sonny stole stealthily along the lake shore towards the buffalo hunters' camp following what he thought were the soft, footfall thuds, of his animals' hooves. He could discern the dying embers of a campfire and heard the drunken snores emanating from the dark shapes of the hunters rolled in their blankets fast asleep. "Huh, a freight train could be going by and those two wouldn't know it," he muttered.

A quick glance at the big dipper and he figured it was somewhere around two o'clock in the morning. At that point, Sonny made out the standing figures of the hunters' wagon horses. Something was amiss, the workhorses stood like statues and then seemed to suddenly move as one and almost glide off into the darkness, the thud of their heavy hooves dying off in the night.

"That was weird," Sonny said. "It's almost as though someone told those clumsy nags to tiptoe out of there." Lengthening his stride, Sonny set out on foot in pursuit of the missing horses, while the drunken buffalo hunters snored on, oblivious to the world and the Indian that had just made off with their draft animals.

Reaching the spot where he had last seen the work-horses, Sonny looked carefully for sign of their departure on the trampled ground, but the animals had been staked out here since early afternoon, and in the darkness it was nearly impossible to discern the direction they had gone. Walking resolutely towards the east, Sonny struck a course towards the direction he had last seen the animals go. Once beyond the trampled picket circle, he soon found in the moonlight the bent grass of their passing. A strong smell of horse manure permeated the air as he began to follow the meandering trail through the brush.

Sonny quickened his pace to a dogtrot in an effort to gain on the departing horses and mule. At one point, he emerged from the brush to a clear patch of grassland that rose gently to the rise of a hill about twenty feet high, and was just in time to see the hindquarters of one of the workhorses cresting the top, before it disappeared from sight. Breaking into a dead run, Sonny raced to the top of the rise and paused to see down the other side. The moon shone bright and clear to reveal a lone Indian, some one-hundred yards distant, at the head of a single file column of his and the hunters' animals. At first, he thought the animals were being led by the redskin, but on closer inspection it became apparent that the horses and mule were following the young brave of their own volition.

Dropping to one knee, the tall cowboy raised his Winchester and drew a bead on the bobbing head of the warrior. He was about to squeeze the trigger when Tornado's head appeared in his sights. He waited, holding his position, but then Hank's big ears were in the way. He dared not shoot his horse or pack mule, or the buffalo hunters' horses either, but the longer he held to get the shot, the more it seemed that the animals were actually providing a shield to prevent him shooting the Indian.

Sonny relaxed his stance and marveled at the luck of this Indian; then to his surprise he saw the young brave break into a fast run at the head of the string of animals, keeping pace with them as the whole bunch galloped out of sight over another ridge.

"That was one fast Injun," Sonny mused, "and those horses... it was almost as though he was telling them what to do and they understood him, even Hank." That was truly a marvel. Sonny had never heard of the legendary Run's With Horses, but had now witnessed firsthand, the young brave's prowess with the animals. Nevertheless, he could not afford to lose Tornado or Hank. He must hurry back to his camp, cobble together an outfit from his gear and get on the trail as quickly as possible.

An hour later, he made his way back to Big Springs to where the buffalo hunters, Sly Kemp and Buff Waistman, were still rolled in their blankets sound asleep. Nudging Buff with the toe of his boot, Sonny said, "Get up, buffalo hunter, the Injuns have stolen your horses."

Waistman sat up and groggily rubbed bleary eyes and stared at Sonny in the dark. "What the hell," he muttered.

"You've been robbed and your horses rustled, so have mine," Sonny said. "Some sneaking Injun has made off with all our stock. I trailed 'im to a ridge east of here a ways, and am going after them. Keep an eye on my pack goods, will you? My stuff is on the other side of the springs. I'll be back as soon as I can with the horses and will bring your horses, too."

"What the hell," Waistman groused again, "how many of them were there?" His comments roused Kemp, who rolled over moaning as he got up on hands and knees to crawl from his blankets and to commence upchucking in the weeds.

"Just one," Sonny said. "Can you keep an eye on my stuff?

"Where's it at?" Buff said.

"Over where I was camping. I'll be back as soon as I can. That Injun seemed to have our animals under some sort of spell, they were following him like well-trained bird dogs."

"Probably that damned Kiowa, Runs-With-Horses," the hunter said.

Sonny paused to turn back, "Who?"

"Some spook the Injuns have who is supposed to magically appear and steal horses. They say he can run as fast as a horse and talks to them or somethin'. He's known all over the plains. If you're going to get our nags back, you got your work cut out for you."

"I better get going then. Just out of curiosity, how'd you and the other fellow get your beard and head all singed up like that? Did the Injuns do that?"

Buffalo Waistman's eyes took on a malevolent glare and he flared up at the question. "Hell no, it weren't no dad-blamed Injun, it were some smart-ass kid with an Injun gal he was cavorting with, right here at this very place. If I ever get my hands on him, I'll skin him alive with a red-hot knife."

Sonny was surprised. "How long ago was that?" he asked.

"Couple a year ago. He and the gal attacked us when we was just tryin' to be neighborly and he set our beards and hair on fire. Hell, we had to run and jump in the lake or we'd been burnt to a crisp."

"The kid have a name?" Sonny asked.

"Said his name was Colt," Buff said, "the son-of-a-bitch, if I ever find him…"

Sonny felt hot ire suffuse through his body at the slur to his mother. It was all he could do to keep from smashing a fist into the filthy hunter's rotten-toothed mouth, but in order to not tip his hand, he held his peace, turned, and strode from the camp.

"What the hell's the matter with you?" Waistman called.

Sonny didn't answer or look back but quickened his pace on the trail of Runs-With-Horses.

"So, Colt had scarred up those two seedy tramps like that. Funny he'd never said anything about it to me," Sonny mused. He was traveling at a fast dog-trot, headed for the ridge where he had been denied the shot at Runs-With-Horses, eager to pick up the trail by sunrise. "I wonder what that was all about. Given the demeanor of those two characters, I'd bet they had it coming. Cavorting with Willow? Huh, that was an interesting take of Buff's. It's more likely that cavorting was what the two of them had in mind, and they just picked the wrong cowboy and Indian gal to mess with."

The sky was graying in the east when Sonny stopped at the spot where he had last seen the Indian and horses disappear into the brush. He bent to peer at the ground and jumble of tracks and detected the faint odor of horse manure. Looking closer he found a piece of drying manure stuck to a willow leaf. "So, Mr. Runs-With-Horses, for all your mystery and magic, you may just be giving yourself away with your sneaky, horse poop tricks." Sonny had heard of Indians who would disguise their scent by rubbing buffalo manure on themselves in order to creep close enough to the herds to get a bow shot, so it was no surprise to realize that Runs-With-Horses had probably pulled the same trick in his capture of the horses. He hurried on, following the scent and the general direction more than the tracks, indiscernible in the dark.

Sonny knew that Colt had returned Willow to a Kiowa Camp in a remote canyon somewhere beyond the Colorado River, and even though that had been over three years ago, it was just possible that they may once again be encamped there. If Sonny could not catch up to Runs-With-Horses, he would head for the canyon.

The stream flowing from Big Springs drained into the Colorado near Pecan Crossing, the place where the Goodnight-Loving Cattle Trail crossed. From the Colorado, Colt said they had followed Sweetwater Creek to a hidden trail that led to the Indians' encampment. The Sweetwater had become a well-known route since the cattle drives, although Sonny had never traveled this part of the country himself. For now, he would continue pressing on the trail that was becoming clearer with the dawning light of day.

———

Runs-With-Horses ran easily ahead of the Thunder Horse and the rest. The clumsiness of the big work horses and their lumbering gait set an easy pace for the young Indian. He was certain the Buffalo Man would follow, in an attempt to recapture the Thunder Horse, and he must be ever vigilant to throw the tall Tejano off the track. He smiled inwardly at the trick he had pulled on the Buffalo Man by coaching the horses and mule following him to keep between him and the White-Eyes' rifle. He had directed his thoughts to the animals and they had responded, something that others seemed unable to do; still, he did not see what was so hard about speaking with horses, as long as one kept his mind occupied with the animal's thoughts.

When the young Indian came to a branch water drainage, he halted and told the following animals to graze but not wander far while he cleaned up. Quickly stripping, the brave entered the stream and bathed his body free of the dried horse manure. Retrieving his deer-skin shirt, he hurriedly dried himself as he shivered in the frigid air, dressed and called to the horses and mule that it was time to move on. It was then that he found the animals were somewhat reticent to follow him.

Walking to the Thunder Horse, he had to snatch the lead rope and pull the big horse's head around and look long into his eyes while blowing in his nostrils before the stallion would once again follow him, and he had to repeat the performance with each of the other animals as well. The mule proved to be the most difficult, and finally Runs-With-Horses found it necessary to tie the mulo's lead rope to the tail of one of the draft animals in order to move on, but not before Hank broke out into a raucous braying. The Indian wondered if the change in his scent had confounded the animals and their ability to understand his thoughts. It was just as well, the animals were accepting him again now.

Runs-With-Horses led his little convoy into the stream, directing the animals to not leave any track on either bank and keep to stony ground. He pressed upstream for some distance until he came to an outcrop of bedrock that rose from the stream bed and here he led them out. At this point he gathered a handful of the Thunder Horse's mane and vaulted effortlessly onto his back. The dark horse snorted and then, at the brave's urging, broke into a trot, keeping to the stony ground that his rider's eyes searched out for him. The other animals followed with the mule the only resistant one.

Was the mulo aware that he was being led to his death? Runs-With-Horses did not think so and was careful to not think along such lines, but it was becoming increasingly difficult not to as the cantankerous animal grumbled and chuckled behind the stolid workhorse he was tied to. Finally, the young brave stopped and slid to the ground. He walked to where the mule, now white-eyed at his approach, was lunging against his tether. Taking a firm hold of the animal's halter, he stared deeply into the mulo's eyes and blew a breath steadily into the mouth of the animal when he opened it to bray.

Hank calmed then and allowed the Indian to untie him. Runs-With-Horses had led him to a point away from the others and, while fixing his mind on the rising sun, he quietly drew his knife and was about to slit the mulo's throat when a shot rang out and a bullet sent the knife spinning from the warrior's hand. Runs-With-Horses was startled to see the Buffalo Man standing on a ridge back towards the creek they had just left, aiming his rifle for another shot.

Ignoring the work animals, and with the feeling gone in his numb and bleeding hand, he ran to where the Thunder Horse stood watching with ears erect, to fling himself astride. Uttering a wild cry to the big stallion to get them away from danger, the two of them raced away while bullets spanged off the sheltering rocks around them.

————

Shortly before, Sonny had peered at the scrape of white on the bedrock that disappeared into the water of the small stream. "That was made by a horseshoe slipping into this stream," he said. "No sign of it coming out on the other side either, I'll bet Runs-With-Horses has taken to the water to hide the trail." Sonny had paused a few moments to determine whether the Indian had gone upstream or down with the animals, when a bit of leaf and moss floated by in the pre-dawn light. "Upstream," he said and turned to move rapidly along the shallow streambed, his eyes searching either side for any sign of his quarry's exit. He had just passed an outcropping of bedrock when in the distance and beyond a low-lying hill, he heard the braying of a mule.

"Hank!" he said, and turning on his heels he nimbly jumped the creek and raced towards the top of the ridge. Before him, he saw Runs-With-Horses slip from the back of Tornado and walk to where Hank was balking behind one of the work horses. The Indian was calming the mule, but Sonny could see that the cantankerous jackass was delaying the brave's progress. "Hank, I wouldn't give two hoots and a holler for you living to a ripe old age unless..." Sonny did not finish the sentence. Instead, he lifted the rifle and drew a bead on the Indian, but Hank was again in the way for him to get a clean shot. What he could see clearly was the knife blade the Indian drew from the sheath at his side and the hand that held it. It was a long shot, but Hank's life hung in the balance. Sonny squeezed the trigger.

When the Indian ran towards the horse, Sonny quickly worked the lever of the Winchester and sent several shots after him, but in his efforts to avoid hitting Tornado, he fired to no affect. Glumly he watched the horse and its rider gallop out of sight.

Rounding up the two workhorses and the mule, Sonny stood looking after Runs-With-Horses departure atop Tornado. For a moment, he considered trying to follow on Hank, but soon gave that up as a bad idea. He'd take the draft animals back to Waistman and Kemp, then go on with Hank and his outfit to try to find the Kiowa camp. If they could steal his horse, he'd just have to steal it back. Throwing a long leg over the reluctant Hank and grasping the lead lines of the work horses, he urged the long-eared mule back the way they had come, his feet just barely clearing the ground.

When he finally rode into the buffalo hunters' camp, he was surprised to find the two of them up and about. In fact, it was apparent they had already recovered his camp gear from the other side of the lake, for they had already divvied it up into two piles and were going through his stuff to see what of value or interest they might find.

"What are you two knot-heads doing going through my stuff?" he said in a loud voice that hauled the pair of them up short to turn guiltily around and face him.

"Just puttin it in order for ya," Sly Kemp said, his face red with guilt.

"Wal, ain't you a sight, seated on that jackass," Buff said in an attempt to allay suspicion of his own actions. "I see ya got our horses; too bad about your'n."

"Put it back," Sonny's voice cracked like thunder, "All of it!"

The two grungy hunters looked at each other and then stepped away from the pack goods and stood a few paces apart.

"Now, there ain't no call to get your dander up," Waistman whined, "we was just seein' if everythin' was there."

"I suppose that includes my money belt sticking out of your back pocket, too."

Waistman looked like a chicken-killing dog with feathers hanging from its chops. "Hell, man, I was just hangin' on to it for ya, I was goin' to give it back." He sheepishly pulled the belt from his hip pocket and tossed it onto the rest of the pile he'd been rummaging through.

"Hey, you young pup," Kemp snarled, "you got no call stomping in here and accusing us of skullduggery after we went to all the trouble of packin' your junk clear round this pound. Why don't you leave those horses, take your trash and that miserable jackass, and get the hell out of here?"

Winchester in hand, Sonny walked over to where the older man was bristling, and said in a low voice tinged with danger, "Kemp, Sylvester isn't it? On these plains out here, a man's horse and possessions can mean the difference between life or death, and to contravene upon either is to put one's life in jeopardy. His and yours. Now I have recovered your horses at the expense of gettin' back my own. The least you could do is to have the decency to not go ferreting through my personals. I'd be obliged for you to put my belongings back where you found them."

"Aw, do it yourself, I ain't nobody's nigger." Kemp said. He had started to turn away and then as an afterthought, he turned back to the tall cowboy and began to poke his finger against Sonny's chest, saying, "And another thing, you could show a little more respect to your elders, we ain't some dirt-poor sodbusters ya know. We happen to be prosperous businessmen of commerce, turnin' an honest buck out here and riddin' the west of all these damn buffalo. You ain't got no call to be accusing us of going through your stuff."

Sonny reached his free hand up and grabbed Kemp's fingers in a vice-like grip and bent them slowly backwards, causing the older man to rise up on his tip toes and yowl with pain.

"Then why did you?" he said.

"Dammit, I've got arthritis in those fingers, you dumb nimrod, let go afore I bust you one in the chops."

"Soon's you put my stuff back," Sonny said, "all of it... the stuff in your pockets too." Sonny bent the fellow's fingers further back until Sly yowled and dropped to his knees beside the packs. Letting go of Kemp's hand, Sonny motioned towards the spilled pack with his rifle and said, "Get to it."

Cursing under his breath, Kemp hastily began to stuff the contents of Sonny's pack back into the bag. When Sonny looked over at Waistman, Buff, who had been watching the proceeding, quickly bent to follow suit, replacing the things he had taken from the other panier and the two worked until everything was ready to load.

"Good," Sonny said, "I'll take it from here."

Quick and efficient, he saddled the sawbuck on Hank and loaded the mule, then finished up by adding Tornado's saddle to the top of the pile. When finished, he turned to the two buffalo hunters who had been sullenly watching him all the while and muttering under their breaths.

"Now, you important and prosperous gents of commerce, I have just one parting bit of advice for you. The next time you make a neighborly visit to some cowpoke and his Injun gal, make sure you come in the daylight. My brother, Colton, has always been a might jumpy after dark."

CHAPTER ELEVEN

Dodge City and Abilene

The Indian Nations, March 1871

I HAD NEVER BEEN NORTH OF TEXAS AND once we left the Red, I was impressed with the country. Somebody was going to have a fine ranch, settling on the range here someday. Bluestem grass was as high as my stirrup and the cattle grazed contentedly along toward a mountain shaped almost like a teepee, in the distance. There was good water and our next river crossing was on Elk Creek. A horseshoe bend here allowed the young and feeble to be pushed across on a gravely bottom, and it made our job trailing on the drag easier. Ben Martin rode up alongside me and pulled up to roll a smoke.

"By golly, Pecos, this is some country," he said.

I nodded and studied a wobbly-legged calf hesitating at the edge of the shallow-running creek. Its momma had already crossed and was bawling for it to follow.

"If the Nations is all like this, a feller could become another Bob King up here," Ben went on, "I think when this drive's over I'll come back here and start a ranch."

"Won't do you much good," I said.

"How come?"

"The Yankees won't let you. They're holdin' this part of the country for the Indians."

Martin got a disappointed look in his eye. "Aw heck, Injuns ain't never gonna run cattle on it."

I nodded and touched Lightfoot with my spurs and headed towards the chickenhearted calf. I stepped down and picked the newborn up and set him on the back of the horse, then climbed back aboard in a hurry when the mother cow came charging back across the creek with an angry bellow. Ben expertly headed her off while I regained my seat, rode across the water and deposited the calf on the other side.

Ranching was the last thing on my mind. I had been troubling some on the wanted poster and was hoping they had not circulated as far north as Dodge City. If they had, someone might recognize me. I needed to find a place in the West to disappear. At that point Hardin came riding up.

"What you foolin' with that newborn for?" he demanded.

"Critter wouldn't cross the creek," I said. "Charley Goodnight had a wagon for newborns."

"I could care less what Goodnight did." With that comment he rode over to where the calf was nuzzling at its mother, crowded it away, drew a pistol, shot it in the head, and galloped off.

It was cold-blooded and hard-hearted, but not an uncommon occurrence on the trail. Newborn calves hampered the movement of the herd, but what bothered me was that John Wesley seemed to enjoy the killing.

We traveled about twenty miles a day and it was a relief to find the weather finally warming up some. We were all resting better and it was great to see the prairie coming to life. We were eating good and had a lot of veal since baby calves were dispatched as soon as they were born, on John Wesley's orders, so Hic had plenty of meat.

When we finally reached the Arkansas, the river was swollen from spring rains and runoff and Hardin ordered the lead steers across. It was against my better judgment and I told Lightfoot so, "A trail savvy boss would wait for the water to go down, he's going to lose more beef." My horse just snorted and acted like it was okay with him if we lost all of the slow-pokey things. By the time we came up with the drag, the herd was strung out a half mile down the river, a snaggle of long horns bobbling in the water like so much pointy driftwood. The cowboys riding flank were doing their best to get the cattle lined out toward the opposite shore but a high bank was keeping the leaders from gaining any footing, so they just kept drifting down-stream. I watched until they finally drifted to a low, flooded shelf on the opposite bank, and there they were able to gain the opposite shore.

Big river crossings always got everybody soaking wet, but they were about the only chance anybody ever had, or took, to get a bath and wash their clothes. If you wanted anything kept dry, you better have it in the chuck wagon, which always crossed first. All hands rode alongside with ropes attached, steadying the wagon, and Hic was across with a cook fire blazing and hot coffee ready by the time the last of the herd crossed and was spread out grazing along the river bank.

We camped early that afternoon and some of the fellers took the opportunity to wash their clothing and go swimming. Martin and I dug out some fishhooks and tried to catch some channel cats. We landed a couple using bacon rind for bait and Ben was telling me how they used to noodle the big cats when he was a boy.

"You mean to tell me you would catch these fish with your bare hands?" I said.

"Yep."

"How come? We always used a hook and line."

"Couldn't afford hook and line," Ben said. "Ma told us, if we wanted catfish and dodgers, we had to catch 'em like that."

"Seems to me that stickin' your hands into some big catfish's mouth is asking to get it bit off," I said.

"Well, they never did, they just laid there and let us feel along 'em until we could grab them and haul them out on the bank. Hey, I got another one on." Martin was pulling in another nice catfish when a commotion was heard upstream where some of the boys were swimming and washing their clothes.

"Wonder what that's all about?" I said.

We found out later that Jimmy Clements had found a water moccasin hiding inside his underwear after he had left them dangling from a branch in the current to wash. Seems as though the boss's fearless cousin was deathly afraid of snakes and had thrown some kind of a hissy fit when he pulled in his long johns and found Mr. snake in there. All the boys were giving him a hoorawing over it after supper and the talk naturally turned to snakes.

"I hear tell there's bluetail racers in this part of the country," the cowboy called Schnoz said.

A couple of the hands looked uncertainly across the fire at him, Clements was one of them.

"Dang, I hate them," Dixon put in. He was a rider from Fort Worth. "I seed one of them run down a cow one time and suck her dry. Her calf was a bawlin' and the farmer couldn't figure out why the calf wasn't gettin' no milk, and so he set me to watchin' to see what was going on. I was a kid at the time and riding a lop-eared old mule. Along about noon I sees one of those blue tail racers chasin' this cow across the field. It got her cornered in the fence and then commenced to sucking til she was plumb dry. That poor calf wasn't gettin' any milk at all."

"Jimmy, you guys have bluetail racer down round Gonzales?" Schnoz asked.

"No! I don't know… I hate the damn things. I blew the head off that damn moccasin today."

I could see the boys were warming to their task and gave Martin a wink. "Ben," I said, "Didn't you guys have problems with bluetails in Fort Smith?"

"Our biggest problem was when one of 'em would run a man down," Martin said. "The darn snakes would take their tails in their mouth and turn themselves into a hoop and get to rolling and they could roll faster than you could run."

"You're kiddin'," Clements looked aghast. "Why would they want to run a man down?"

"Why, to get in his underwear, why else?" Ben said.

Jimmy Clements took it pretty good, and when the laughter died down, somebody said, "Well, snakes do like to crawl into a feller's bedroll. They are cold blooded and look for some place warm. I've known more'n one cowboy who's had to jump up in the middle of the night and shake out his blankets." Some of the others nodded sagely and murmured assent.

"Best way to prevent that is to place a coil of rope around your blankets," Hic said.

"Coil of rope?" Jimmy looked uneasy, "What's that supposed to do?"

"Keeps the snakes from crawling into your bedding," the old cook said.

"Aw, bull, how's it do that?"

"Snake won't crawl over a rope."

"I don't believe you," Clements flared.

"You ever see a snake crawl over a rope?" Hic asked.

"No."

"They won't," the cook asserted.

"I've heard that, too," Schnoz put in. "It's a good way of keeping the critters out of your bed.

"How come you guys don't do it then?" Jimmy wanted to know.

Schnoz shrugged, "I ain't never had a problem with 'em. I leave them alone and they leave me alone."

"Aw, he smells too bad for any self-respecting snake to snuggle up to him," Dixon put in.

"You fellers hear about the Comanche chief that was killed by a flying rattle snake?" Heads popped up and everyone was staring at Gopher, a cowboy with little ears that bore an uncanny resemblance to one of those varmints. Someone had hung that handle on him, and he reminded me of a rodent peeking out from under a rock.

"Snakes don't fly," Jimmy said with a nervous grin, but everyone else was stone sober.

"It was down on the Sweetgrass somewhere west of San Angelo just last summer," Gopher went on. "Seems a bunch of Comanche was chasin' these three riders, and was after some horses they had. When the white guys holed up on top of this perfect little, round hill in the middle of a meadow, one of 'em near jumped on a Mohave Rattler. Quick as a flash he flung it at the lead Injun, and the snake wrapped itself around his neck and bit him in the face until he died."

"Sounds like a good way to break up an Indian attack," Schnoz said.

Everybody nodded soberly and then Clements said, "I don't believe it. You guys are trying to yank my chain again."

"Nope, true story. The Injuns figured those ol' boys' medicine was too powerful if they could make snakes fly, so they turned and just rode off. Left the horses alone too."

Later I was crawling into my blankets, my thoughts on what Gopher had said about the cowboys down on the Sweetgrass, and I got to thinking about a place I knew of down there that sounded like where those ol' boys were. I wondered who they might have been. I was reminded too, of a run-in I'd had with a Mohave Rattlesnake on a little hill down there, and it sounded like the same place. There was quite a price tag tied to that memory and I was having a hard time getting it slammed back into my never-mind room and the door shut tight on it, when a commotion erupted over where Clements had rolled out his blankets.

Several of the boys had been real helpful in showing Jimmy how to arrange his rope around the blankets as snake insurance, Ben Martin among them. Finally, the camp had settled down with a symphony of snores drifting skywards when Jim Clements, screaming like a twelve-year-old girl, leaped from his blankets and proceeded to empty both six-guns into his bedding.

I sat up as someone fetched a lantern from the chuck wagon, and noticed Ben quietly dragging his rope out from under Clements' bed role and coiling it up.

"What's going on?" someone yelled.

"Are we under attack?" came another holler.

"Who the hell is shootin' off these hog-legs," groused a third. "You tryin' to stampede the herd?"

"There's a snake in my bed, a snake," cried Clements. He had grabbed the lantern away from the cook and was bent over his tumbled blankets prodding the bedding with the end of his smoking pistol.

"I don't see no snake," the cook said, and nudged the corner of a blanket with a bare toe.

"He was right there," Clements said, "I could feel 'im crawling under me where I lay."

I noticed Martin had walked nonchalantly over, after casually rubbing out with his foot a line in the dust that his rope had made—a line that led from his general direction and disappeared where Jimmy's blankets were piled.

"Did you get 'im?" Martin asked helpfully.

"I don't know," Clements said shakily. "Hold this lantern and let me look."

He began to pick up his blankets one at a time and shake them out. From where I sat, I could see lantern light dappling the bedding through several bullet holes and began to laugh. The tom-fool-idgit had been the victim of an age-old prank and didn't even have a clue. I figured that Martin had waited until Clements had gotten well settled and then began to pull on the rope he had sneaked under his victim's bedroll while he and the other boys had earlier helped rig the encircling snake-proof rope around his blankets. I figured Clements would be gunning for blood if he ever found out what Ben and the others had done, and I was glad it wasn't me. I was in enough disfavor with the boss and was trying to keep a low profile, but still it was pretty funny, especially the way his tough-guy persona had been perforated with those girlish screams... about the same as those blankets.

Hardin had been with the herd and had not heard any of our campfire talk, but when his cousin foolishly discharged his weapons in the dark, the cattle had all come to their feet and began an anxious bawling and milling about. It was with supreme effort that he and the other rider on guard duty had succeeded in calming them down. He came riding into camp like the devil was on his tail, and jumped from his horse.

"What in blazes was all that shooting," he yelled.

"Jimmy got a snake in his bed," Martin said glibly.

Harding looked hard-eyed at his cousin, "Snake, where's it at?"

"I don't know," Clements said, still poking around in his bedding. "It must have crawled off."

"Well, you damn near stampeded the whole herd, you flaming idiot, I ought'a take those guns of yours and wrap 'em around your stupid neck. Get your boots on and go take the rest of my watch."

Clements went meekly out of camp while the rest of us settled back down to rest. I figured Jimmy was probably too boogered to sleep anyway so he might as well go on night herd.

We were getting near the Kansas line one morning as Ben and I were bringing up the drag, when we noticed a bunch of cattle coming up behind us. It looked like a Mexican herd with the cattle all scrawny and undersized but with overly big heads and horns. The drovers we could see wore the big sombreros typical to Mexican vaqueros.

"Would you take a look at that?" Martin said. "Those Mex's are gonna run those skinny critters right into our bunch."

I watched one of the riders gallop his horse up to where we were sitting waiting. The man was dark complected with a neatly trimmed mustache and goatee. He rode a fancy silver-rigged saddle with tapaderos, a martingale breast piece and silver-studded bridle. His costume was of the landed gentry of Mexico and the man's bearing was one of arrogance and irritation.

"Ju need to move deese cattle aside and let us pass through," he said.

I pushed my hand to the back of my head and scratched beneath my hat. "Well, that ain't likely to happen." I said. "Why don't you just go around?"

"Ju people are moving much too slow and are preveenting us from getting to the railhead first."

"Well doggone," Ben said. "Just excuse us all to pieces, why didn't you say so? We sure wouldn't want to be to blame for you not gettin' to market first, what with all that prime beef and all."

The Mexican eyed us both coldly and said, "Who is en charge of dis drive?"

"That'd be John Wesley Hardin himself, and here he comes now," Martin said with a nod over his shoulder.

Wes Hardin pulled up his plunging horse in a shower of gravel and gave the Mexican an ugly look. "What you greasers doin' shoving up our back trail like this? Get them scrawny flea-bags back away from my herd before you infect them with tic fever."

"I am Juan de Castillo La Vega, Segundo for Don Del Louisa Quaitar. Ju gringos are blocking thee progress of my herd, ju must draw your bunch off to thee side and allow us to pass." Several of the Mexican herders had left the cattle and ridden up behind the spokesman who was obviously the boss.

"One of the best things we Texans ever did was take this land away from you pepper bellies and it was just such persnickety ways as this that made us do it," Hardin replied. "Now you pull that mangy bunch of yours back and stay in line and wait your turn. We're first on this trail and it's going to stay that way."

"No, Senor, it is ju who will geet out of thee way," and when he made that remark, Juan La Vega drew a pistol and fired it at Wes Hardin. The bullet went through the crown of John Wesley's hat and whipped it off his head to the ground. It was one of the few times I ever saw Hardin without his fancy cross-draw guns, and I found out later he had taken his vest off at the wagon and was washing up when the fracas started. He had jumped on his horse and raced down here without them.

Hardin bailed off the right side of his horse, scrabbling in his saddle bags to come up with an old percussion cap and ball pistol with a wobbly cylinder. He aimed the weapon across his saddle while his horse fidgeted about, and managed to fire off a round by holding the cylinder in place with one hand and pulling the trigger with the other. His bullet struck Vega in the thigh.

By this time, Martin and I both had our guns trained on the Mexican riders and they had us under their guns as well. It was a true Mexican standoff. Hardin was cussing his gun and trying to get the cylinder to the next firing position while La Vega was seeking to stem the flow of blood that was staining his fancy riding britches.

187

"We will call deese a draw, Juan La Vega said. "There is plenty of range and grass for everyone. There ess no need for further bloodshed."

With that, he waved his men off and they rode back to their herd while we put up our guns. Wes Hardin, however, was livid. Unable to get the old cap and ball pistol to work, he threw it angrily after the departing Mexicans. Mounting his horse, he rode sullenly off towards the front of our drive. Ben and I trotted to catch up to the end of the drag.

"Boy, that was some doin's'" Ben said. "I thought for a minute we were going to have to plug them Mex's."

"We may still have it to do," I said. "From the look on Wes' face, I'd bet he's on his way for his hog-legs right now. Funny, him not having them with him. You ever see him without his guns before?"

"Nope." Martin shook his head.

"Me neither, and if those Mexicans don't back off, there's going to be hell to pay."

The rest of that day and most of the next, the Mexicans kept pushing us, which didn't make very good sense. If they'd backed off about a day, they would have had better grass and water, but for some reason they seemed to have it in mind that they had to be first to reach Kansas. Perhaps it was due to the fact that the first herd in was likely to get the best offers from the several cattle buyers waiting. One thing was certain, their herd would not command as good a price once the buyers saw our cows. Finally, the afternoon of the second day, John Wesley had had enough. He set Ben and me to circling the herd while he took the rest of the crew and rode back to confront the Mexicans. I learned later from Schnoz that John Wesley had ridden up to La Vega, drew his pistols and shot the Mexican boss in the head. A firefight had ensued when they had attacked the Mexicans all along their line, killing six of them, with Hardin bragging that he done in five himself.

We had the herd bedded down some thirty-five miles south of Dodge City, Kansas, when John Wesley and Jim Clements decided to leave us with the cattle and ride in to locate a buyer. The Mexican herd, what was left of it, had been pushed around to the east of us and was continuing on, unopposed. While we waited for the return of the boss, I noted an increasing restlessness amongst the men. Even Hic was unusually cantankerous about the delay and was cussin' the Mexican herd for getting ahead of us.

"I can't for the life of me figure what Hardin has in mind lettin' them sorry cows out in front, and after he went to all the trouble of shootin' down that Don feller," the cook said.

"Perhaps he figures getting' top dollar for our bunch, once the buyers see that sorry lot by comparison," Schnoz said.

"Well, I sure wish they'd hurry up," Ben said. "I'm hankerin for a bath and some clean clothes and for some female companionship."

It was around noon the next day when Hardin and Clements rode in. One look at them and I figured trouble was brewing because their faces were dark as thunder clouds.

"We ain't goin' to Dodge," Hardin fumed. "The damned railroad hasn't gotten that far yet."

"What do you mean?" Hic posed the question for us all.

"We were told in Gonzales that the railroad would be in Dodge by the time we got here, but they haven't even laid the rails yet." John Wesley said. "The trains are not travailing any farther than Abilene. We're going to have to trail these beeves up there."

"You're kiddin'," Dixon put in. "No trains in Dodge?"

"Nope," Jim Clements said, "they got front street wider'n you could throw a cat across and a set of ties laid down the middle of it, but no rails and no trains."

"Well, I'll be dogged," Gopher said. "What's the place like?"

"Oh, it's busy enough," Clements went on. "Everybody is building like mad, new stores and saloons, billiard parlors and dance halls, a couple of hotels and big stockyard pens, but no trains and no cattle buyers. The end of the line is in Abilene. They say the tracks won't be finished before next year."

"We get to go into town, don't we?" Gopher asked.

Hardin gave him a depreciating look, "You'll get separated from your money soon enough, Gopher, we got to get these critters up to Abilene."

I was feeling some relieved for I had been dreading riding into the town with a wanted poster circulating around on me, and had been giving some thought to heading for parts unknown as soon as I drew my pay. But now it looked like I could avoid Dodge City altogether and postpone rubbing elbows with the local gentry until we made Abilene. Of course, I would have it to deal with there too, and to make matters worse, I was told Wild Bill Hickok was the marshal. I sure didn't need his hard eyes sizing me up.

A couple of days later we were on the outskirts of Dodge City, and that evening Ben Martin sidled up next to me and said, "A bunch of us boys are ridin' into town tonight, you wanna go?"

"Naw," I said.

"Are you crazy? It's past time we washed some of this trail dust out of our gullets. Come on with us, we'll have a high-o time."

"I don't think so," I said. "You boys go on ahead, I'll stay and nighthawk the herd."

"You're a funny galoot, Pecos, all these days on the trail and you have no yen to let off a little steam?"

The truth was, I did have a yen to let off some steam. Trouble was, I was afraid it might just scald the wrong

people and I needed to stay on the down-low. A sarsaparilla would have slid scoozy-oozy down my throat about
now, but I'd probably have to bust some wiseacre in the
snoot for drinking one instead of red-eye.

"You go ahead, drink a sarsaparilla for me."

Martin gave me a funny look, then shrugged and went
off to find his horse.

Later, Hardin and Clements rode in from the herd and
wanted to know where everybody was.

I said I figured they was around somewhere, mounted
Lightfoot and started for the herd. I took two shifts that
night, practicing my singing, and kept the cows near
boogered because of it, but come daylight they were all
still with us.

Two weeks later we were holding the herd outside
the town of Abilene, Kansas and Hardin was in town,
shopping for the best buyer. He had already brought out
two gents from a big Chicago firm. He let them wine and
dine him and buy him expensive cigars, but would not
commit to a price. Finally, on the third day, he sold to a
Mr. Greenfield at thirty dollars a head and was to pay us
off in a saloon called the *Bull's Head Tavern,* owned by a
Ben Thompson and a Phil Coe. Hardin had warned us all
to call him Wesley Clemens, or better yet, Little Arkansas,
since he was wanted by the law back in Texas, and he
didn't know if Wild Bill Hickok knew about it or not.

We were all lined up at the bar with most of the boys
enjoying cold beer. I was nursing a sarsaparilla and trying
to blend into my surroundings while Hardin was paying
each of us off. I had just pocketed my earnings after getting a hard look from the boss, when Ben Thompson
asked, "Which one of you is Wes Hardin?"

You could have heard a pin drop in that place, then
Wes said, "Who wants to know?"

Thompson shrugged, "Heard you was a hand with a gun and I thought you might go shoot that damned meddling Hickok."

Wes looked puzzled and then said, "Why would I want to do that?"

"Think about it man, you takin' down Wild Bill, why you'd be the talk of the West."

"I ain't got nothing against Hickok, he ain't never done me no wrong. Why you so peeved at 'im?"

"He wrecked our bull," Coe interrupted.

"Wrecked your bull?" Hardin looked confused. "What are you talking about?"

Ben Thompson leaned his elbows on the bar and with malice, explained, "We went to all the trouble of having a big colorful bull painted on the side of the *"Bull's Head Tavern,"* and when the townspeople complained about a large, erect penis on the bull, which we properly refused to remove, Wild Bill came and painted it over himself. Therefore, he needs killing."

"Well, if you want him kilt so bad, kill him yourself," Hardin said and then turned and walked out the door.

I finished my nickel drink, paid the man and left the bar. I had just reached the end of the boardwalk when I near bumped into a man with long hair and a curling mustache. He said, "Hold up there, mister. I see you're wearing a sidearm. All cowboys must check their guns at my office until you leave town."

I knew this was Wild Bill Hickok, and not wanting him to recognize me from the handbills that were going around, I mumbled that I was leaving town now and riding back to the herd.

Hickok gave me a steely glare and then said, "See that you do."

I mounted up and rode back to camp and soon was fast asleep. Somewhere in the wee hours of the morning I heard horses running and sat up in my blankets to see some of the boys riding in. Martin spied me and came over to roll out his soogan next to mine.

"You awake," he said.

"No, I usually sleep sitting up like this."

"There's going to be hell to pay for this night's work," he said.

"What happened?" I said wearily.

"That stupid Hardin just shot some guy for snoring."

"For what?"

"Snoring," Ben said. "A bunch of us boys had tied one on, and later we had put up at the *American House Hotel.* We was all settlin' down, but some guy in the next room was snoring so loud it got to where we couldn't go to sleep. We were joking about it and Gopher said, 'Somebody ought to shoot the son-of-a-bitch,' and John Wesley said, 'I'll do it,' and before we knew it, he had drawn both of his pistols and started shooting through the walls and ceiling at the guy. Well, of course the management came checking, and it turns out one of Hardin's bullets killed a man sleeping in the next room."

"Wha'd ya do?" I asked.

"Hardin and the rest of us crawled out a second story window figuring we would be in trouble with Hickok for Wes firing his weapon within the city limits, and sure enough, just as we climbed out on the roof, we saw Hickok and four deputies entering the front door of the hotel."

"Where is Hardin now?" I said.

"The last I saw of him, he was hiding in a haystack in his underwear. I put my pants on and lit a shuck this a-way."

By morning Hardin and Clements had ridden in on stolen horses. They were minus their boots and pants and were a sorry sight to be sure. The rest of us were sittin' around just finishing up breakfast, and I personally was enjoying the sight of John Wesley Hardin running from Wild Bill Hickok, but I had enough presence of mind not to say so.

"Somebody lend me a pair of pants," Hardin called. "There's a couple of deputies trailin' us."

Nobody said anything until finally Gopher got up and rustled through his bag and pulled out a patched pair of jeans. Wes pulled on jeans that were too short for him, found a pair of boots and grabbed a double barrel shotgun from off the chuck wagon, and then went back to the horse he'd rode in on. Mounting, he said, "Hickok would a killed me if he had caught me in a defenseless position, just to add to his reputation. Now, I'm going to buffalo this Tom Carson and his two deputies to add to mine."

Hardin rode out and I heard later he had ambushed Carson and the other two, but did not kill them. He made them strip all their clothes off and walk back to town naked and barefoot, some thirty to thirty-five miles.

———

"What you going to do?" Ben was asking.

I finished tightening the girth on my saddle and swung up on Lightfoot. "Figured I'd head over towards Colorado and the gold fields," I said, "see what's around the next bend. You are welcome to join me."

Ben shook his head, "Naw, I wanna go down and scare some of the wild mavericks out of that South Texas brush and bring a trail drive of my own up here," he said.

I nodded and touched the brim of my hat. "Well, so long, pard, it's been good to know ya. Watch out for snakes… all kinds." I touched spurs to Lightfoot and rode out, leaving Ben with a big grin on his kisser. If the West had a few more men like him, it'd be a whole lot better place.

CHAPTER TWELVE

The Buffalo Hunters and the Gambler

Confluence of the Concho and Colorado Rivers, April 1871.

THE MAN CALLED FRENCHY ABSENTLY SHUF-fled a deck of soiled playing cards, and looked down from the top deck of the sternwheeler as the two grungy buffalo hunters poled a flat bottom boat piled high with hides to the rickety pier. The big riverboat had tied up and was taking on a hide cargo from several flat bottom boats that had made their way down the Concho. Frenchy leaned against the rail and watched the two hunters trying to secure their barge against the current. It seemed to the gambler that here was a pair of obviously incompetent sailors. He guessed from the look of their cargo they were more adept at killing and skinning buffalo than handling a river barge.

"Sly, get that back line tied off before we lose the whole thing to the Gulf of Mexico, what are you doing?" the bigger man said to the other, whose foot had become entangled in the rope.

"Keep your britches on, Buff, can't cha' see my foot's caught?"

Frenchy scoffed and spat disgustedly into the river, then turned away from the two arguing men. He pulled a rolled-up poster from the inside of his frock coat, and his eyes narrowed as he unrolled it and stared again at the youth pictured there. "Ah, monsieur, we shall meet again. I have not forgotten what you did to me and a day of reckoning is coming." Frenchy rolled the poster back up and went down the stairs to the lower deck. He would see if he could secure passage on one of the flatboats back up the Concho to San Angelo. He had hopes of finding a lead on the whereabouts of Colton Saber, find the insolent young man, collect the reward and seek his revenge.

Pierre LaRoush had assumed the prestigious-sounding name of Alphonse Adalard Beaumont, but everywhere he went, folks just called him "Frenchy." It was a title that had long ceased to irritate him as he sought to blend into the riverboat and waterfront crowd of the West. LaRoush had made good his escape from Saint Louise and the ports of the Mississippi, after his escape from the police wagon, and had hidden for two days in a culvert until the police had stopped searching for him. He eventually stole clothes from backyard clothes lines and found a cold chisel and hammer in a shed with which to strike off his shackles. He then stole a skiff and drifted down the Mississippi to New Orleans. Here he was able to finagle a loan from Madam Dolly, on threat of exposure, and spent the next two-and-a-half years as a gambler, working the waterfront parlors and casinos along the coast until he reached Galveston, Texas. It was only by the merest chance that he had stumbled across the wanted poster for Colton Saber. He had just taken the last dollar off a down-on-his-luck cowhand and sometimes bounty hunter, who offered the poster and a brass pocket watch for table stakes, and was about to laugh the poor man to scorn, when he recognized Colton Saber's picture, the young man who had caused him so much grief back in Saint

Louis. He had accepted the ante and won the poster and watch handily by bottom dealing.

Frenchy had long chaffed under the humiliation and exposure he had suffered at the young man's hand and had kept a watchful eye out in hopes of finding some lead to his whereabouts, for he had sworn an oath to himself that he would be avenged on the fellow. Now he had information that Saber was wanted and he had set out up the Colorado with plans to visit the developing frontier towns in hope of finding and punishing him for his effrontery.

The Frenchman had barely stepped off the gang plank onto the dock when his valise and traveling bag hit the deck beside him with a thud. "Frenchy," the captain yelled down from the bridge, "Don't ever set your cheatin' carcass on my riverboat again. If you do, I'll have you thrown overboard."

Frenchy turned to retrieve his belongings, his ears burning red with embarrassment, as the dock hands and boatman looked on with amusement. Only the two buffalo hunters seemed to have missed his latest humiliation as they were busy collecting the money for their smelly hides at the far end of the pier. They had not witnessed his unceremonious dismissal from the paddle wheeler. Spying a string of flat boats with the name *Hanson's General Store* painted on the bow, he approached a stalwart Irishman who seemed to be in charge of the crews handling hides.

"Excuse me, bon ami, I am seeking passage up zee river, are you returning to San Angelo?"

Paddy O'Malley looked at the threadbare gambler, having witnessed what just took place, and shook his head. "No can do, we do not take passengers."

"I can pay, monsieur," Frenchy said.

"Nope, no riders," O'Malley shook his head.

At that point, Buffalo Waistman and Sylvester Kemp walked past while counting their money, and Buff elbowed

Sly in the ribs. "You hear that?" he said. Sly looked questioningly at his partner. "He just said he'd pay someone to take him up river," Waistman said. He stepped over to the river boat gambler and said, "Mister, we can take you to 'Angelo for twenty bucks, but it will be a working passage."

"Ah, oui, oui, monsieur, what ees a working passage?"

"You have to take one of the poles and help us pole the scow upstream," Buff said.

"I will pay you fifty dollars and you pole the boat, monsieur," Frenchy said.

"Pay us each fifty dollars and you got yourself a deal," Kemp growled.

Frenchy pulled out a roll of bills and peeled off two fifty dollar notes and handed one to each of them. "Please take my luggage to a dry space in zee boat," he said, and then walked off with head held erect, amidst the jeers and cat-calls of the laughing dock hands.

Kemp flashed Waistman a look of annoyance, hesitating to pick up the travel bag. "Go ahead, Sly," Buff said. "Did you see that wad of bills? Do what he asks and we'll get the rest of it up river."

Two days later found the trio up river. There had been little exchange between the gambler and the buffalo hunters, with the former relaxing in the stern of the skiff on a pile of gear, spending most of his time playing solitaire while the two hunters poled, pulled, and at times drug, the shallow flat-bottom boat upstream. The first night, they had managed to bum a meal off a poor farmer who had a black river-bottom cotton farm, and had found sleeping arrangements in his haymow for the night. The farmer's daughter had succumbed to Frenchy's polished continental accent and beguiling ways, and ended up visiting him with an extra blanket later in the night. The two of them were nearly caught when the big Danish farmer came looking for her, and all three men had to run for the river dodging shotgun blasts of rock salt. Fortunately, it was still dark and only a few pieces of the shot found their targets.

The second night they made camp on the shore and shared a fried catfish dinner with some fish Frenchy had caught during the day. Again, there was little conversation as the two buffalo hunters were still nursing grudges against their passenger for the previous night's affair. Kemp, in particular, was miffed as he had received the worst of the rock salt, and Buff had tried to dig it out of his posterior with the point of a knife.

"Why don't we just knock him in the head and feed him to the catfish?" Kemp had grumbled to Waistman. "All he does is sit on his duff and play cards."

"Well, he did catch the catfish for supper," Buff said in his defense.

"I'm tired of dragging him along. It's bad enough we have to drag this old scow back to 'Angelo without having to haul his dead weight too."

"Don't forget that wad of bills," his partner reminded him. "When the time's right, we'll conk him one and improve our financial horizons."

Frenchy was rather enjoying the trip. He found fishing to be a challenge, and his dalliance with the farmer's daughter amusing. She had been innocent as to the ways of men and women, but he left her a little wiser, with her virtue still intact, thanks to papa and the rock salt. He smiled inwardly at his two rough companions. It looked to him as though they had made a pretty good payday with the hides, and he was wondering just how much money they had stashed away. They thought they'd held him up pretty good with the hundred dollars he had paid them, but he knew he could win it all back, plus more, once they neared San Angelo. He would lure them into a poker game then and take all their money.

Due to the necessity of avoiding the current, Kemp and Waistman kept close to the shore where slower water could be found. At times, it was easier to pull the skiff along by walking the shoreline, but whenever trees and brush hugged the water's edge, the two of them would pole around such obstacles. Travel was slow, and by the third day Frenchy was feeling the boredom. The smell of the skiff as well as the two hunters reminded him of dead carrion, and he began to feel a compelling need to take a bath and clean up. Perhaps he might give the other two an idea about cleaning up themselves if he were to take a swim. That evening after a supper of beans and bacon, he said, "I am going for a swim. I am starting to smell like a gut wagon. You two want to join me?"

Both hunters looked up at him with a skeptical look. What was this two-bit gambler trying to pull. Neither of them was about to pull their clothes off and go cavorting in the water with this *frog*.

"No, really, ma amis. Who knows when we may reach another farm. Would it not be better to make ourselves more presentable when seeking a meal?"

"You sure that looking for supper is all you have in mind?" Kemp accused.

"Or whatever," Frenchy said.

"There ain't no more farms between here and 'Angelo," Waistman said. "We don't take no baths lessen we have to."

"Suit yourselves, I am going to clean up." The gambler walked off towards the river, unbuttoning his blouse and shedding his coat.

"Wait," Buff cautioned his pard. "Let him shuck his clothes and then we'll sneak up and go through his pockets… see what we can find."

When they heard the Frenchman splashing around in the water, the two hunters crept over to where his clothes lay in a pile. The first thing they noticed was the rolled-up wanted poster sticking out of one side of the frock coat.

"Take a look at this," Waistman said. "He's carrying a wanted poster on some guy worth a thousand bucks."

"Look who it is," Kemp said. He was peering over Buff's shoulder staring at Colt Saber's picture.

"Well, I'll be go-to-hell, it's that damned fire burning kid from Big Springs. Says here he' s Colton Saber and the Sheriff in Wade's Landing, Texas wants him. If I ever get the chance, I'll draw and quarter this Saber."

"You want to go to Wade's Landing?" Sly asked.

"No, he ain't there no more. Don't you remember, that feller that got our horses back from the Injuns last fall? He said this guy was his brother and he was looking for him... said he rode a sorrel horse with white feet and a blaze face and figured he was headed for the cattle trails."

"He never said he was headed for the cattle trails," Kemp said.

"Well, where else would he be headed for? Figure it out, if you was a cowboy on the run, where'd you go?"

"You want to go kill him?" Sylvester said with a glint in his eye.

"As shore as God made little green apples, but slowly. I wonder what the Frenchy's doing with this poster."

Frenchy had walked up unobserved and said with passion, "I em going to cut out hees heart and feed it to zee birds; if you gentlemen have any inclinations that way, you weel have to get in line behind me."

"Why, wha'd he ever do to you?" Kemp demanded.

The French man picked up a towel and began to dry off. "He attacked me, enterfeered en a relationship I was involved en, told lies about me, got me arrested with a death sentence and messed up a very lucrative beesiness I had going, that's what. I will find him and I will kill him, slowly and painfully."

"Well, ain't that just too bad, we know where he is," Kemp said. "We are going to get him first 'cause he burnt us. See these scars? He did that."

The Frenchman got all conciliatory then and said, "Let us team up and keel him together, three of us have zee better chance than one or two. Then we will split up the reward monies in equal shares."

"We got us an outfit in San Angelo," Buff said. "If you want to spring for the grub and supplies you can trail along with us and we will cut you in on the reward."

"Deal, ma amis," Frenchy said, and stuck out his hand.

The two buffalo hunters shook it and wondered what they had let themselves in for.

San Angelo in 1871 had become an important center for supplies, outfitting the buffalo hunters and buying the hides. The cow outfits driving cattle up the Western Trail often stopped here, and the Army at Fort Concho was in constant need of goods as were the farmers and settlers coming into the country.

Joe Hanson's General Store was doing a thriving business, but was off limits to Waistman and Kemp. When Frenchy asked them why they were not allowed in the establishment and had insisted he go in to make the purchases for the trail instead, they replied, "That scoundrel, Saber, interfered with business dealings we had with Hanson, too, and ever since then we have been black-balled from his establishment. We always had to pay someone else to get our supplies from the merchant."

Frenchy had just walked into the store with a list of things to buy when a tall, dusty cowboy pulled his pony up at the hitching rail and stepped down. He took his hat off and dusted his britches, ran his fingers through his hair and replaced the hat, then stepped up onto the boardwalk and walked towards the door. He was intent on picking up some things for the trail south when a picture on a poster nailed next to the door arrested his attention.

"Wal, I'll be dawged," he said. He reached up and plucked the poster from the wall and walked in to confront Hanson at the counter.

"Howdy," Joe said. "I see you got a copy of my friend's picture there. Do you know him?"

"I should smile I do," the cowboy said. "So, he's Colton Saber then."

"That would be him," the storekeeper said. You know him?"

"Yeah, my name's Ben Martin and we just finished delivering a train load of beeves to Abilene, 'cept I knew him as Pecos. What's he wanted for?"

"It's not what you think," Hanson said. "A truer man never rode trail than Colt. Oh, he had his troubles alright, but he was there for me in the clinch."

"How's that?"

"He stopped a couple of no good buffalo hunters from shooting me in the back over a hide deal. I owe my life to this cowboy. The whole thing's been one huge misunderstanding."

"He was my pard on Hardin's drive," Ben said.

"Hardin? You mean Wes Hardin?"

"That'd be him."

"Half the State of Texas is looking for him," Hanson said. "I hope Colt didn't get mixed up in no shenanigans with that gunslinger."

"No, he came near to plugin' him once but a stampede intervened. That was a strange deal, it was like Pecos... Colt didn't care if Hardin shot him or not."

"He probably didn't," Hanson said.

"How come? I figured he was probably on the dodge but I never asked and he never said."

"It was over a bum deal gone sour with his girl," Hanson said. "We got word out of Fort Bliss in El Paso that Colt got bushwhacked a few years ago, and ended up with amnesia, didn't know who he was. He got sold into slavery down into Mexico working the mines. He finally came out of it and made his way home after being gone for over two years. He got back just in time to see his brother kissing his girl."

"Why would his brother be kissing his girl?"

"The family had found the dead body of a stranger dressed in Colt's clothes but the face was eaten off by buzzards, so they were pretty certain Colt was dead, but his girl, Suzanne, would have none of it. She said he was still alive, that it wasn't him. They knew how much the two of them, Colt and Suzanne that is, were in love and figured if he was alive, hell or high water couldn't keep the two of them apart. Suzanne was true blue, but finally she figured him for dead, too, and allowed the older brother to become her beau. Sonny and Colt had been close before his disappearance and it hit Sonny hard, his death, but nothing compared to how hard it hit Suzanne. Sonny set out to help her through it all and in the process, fell helplessly in love with her himself. The day Colt rode in, he found Sonny kissing Suzanne for the first time and he lost it, drew his gun and shot his brother in the chest."

"Shot him in the chest?" Martin was puzzled.

"Yep, funny thing was, a heavy Indian medallion Colt had given Sonny one Christmas stopped the bullet and he survived, but Colt had rode away by that time, thinking he had killed them both. Poor Suzanne and Sonny—and the whole family, are desperate to find Colt and tell him they are alright but no one knows where he is."

"My Lord, how awful," Ben said. "I had no idea. I know where he is."

"Where?" Joe asked breathlessly.

"Well, I left him in Abilene, but he was heading for Colorado and the goldfields the last I saw of him."

"You're sure this is him?" Hanson held up the poster and peered at it.

"Pretty sure, that's got to be an old picture and he has grown a beard and his hair long. Probably doesn't want anybody to recognize him, although I don't know if he knows about these posters."

"Son, you may have just put a lot of troubled minds to rest. I will get a telegram to his folks right away. Thanks, thanks a lot."

The storekeeper took off his apron and hurried out the door towards the telegraph office. Neither he nor Ben Martin saw Frenchy standing in the shadows behind some dry goods, a wicked smile curling his lips.

Waistman and Kemp walked past the sheriff's office on the boardwalk heading towards the livery yard when Buff stopped to stare at a handbill pinned next to the door. "Say, ain't that Frenchy?" Sly stopped to look at what his pard was studying and saw the faded *"Wanted Dead or Alive"* poster on the Frenchman. They read that the man named Pierre LaRoush was an escaped convict, sentenced to death for the kidnapping and rape of several young St. Louis ladies, and recognized him as their traveling partner, Frenchy.

"Five thousand dollars is a lot of money," Waistman said with an evil glint in his eye.

"Let's go tell the sheriff where he is right now," Sly said.

"Now hold on pard," Buff pulled the handbill loose and folded it up and put it in his pocket. "We will just hang onto this and let him help us collect Saber's scalp first, then we can hang him out to dry."

Kemp nodded his head, "Good idea," he said. The two of them walked on to the wagon yard to hitch the team and meet Frenchy at the General Store.

They were two days out on the Western Trail heading for Dodge City, Kansas, and had pitched camp for the night. Supper had just finished when an argument broke out between Frenchy and the buffalo hunters.

"I say we follow that new Goodnight-Loving trail to Colorado," Frenchy said. "It's the fastest route from here."

"Naw, we need to pick up his trail in Kansas, see if we can run into anyone who has seen 'im. Buff said.

"I side with my pard," Kemp said.

"Tell you what, let's cut for it." He pulled out a deck of cards and started shuffling it against his knee.

"We'll cut, but I'm shuffling the deck." Buff said, an accusing look in his eye.

Frenchy shrugged and handed the deck to the older man. Frenchy deliberately drew the top card and turned up a two of clubs and then disgustedly threw it on the ground amidst the rough laughter of the other two. Buff easily won the cut with a ten of diamonds, and with smug smiles the two hunters settled into a poker game with Frenchy, but the smiles soon faded as they began to lose heavily to the conniving Frenchman, a pattern that had been developing over the past two evenings.

CHAPTER THIRTEEN

Kiowa Winter Camp

December 1870, Sweetwater Canyon.

SONNY SABER TIED HANK BACK IN THE pines and then crept forward to the edge of the rimrock and peered down into the wide valley below. A large circling encampment of teepees clutched the narrow embankment of a meandering stream, and smoke from two or three campfires drifted lazily skyward in the afternoon sun. The tall cowboy saw several children playing about and women busy scraping hides and attending to other camp tasks, but the camp seemed to be devoid of men other than a few old warriors sitting around one of the fires and passing a pipe.

"I wonder where all the men-folk are," Sonny mused. "Probably off on a hunt or raiding party, I'll bet." His eyes lifted to a meadow that was on the wide flood plain of the valley and he quickly looked over a herd of horses grazing there. To his disappointment, he saw no sign of Tornado among the bunch of Indian ponies.

"Shoot, I figured this for the band of Kiowa Willow was from. I had hoped Runs-With-Horses brought my horse here."

Sonny had spent the past week leading and sometimes following Hank over a sketchy trail from the Colorado

207

River and had lost two days locating the trail head to this hidden canyon. He wished he'd paid better attention to Colton's story about returning the Indian girl to her people for it had cost him precious time in his search for the horse and Indian. Now, as he gazed at the camp below with no sign of the horse or Runs-With-Horses, he was at a loss as to what to do next. He was determined to find Tornado, but where to look. His thoughts were disrupted by a commotion at the upper end of the valley and looking in that direction he spied a large band of Indians riding towards the encampment. The camp below came alive with women and children yelling and running about and the camp dogs barking and raising a fuss. Sonny wondered if the camp were under attack right before his eyes, but soon the shouting and friendly gestures led him to believe that this war party was returning in triumph from a successful raid.

He saw women and girls riding double behind some of the braves and a bunch of horses being driven up in the rear of the procession. A lone Indian brave, mounted on his big grulla, was herding the band of ponies.

"Tornado," Sonny said.

This returning raiding party had captured women and horses, and there was much jubilation and shouting as the warriors were greeted and led back to the teepees by the women and children of the band, even the dogs seemed to feel the general excitement, strutting at the edges of the procession and scratching at the grass in important posturing. Sonny watched the chieftains dismount, followed by the rest of the braves while all were greeted by wives and children. Those braves who had brought new women turned their captives over to their wives and mothers who quickly took them in hand and led them away to their several lodges. Sonny's eyes followed the bunch of horses as they, along with those of the warriors, were driven out to join the other ponies in the meadow.

Soon, he saw Runs-With-Horses return to the encampment astride Tornado where he was greeted by several young maidens, and he smiled as he observed the reckless young brave effortlessly vault from the back of the big stallion and land in a crowd of fawning young women. The Indian youth carelessly slung his arms about the shoulders of two of the maidens and disappeared inside one of the lodges. Tornado stood looking after his departure until a lad came and led him to water on the banks of the stream. Runs-With-Horses stuck his head from the lodge and shouted something to the boy and then disappeared back inside. The boy led the dark horse back to the lodge and tied him to a picket post, then wandered back to where the elders of the tribe had formed a council circle. Here one after another stood to address the crowd.

"Well, there will be partying tonight," Sonny muttered. "I better hunker down here and wait until dark. Once everybody's celebrated to the full, I'll mosey down and get my horse."

It was past three o'clock in the morning and the camp had finally settled down after much feasting and boastful talk from those who had been part of the raid. Runs-With-Horses had spent a leisurely afternoon with Yellow Bird and her cousin, Little Cloud. The two girls had vied for his attention and he had repaid their affections amorously for most of the afternoon and evening, but now he was tired and wished they would stop their chatter and leave him be.

His thoughts turned to the beautiful Seeaugway, Spotted Buffalo's daughter. Ever since she had been captured by the Comanche, the girl had been somewhat aloof and distant to him and he wondered just what had happened to her while she was gone. He had heard the stories about the white-eyes the Comanche called the Kwihnai Killer, and of his rescue and safe return of the maid, and wondered if the Eagle Killer had stolen her heart for she showed no inclinations towards him, or any other of the potential suitors in camp since then. The talk of her rescuing the white man from a flight of the arrows test at the time of the council of the bluffs, an event Runs-With-Horses had missed while off on a horse-capturing quest from the Arapaho, and that he was brother to the Buffalo Man, gave the young Indian to know that he was up against strong medicine. Had the Kwihnai Killer bewitched her? If he was a powerful shaman and friend of the Great Spirit's Son, then Runs-With-Horses must draw upon even greater medicine to recapture Seeaugway's heart. Perhaps if he were to offer the Thunder Horse to her father as a dowry, she would relent and share a courting blanket with him.

The two girls, one on either side of him, were already asleep when the young brave finally drifted off. A restless dream of scolding by the Thunder Horse for taking him from the Buffalo Man, and insisting that he walk from now on and ride him no more, troubled the young brave's sleep and he paid no attention to a dog fight and snarling over food off in the distance, for it too seemed like part of the dream.

———

Sonny's head popped over the edge of the creek embankment and he cautiously studied the sleeping camp. Sparks from the council fire spiraled into the air when an ember popped and a dog gave a startled yip at the sudden noise. The dogs will be a problem unless I can distract them, he thought. The young Texan had just spent the last hour and a half quietly working his way off the ridge from where he had observed the camp earlier that afternoon. Hank was safely picketed on a lead line back of the ledge, and now Sonny had snuck along the streambed to his present vantage point at the upper end of the village. Tornado was tied outside a teepee about one third of the way around the circle, and he would have to make his way past the dogs to the outer perimeter of the camp to reach him. He tested the breeze and felt a slight wind in his face blowing towards him. This was good, as long as all the camp dogs were in front of him.

Boldly, Sonny stepped up from the creek bed and walked deliberately towards a meat drying rack and began to collect several hunks of buffalo meat hanging there. While he was thus engaged, a dog, curled up in front of the closest teepee, woke up and looked at him. The animal growled and leaped to his feet, his hackles erect on the back of his neck. Sonny quickly flung a hunk of meat onto the ground in front of the cur, and a bark caught half way in its throat as the dog lunged towards the choice morsel. But the cur's good fortune did not go unnoticed as several other dogs caught wind of the animal's actions and rushed with eager barking toward their camp-mate, Sonny, and the meat rack.

Sonny knew the commotion would attract attention so he quickly toppled the rack over in front of the charging canines and ducked around the back side of the nearest teepee. The dogs converged on the feast, barking, snarling, and snapping, interspersed with an occasional yelp. Low muttering was heard from inside the lodge and finally a man's voice spoke. From the tone of it, someone was complaining about the upset meat rack and the ravening dogs, and soon a squaw emerged to holler at the beasts and hurl stones and sticks to drive them away from her spoiled supply of meat. Eventually the snarling, snapping, and shouting died down, but by this time the cowboy had reached the edge of the lodge where Tornado was picketed. He stepped around to greet the slumbering horse with a quiet hand over his muzzle. Stealthily, he loosened the rope from the picket stake, paused to listen for any sign of detection, and then quietly led the stallion downwind from the Indian encampment.

Once Sonny was far enough away to avoid discovery, he mounted the dark horse and rode down the valley with a wary eye on his back trail. Sunup found him leading Hank off the ridge and back towards the Sweetwater. The theft of his horse had cost him several days in his pursuit of Colton and now he was left with a cold trail. He decided to work his way to Stretch and Gwen's place on the Brazos and see if anyone there might know of his brother's whereabouts.

———

Kicking Bird watched through narrowed eyes as the Buffalo Man led the Thunder Horse from the encampment. The tall, lesser chief of the Kiowa recognized him as the young son of the long knife and the brother to the Comanche's Kwihnai Killer. He grunted approvingly at the young cowboy's daring. It was no wonder the sons of Saber were gaining such renown on the prairie with feats of courage such as this. But still, this would not put his quest for peace between the Gaigwu and the white-eyes in a favorable light. Not only was this capture of the Thunder horse a slap in the face of Runs-With-Horses, it was an affront to the whole band.

The principal chiefs of the tribe, White Bear, Sitting Bear, and Big Tree, continued their campaign for war with the Texans, and now that the white men had settled their war with each other in the East, they were certain that more and more of them would invade their lands, slaughter the buffalo, and kill their women and children.

It was men such as Saber who dealt fairly with the tribes that Kicking Bird held out the most hope for, and he wondered if he might not convince the people to listen to the wisdom of making peace with the Texas ranchers, but he must convince the Buffalo Man to come and talk to the council. It was a risky plan and could easily put the young Saber and himself in danger, yet he knew he must try. Silently, he untied his horse and led it off into the dark in the same direction the Buffalo Man went.

Sonny made camp for the evening and was just finishing a supper of beans and bacon when a glimpse of movement in the sage beyond his circle of firelight alerted the young man to danger. Quickly he sprang to his left while drawing his six-gun and tried to focus on the intruder.

"Who goes there?" he called.

"How, Son of Saber," Kicking Bird replied, and stood from his concealment with palms upheld and extended.

"Keep your hands up and come into the light," Sonny commanded.

The tall chieftain walked carefully forward, a rifle cradled in the crook of his arm and a blanket around his naked shoulders. When Sonny saw the lightning tattoos on the Indian's cheeks, he at once recognized Kicking Bird as the Kiowa chief he and Colt had shared lunch with a few years back.

"Kicking Bird, what brings you to my camp?"

"I come speak with Buffalo Man."

"Buffalo Man, who's the Buffalo Man?" Sonny was confused.

Kicking Bird squatted by the fire and sniffed the air, a lingering odor of bacon and beans still evident to the tall Indian. He looked steadily at the white man and said, "You Buffalo Man, heap big medicine."

Sonny took a tin plate that was turned upside down on a rock and removed the lid from a left- over pot of beans.

He then looked back at Kicking Bird while spooning some of the food onto the plate and asked, "Why are you calling me that?"

In halting English, the chief replied, "We know you reborn from great buffalo—you bet."

"I don't understand," Sonny handed him the beans.

"Two Dogs, chief of Comanch, see you kill great buffalo, jump on back, go down in great run, rise from dead remains to talk to brother coyote. Now you Buffalo Man... big medicine."

Sonny was dumbfounded. Had this Two Dogs seen his near-death experience in the buffalo stampede? It never ceased to amaze him how the Indians interpreted things.

"Kicking Bird, I was nearly killed in that stampede, medicine had nothing to do with it. It was only by the grace of God I am alive."

The Kiowa chief nodded slowly and took the last bite of beans, "Ugh, White Man's Great Spirit give medicine of great bull you kill in stampede. You back from dead, like Son of Great Spirit we speak of many moons ago."

Again, Sonny found himself at a loss for words. This wild man of the plains was more insightful into those recent events than even he had been. Sonny had been mindful of his miraculous deliverance in the buffalo stampede, but had not once considered it as a rebirth-back-from the dead experience. Now the simple reasoning of the red man had drawn a parallel to the story of Jesus' death and resurrection that Sonny and Colt had preached to him three years earlier.

"Kicking Bird, I did not die under that buffalo, I was just knocked out. Its huge bulk is what spared me from being trampled to death, and as for that dumb coyote, he was chewing on my boot and I only let loose some coyote yips at him to scare him off, that's all. I can't talk coyote any more than you can. Why are you saying such things?"

"You come, make straight talk to Satank, Big Tree, White Bear. Buffalo Man favored by Great Spirit and Son, medicine heap good. They listen, maybe no, but you come, stop war talk, bring peace with Gaigwu and white-eyes before too late for the People."

"Kicking Bird, I have no medicine the chiefs will listen to. Better men than I have held peace talks with the Kiowa and Comanche and still the tribes make war against the settlers. Why, if I rode into your camp they would most likely spit me over hot coals. I can't do it."

"Buffalo Man favored by the People, big medicine, you come, talk straight, people hear, stop killing."

"Kicking Bird, I am nobody's favorite and I cannot go with you for I must find my brother, Colton. He has gone off with the mark of Cain on him. I took his girl and he tried to kill me but did not succeeded. I must tell him the girl is his."

"What mark of Cain?"

"In the Bible, God's book, the first two brothers, Cain and Abel. Cain killed Abel from jealousy, and it left a mark on him. Colt thinks he killed me and it has left its mark on him, too. I must let him know I am alive and that the girl, Suzanne, still loves him and looks for him also."

"I know Col-ton, him medicine good, make crossed stick sign. You come to council fire, talk straight talk to chiefs, stop bloodshed, then... Kicking Bird help find Col-ton."

Sonny knew the plight of the plains Indians and could not help feel the appeal of this chieftain for the preservation of his people, but it seemed a hopeless quest. The chance that he would even be heard was remote at best and the interruption to his search for Colt would cost him valuable time. Still, if he could somehow trade on the notoriety they were evidently attributing to the "Buffalo Man," maybe he could do some good in cowboy and Indian affairs. Perhaps the aid of the Kiowa might help him locate Colton as well.

215

"Kicking Bird, I will accompany you back to the encampment, but I will retain my weapons and my horse. I will give you two suns to make the peace talk, then you must help me find Colt."

The tall chief nodded his head and stood to stride over to where he had left a spotted pony in the brush. He led the animal over to the firelight, stripped a blanket from the animal and spread it on the ground, and then he lay down and was soon fast asleep.

Sonny wondered what he had let himself in for.

Dogs were barking and dark eyes were peering questioningly from the doorways of the circle of lodges as Kicking Bird rode his pony ahead of the Buffalo Man into the council circle. From in front of the head-chief's lodge, Satanta rose from his breakfast of cornmeal mush, his White Bear emblem displayed boldly on the sides of the teepee. He scowled as the lesser chief led his enemy into the campfire circle. Satank, his brother chief, came to the door of the next lodge. It had a painting of a sitting bear, and the next lodge to that depicted a big tree on its walls. "Big Tree"—Adoeette, Sonny recalled. He was facing the three principal chiefs of the Kiowa bands encamped here.

"Kicking Bird, why you bring this enemy of the people into camp?" White Bear demanded as the white-man and tall Indian stopped their ponies.

"Buffalo Man come—make peace talk."

"No, Buffalo Man speak with forked tongue, he not trusted."

"Buffalo Man back from dead with strong medicine of Great Spirit, him speak straight talk. He know path of peace for Gaigwu and Texicans. He son of Long Knife of boarder riders. Long Knife, Saber, always treat the People fair. The Buffalo Man can be trusted."

"Then why does he enter the encampment of the people with weapon? You endanger all our women and children?"

Kicking Bird said, "He comes as friend to Gaigwu, not as captive. Would you dishonor him, pare his claws, and pull his teeth?"

"Why he ride Thunder Horse, is this not same pony Runs-With-Horses capture while Buffalo Man sleep?"

"Runs-With-Horses repaid in kind, the Buffalo Man take while White Bear and Runs-With-Horses sleep in the night. I see daring—Buffalo Man's medicine—understand the sign. The Great Spirit send him to the People— make peace talk. He speak language of blue coats. Him medicine allow him enter the People's camp unopposed, recover stolen horse. It heap sign to hear his words."

Sitting Bear and Big Tree had stepped next to White Bear, one on either side. They spoke briefly together and then turned to the waiting lesser chief and the white-man, their arms folded resolutely across their chest and their faces inscrutable bronze masks. Sonny could not understand the words, but he could see that Kicking Bird's offer for peace was not going well.

White Bear rose to his full height and held up his hand and spoke loudly to the gathering Indians. "The Buffalo Man is not welcome in our camp, him come in night as enemy, take Thunder Horse—ride away. Runs-With-Horses is dishonored and must treat with Buffalo Man for satisfaction. He decide. Where Runs-With-Horses?"

"Runs-With-Horses tracking Buffalo Man and Thunder Horse." A tall Indian had stepped forward from among the others, "When he found Thunder Horse taken, he went to bring him back just after sun come up yesterday."

Sonny saw this Indian had been standing beside a girl he thought looked like Willow. What was it Colton had called her, Seeaugway? He wondered if this warrior was her father. He looked over at the Indian maiden and saw her drop her eyes and turn away. She seemed distressed and Sonny wondered if she had recognized him from the time Colt had brought her to the ranch.

"Take Buffalo Man's weapons, tie Thunder Horse in front Runs-With-Horses lodge. We wait for Runs-With-Horses' return."

"You must not dishonor Buffalo Man in this way," Kicking Bird cried. "I give word he would be treated fairly."

"You have spoken beyond your authority," White Bear said, "and brought a notorious enemy of the People into our midst. Take care you do not go too far... to do so will be at your own peril." With that the head chief turned and stooped under the flap of his lodge and disappeared.

A rush of Indians took Sonny by surprise, he was pulled from Tornado's back and stripped of his pistol and belt knife while Kicking Bird yelled in protest, but the lesser chief was blocked from interfering, as Sonny's hands were tied and he was led away to a lodge. Here he was propelled into the dark interior where a hideous old hag of a squaw sat with an evil, toothless grin. As Sonny stumbled forward to land on his face on the ground, the old woman picked up a club and began to beat him about the head and shoulders. Her blows, though painful, were not severe enough to do any real damage, but at this final indignity, Sonny had had enough; rolling over onto his back he raised both legs and kicked his attacker full in the stomach, sending the old squaw over backwards into her cooking fire where she landed with a crash, scattering pots and pans about. The buckskin fringes of the old hag's dress burst into flame and with a dreadful cry she sprang spryly from the fire pit and raced out of the lodge leaving a trailing stream of smoke to mark the path of her departure. Outside all was silent and the cowboy waited, wondering what might become of him. He had heard many stories on the frontier of captive white men and the barbarities inflicted on them by the Indians. Was that to be his fate?

A scrabbling at the entrance brought the cowboy's head around to spy a mongrel dog inquisitively nosing his way inside. Spying the captive white man, the dog bristled and withdrew its head. Sonny immediately gave a low whistle and called softly, "Here boy." The dog's head reappeared, his ears cocked questioningly. With soft words and sucking air through pursed lips, Sonny encouraged the dog to come inside the teepee. The whites of his eyes showing, the cur began to lick cautiously at the spilled food on the floor, as if expecting at any moment to be set upon by some irate squaw.

"Good boy," Sonny said, "Good boy."

The dog wagged his tail and stuck his head into the spilled pot, lapping noisily while Sonny squirmed close and reached out to soak the rawhide bonds on his wrists in the spilled broth.

"Here boy, lick this," and Sonny held out the bonds to the dog, whose head had reappeared from the kettle. The animal gave the man a puzzled look and went back to eating. It took several minutes more before the dog had cleaned up sufficiently to turn back to the coaxing captive and sit on its haunches before him, studying the human with head cocked to one side.

It was at that moment that the old squaw and a younger girl carefully poked their heads in through the teepee door and saw the Buffalo Man in conversation with the dog. The dog was listening attentively to the prisoner. The two Indian women drew their heads back in amazement and hurried over and began an excited chatter with several other women who were grinding corn meal nearby.

"The Buffalo Man is a sorcerer," avowed the old squaw. "He speaks to the animals and they understand him."

The younger woman nodded her head in affirmation, while the others looked nervously at the teepee and began to whisper amongst themselves.

"He brings the evil spirit of the white-eyes into our midst," the old hag went on, "he must be purged of the evil, but when I tried to beat him with a stick, he turned into a buffalo and kicked me in the stomach, knocking me into the fire. It is only by the merest chance I escaped serious harm. Who will tell White Bear of these new sorceries?"

The younger girl held up her hand and said with a shy smile, "I will go speak with White Bear, he will hear me."

"Go, Little Cloud, you have favor with our chief," said the old squaw.

White Bear listened as Little Cloud told of the old woman's experience with the captive white man, how he had turned into the buffalo long enough to kick old Magpie into the fire and then had coaxed the meanest cur in the entire encampment into the teepee after she left, and was speaking dog talk with him. "The women are fearful he is a sorcerer who might turn into a ravenous wolf, or bear, or perhaps a devil, in the night and murder the entire camp in their sleep."

White Bear told Little Cloud to wait while he summoned the other chiefs to the council fire and once all were assembled, he had her repeat her story. When she had finished, the council was silent, all eyes on their head Chief. Finally, Big tree stood up and addressed the gathering.

"Two Dogs of the Comanche has told of the Buffalo Man's magic and how he witnessed him return from the dead out of the great bull buffalo. It was afterward that he spoke with that rascal, brother coyote, and we all know that that can come to no good. If he is now speaking with the camp dogs, who knows what mischief may befall us. It is my council that we enslave him and keep him closely guarded while him do woman's work and menial tasks. This should break the fierce spirit in him."

A mummer of voices swept around the circle in agreement with the chieftain until Kicking Bird rose to his feet.

"Brothers, do not make such a mistake. The Buffalo Man has demonstrated great medicine and talks first hand with the Great Spirit himself. We will bring much wrath down upon our heads if we fail to heed his words. He came with me willingly, as friend, while searching for his brother. Do not betray him, do not betray me by doing such a thing. Hear him, he is a man of good will towards the Gaigwu."

"Enough," Satanta rose to his feet. "The Buffalo Man will remain our captive until Runs-With-Horses returns. His has been the offense, he shall decide." With a wave of his hand he dismissed the council and one by one they rose to their feet and left the circle.

Runs-With-Horses held the Thunder Horse by the bridle and looked deep into the animal's eyes. The big grulla tossed his head nervously and danced from side to side under the young brave's scrutiny. Softly, Runs-With-Horses blew his breath into the stallion's nostrils and the horse calmed down to stand quietly, his ears pricked forward. The youth turned an angry look upon the Buffalo Man.

"I claim Thunder Horse by right of capture," he said.

"Right of capture?" Sonny said, "I took this horse from the wilds and broke him to ride. This horse is mine."

"You trespass on Indian land and steal this horse from his band along with many others. I was to take him from the band before you intruded."

"How was I to know that?" Sonny said. "I found him running wild and free, now he runs with me, his spirit yielded to my will. How can you say he is yours? Yours are the words of a thief for you came in the dark and took him and the mule. My only crime is that I took my property back. Under white man's law you would hang for what you did."

At this declaration, the watching crowd of Indians went quiet and Runs-With-Horses whipped out a knife and lunged at Sonny. There was a scream and Seeaugway, who had been standing near the bound prisoner, quickly jumped in between the Buffalo Man and Runs-With-Horses whose knife plunged into the arm of the Indian girl. With a gasp, Willow fell at Sonny's feet, blood welling from a long cut in her white buckskin sleeve.

Runs-With-Horses gave a worried cry as he dropped to his knees and tenderly lifted the wounded girl into his arms, then without looking back he carried her to her father's lodge. Rough hands grabbed Sonny and led him away to the same teepee where he previously had been held captive. It had only been a few hours since his earlier imprisonment here. Sonny had finally gotten the dog to lick his rawhide bounds, wetting the strands and causing them to stretch, when several braves entered the lodge and brought him out to face the humiliated Runs-With-Horses. Now he wondered what would happen at this new turn of events. It was obvious the Indian youth was not going to give up Tornado without a fight. Maybe he should just give the lad the horse, he certainly had no desire to kill the young Indian. The thing was, would Tornado go with him or the Indian? The redskin certainly had some sort of charm over the horse. And what was his connection with Willow? It was obvious he cared for her, dropping the knife and picking her up like that.

Sonny did not have long to wonder. In short order, several braves returned and physically drug him from the lodge to stand before a glowering Chieftain who spoke rapidly in Kiowa while many of the men of the camp stood around. Kicking Bird gave a rough translation to the cowboy as Runs-With-Horses was summoned from Spotted Buffalo's lodge.

"The Thunder Horse will choose," Kicking Bird said.

"What?" Sonny's eyes watched Runs-With-Horses walk up, and then turned to face the lightning-tattooed chief.

"White Bear has decided. The Thunder Horse shall choose between the two of you. We will see whose medicine is best."

So, that was to be the way of it then, Sonny thought. Well, he would soon find out how well he and Tornado were bonded. He was also very interested in watching the young Indian work with the grulla for he obviously had a way with horses.

What Sonny had not expected was the nature of the test. Tornado was led outside the circle of teepees and picketed to a solid stake driven into the ground. Sonny could see the horse still had his saddle and belongings on him. Apparently, it was to be winner takes all. The big horse watched curiously as three or four riders rode out to the horse herd while the rest of the band gathered some distance away to watch.

Sonny was pushed out to stand a hundred feet away from the stallion while his hands were untied, his feet having been previously loosed. Runs-With-Horses took up a position about ten yards to Sonny's left, and an equal distance from the horse. He eyed the tall Buffalo Man with both amusement and self-confidence.

Soon the riders returned in a cloud of dust, leading a mare between them. With much kii-yiing and yipping, they jumped from their mounts and tussled with the mare until they had her tied off to a stout post some fifty feet the other side of the stallion. She was obviously in season and Tornado's head came up and he began an anxious fidgeting against his picket line, making a throaty nickering after he caught her scent.

Once again, White Bear spoke loudly so that all could hear, and then Kicking Bird explained to Sonny that both he and Runs-With-Horses would be given equal opportunity to untie the stallion and lead him away from the mare and back into the circle of lodges. Whichever one the horse followed would be declared the master of the animal. If neither one could entice the stallion away from the mare, the two of them would face each other in mortal combat to decide the winner. Runs-With-Horses was to go first.

Runs-With-Horses confidently walked up to the agitated stallion and reaching up, he grabbed the stallion's forelock and pulled his face around to stare deep in the horse's eyes, all the while speaking softly in a low voice. The horse slowed his prancing and came to a standstill, his neck bowed and nostrils quivering and blowing. The Indian blew a long, steady breath into them and the Thunder Horse suddenly jerked his head up with a short squeal and then returned his attention back to the young brave. Runs-With-Horses continued to speak in a low sing-song voice while untying the picket rope from around the animal's neck. The horse remained motionless until Runs-With-Horses turned his back on him and then when the Indian gave a low command, the animal began a slow, methodical plodding behind him as the young warrior led him towards the circle of lodges.

Sonny watched this whole process with amazement and marveled at the young Indian's way with the horse. He did indeed seem to hold some kind of spell or at least understanding with the animal. It was at this point that the mare gave a high-pitched whistle and upon hearing it, Tornado whirled about and raced away towards where she was tethered. It was a marvel to see, the big stallion running towards the mare with obvious intent, but holding his head in a sidelong glance back towards the confounded Indian brave who saw his chance for the

Thunder Horse slipping from his grasp. It was as if there were two forces at work in the horse, the call of the wild to his own kind, and yet another call from the Indian that was growing fainter and fainter the closer he drew to the mare.

Sonny took one step forward, placed thumb and fore-finger in his mouth and with all his might sent a piercing whistle after the fleeing stallion. The result was even more amazing to the watching band of Indians than what had happened previously. The stallion had nearly reached the dancing, prancing mare, when the shrill whistle of the cowboy hauled him up short in a turf-plowing stop. The call of the cowboy was not to be ignored; with mus-cles bunched and forelegs pistoning, Tornado bolted back in a mad dash towards the waiting Texan. As the horse approached him, Sonny made a hand signal, and Tornado thundered on by him while he reached up and grabbed the saddle horn, vaulting into the saddle. With a wild Texas yell, the Buffalo Man raced out of camp, to freedom and away from the bewildered Kiowa band.

CHAPTER FOURTEEN

The Girls, The Bull, and the Englishman.

Spring 1871, Wade's Landing. Texas

GARETH HAZELHURST STOPPED HIS BUGGY in front of the Kluesmans' house and stepped down. Carefully he withdrew a hitch weight from the back and dropped it. Snapping a tie-down lead to his horse's bridle, he then purposefully turned, opened the gate and strode up the walk. A firm rap on the door led to the sounds of footsteps within and soon an inquiring middle-aged woman stood in the open doorway.

"Mrs. Kluesman, I presume," Hazelhurst said, removing his large hat.

"Yes?" Mable Kluesman replied.

"My name is Gareth Hazelhurst of the Box 7 Ranch. Is your husband about?"

"You will find him at the blacksmith's shop in town," she said. "Can I be of assistance?"

"I have a proposition to put before him," Gareth said. "Is Suzanne here?"

"No, she would be at school this time of day. What is this about?"

The big rancher shifted uncomfortably on the porch and then replied, "Well, I understand your daughter may be thinking on a trip to Dodge City, or maybe Abilene, and since I have some business up that way, I was wondering if she might need an escort."

When Mrs. Kluesman looked at him in confusion he went hastily on to explain. "I will be taking a couple of my ranch hands, 'Two Bits' Thompson and Buddy McLeod, and an outfit to Abilene to pick up a registered bull I am having shipped in from England to the railhead there. I don't know if she told you or not, but I have made your daughter's acquaintance along with a friend... a Miss McClusky, and since I understand the girls are already acquainted with Bud and Two-Bits, I thought it might be helpful, in light of the present circumstances, for Miss Kluesman to accompany us. We would extend to her the utmost care and protection on such an arduous journey."

"That is something you will have to take up with Suzanne and Mr. Kluesman," Mable said. "It might be helpful for you to know that Miss McClusky is on her way here now, and the two of them do have plans to go search for Colton Saber."

Gareth Hazelhurst smiled and nodded his head. "Miss McClusky would be welcome too," he said.

———

Suzanne galloped her spotted pony up the lane to the Sabers' two-story house and sprang from the saddle, leaving the horse to find her own way into the barnyard. Out of breath, she rushed up onto the porch and hammered a small fist on the door, then without waiting for an answer she opened the door and burst inside, crying, "Mrs. Saber... Mom, Dad Saber, where are you?"

A rush of feet brought first Pearl and then Becky treading down the stairs, followed soon by Mrs. Saber who had been on the back porch gathering kindling.

"Suzanne, what in the world?" the rancher's wife asked worriedly.

"Look at this!" Suzanne said, holding aloft a telegram. She handed the piece of paper to Jessica Saber who quickly scanned its contents and then reread the brief message more slowly.

Becky and Pearl were attempting to read over her shoulder until finally the younger girl said, "What is it, what's going on?"

"It's about Colt," Suzanne said. "He has been seen in Abilene, Kansas. The telegram is from a Joe Hanson of San Angelo and was sent to the Sheriff here. He said a cowboy stopped in at his mercantile and saw the poster and said he knew Colt and that he had just finished a cattle drive with him. He said Colt was headed for the gold fields in Colorado and that he went by the name of 'Pecos'."

"Pecos?" Pearl butted in, "Why would he go by Pecos? He told me his name was Woody Stover."

"Woody, Pecos… who cares, it's Colton," Suzanne cried joyfully and grabbing Jessica Saber in a big hug she began to dance up and down gleefully while the two younger girls encircled the pair with hugs of their own and joined in.

Mrs. Saber dabbed at her eyes with her apron. "Pearl, run and tell Grant and Tommy that Miss Kluesman is here."

Pearl dashed out of the house and ran to the barn where the rancher and Tommy were working. "Hey," she yelled, "Mom wants you and Dad inside on the double."

Grant looked up at the young teen and then set aside the harness he had been mending, heaved himself to his feet and started towards the house.

"You young'uns stop your arguing and come on in." he said.

Tommy had already challenged Pearl, "What's so all-fired important that you have to come running out here like a house on fire and spook the chickens out a layin' eggs?"

"Come inside, you'll find out," Pearl said.

Tommy looked skeptically at their new-found house guest and was beginning to feel the by-now-familiar sense of irritation that seemed to gyrate around the girl whenever she put in an appearance, especially whenever they were by themselves. It was something he didn't question, it was just there and he never failed to rise to its provocation. If one would have questioned him about it, he would have been surprised that anyone should find it unusual. Wasn't this the way it was? Dogs and cats, cows and horses, girls and boys? The challenge is always there.

"Why don't you just tell me," he said.

"Because I know something you don't and its really good stuff." Pearl said.

"What's it got to do with?"

"That's for me to know and you to find out."

"I'll find out, you can bet your boots on that." Tommy said.

"Not from me, you won't."

"Huh, probably has something to do with the notional ideas you have about my brother."

"Well, it just so happens that it does, Mr. Know-It-All, and now we are going to find him."

"We?" Tommy said, "You got a mouse in your pocket?"

"No smarty, Miss Kluesman and I are going to Abilene, Kansas and find him and bring him back, and then I am going to marry him, just like I said."

"Aw rotten eggs, you're too danged young to marry anybody. You don't know the first thing about being married."

"I do so, I know a whole lot more than you do."

At this point, Tommy had forgotten the more persuasive issue of Pearl's news, and was intrigued by what she may reveal regarding the relationship she was compelled into with the old coot Colt had found her with.

"So, what do you know that I don't?" Tommy challenged.

"I know stuff," Pearl said. "Stuff that you have no clue about."

"Oh really, I suppose you mean stuff about having babies and the like," he said.

Pearl grew silent, then quietly said, "Maybe."

"I know all about that stuff, good heavens, girl, I live on a ranch and see that stuff going on all the time," Tommy boasted.

"Not between human beings," Pearl avowed.

Tommy, a little subdued, said, "What could be so different?" Although he knew there was a difference—a big difference—and while a part of him was very curious about that difference, another part warned him to tread carefully with this girl who had experience beyond her years. Experience that still went way beyond the curve of knowing what had happened to her. Shoot, he didn't even know what had happened to her himself.

Pearl had bent down to pet the old tomcat that had walked up to rub against the back of her leg, "The thing is, I know stuff and you don't, so why don't you just accept it and quit being such a kid."

Stung by the remark, the boy bristled, "I ain't no more a kid than you are, in fact you are such a kid there's no chance Colt or anybody else is ever going to marry you. Quit petting that mangy cat."

Pearl looked up in surprise. "What did this poor cat ever do to you? She likes to be petted," she knelt down and petted the tomcat until he was purring like a windmill in a gale.

"Ha," Tommy said, "that proves you don't know much. That dumb ol' cat is a tomcat, not a tabby cat."

"So, it's still a cat. Cats are for girls and dogs, ugh, are for boys," Pearl declared with finality.

Tommy seemed to hang up on this logic, which at less contested times he might have been inclined to agree, but at the peevishness he was feeling towards the girl at this point, all he could think of to say was, "Oh yeah!"

Pearl turned her head away and, still petting the barn cat said, "Yeah."

The two youngsters went silent then, glaring at each other with obvious disdain. Finally, Pearl said, "What's its name?"

"What's who's name?"

Pearl gave him an exasperated look, indicating the purring cat in her lap.

"Oh—cat." Tommy said.

"Cat?" Pearl was dismayed, "you mean you haven't even given this poor kitty a name?" She lifted the tomcat up with her hands under its front legs and cooed, "Poor kitty, I'll give you a name," and she kissed the animal on the nose.

"You better watch out, you're going to get ringworm messing with that scruffy cat."

Pearl let the cat back down and looked at Tommy skeptically. "This cat doesn't have ringworm."

"You never can tell," Tommy said. "He for sure has mange, just look at his hide, the Lord only knows what else he's got."

"Poor Petunia," Pearl said, fussing over the cat. "No one ever takes care of you."

"Petunia," Tommy scoffed. "That's about the dumbest name for a cat I ever heard of."

"It is not, it is a very good name."

"Naw, Boone, or Crockett or Wetzel, or even Magoozalem would suit this cat better'n that. He's a hunter."

"Magoozalem, have you taken leave of your senses, boy?" Pearl got to her feet, but still in a crouching posture, continued to pet the cat.

231

"You're going to get mange," Tommy declared. "You keep on rubbing that dumb cat and your hair will all fall out."

Pearl straightened up and looked doubtfully at the cat. "People can't get mange," she said with uncertainty.

"If I was you, I would treat that cat before I did anymore cuddling up to it," Tommy said.

"Treat it, how do I treat it?" Pearl asked.

"Rub it with horse liniment, I guess. . . no—wait, turpentine. Use turpentine, that will cure that cat of anything," Tommy declared.

"Well, where will I find turpentine?" she said.

"In the workshop on the paint shelf. Be sure and rub it on him good, especially under his tail."

Pearl picked up the tomcat, its tail switching, and holding it at arm's length, she headed towards the workshop by the barn. Tommy turned on his heels and made a beeline for the house.

———

Suzanne watched the stagecoach roll to a stop in front of Munson's General store and spied through the open window, the red hair of Kathreen McClusky as her young friend bounced to a final stop on the hard seat of the conveyance. The door popped open and Kathreen began to climb down the steps while fanning the dust away from her face with a lace hanky. The young Scottish lass was dressed in an emerald green traveling outfit with a heavy brown shawl over her shoulders and was looking the worse for wear from the long trip.

"How come this place hasn't got a train station yet?" she complained.

Suzanne stepped to hug her neck, "Kate, I am so glad to see you, now we can get started after Colt."

"Good gracious, Suzanne, I just got here. Let me at least get a bath before you go dragging me off across the prairie on a wild goose chase, and I do mean *Wild Goose.* What is the matter with that Colton anyway?"

"Colt didn't understand," Suzanne said, "we thought he was dead and..."

"Save it, Suze," Kathreen interrupted, "if he'd had half a brain he would have asked questions first and shot you later."

"Oh, forgive me, Kate, it's just that we have been waiting for you to get here. Gareth Hazelhurst has been ready to leave for the past week, and now that you're here, I am so anxious to get started."

"Now what's this business about Hazelhurst and do you even know where Colt is?"

"A cowboy who rode with Colt on a cattle drive to Abilene saw his poster in San Angelo and told the store-keeper there, and he sent us a telegram that Colt was heading for the goldfields in Colorado. Mr. Hazelhurst needs to travel to the railhead in Kansas to bring back a prize bull and has invited us to go along. I hope to pick up his trail in Abilene and go find him."

"So, the two of us are to go traipsing across Texas with the most eligible bachelor west of the Mississippi then?" Kathreen said with a big smile.

"Yes, Texas, the Indian Nations and most of Kansas. Isn't it just an answer to prayer? You know Two-Bits and Buddy are going along don't you?"

"Huh, those two ninnies, um. This could prove to be an interesting trip, a rich man to spoon with and a couple of cowpokes to pull our boots off."

"Kate, are you still heckling poor Two-Bits and Buddy? I thought Two-Bits and you were writing to each other."

The two girls had walked the distance from the stage to Suzanne's house while carrying Kathreen's luggage. A steamer trunk was left on the porch at the store for Gunner to pick up later. Miss McClusky turned towards her friend, after setting a valise on the porch step with a grunt.

"Well, Godfrey did write me one or two letters that were about the equivalent of what a first grader needing to be held back a grade or two might write, then he just stopped writing and that was the end of that torrid love affair."

"Did you even write back to him?" Suzanne asked.

"I was going to, but I guess I just never got around to it," Kathreen said dismissively. "Now where do we find Mr. Hazelhurst?"

Two days later the heavy stock wagon cleared the last of the sand hills and rolled out on the high prairie to points east. Several extra water barrels had been filled from Sand Creek and attached to the sides of the wagon for the eighty plus miles they would have to travel without water until they reached Big Springs, for it was Gareth's stated intention to try and follow the Goodnight-Loving cattle trail east. He had hopes to make it to Fort Griffin before encountering any major cattle drives that would be westbound this early in the spring. Once at Griffin, they would swing north on either the Western or Chisholm cattle trails and hopefully find a northbound herd to Abilene and travel with them.

Suzanne was mounted on Checkers and Kathreen rode a fine bay gelding that Gareth Hazelhurst had provided. Gareth rode a big black gelding with a white blaze face, and was leading the way. He was followed by the two girls. Next came the wagon while Two-Bits and Buddy brought up the rear, herding five extra saddle horses, one for each of the party to trade off with. The wagon, built of heavy planking to carry the bull, was pulled by two sturdy workhorses, and the Chinese cook, Wong Wey sat on the high seat handling the reins.

"Who was that kid making such a fuss back at the Sabers' place?" Kathreen asked.

"Pearl?" Suzanne said. "She's the girl I was telling you about, the one Colt rescued and sent to his folks."

"Why did she think she was going with us on this trip?"

"She has it in mind to marry Colton," Suzanne said with a sigh.

"Marry Colt! Why she's barely out of diapers herself. What put that notion into her head?"

Suzanne gave her friend a thin smile. "What... or better yet, who do you think?"

"Oh, Colt's old fatal charm at work again, was it? I think I understand. Poor kid. Did she get into some kind of trouble at the ranch?"

"I think so, something about their old tomcat and trying to doctor it with turpentine."

Kathreen burst out in a sudden peal of laughter and then regaining her composure asked, "Whatever possessed her to do that?"

"I am not sure but what I understand is that Tommy put her up to it. Apparently, the girl had no clue what affect the turpentine would have on the cat and, at his instigation, decided to treat it for mange."

"Well, that little devil, surely he knew what it would do," Kathreen was still giggling.

"I feel sure he did," Suzanne said. "At any rate, it earned both of them a good spanking and in no uncertain terms, Grant Saber let Pearl know she wasn't going anywhere, especially with us."

"You better watch out, Suzanne," her friend said, "this Pearl is liable to upstage you with the mysterious Colt Saber."

The girls rode along in silence then, following Gareth Hazelhurst, and drinking in the greening beauty of the range as it awakened to spring. There was a fresh scent of sage and growing things in the air and a stirring of life all about them. Suzanne felt the familiar longing overtake the fear that had shadowed her thoughts of Colt of late, and she realized that a dread had lodged next to his place in her heart... a dread that she had not 'til now even recognized and she wondered at it. Why was it tarnishing her deep love and hope for Colt Saber? Was the awakening of spring all around reconnecting her both with what was, and provoking a fear that he would no longer feel for her as he had?

"Kate," Suzanne said, "Do you think Colt ever thinks about me?"

Kathreen turned in her saddle to look at her friend. She was struck by the sad beauty in Suzanne's question and the innocent, somewhat hopeless, yet hopeful, expectant picture she made riding next to her.

"Golly, Suze, how could he not? If he's alive and breathing he thinks about you, probably all the time."

"But, he thinks he killed me—that I'm gone."

"Yeah, what do you think that's like? It has to make him feel pretty desperate and lost. I'll bet he probably doesn't give a darn whether he lives or dies—with you gone."

"Oh, Kate, that hurts my heart so, to think of him like that. He was so full of life and love and hope. I must hurry to find him and let him know I am alright—that Sonny is alright. That we are not killed."

Kathreen rode in silence then, thinking about what Suzanne had said. For Colt to have left everything and disappeared, leaving no word at all to the folks he cared about the most, and just ride off, showed the desperation he was feeling at the tragic moment of the shooting. But for him to have remained gone, to have made no effort to contact anyone, least of all her, led her to believe that he was indeed a lost soul probably battling it out with God in some dark, forlorn, forgotten place, as to the why of it all. She knew she would be, and even though she still held a special place, deep down in a dusty corner of her own heart for Colt, the fact that he had made no effort to contact her either had reaffirmed to the young lady from

Saint Louis that her role in this adventure was subordinate to that of Suzanne, that she held no special place in Colt's world, and in fact, she was pretty sure that was the way she wanted it anyway. There was still the matter of Sonny and his relationship to Suzanne and his choosing the young school teacher over herself as well. Her temper stirred a little then and she gave a disgusted huff at being reminded of it. Setting a determined jaw, she allowed as to how she would make every dad-blame cowboy pay, and Sonny Saber was at the top of the list.

Two-Bits Thompson drug up a section of log and dropped it on the fire and paused for a moment to look at the two young ladies sitting there as their eyes followed the shower of sparks rising into the night air. Without saying a word, he turned on his heels and walked out of the circle of light to where his friend was rolling out his bedroll. Buddy McLeod looked up as his pard approached.

"Got em all tucked in for the night?"

"Not my job," Two-Bits said tersely.

"Shucks, pard, thought you was sweet on that red-headed gal."

"Wal, that turned out to be a one-way wagon track," Two-Bits drawled. "I think I better find me one of those down-home girls and forget about the big-city ones... there'd be too much I'd have to teach her."

"Makes sense to me. If'n I was fixin' to hitch up, which I ain't, that'd be the kind I'd slap my brand on."

The two cowboys sat on their bedding and looked back at the fire while rolling a smoke and said nothing more until they had twisted the ends and lit up.

"Looks pretty as a feed-store calendar, doesn't it, them two sittin' over there?" Bud said.

Two-Bits exhaled a long puff of smoke and said wearily, "Yeah, kinda makes you feel good bein' around such be-oo-ti-ful girls, even if they cain't see you apart from the rest of the scenery."

Bud grinned in the dark and nodded his head in agreement. "Guess we're just along for the ride, we might as well enjoy it while we can."

Hazelhurst was quietly puffing on his pipe while staring into the fire. He was seated across from the two girls on an over-turned bucket when Kathreen nudged Suzanne in the ribs.

"Mr. Hazelhurst, what do you hear from England?" she said.

The rancher withdrew the pipe from his mouth and looked up with a reflective smile. "Mother says I need to come home and tend to the family's affairs. She thinks I should forget about 'this foolishness in Texas,' as she calls it."

"Are you going?" Kathreen sat up in interest.

"I will have to soon, there are some pressing family matters that only I can attend."

"I wonder what it would be like to visit England," Kathreen said. "I think I will persuade poppa to take mother and me to London when this business is over."

"Speaking of that," Gareth said. "What plans do you young ladies have once we reach Abilene?"

Suzanne seemed a little doubtful and was about to speak when Kathreen interrupted her and said, "We will find our way to Denver and make inquires after Colt Saber until we locate him and then straighten that poor misguided soul out."

"How will you travel? I don't believe the railroad has made its way to Denver yet."

"I beg to differ with you, Mr. Hazelhurst," Kathreen said. "The Kansas Pacific Railroad completed its line to Denver last August. People can now ride non-stop by rail from the Atlantic to the Pacific."

"That is truly a marvelous feat of technology but it was bound to come," the Englishman said, "What advancements are yet to happen? It is bound to change the face of this country."

"Well, folks still have to take a trunk-line from Denver up to Cheyenne to connect with the Union Pacific for points west," Kathreen said, "but now you can ride all the way by rail without having to take a barge across the Missouri at Omaha."

Suzanne barely heard the conversation, her eyes staring into the fire while lost in thought. What would Colt do when he saw she was still alive? Would he still want her? Was her misstep with Sonny of such consequence that she'd been torn from his heart? Oh, how she dreaded that thought. The oppression surrounding her heart made it difficult for her to breathe and she had to periodically take a deep breath and let it out with a sigh. At length both Gareth Hazelhurst and Kathreen noticed this, and the rancher nodded slowly towards his young charge.

"I think it is time for us to seek our repose," he said with a knowing glance to Kathreen on Suzanne's behalf. Rising to his feet, he stretched, then walked off stiff-legged to where his bed was rolled out under the stars.

Kathreen nudged her friend and the two girls walked out some distance from the firelight, soon to return and climb into the bedding rolled out under the wagon. In the distance a lone prairie wolf howled mournfully at the moon.

The next morning the camp woke to a heavy frost that had stiffened the top blanket of their individual bedding. Wong Wey was slamming pots and pans around on the tailgate of the wagon where a makeshift food box had been mounted, and was grumbling over having to climb in and out for his breakfast provisions.

"Why no makee step ladder so Wong Wey can get crummy things?" he said to no one in particular.

"Hey, Wong," Two-Bits called, "You got some coffee made for us Americans yet? We don't drink no fureign tea, ya know."

"You shutee you yap," the little Chinaman yelled back. "You one Amelican with belly bad manna'. In China, you..." and here the irate cook launched into a tirade of Chinese at the grinning cowboys who were crawling from their blankets and pulling on their boots.

"You shouldn't had ought a be rilin' the cook that-a-way, Two-Bits." Bud said, "He's liable to put some slippery elm into your coffee."

"Aw, the little chink's alright, it's funny to see him get all het-up over nothing. Let's go get some of that mud he calls coffee."

The two pards walked over to the wagon and peeked under it to where the two young ladies were sitting up and rubbing the sleep out of their eyes.

"Mawnin', ladies," Bud drawled, "You all need help with anything on this frosty morn?"

"Well, a cup of tea does sound very inviting, Bud," Kathreen said sweetly. "Do you suppose Two-Bits might persuade a cuppa out of Mr. Wong?"

"Shore thing, darlin'. Hey Two-Bits, Miss McClusky wants you to get her a cup of tea."

Two-Bits squatted on his heels and peered with raised eyebrows at the big-eyed, mock innocence of the girl sitting there in her wrinkled bedding. With a thin-lipped smile, he slowly nodded and then rose to his feet and turned to face the cook.

"How 'bout it, cookie, you brew up any that fureign tea for you and the boss?"

The Chinaman scowled, "You no havee tea. Tea for bossee man, and for Wong Wey, you drinkee coffee." With that the little cook scurried over to clutch up a china tea pot that had a slow curl of steam drifting from its spout into the cold morning air. "You drinkee coffee," he repeated.

"Now hold on here," Two-Bits said, "You mean to tell me you have no tea for the ladies? Miss McClusky here's from over by England, shucks, everybody over in that part of the world drinks the stuff. Surely you will not deny her a cup of your ol' tea."

"Oh, allee right, the Missy can have some tea, but no tea fo you."

Bud watched the whole proceedings with a big grin on his face while helping himself to the hot black coffee and then pouring a cup for his friend. Kathreen and Suzanne, still sitting up with the blankets around their shoulders to ward of the morning chill, smiled at each other as they watched the little Chinaman carefully fill two fine china cups with the amber liquid and then hold them out to the waiting Two-Bits.

"I'll take two lumps, milk and lemon," Kathreen called from her spot beneath the wagon bed.

"No! No!" Wong Wey called. "No lemon, Missy, no milky, jus belly good tea, Oolong tea." he smiled at the redhead and nodded positively.

Two-Bits turned and walking carefully over to the girls, he squatted on his heels and held out the two steaming mugs to the young ladies, who took them gratefully and began to cautiously sip the contents.

"Sorry ladies," he said, "looks like Wong Wey drinks his tea the wrong way."

"Two-Bits, don't you think that joke's getting a little old?" Kathreen said. "Why don't you come up with something a little more original than that?"

"Oh, you mean like, 'Very well, Mr. Two-Bits, I shall be happy to correspond with you once you have written to me first,'" he said.

Suzanne turned toward her friend with eyebrows raised and a look that said, *"Well Kate, what about that?"*

Kathreen made a snide grin as though tolerating a small child and said, "Remember I also said something

about 'if I could find the time amongst my other suitors'?"
She took another sip of hot tea.

Two-Bits' face went white. "No, you didn't, you said
you would add me to your list of would-be suitors, and
be happy to correspond with me once I had written first.
I wrote you two letters. Didn't you get them?"

It was Kathreen's turn to blush. "I got them," she murmured into the mug.

"That's what I thought," Two-Bits rose to his feet and
turned his back on the two women. "Pard, where's that
cup of mud you poured me? No use lettin' it get cold while
I senselessly flap my gums in the wind."

It took the small party three days to cross the eighty-
mile stretch from Castle Gap to the first water east of that
tormented bit of land. The trip was without incident since
they had packed plenty of water with them. Kathreen had
taken to riding up front along with Gareth Hazelhurst and
bedeviled the patient Englishman with many questions,
sprinkled liberally with much flirting.

Suzanne rode most of the time in single file behind
them or a little off to one side to avoid the dust kicked
up by their horses' heels, and was for the most part lost
in thought in some dark place. The Chinaman wrestled
with the team, keeping his seat on the hard wagon bench
and freely demonstrating that his prowess as a teamster
lagged some distance behind his abilities as a cook.

Bud and Two-Bits tended the remuda, happily saddled
and bridled the mounts for each day's ride, and hitched up
the team. They, for the most part, kept their own council,
keeping an eye on the trail and watching for danger like
the good men of the range they were. There had been
a decided briefness of conversation between Kathreen
McClusky and Two-Bits Thompson for the past two days,
and Bud was pretty sure his friend was nursing some hurt
feelings like one might a sore toe, that is, walking around

certain things—or ones, real careful like. He hoped his pard's usual, "World-by-the-tail-with-a-down-hill drag," demeanor would soon return and figured to just ride it out with him, until it did. Thus, it was that they eventually came to a creek which led them on to Big Springs. Here it was decided to call a halt for a day, rest up, and do some laundry while taking advantage of the lake's swimming hole.

CHAPTER FIFTEEN

Trailin' to Colorado

May 1871, Smoky River Trail, Kansas.

I PEERED AT THE ROUNDED HILLS OFF IN the distance that seemed to have a smoky haze about them and said to Lightfoot, "That's why they call this country the Smokey River Hills." Lightfoot just nodded his head once and went on back to eyeing the choice tidbits of grass alongside the trail we were riding. According to the papers I'd read last winter, this trail was the old Butterfield Overland Dispatch route and not to be confused with John Butterfield's mail route down in Texas. It had survived less than a year before David Butterfield, no kin to John, sold out to rival Ben Holladay, who turned around and sold it to Wells Fargo. The Kansas Pacific Railroad was also pushing for the goldfields by this time last year and so the stage was no longer needed and the Wells Fargo equipment was moved north to the company's Platte River route.

Due mostly to the wanted poster, I decided to trail over this old route and avoid the train. There was a good road with stage relay stations posted every twelve miles or so, most of these were pretty much abandoned and sodbusters, or somebody, had scavenged all the lumber from the buildings and corrals, but the sites are mostly situated on good grass and water, so I figured it would make for easy traveling. The new Kansas & Pacific Railroad's tracks more or less followed this same route and occasionally a train would go puffing by. Sometimes the wiseacre engineer would blow his whistle and make Lightfoot jump like a jackrabbit in a rattlesnake's nest and he'd go to bucking and have me pulling leather. I guess it was good entertainment though, for I could see through the windows of the Pullmans, the rich folks drinking coffee, pointing their fat cigars, and laughing at me.

After this happened a few times I could tell Lightfoot was wondering why I didn't pull my hog-leg and shoot the blamed thing.

"Shucks, Lighty," I said, "I'm tryin' my best to keep it on the down-low and you want me to ventilate that puffer-belly? That's the reason why we ain't ridin' it in the first place, that'n because it'd cost me my drover's and winter's wages to freight your sorry hide all the way to Denver."

The horse just snorted his disgust. He didn't like me callin' him Lighty, and he didn't like trains, although the idea of ridin' in a nice new stock car did have some appeal to him.

"We'll just mosey along easy like, take our time and enjoy the country. I've never seen this range before, have you?"

Lightfoot just chuffed and shook his head, rattling the reins. He figured it wasn't all that much different than Texas except that the grass was watery tasting. It had been something of a wet spring alright, we'd had to scrape mud off our boots more'n once on our way up from Texas. I should a kept those ideas hogtied because I had no more'n thought it, and it started in to raining again. I pulled the red horse up and reached for my slicker, then kneed him on up the trail in a cold, misting rain.

By evening, I reached what was left of Fort Harker and was reminded of something I'd seen in the paper back at Fort Griffin about this place. A feller had written back home to his wife at the end of the war and gave it a less than colorful description. He said she would laugh if she could see what they were calling a Fort, for it was no more than a group of log shanties covered with dirt with most of the windows made of boards hung on leather hinges to swing open when they wanted light and shut to keep out the weather. Some of them had half a window with glass panes in them and he figured the upper crust resided in those. He said the log buildings were in a row and you could throw a cat between the logs, or something like that. The soldiers lived in caves dug into the bank in the winter time and you could look off and see nothing but high stony hills and valleys. He figured the place ought to be left to the Indians and wild beasts.

I had to admit, it wasn't much of a place now, with only a few soldiers about. Most of them stared hollow-eyed at me as I rode on past to find a place out of the wind down by the river where I made camp. I was sure wishing for a tarp, but managed to get a shelter of sorts constructed—a lean-to affair covered with some tules I pulled up from alongside the river and some wind-fall branches. I got a fire going and sat huddled up close under my slicker and stared off at the stony hills. I ate a cold supper of jerky and biscuits and managed to pass the night in relative comfort with just a few drops finding their way through to splatter on my slicker. By dawn we were on the trail again and we'd rode nearly all the way to Ellsworth before Lightfoot got the hump out of his back and settled down to his usual steady gait. I don't think he was too pleased with me using his saddle blanket for a ground pad the night before. It was some damp when I stuck it on him this morning.

Ellsworth, Kansas was fast becoming the new cattle center for Texas beef since the folks around Abilene and Dodge were griping more and more about the tick infestations coming up on the longhorns, and I was about to learn first-hand of its tawdry reputation as the *"Wickedest Town in the West."*

The town was situated on a broad flat some distance above the river, and the wide main street was a churned-up sea of mud from all the rain and the numerous hooves of freight animals, cowboys' and soldiers' horses, and the teams of nesters and farmers. I could only imagine what it might look like when the cattle drovers rode in with their herds heading for the new stockyard. A long row of new-sawn lumber buildings, some of them two and even three stories high, lined one side of the street, and I made out at least two, maybe three grocery stores, a hardware store, a boot shop, a dry goods store, and numerous saloons. Lightfoot tip-toed across the mess to where I pulled him up in front of one of the grocery stores. I was fixing to add to my grub supply and then go get a light tarp from the hardware. He snorted me one and stretched his neck down to rub his nose against the once white fetlock of his left front foot. I could tell he was peeved at me riding him through all that muck.

"Not to worry, boy," I said to the horse, "from the looks of them clouds, more rain's a-coming and your pretty white feet will get all spiffed up again."

"Young feller," a grizzled old man sitting on a bench in front of the store window called. "That's a mighty fine lookin' animal you're ridin' there."

"Shh," I hissed, "Don't be saying things like that so loud. He might hear you and his vanity's already bigger'n mine. I am barely able to sit 'im as it is."

"Huh?" the old man looked puzzled. "I heard you talkin' to him, you don't reckon he understands plain English, do you?"

"As clear as a bell, why one of these days I expect he'll bust right out talkin' back to me and I 'low as how he'll have plenty to say when he does." At this point, Lightfoot nodded his head two or three times and then turning his gaze on the old geezer, curled his upper lip back over his chompers, opened his mouth and let loose a loud horse laugh.

The old man jumped spryly to his feet and took a couple steps towards us. "Gol-dang, I believe he does know what you was talkin' 'bout," he said rubbing his hands together. He turned to a couple of passersby and said, "Folks, you wanna see a talkin' horse?" The young couple stopped for a moment, took one look at the old-timer, then at Lightfoot who had hung his head and was dozing. They muttered, "No thanks," and then hurried on up the boardwalk.

"You don't know what 'cher missin'," he called after them.

"Say, old timer, how about you keeping an eye on Lightfoot here while I go in and fetch some groceries?"

"Sure, sonny, I'll see if I can get him to talk while you're gone."

I paused for a moment when he called me sonny and gave him a curious look that hopefully didn't register the pang I felt in my heart at the mention of that name. I stepped on into the grocery store and swallowed down the cotton-ball-sized wad of regret that was about to strangle me, then let my eyes roam over the place, and I was amazed at all the stuff for sale. It looked like there was a butcher shop and a bakery, right there in the same store. I wandered around for awhile, just enjoying seeing the produce and cheese and eggs and butter and stuff, and was thinking I could fill a couple of gunny sacks full of grub and hang them over my saddle bags. No doubt Lightfoot would have something to say about that. I finally settled for more jerky, a dozen or so of some bratwurst all strung together, since I remembered how good the ones the mom of a girl I once knew had fixed on a camp out, but I soon chucked those thoughts and zeroed in on how to take some butter and eggs along. The store keeper suggested I break the eggs into a Mason[1] fruit jar, add some milk and screw the lid down tight with some waxed paper to keep it from leaking in my saddle bags. It worked pretty well, too. I drank the rest of the bottle of milk while munching a couple of oatmeal cookies from a dozen I picked up, and then I bought some cheese, two good size slabs of smoked bacon, a couple of onions and bell peppers, some taters and a half dozen red apples. I sure didn't know where he was getting such nice apples this time of year, but the storekeeper said they were out of California and came in on the train. I wondered what the world was coming to. I got two loaves of fresh baked bread and a baker's dozen of biscuits, some canned peaches and green beans, as well as dry beans, and finally added tins of salt and pepper. The man behind the counter gave me two gunny sacks and helped me load my goods into them and then let me leave them behind the counter while I went over to the hardware store. I paid for the groceries with the last of my cash, and asked the store keeper if there was an assay office or bank in town. He told me there was a bank up the street and I thanked him and left.

When I walked back out on the porch, the old man had engaged two seedy looking characters in conversation about my horse. He was explaining how Lightfoot could understand everything folks said, and could almost talk back to them.

"That durned horse can answer you, yes or no, just by noddin' or shakin' his head."

"Aw, that's bull," the bigger of the two new guys said.

"Go ahead, ask him somethin'" the old man replied.

"Shucks, Johnson, why not make it a sportin' venture?" the other fellow said.

"Good idea, Craig," the big man said. "I got twenty bucks that says that nag don't understand a word I say."

"All's I got's a ten-spot," the old man said.

"That's good enough," Johnson said. "Hey horse, is it ever gonna stop raining in this damned country?"

Lightfoot just stood there, his head drooping and eyes closed. I knew he heard the question and was just being contrary. I swear that horse's got mule blood in him somewhere.

"Ha, I told you so," Johnson said, "pay up, you old buzzard."

"Now, hold on," the old man said. "Give him a chance to answer, he was snoozing and probably didn't know you were talking to him. Ask him again."

Johnson and his friend Craig turned to stand on the boardwalk in front of Lightfoot. Johnson stomped his feet up and down a couple of times and the red horse jerked his head up with ears pricked forward.

"When's it going to stop raining around here?" Johnson yelled loud enough so that some folks across the street turned to look back in our direction.

Lightfoot huffed, hip-shot his right rear leg and lowered his head again.

"He heard me that time, pay up." Johnson held out his hand to the old gentleman, palm up.

Grumbling, the old man said, "Well he was doin' it a little bit ago. Say, there's the cowboy that rode in on 'im. He'll show you the horse understands what you're sayin'."

The two hard cases turned to look at me and I just grinned and shrugged my shoulders.

"Don't think he feels much like talkin' right now," I said.

The two of them looked a little puzzled and Craig was scratching his head which made his hat fall off onto the board walk. While he bent over to pick it up, Johnson said to me.

"That your nag?"

"Yeah, Lightfoot's a might sensitive about being called names though, he's probably miffed at you for calling him one. I'd bet that's why he's not talking to you."

"Miffed at me! What the hell is that?"

"Peeved, Pee-ohed, upsetted, provoked, take your pick."

"I don't believe that crow-bait knows his ass from a hole in the ground, and I am beginning to suspect that you and the old codger here are in cahoots tryin' to bilk folks into thinking he does. Here's my twenty, let's see you make him talk."

"Nah, I got better things to do than tryin' to convince you mental giants that my hoss is smarter than the two of you put together. Let me have a word or two with him and then you can pay off the old timer there."

I turned to look at Lightfoot while Johnson and Craig stood scowling at me. I could see they figured there was some kind of an affront in what I had just said but were having a hard time wrestling it out into the light of day.

"Lightfoot," I said, "Are you deliberately ignoring these two town characters?"

Lightfoot nodded his head up and down.

"Did you hear the man's question?"

Again, the horse nodded his head.

"Well, are you going to answer him?"

Lightfoot shook his head, rattling his bridle.

"Why not?"

Lightfoot nickered low in his throat and fixed a malevolent stare on Johnson and Craig.

"You think he owes you an apology for calling you a nag?" I said.

Lightfoot once again bobbed his head up and down.

I turned to the men on the porch. "Lightfoot won't answer you until you tell him you're sorry for calling him a nag."

"What!"

251

"You called my horse a nag, he won't answer your question about the rain until you offer your apologies," I said.

"That's a crock of horse manure and you know it. I ain't a-gonna apologize to no dumb an-i-mile, I don't care if you can talk to him or not," Johnson said.

"Ha!" the old man hooted. "So, you admit the horse was answering him, just like I said. I'll take my ten bucks, thank you very much."

I grinned at the old-timer as he danced around on the porch while holding out his hand to Johnson. His eyes were sparkling in triumph.

Johnson had had all he could take. He grabbed the old man by the front of his bib overalls, and began to man-handle him, jerking him back and forth and yelling, "Give me my ten dollars, you toothless wonder, before I break your scrawny neck."

"Hey," I said and stepped up behind Johnson gripping him by the shoulder. "Pick on somebody your own size."

Johnson whirled about, an angry snarl curling his lips and said, "Why you snot-nosed kid, I'll break you of suckin' eggs."

I never sucked an egg in my life, so I plowed a dou-bled-up fist into his mid-section. The breath left his lungs with a whoosh and he stumbled back. His eyes grew round and with an angry roar he rushed at me trying to grab me in a bear hug. I stepped back quickly and stuck out a booted foot that tripped the bigger man as he thundered past. Johnson hit the muddy boardwalk on hands and knees and slid to a stop. Lunging to his feet, the bigger man went for his gun but mine was already in my hand.

A startled look came over the bully's face as he stared down the bore of my .44. Slowly his hand relaxed and he let his pistol drop back into the holster.

"Hell, I ain't going up against no gunslinger," he said. "You some kind of Billy the Kid?"

"Nope, you should just treat old folks better than this, give the old fellow his ten bucks."

The other man, Craig, had been standing silently by the whole time watching, but now he said, "Pay the man, Johnson, we'll go get the rest of the boys and come back. Maybe *Billy* here and his horse will have a different tune to sing then."

I watched as the two of them trudged off in the mud and then turned to the old timer who stood looking after them with a thin-lipped grimace and shaking his head.

"Wal, sonny, I reckon the rocks hit the outhouse now."

Sonny, there it was again and for a moment I was at a loss for words, but then recovered myself. "You mean them two?" I said, "They're crazier than a run over coon. What are you going to do with that ten bucks?"

The old man grinned, "Why, I reckon it'll keep me in beers for a while, but you shouldn't be too quick to write Craig and Johnson off, they head up a gang of ruffians and thieves and do a lot of bullying round town. They are likely to come back and stir up some hate and discontent."

"Well, why doesn't the sheriff do something about them?" I asked.

"Ezra W. Kingsbury?" he said, "Huh, ever since he beat out Wild Bill for the job back in '68 he's been too busy with his *Lady Godiva Saloon* to do much sheriffin'."

"Wha'd you say your name is?"

"Barnaby P. Bingham, Barney to my friends."

"Pecos is my handle, nice to meet cha'," and I stuck out my hand. "The ninety day wonder there's Lightfoot."

"I heard you call him that, he's quite a horse."

I laughed out loud and Lightfoot curled his lip and gave us both a horse laugh. Barney joined in and when we had all calmed down a bit, I said, "Now wait a minute... you mean to tell me that this Kingsbury actually beat out Wild Bill Hickok for sheriff of this town?"

"That's right and we've regretted it ever since," Bingham said, "He'd never done it if it wasn't for the *Lady Godiva.*"

"Lady Godiva, wasn't she some naked lady back in England a couple hundred years ago?"

"That's right, she was the wife of some Earl who imposed taxes on his tenants and she opposed him by riding through town in protest with nothing on except her hair for a covering. It seems this Kingsbury is a direct descendant of those folks and he's made capital on the legend by opening the *Lady Godiva Saloon.* He has a nek-ked saloon gal ride a white horse down Main Street with nothing on but her long hair. He advertises this at the train station and supposedly she is conducting tours of the town, but they always seem to end up at his saloon. It's been a big hit with the sojer boys on leave from the Fort, and now with the Texas cowboys coming up the trail. It made him real popular for the vote back in '68."

"You'd think the city fathers wouldn't allow such goings-on," I said.

Barney shrugged, "What can they do? He's the sheriff."

I nodded in resignation and then said, "Barn, you seem like a decent enough sort, have you ever thought about saving your money?"

Barney seemed confused, "Save it for what?"

"Oh, I don't know, this seems like a booming place, maybe you could invest it."

"Invest it? Invest it in what?"

I was thinking this old gent was just going to guzzle up that ten bucks and maybe I could steer him on a more constructive path, have him buy some property instead of drinking the money away. "You could buy a lot, it would probably take more'n ten dollars, but I'll bet you could get a little lot for around a hundred."

Barnaby Bingham looked bewildered. "What do you mean? A lot to buy little or a lot to buy ah…a lot, which is it?"

"A lot of land," I said, "It would be a good investment."

"What would I do with a lot of land?"

"You don't want a lot?" I asked. "The way this towns growing it might be worth some money someday."

"Well, sure I want a lot, but ten bucks ain't hardly going to buy a lot."

"If you had ten times ten bucks that'd buy one."

"One? I thought you said it would buy a lot."

I could see that Mr. Bingham was having trouble understanding what I was driving at and I began to get a clearer picture as to why he spent so much time perched on this bench in front of the grocery. It had been a while since I had anyone but Lightfoot to talk to, so I decided to pursue this conversation and see just where it might lead.

"It would," I went on, "it could buy one lot."

"One lot? You're not making much sense, Pecos, which is it, one or a lot?"

Now this was getting fun. "Barn, I'm talking about a parcel, a parcel is a lot."

The old man took his hat off and scratched his head. "You're tellin' me a parcel is a lot? How much?"

I'm chuckling now but tryin' not to let him see me. "One," I said with a blank poker face.

"One parcel is a lot?"

"Yes, usually."

"One is not a lot," he said in exasperation and threw up his hands. "Two is not even a lot, it takes more than that to have a lot, a lot more."

"Not if it's a lot. Now you take that there ten dollars there and salt it away in a coffee can and when you get some more you save that too, then you could buy a little lot."

"Little lot? There ain't no such thing as a little lot."

"Sure, there is, there are lots of little lots for sale on the edge of town."

"Now just a dad-burn minute. A little is a little and a lot is a lot but there's no lots that's little and no little that's lots, don't 'cha see?"

"Barney, you're making my head hurt. You could save your money and after a bit you could buy one of those little lots."

"Wal, I'm sure I could, but a lot of what, a lot of parcels?"

"No, just one parcel."

"I told you, one parcel's not a lot."

"Sure, it is, one parcel and one lot are the same thing."

"I'm beginning to think you've been grazing in a loco weed patch, son. There's no way one parcel, or one of anything else can be called a lot, and I sure ain't going to be saving my ten bucks for a whole lot of nothing," Barnabas said in frustration, "Now I'm going to go over to the *Lady Godiva,* and get me a lot of little cold beers and you're welcome to come along if you like, and I'm going to forget you ever said anything about saving up for a lot of nothing."

"You go ahead, Barn, I need to stop over at the hardware store and pick up a few things for the trail before I head out. You take care now," I said, chuckling.

"Yeah, you too, keep your head low, that Craig 'n' Johnson outfit'll be lookin' to pin your ears back."

The old man got up and hurried off up the street as though he was glad to be shut of my company. Grinning, I gave Lightfoot a wink and turned to head for the hardware. Lightfoot gave me a look, shook his head and snorted, then turned to stare off after Barnabas P. Brigham as though he considered the whole human race a lost cause.

After I picked up a tarp at the hardware I decided to go over to the dry-goods store and buy a clean shirt and jeans. My black outfit was some frayed around the edges and I figured there was no need of attracting undue attention after Johnson's mistaking me for a gunfighter. I didn't need that kind of notoriety. Once I picked up the clothes, I figured it wouldn't hurt to get my old duds washed so I stopped in at a Chinese laundry and then helped myself to a hot bath while I was waiting for my wash. It felt mighty good to soak in the hot water and I kept the little Chinaman busy hauling more of it while I relaxed. Finally, I got out, dried off and went over to collect my groceries and get stuff packed onto Lightfoot. By the time that chore was finished and I had endured several uncomplimentary snorts and grumblings from my horse, I went back and picked up my clean clothes.

It had started to rain again so I led Lightfoot in under the overhanging porch of the feed store and worked my clean duds into the saddle bags and then covered the whole affair with my new tarp. Lightfoot's objection that I looked more like a Yankee peddler and he like a plow-mule went largely ignored as I snubbed him off to the hitching rail. After securing a bag of the gold I had brought out of Mexico, I set off to the bank to convert it into cash.

There were a number of heads turned to watch us, as I followed a short balding man into an inner office where he weighed out twenty-four and a half ounces troy of the gold I had and gave me five thousand dollars in green-backs. He offered to keep them in his safe for me until I left town, but I declined his offer and headed back for my horse. I was anxious to leave town as it was already past noon. Next I went to the railroad express office and wired four thousand dollars to Wade's Landing, Texas, for my folks. The rest of the money I kept for trailing.

When I stepped out of the express office, I stopped. Several rough-looking hombres were sitting their saddles and had my cowpony surrounded. I could see Craig and Johnson among them. It looked like the hate and discontent that Bingham had spoken of was about to bubble to the surface like last year's swamp gas.

They hadn't noticed me yet, probably looking for some fella in a black Billy the Kid outfit, so I sidled off the porch towards the river and slipped over the embankment down to where the willows grew. It was my intention to get back behind some buildings unnoticed and see if I could wait out the gang. It was still raining and I figured no matter how much of a mad they had on, some of them would get tired pretty soon and head for more comfortable diggings.

I was ducking around and through the willows trying not to get too wet when my hand grabbed a branch that produced an angry buzzing sound. Quickly I let go and stepped back. Attached to that branch was a hornet's nest the size of a man's head. One or two hornets buzzed out and flew around me for a few moments, but I just held my breath and prayed they wouldn't sense my fear. In a few moments, the hornets returned to the nest and got in out of the rain. I breathed a sigh of relief. Then an idea hit me. I remembered a story from Sunday School when God used hornets to defeat Israel's enemies and I figured if it worked back then, it might just bail me out of a tight situation now. I was somewhat annoyed with Johnson and Craig, and a part of me wanted to walk back up there with my guns a blazing and send them hightailing it, but I didn't think any of their so-called offenses were worth killing anybody over... still, maybe I could introduce them to these hornets and sort of accomplish the same thing.

Stooping down, I picked up a wad of mud, rolled it between my fingers until it took the shape of a plug and then carefully and swiftly plugged the entrance hole to the nest. There was a wild buzzing and the nest bobbled up and down on the branch while I ducked for cover and watched to see if any hornets flew out. It looked like my plug was holding so I drew my knife and carefully sliced off the branch a foot or so below the hive, and then holding it out away from me, I climbed back up the bank to the muddy street.

"Hey!" I hollered, "You boys looking for me?"

Startled, the riders jerked erect and turned to see who was calling. When they recognized me, they turned their horses and the whole bunch of them came splashing through the puddles towards where I stood, Johnson and Craig in the front.

I waited, my right hand holding their big surprise out of sight behind my back. The riders drew up about twenty feet from me, and Craig said in a rough voice. "Young bucko, I don't know who you think you are, but me and the boys here figure you're a little too uppity for your own good and we're going to whittle you down to size."

I was feeling some nervous for there were eight of them and I only had a six-shooter and the range was a might close for a lot of bullets flying around; besides that, the hornets weren't getting any more sociable from the sounds of them in my little surprise package. I wasn't sure how long it would take before one of their scouts found a way out and onto my backside. I didn't really want to shoot anybody over a lot of nonsense either, but it was plain these boys had been bulling their way through the herd for far too long and it looked like it had fallen on me to haul them up short. I pasted on my most insolent smile.

"How you and this pack of meat-heads plan on doing that?" I scoffed.

An evil grin spread across Craig's face, "First we'll hog tie ya and then drag your smart ass through this mud until you look like an Arkansas shoat and then hang you upside down to dry by the fire until the mud has baked some of that sassy tongue out of ya."

"What you gonna do if I shoot you out of your saddle first?"

"Hell kid, you can't shoot us all."

"Well, no, but I can sure shoot you and Johnson there and probably two or three more of those other baboons before I'm out of bullets."

259

"Yeah, and we will shoot you to rags in the meantime," Johnson put in.

"I don't care, go ahead and shoot me, but plan on making the trip with me, you big tub of guts."

The two gang leaders seemed to be stymied at this announcement. Seldom if ever had they been challenged in their bullying of people, but here was a devil-may-care kid standing up to the whole bunch of them, and he appeared to be holding something behind his back. He had the tied-down holster of a gunfighter and it was starting to occur to the whole bunch of them that this kid may be dangerous as a hydrophobic skunk.

"He's got something behind his back," Johnson whispered hoarsely to Craig.

"I know it—shut up." Craig gritted through his teeth, then in a louder voice he said to me, "What you holding behind your back?"

I just gave him a big toothy grin and said, "This!" and I carefully withdrew the hornet's nest and held it up for all of them to get a good look. "I brought this along to liven up the party and I want you all to have it." Then I hurled the hornet's nest up over the heads of the whole bunch of them, drew my pistol and put two quick shots through the spiraling missile. The heavy slugs ripped through the paper-mâché of the nest, tearing it apart and spilling angry hornets all over the outlaws. After that, all I had to do was step back under the porch of a nearby building and enjoy the show.

I watched until the last of the gang disappeared up the street with the angry hornets in hot pursuit, then turned and made my way over to where Lightfoot stood looking like some homeless tramp with my stuff piled all over him. I dug the stirrup out from under a gunny sack, put my foot in it and attempted to swing up over the pile and get into the saddle. I couldn't do it; my leg wouldn't reach that high. Lightfoot began to dance about and then my muddy boot slipped out of the stirrup and I landed back on the ground. If I hadn't been holding on I'd a landed on my butt in the mud.

"Hold still you jackass," I snapped.

Lightfoot laid his ears back and he got that look in his eye... the same one he'd had back on the Clearwater in the Palo Duro. I swallowed a couple times and said, "Alright, sorry 'bout the name calling."

Lightfoot snorted his acceptance of what we both knew was a lame apology and stopped fidgeting. I knew he hated me loading him down with all the travel gear; he was a high-stepping, free-and-easy spirit, and I could tell he was wondering why I just didn't go and get a pack horse. It wasn't like I didn't have the dinero.

"Well, I guess I could go and get a pack animal," I said. Lightfoot shook his whole body, rattling the saddle and my pack goods so I figured he was in agreement.

I led the horse over to the livery stable and asked the man if he had a good pack animal for sale. He showed me some mules and a few broke-down pack horses showing white hair patches from previous saddle-sores. He told me I could have my pick for twenty bucks. I saw a husky bay gelding that had good bottom and told the livery man I'd take him.

The man said, "That horse will cost you a hundred dollars, he's packed for Custer in the Indian wars and is battle wizened.

I said, "I ain't planning on no Indian wars or any other kind for that matter. Here's fifty dollars and you can throw in a pack saddle."

"Huh, where do you think you are, downtown Kansas City? For fifty dollars, you can have one of these others and maybe a used pack saddle."

I learned a long time ago that the quickest way for a man to double his money was to fold it over and stick it back in his pocket, so I shook my head and turned to leave, but that danged Lightfoot balked and butted me with his head until I turned around and made the deal with the owlhoot posing as a livery man. I got the horse and pack outfit, but it did cost me the full hundred. When I left, the stable man was counting his money and grinning like a jackass eating cactus.

Two days later I was nearing Fort Hays. It was along towards evening and I decided to pitch camp near the river and fix a nice supper, turn in early and get a jump start on the day, come morning. I found a grassy spot surrounded by cottonwoods and willows with a big, dead-fall tree that would provide abundant camp wood. It was high enough above the river so that the ample rain we had been getting wasn't likely to sweep me and my blankets downstream. Soon I had the horses picketed on the grass, the tarp tented over a rope stretched between a tree and a pole, and a small but cheery fire burning. Canned green beans, a couple of roasted bratwurst, some fried spuds, onions and bell peppers, all made a tasty meal along with some bread and butter, and hot coffee to wash it all down. I finished up and was just sitting on a chunk of wood by the fire, eating an apple and thinking about getting up and scrubbing out the frying pan when movement caught my eye.

I looked up towards a long rolling hill that was just across the river and thought I saw a light over there. It was hard to make it out, but looked like someone or something was moving along the crest of the hill in a funny kind of blue light. It was puzzling, I had never seen a light like that, pale blue and moving along like something floating on water. I watched it for awhile until it finally disappeared behind the brush on the opposite side of the river. I waited for it to reappear but saw nothing so finally got up, gathered up my few dishes and made my way down to the water and cleaned them up.

"That was a funny light," I said to myself. "Never saw one quite like that. Didn't look like someone was carrying it or that it was jouncing along on a wagon, there was no up and down movement. It just floated along, I wonder what it was?" I went back to camp, washed up, scrubbed my teeth with a toothbrush I'd got back in Ellsworth and went to bed.

Sleep didn't always come easy for me these days, there were still way too many memories that would rumble to the front of my mind the minute I tried to disengage from the present and find some rest. Memories of a big-eyed girl, memories of those blue eyes registering shock and the soul-numbing memory of the light going out of those same big eyes. There was the other too, that of a tall lean cowboy with an infectious, lop-sided grin and a ready tongue that always had a final quip to say. What had I done? I chased the mice of regret and bitterness, sadness and shame in my mind until I finally dozed off into a fitful sleep.

I woke in the early hours of the morning and lay for a moment in confusion while firelight danced on the ceiling of my tent. I couldn't put my finger on what had awakened me, but then realized that my campfire had flared up and was burning brightly. I sat up in bed alarmed and reached for my six-gun. Somebody was out there putting fuel on the fire. First I thought of Indians, but then realized that was highly unlikely with me practically in the very shadow of Fort Hays. I wondered if Craig and Johnson had gone to the trouble of tracking me down.

What in the world? First I saw the long flowing ruffle of a woman's skirt, then a trim young lady clad in a long flowing blue dress, a knit blue shawl and a stylish white bonnet. She stooped to put another stick of wood on the fire, then took a seat opposite my position and sat staring into the flame.

I sat mesmerized for a moment studying her features. She seemed young and had a pretty face, though her face was somewhat shrouded by the bonnet. She looked up and stared at me and her eyes were like nothing I've ever seen before, like blue ice and they seemed to see right into the very core of my being. Totally unnerved, I sat there, helpless under her gaze.

"Suzanne and Sonny are looking for you," she said.

Her words hit me like a thunderbolt and I fell back in my blankets, my mind scrambling to wrap around what she had just said. Quickly I sat back up and blurted out, "What did you say?" But there was no one there. Frantically, I scrambled from my blankets and crawled to the entrance of my shelter. I saw the blue lady lit up in an eerie blue light gliding across the river above the water without touching it. I heard Lightfoot snort and I looked over at my horse. Both he and the new pack horse stood staring after the apparition, their ears pricked forward and nostrils flaring, testing the wind. I was not the only one to see the blue lady.

CHAPTER SIXTEEN

Bodalk Inago—The Buffalo Man

Chief White Bear's Encampment, Late December 1870

SONNY HAD A PROBLEM. HE HAD MADE good his escape, but his outfit and Hank were left back in the Kiowa camp. If he was to continue the search for his brother, he would need the mule. Reigning Tornado in, Sonny urged his horse down the shallow embankment to the stream and into the water. Once there, he pulled the stallion up and listened for any pursuit. Off in the distance he could hear the Indians yelling and making war cries. It was obvious that some of them were already mounted and following his trail. He clucked to the horse and urged the animal into a slow walk back up towards the encampment, while holding to the brushy cover of the stream bed. "The one thing these redskins don't expect me to do is head back into their village," he muttered.

He had last seen Hank tethered with some ponies to a patch of willow, not far from one of the central cooking fires. Sonny's pack had been pulled from the mule and carried over by the fire area and its contents gone through. With any luck his stuff and the animal would still be there, hopefully unattended.

About twenty yards from the circle of lodges, Sonny stopped his horse and dismounted. He quietly tied Tornado to a bush and crept up to peer over the bank at the camp. Good, Hank was there and so was the pack. He heard quite a lot of noise off in the distance and it appeared as though the whole camp had gone out to witness the warriors chase the Buffalo Man. There were sounds of some of the people coming back and he knew he must hurry for it would not take the Indians long to discover he had doubled back upstream. Hanging his hat on his saddle horn and slinging his gunbelt around his hips, he pulled his shirt off and draped it over the saddle. He paused momentarily to finger the Snakeman medallion hanging around his neck. For reasons never clear to him, he continued to wear it. Perhaps he would one day show Colt the damaged piece with the spent slug in it. For now, a handful of mud smeared on his chest and face, while naked to the waist, may cause anyone looking from a distance to see him as just another Indian of the camp. The medallion would lend itself to the allusion.

Sonny stood and walked boldly up from the creek bed to where his pack lay. Squatting, he began to place items of his gear back into the panniers and then picking up one of the boxes, he carried it back to the cover of the brush along the water. He returned for the second box and made it back without discovery, then went to the mule. Hank recognized him and began a raucous braying until Sonny pinched his muzzle and told him, "Quiet down." The pack saddle lay in a heap and the cowboy hefted it onto the mule's back, then cinched it down while keeping Hank between him and the rest of the encampment. Turning, he took the lead and led Hank down to where he'd left the packs. He put his shirt back on and was just finishing securing the last pannier to the sawbuck when there was the noise of running horses. Hurriedly he led the mule to where his horse was tied, but when he reached Tornado he was too late. A band of Kiowa braves had him encircled, each holding a lance or rifle pointed in his direction.

Sonny was herded back into the circle of teepees, along with his animals and brought back in front of White Bear's lodge. Satanta stood with arms folded across his chest, his face a dark thundercloud of anger.

"Buffalo Man make sport of the People," he said.

"The dark horse is mine," Sonny said simply. "The test proved that, I merely took him and went on my way."

"Not good you go—I no say go."

Sonny just shrugged, "I understood that if I won it was my chance to leave, so I took it."

"Buffalo Man not to be trusted, must die."

Kicking Bird stepped between White Bear and Sonny. "Buffalo Man's heart is true," he said.

"No, Kicking Bird. White man's heart is false, him leave, he bring back blue coats to hidden camp."

"I am trying to find my brother," Sonny said. I haven't the time to go looking for the soldier boys."

Kicking Bird nodded his head slowly, "Yes, he look for the one with Cain mark, me help."

"You no help Buffalo Man," Satanta said loudly. "Buffalo Man no leave, him die by fire."

Kicking Bird scowled at his chief. "I make promise to help if him come—make peace talk, my word is true."

"You talk against council of your chief, speak malo talk. I have spoken, him die, you must stand aside."

Kicking Bird's face grew angry, "You shame Kicking Bird in front of the People. I challenge White Bear's word—it is a bad word."

"You have the bad heart of the white-eyes and betray your people, this not way of Gaigwu," Satanta said.

"White Bear does not see as Kicking Bird," the lesser chief said, turning to the gathered crowd of Indians. "His vision is little," and he held up his hand with thumb and forefinger close together to illustrate. "Soon the blue coats will come and force the people onto the reservations to eat the white-man's beef and take all the buffalo for themselves. It is best we sit at their council fires and treat for good hunting grounds and for our own buffalo."

At this open defiance, Satanta grasped a lance from a nearby warrior and stabbed it into the back of the lesser chief, driving the point through his body to where it protruded out of the front.

"No!" Sonny yelled as blood gurgled from the lean Indian's lips and he fell forward to his knees.

"Tell me his name," Kicking Bird gasped to Sonny.

"His name?" Sonny was puzzled.

"Your friend—Son of Great Spirit."

"Jesus, his name is Jesus."

For a moment Kicking Bird stared wildly at the young cowboy, his lips flecked with blood, and choked out, "Jesus," then his eyes glazed over and he toppled forward onto his face in the dust.

White Bear pointed a finger at the cowboy. "Take Buffalo Man captive, prepare him for the stake. Kicking Bird had the heart of a woman and was too timid to make war with the white-eyes. We will fight for our lands and our people."

Sonny was incredulous at this grave injustice done to probably the only friend the white man had with the Kiowa. A well thrown war club then struck him a resounding blow on the back of the head, lights exploded and he felt himself sinking into deep blackness.

A cold rain was falling, chilling him, and Sonny felt himself being handled, stripped naked, and drug along over rough muddy ground. In his dazed condition, he was having difficulty recalling where he was or what was going on. Eventually he was bound to a post and, shivering in the cold, he lost consciousness.

The Buffalo Man presented a doleful picture to the watching Indians and a gleeful Medicine Man danced a confusing pattern about this so-called shaman with the buffalo spirit. Black Claw, for that was what the Medicine Man was called, continued singing weird and strange enchantments as he danced about while some warriors drug up brush and logs to arrange them about the white man's feet. It was plain to the watching villagers that the Medicine Man saw this capture and destruction of the Buffalo Man as a significant victory over the hated white men and a potent display of the medicine of the Kiowa camp in general and of Black Claw specifically. Drums had started up and the Medicine Man's dance became more frenzied as did his chanting and howling until he was leaping about in impossible angles, his body contorted and glistening in the falling rain.

Suddenly the drums stopped and Black Claw dropped into a crouch, hissing like a snake while shaking a gourd rattle at the prisoner. Two warriors with torches were attempting to light the brush pyre with little success as the rain was increasing in intensity. It was at this point that Sonny regained consciousness. Quickly his mind focused on his plight and he realized his doom, that short of a miracle this could spell the end of the so-called Buffalo Man. Remembering Colt's tale of encounter with these same Indians, he gave a heartfelt cry of desperation and called on the name of the Lord.

"In the name of Jesus I command that you stop this savage outrage immediately!"

All went silent, with only the crouching Black Claw glaring and hissing like some other-worldly creature, then one of the torches finally caught the pyre and blazed up. There was a cackle of triumph and the Medicine Man resumed his leaping and crazed chanting while a loud collective shout of approval broke out amongst the watching Indians. Soon the second torch took hold and the light from the blaze fully illuminated the doomed Buffalo Man as his face lifted towards the sky calling to his God. In fascination, the on-looking villagers watched to see their enemy die, but sometimes the simplest things can bring unexpected triumphs, and for Sonny it began to rain harder.

Two things happened, as the rain turned to a downpour; first, it began to wash the mud and grime from Sonny's upper torso until at last the Snake-Man medallion became visible to the watchers as it dangled about his neck, and secondly the rain prevented the brush pyre from catching and burning the Buffalo Man. To the astonishment of those watching, the fire dwindled and went out.

In a very real imitation of a wounded crow with a broken wing, Black Claw hopped over to the bound white man and, reaching out with a crow's foot, he hooked the claw behind the medallion's thong and pulled it over the Buffalo Man's head. He dropped the foot and rattle and clutched the medallion in both hands, studying it closely. When he discerned the silver snake image with the lead bullet embedded in its center, he let out a piercing scream and rushed to where the group of chiefs stood and passed the trinket to White Bear. The head chief examined it and wondered at the significance of its being in the possession of the Buffalo Man. He handed it to Sitting Bear, who then handed it to Big Tree, while all the while Black Claw was jabbering on about the medicine of the Bodalk Inago as a part of the Buffalo Man.

Sonny's head drooped and his eyes closed as the last of the flames were extinguished. It looked like once again that fool ornament Colt had given him had saved him from certain death. He felt rough hands loose his bounds and a warm buffalo robe placed around his shoulders. The medallion was replaced around his neck while curious fingers traced the pattern the medallion had imprinted in his chest when Colton's bullet had struck it there. With conciliatory tones, his captors led him to a place inside a warm tepee where more soft robes and a hot broth were given to him. It was with awe and wonder that the Kiowa clan of White Bear began to grasp the magnitude with which the Comanche regarded the Buffalo Man and his medicine.

———

Frenchy pulled up with an angry scowl and turned in his saddle to look back at the lumbering hide wagon of the buffalo hunters. He figured they were two days before they reached town. It had taken well over a month to travel through the Indian Nations; the hide hunters were ridiculously slow, plodding along as though they had all the time in the world. He was becoming extremely fed up with their insults and bullying. Soon he would put an end to it all and get on with the business of finding Saber and settling accounts. It had been awhile since he had spent any time in a town and he was looking forward to getting some action in Dodge or Abilene. He had cleaned out both Waistman and Kemp of their hide earnings a couple of weeks ago, and thereby had earned their enduring scorn. The fact that they had continued to gamble with him each evening using his share of camp chores as stakes, had only further infuriated the two buffalo hunters, for he easily cheated them on that score as well, and was now enjoying a free ride at the two hunters' expense. He had a growing suspicion that the two were plotting against him and deliberately delaying the journey. To what purpose, he did not know.

"I'd like to throttle that slippery Frenchman," Sylvester Kemp said.

"A little longer now, and we will fix 'im for good," Buff Waistman replied.

"Hell, what are we waitin' for? I could easily drop 'im from here with this buffalo gun."

"Yeah, and who knows who'd be watchin' out here in the open. Just hang on, soon we'll be near town and we can cash in his chip. We'll want to turn in his carcass for the reward."

"If I have to hand that smiling faced frog one more cup of coffee, I'm liable to cut his throat instead."

"Sly, think about it a minute. He's got all that loot he brought with him along with our money. Have patience, man, it's all ours for the takin'. One of these times while he's sleepin' the deed will be yours to do. Meanwhile, keep your temper simmering on the back of the stove and don't give anything away."

An hour later, Buff pulled the wagon to a halt alongside of where Frenchy sat his horse at the top of a long rolling hill with a trail that led down into a section of jumbled cut-banks, canyons, and arroyos. "Ah, Monsieurs, looks like we will have to unravel zee trail through rough country, no?"

"Just more stuff to slow us down, and make it harder to watch out for Injuns," Waistman groused.

"Speakin' of Injuns," Kemp said, "Lookee yonder over there, is that smoke I see?"

The three travelers turned to study a plume of smoke that Kemp was pointing to. About a mile away it was obvious someone had a camp, and it looked to be ahead on this trail.

"Kemp, you stay with the wagon," Buff said and handed him the reins. "Me'n Frenchy will ride on ahead and scout out the trail. The last thing we want to do is bust in on some Injun war party."

"Oui, it is a good idea," Frenchy said.

Buffalo Waistman got off the wagon and mounted one of the horses and rode him around to where the

Frenchman waited. "If we are not back in an hour, you come hauling ass down this trail with guns a ready."

A quarter of an hour later Frenchy and Buff pulled up their horses and tied them to some willows off the trail. They crept forwards to a low knoll between them and where the smoke of the campfire was.Peering over the top from the concealment of brush they made out the remains of a camp, the fire pit still smoldering.

"Looks like whoever was here has moved on," Buff said.

"Oui, but what a fine place to camp," Frenchy said.

It was a beautiful little sylvan glade complete with a babbling brook and good grass. Signs of wild game were in abundance and at Frenchy's suggestion the two agreed to make camp here for the night. Frenchy would rustle up more camp wood while Buff went looking for some wild game for supper. They would wait for Kemp's arrival, make a long evening of it and rest up before pushing on tomorrow.

Grumpily, Sly Kemp got down from the wagon and started hauling out the cooking gear.

"How come we're camping so early? There's plenty of daylight left."

Buff looked up from the two sage hens he was dressing and grinned. "It's too good a spot to pass up," he said.

"How do you know it wasn't Injuns who were camped here and that they mightn't come back?"

"Oh, no monsieur, the Indian would never leave zee fire burning," Frenchy said. "Besides it es much too close to town, they won't be back."

"You better drop on your knees and pray to God they don't."

An evil light flickered in Frenchy's eyes and a snarl curled his lips. "Do not speak to me of God He does not exist and if He did, I would keel heem. I pray to no one."

"Aw, what the hell do you know about God?" Kemp groused. "There ain't no way you could kill God, He'd take you out just like that," and Sylvester snapped his fingers.

"One would theenk you would know better than to believe all this God-stuff." Frenchy said in scorn.

Sylvester Kemp gritted his teeth and muttered something decidedly uncomplimentary under his breath about the Frenchman and the latter's ears burned hot with anger at the rude allegation.

"Alright, you two," Buff said, "let's have no strife. We got us a purtty little place, some good sage hens and we'll have us a fine supper, maybe haul out the jug and get Frenchy to stake us on a card game after we eat. How about it, Frenchy, our credit any good?"

Frenchy gave a sly smile and nodded his head while Kemp looked up at him, his eyes glaring under lowered brow.

"Oui, oui, my friends, I am sure we can find some table stakes once you finish cooking and setting up the camp for me. In the meantime, I will roll out my blankets under that tree and take a little nap. Wake me when supper is ready."

The two buffalo hunters looked at each other and a silent signal passed between them. It was then that Sly Kemp understood this would be the Frenchman's last nap. Suddenly his spirits rose and he went about setting up camp while whistling a tune.

The hens had roasted to a golden brown over the hot coals of the fire and Buff was putting the final touches on some spuds and onions when Sly passed him back the jug. The two had been sipping whiskey for the past hour while taking surreptitious glances at their sleeping companion.

"When we gonna cool 'im?" Kemp whispered.

"Shh, in a minute. You sure he's asleep?"

"Yeah, heck, I been bangin' around here for the past hour and he ain't stirred nary a muscle."

"Let's make a clean job of it," Waistman said, "you take that wet towel and sneak over there and smother him with it while I hold him till he quits struggling."

"Good idea," Kemp leered evilly, "it's about time we shut him up."

Sylvester Kemp crept noiselessly towards the head of the sleeping gambler while Buff Waistman circled around towards his feet. They crawled to within striking distance on hands and knees until Kemp, grasping the wet towel in his hands, rose to clasp it over the sleeping victim's face.

"Now!" Waistman cried, and lunged to grab Frenchy's feet. Kemp reached to press the gag over the sleeping man's face, when suddenly there was a loud explosion and a pistol discharged from inside Frenchy's blankets, the heavy slug caught Waistman in the chest and knocked him over backwards. Almost instantaneously the Frenchman plunged a knife upward and backward, driving the point through the startled Kemp's neck. The stricken buffalo hunter rose to his feet with a gurgled yell, stumbled backwards and fell to rise no more. His companion likewise lay as silent as the quiet that once more settled into the little glen. Frenchy went through the buffalo hunters' belongings, rifling through their clothes and discovered the wanted poster on him that Waistman had concealed inside his coat. "So, et looks like there was zee method to your treachery, ah? It serves you right, you rotten skunks."

Having disposed of the buffalo hunters' wagon, team and outfit down at the wagon yard in Abilene, Frenchy stepped up on the boardwalk, pushed through the swinging doors of the "*Bull's Head Tavern*" and went in. It was his kind of place—loud music, a rowdy crowd and plenty of trail-rich cowboys to bilk out of their money. The next several days saw him gambling, but with always an ear to the ground for any information on Colt Saber.

———

The Hazelhurst party rumbled the bull wagon down the main street of Fort Griffin and pulled up at the wagon yard. The girls checked into the hotel, while Gareth Hazelhurst rode his black up Government Hill to report to the post commander and check for any wires from home.

The next day, while replenishing supplies at Conrad & Rath's trading post, Suzanne noticed a pretty dark-haired girl addressed as Miss Elizabeth by one of the patrons of the store and waiting until the clerk was not busy, she approached her.

"Miss Elizabeth?" she said.

"Yes," Elizabeth said.

"You don't know me, but my name is Suzanne Kluesman of Wade's Landing, Texas. I wonder if you would take a look at this hand bill I have?"

Suzanne dug from her bag a copy of the handbill she had on Colton while Elizabeth looked on with interest. "Do you recognize this man?"

Elizabeth Boyle studied the picture for a moment and then said guardedly, "Why do you want to know?"

"This man is Colton Saber, my fiancé, and we are trying to find him. Was he here in the company of a young girl by the name of Pearl, Pearl Harmon?"

"Pearl, you know Pearl? Is she alright?"

"Yes, Pearl is fine, she is with Colt's parents and they are taking good care of her. What can you tell me about Colt? I believe he went by the name Woody when he was here."

"Yes, Woody was here. He spent the winter cutting wood for the army and signed on a month ago with a cattle outfit headed for Kansas. Are you the girl that so haunted his dreams?"

"I'm afraid so."

"What happened between you two?" Elisabeth asked.

"It's a long story. If you are allowed a lunch break, I can buy you a cup of tea at the hotel and tell it to you."

"I would like that," Elizabeth said.

The two of them spent a long hour in which Suzanne confided in Elizabeth the story of hers and Colton's great love and of its tragic end, at least to this point. It seemed to help, to share her story with this sensitive young woman who had known Colt, albeit only briefly. Sharing with her and hearing Colt had been there seemed to draw her and Elizabeth close, kindred spirits of sorts, and when they parted Suzanne promised to keep Elizabeth informed as to the outcome of her search for the man they both knew was adrift, wandering aimlessly and looking for he knew not what.

CHAPTER SEVENTEEN

Colorado Goldfields

Smokey Hill Trail, Kansas, May 1871

THE HAIR WAS STICKING STRAIGHT OUT ON the back of my neck as I gazed back across the river. The blue light lady could no longer be seen. Lightfoot rattled his headstall and when I looked back at him, both he and the pack horse were looking in my direction as if to say, "Well?" I noted the pack horse was right alongside Lightfoot, his head reaching over the sorrel's withers, and the both of them looking at me like a couple of school boys that had just watched the burning of the school house.

"Don't look at me," I said. "I don't believe in ghosts."

Both of the horses bobbed their heads up and down and just kept looking in my direction. It was the craziest thing I ever saw. It was as if they knew what I refused to believe, and that got me to thinking that my crazy horse and his goofy sidekick were convinced that the blue light lady had been here. What did I even know about ghosts? I hadn't ever really thought about it much. Oh sure, I had heard things go bump in the night but always figured there was a good explanation for it: the wind blowing over a bucket, the cat out on the porch knocking over the broom, but this thing was a full-blown, wide awake experience that not only I saw, but my horses did too.

So, what were ghosts anyway? Disembodied spirits, the souls of the dead, fallen angels—demons? My theology was pretty sketchy along these lines and although the Bible had plenty to say about it, I guess I never took it much to heart. Jesus had told Thomas to touch him that time in the upper-room where they had all been hiding out after his resurrection. He had appeared to the disciples and said, "Touch me and see that it is I, for a spirit does not have flesh and bone as I do." For the first time, I saw that Jesus was acknowledging something about spirits—ghosts. If He acknowledged there was such a thing, then there must be. He had many encounters with unclean spirits—was there such a thing as a clean spirit—and if so, who or what were they, and who or what was this blue lady I had just seen? I'd heard about angels unawares, was she one of them?

I lay back down on my blankets and stared up at the darkened ceiling of my canvas, but sleep was a long way off for me. What was it she had said, "Suzanne and Sonny are looking for you"? How could this lady—this ghost, know about them? Had the departed souls of my dead... no, murdered sweetheart and brother, sent her to haunt me for the foul deed I had done to them? Were my former sweetheart and older brother looking for me somewhere on the plains of heaven? Did she mean they were waiting for me to join them, and if so, what would be in store for me when and if I even got there. Once again, for the thousandth time, the enormity of what I had done rolled over me. In my mind's eye, I saw again the bullet I had fired in anger and despair plow into the chest of my older brother, saw it pass through him to strike my lovely Suzanne, saw that beautiful blue light in her eyes turn to shock and then glaze over in death. In one incredibly stupid moment of passion and rage, I had snuffed out the life of the two dearest people in my world, and it was these cold hard facts that I had been unable to reconcile to. It was still irreconcilable to me. This is what drove me, what I was running from, but I was having no success in escaping its reality, and life seemed to hold no real promise of sunshine or light or good days anymore. Maybe death awaited me on the trail ahead. Maybe I would be joining the searching souls of Suzanne and Sonny. There was a dark, sinister, almost macabre expectancy that sidled up to me and kept me company for the rest of the night.

Hays City, less than a mile away from the Fort, had sprung up as a railroad terminus for the Kansas Pacific and was a large staging center for the U.S. Army. Buffalo soldiers as well as, for a time, the 7th Calvary were bivouacked here and as many as six hundred troops were stationed here at various times. The town was not unlike Ellsworth for a reputation of being a wide open, wild-west cattle town. It had a large mix of cowboys, soldiers, prospectors and railroad men, along with the usual farmers and emigrants, and when I rode up the main street the next morning, I was more than happy to be swallowed up in the hustle and bustle of the place.

I was still feeling the melancholy of my ghostly visitor from the night before, and I could have sworn Lightfoot and Sidekick were carrying on a running conversation about it as we rode along. I decided Sidekick was a good name for my pack horse as he seemed to be filling that role with Lightfoot and I was glad to see the two animals had become buddies. It was trouble enough managing two horses on the trail without them being at each other's throats all the time. It was plain Lightfoot was the boss of the pair, and Sidekick seemed content to stand end-for-end in his shadow and enjoy the mutual fly-swatting benefit of their tails when not otherwise employed.

I rode past a storefront window and caught my reflection in the mirror and abstractly wondered who that scruffy looking character was with horses that looked like mine.

When I realized it was me, I couldn't believe my beard and hair had grown so long.

"Maybe I ought' a get my hair cut," I said out loud. "Wha-da-ya-think?"

Lightfoot and Sidekick ignored me, but then I rode up close to where a couple of little kids were playing in the street and they ran off crying after they'd got a good look at me.

"Well, that settles it, where's me a good barber shop?"

I eventually spotted one and, tying my animals to the hitching rack, I got down, dusted off my clothes with my hat and went on in to what turned out to be a two-seated barbering establishment. There were a couple of soldiers in the chairs and a thin hawkish looking gent with a soup-bowl haircut was giving one of them a shave. The other barber was clipping a black soldier's kinky curls in a close crop cut. He appeared to be a jovial fellow, short and balding with a pair of suspenders desperately trying to hold his britches up over a heavy belly.

I took a seat and sat down to wait my turn.

"Howdy, cowboy," the short barber said. "Be with you in a second."

I nodded and picked up a copy of the local paper and was letting my eyes run over the headlines when I overheard one of the soldiers mention that there had been a haunting again over by the Fort the night before. I was all ears.

"Yas, suh, Miss Elizabeth was out strollin' on Sentinel Hill again las night," the black man said.

"Aw, I don't believe that hog-wash about no Blue Light Lady wandering the hills east of the Fort." the thin barber said.

"Tis so, boss," the negro said. "She done lost her life nursin' the sojer boys back in the cholera epidemic of sixty-seben. [1]Miss Elizabeth Polly is her name. She nursed all dem dying sojers night 'n' day till she took sick herself and up and kicked de bucket, but not before she got dem to promise to bury her out top o' Sentinel Hill where she took de walks to gets away from all de sickness and dying and sech."

"I've heard it all before," the barber said. "I don't believe in ghosts."

"I don't know, Joe," the other barber said, "lots of folks claim to have seen her."

"You ever see her?" Joe asked.

"Well, no."

"How about you soldiers, either of you ever see her?"

The first soldier shook his head, but the black soldier said, "I ain't never seed her, but I's talked to plenty ob de boys who did. They say she trying to get her grave to the top ob de hill where they promised to bury her so's she can finally be to rest. They went and buried her at the bottom of Sentinel 'stead of de top cause the ground was too rocky up dere."

I was dumbfounded. Here was the mystery of the Blue Light Lady laid out before me without me having to say nary a word. I was wondering about speaking up when the skinny barber looked over at me and said, "How about you stranger, you ever hear such malarkey?"

I shrugged my shoulders and said, "No, can't say as I have, not leastwise before last night I hadn't, but when she came into my camp in the middle of the night and woke me up by fixin' my fire and then told me my former sweetheart and brother were looking for me, well you could of knocked me over with a feather."

You could have heard a pin drop in there, all eyes were on me. Old hawk nose was scratching his chin, the two soldiers were staring wide-eyed and the other barber's eyebrows seemed to be raised high enough to hold up the ceiling. Finally, the skeptic barber spoke.

"You shouldn't be spreading yarns around like that, son, it ain't Christian to be untruthful."

"You think I don't know that? Why even my horses saw her. You can't fool horses about stuff like that you know."

"Your what?" Joe said.

"My horses, my saddle horse and my pack horse. They both saw her the same as me, and they was watching her glide across the river, their ears pricked forwards and nostrils testing the wind for her scent."

"Now hold on, Joe," the other barber said, "maybe he did see Elizabeth Polly. Lots of folks swear to it, some of 'em good God-fearing people, and if his horses saw her, that pretty much proves we got Liz's ghost wandering around here."

"Wha'd she say to you?" Joe remained doubtful.

"She said Suzanne and Sonny are looking for me."

"Who are they?"

Now I was in a bit of a bind. I didn't really wish to reveal that I had killed my sweetheart and my brother, but I had already over spoke, so I said, "They are a couple of dead people."

"Oh, so now you are getting messages from the dead, huh? Young feller, you need to know that kind of stuff is frowned on around here. There are plenty of God-fearing folks who will not allow any truck with that kind of stuff here in Hays City."

"I should hope not," I said. "I didn't conjure her up, she just showed up all on her own when I was camped across the river from your Sentinel Hill. She gave me the message, then she up and left. It like to scared me half to death."

"I wouldn't be noising that around town, if I was you," Joe put in. The rest just sat looking at me like I had corn-cobs growing out of my ears.

"Alright," I said, and held up my hands. "Forget I said anything. Can I get a haircut and my beard trimmed?"

"We don't do business with no necromancers," Joe said. "You need to leave these premises now."

I could see I wasn't going to get a shave or haircut with old Joe around, although the rest of them looked like swelled up toads about to bust with curiosity, so I shrugged, got to my feet and left this discriminating establishment and went in search of a more broad-minded place to get my ears lowered.

Leaving the barber shop and a little preoccupied, I didn't see the rough looking character with the tied-down gun when I stepped out the door and I nearly knocked him over. He let out an angry, "Hey!" and would have fallen if I hadn't reached out an arm and quickly grabbed him.

"'Scuse me," I muttered, "I didn't mean…"

"You dumb cow nurse, why don't you watch where you're going?"

"I'm sorry Mister, I didn't see you," I said and tried to brush out the wrinkles in his sleeve where I had just grabbed him.

He jerked his arm away and stared hard at my face.

"Don't I know you from somewhere? You look awfully familiar. What's your name?"

I gave him an uncertain look and feeling nettled at his rude demanding of my name, I guess I got a little snide.

"Could be Puddin' n' Tane, but it ain't."

"Well now, ain't you the Cock 'o the Walk? I've half a notion to box your ears for ya.'"

"You'd better save it until you find the other half," I said.

The rough character's eyes swept up and down my frame and settled on my gun. I guess he figured all his blustering and bellowing wasn't going to get him anywhere and it was now time to take it to the next level. In the meantime, a small crowd had gathered to watch what looked like a fight a brewing. My would-be adversary had just stepped back, his hand hovering near his gun and I thought to myself, *is this idiot actually going to draw on me over something so trivial as a little bump on the boardwalk?*

"I said I was sorry, mister, why don't you let it rest?"

Mr. Gun-hand turned to the watching crowd and said in a loud voice, "It ain't a going to rest until one of us rests in Boot Hill."

He was backing off the boardwalk and out in the street when old hawk nose Joe opened the door to the barber shop and found me standing there with a whole lot of people gawking in our direction.

"What's going on here?" Joe hollered. Then he recognized me.

"You," he said, "I thought I told you to get."

At that point ol' Joe whacked me on the backside with a broom he was holding and announced to the crowd, "You folks better look out, this stranger's mixed up somehow in the speaking with the dead, claims he saw and talked with the Blue Light Lady last night. I wouldn't trust him any further than I could throw 'im." Then turning his attention back to me, he walloped me one more time with the broom and said, "You get!"

What could I do? Folks were looking sideways and backing away from me, and even my gun-hand opponent started moving off up the street, dissolving with the crowd once he had lost their attention. Joe glared at me, turned on his heels and went back into his barber shop, slamming the door. I shrugged, cast a backward glance at Lightfoot and Sidekick and headed on down the boardwalk. For a moment, there I thought my horses actually looked like I had embarrassed them.

Walking along, I came to a small barber shop that was run by an old negro, and upon closer inspection found that no one else was ahead of me so I went in and spent a pleasant hour with the old colored man hearing how Buffalo Bill Cody and a man named Rose had tried to start up a town named Rome about a mile away. When they refused partnership with a Dr. William Webb, who apparently had authority to establish towns for the railroad, it caused Webb to form the Big Creek Land Company, which established Hays City on the present location. Rome began bleeding businesses and occupants to Hays City in order for folks to be near the railroad, and in a last-ditch effort to save the town, Cody and Rose tried giving lots away, all to no avail. Within a year, Rome was gone with most of the buildings ravished for lumber or moved to Hays City.

When I left, I had a nice trim on the hair, and my beard was a master piece of grooming, full but not too long with a well-waxed handlebar mustache. I found a general store with the name of *Moses & Bloomfield* and went in to replenish some of my supplies. I had just finished putting them away in Sidekick's pack when I was once again confronted by the ruffian with the tied down gun that I had run into earlier.

"Colt Saber, you are wanted by the law in Wade's Landing, Texas and I'm taking you in for the reward," he said in a loud voice.

I turned and looked at the man with a thin-lipped grimace and shook my head. "I don't think so, mister, not today."

My antagonist was standing in the street holding up one of the wanted posters on me and was watching me with cat eyes, his hand once again hovering near his gun. "Yes, today. Drop your gunbelt and turn around."

Another crowd had started to gather as I ignored the man and stepped up into my saddle. Cautiously I thumbed the thong from the hammer of my pistol. I turned to ride towards the man, noting his uncertainty as he drew his gun. When I got next to where he stood, I leaned out of the saddle and said in a low voice that only he could hear, "If you haven't holstered that gun by the time I count to three, I am going to turn in my saddle and shoot you right between the eyes."

I sat back up in my saddle and nudged Lightfoot forward at a walk. "One," I said loudly. There was a murmur heard among the watching bystanders. "Two!" I listened and just as I was about to say "three," I heard the faint sound of his pistol sliding into leather. I never said three, just goosed Lightfoot into a trot and took the trail west out of town without looking back.

By the time I'd cleared the city limits, my heart had settled down to a dull roar. I thought Lightfoot was complaining to Sidekick about the jeopardy I had put both of them in, something about what would I of done if that guy had shot me instead of putting his gun away... that there would have been bullets flying every-which-a-way and they were much bigger targets than I was. It sure seems like he complains a lot more since that pack horse joined us.

Riding along, I wondered about it. There was an emptiness I felt inside, almost a disappointment that I was still on this side of the world and not the other. That bounty hunter could have answered a lot of questions I was having about Suzanne looking for me, if he had just pulled that trigger. Was I missing her so bad that I was ready to relinquish my hold on this life just to be where she was in the next? And who's to say the Blue Light Lady was speaking true anyway, most everything I had ever heard about familiar spirits was that they were bad, full of tricks and lies and deception and bedevilment. Was I being enticed to throw away this life by such a spirit? I knew folks could get deceived, talked into believing things because they wanted so bad for them to be true. What else could the Blue Light Lady have meant, surely not that Suzanne and Sonny were alive and looking for me here? Was all this what was behind my death wish if, indeed, I even had one? My reckless challenge of Wes Hardin, and the Jones and Carol gang, and now this careless deal with the bounty hunter? It just didn't make any sense except for someone who really didn't care whether they lived or died. Was I that person? Really? Nothing mattered to me anymore. Not me, not God, not family...? My mom mattered to me. I didn't wish to see any more hurt or grief come to her—or my dad or Gwen or Becky or Tommy; and what about Pearl? Golly, I'd almost forgotten about that spunky kid. Pearl was the very picture of someone with a choke-hold on life. Somehow, she mattered to me and without understanding why, I knew she was counting on me, and that knowledge began to work on the dried and cracked leather of my heart and began to let in a little light for me to look at the things I had done, what I was becoming and where I was going. Frankly, the thought of having to handle all those buried feelings scared me more than any Blue Light Lady, insane killer, outlaw gang, or ruthless bounty hunter ever could have.

The next week, I was just beyond Fort Wallace on the trail to Cheyenne Wells when I heard rifle fire. A train had passed me earlier, and it sounded like it was under attack. Perhaps the Cheyenne or Arapaho had blocked the tracks and were attempting to massacre the Iron Horse's occupants. I urged my pony into a gallop and topping a small rise, I pulled up to gaze at the spectacle before me. Stretched out, nearly from horizon to horizon in the valley below, was a heard of buffalo and the train was stalled as their numbers covered the tracks in front and back. But the train was not what was under attack, it was doing the attacking. I saw rifle after rifle firing from the windows of the passenger cars as their occupants laid down a murderous fire, killing and maiming the bison in a wanton and useless slaughter. Already, numerous animals lay dead or dying while the shooting continued.

I shook my head in disgust. What was wrong with people anyway. This senseless waste was so some dude from back east could go home and brag how he had killed a buffalo in the wild west? I was helpless to stop the carnage and sat there watching until finally the engineer was successful in clearing the track by repeatedly blowing his whistle and bumping animals out of the way. Slowly the train with its advancing civilization moved on across the valley.

It was with a sinking feeling of things real and wholesome having been violated that I rode down to the killing field and made an effort to salvage some of the meat. I carved some medallion stakes of back-strap from a young yearling heifer. I was storing them in one of the fruit jars, and had managed to get the animal's tongue, which I planned to jerk and smoke over my campfire that night, when movement across the valley caught my attention.

Coming towards me about a mile off was a band of Indians moving to where I and the dead buffalo were. They were moving slowly with women and children in their midst and I figured it was time for me and my horses to hit the trail. Thrusting the rest of my stuff and the meat into my pack, I tightened the tarp and hit the road on a run for Cheyenne Springs. I didn't slow down until we were well beyond the railroad.

Cheyenne Springs was the headwaters of the Smokey Hill River, and here the trail divided into three separate routes for Denver. The northern route, the middle route called starvation trail, and the southern route. Since the railroad followed the northern route and I had had my fill of its noisy shenanigans, and I had been told the middle route lacked good water, I decided to take the southern route, being somewhat uncertain as to where I was actually headed. Gold strikes had been booming at a place called Cripple Creek on the west side of Pike's Peak, Cherry Creek near Denver and farther south on Clear Creek. Since it was my intent to get lost in some mountain hideaway and enjoy the solitude, I pointed Lightfoot's nose down the southern route.

I crossed into Colorado at last and was heading towards the eastern slopes of the Rocky Mountains. I could see the Front Wall of the Rockies rising majestically on the horizon and felt an unexplained quickening of my pulse. I rode on through a changing countryside with grasslands, sage, and sedges changing to scrub oak, pinion, juniper, mahogany trees and sumac, bitterbrush, and buckbrush. There were the usual willows and cottonwoods that grew from the prairie floor and followed the stream courses and drainages right on up to the higher elevations from what I could see. Here also grew wild raspberries, currents, and goose berries found in areas that the trail wound through. In the sub-alpine places above, there were thousands of lodge pole pine, Ponderosa pine, and Douglas fir with stands of alder, wild cherries, and mountain maple scattered about by the hand of some unseen gardener. On the slopes above nine thousand feet were seen the tall spires of balsam fir and Engelmann spruce piercing the sky like cathedral steeples. Interspersed among them were blue spruce, sub-alpine fir and white spruce. Here also was the quaking aspen that, come October, would change the mountaintops and valleys to a splendid kind of gold all their own. I have always loved these trees, in the summer the bright green leaves never stop their "Nervous-Nellie" quivering and the white-blotched trunks seem to gleam, clean and bright against the mountainsides. The smell of an aspen grove in the fall satisfies a deep yearning of the soul, a kind of gold with no monetary significance whatsoever.

As I rode towards the next settlement, the country was already changing to forested parks of ponderosa pine with large open meadows and there was evidence of farms and ranches being established in this area. I told Lightfoot and Sidekick this looked like good cattle country and they looked it over as we rode along, giving it their general approval. I was pleasantly surprised at seeing herds of Texas Longhorns and absently wondered if these were some of those brought up on the Goodnight-Loving trail.

"Boys," I said, "some of those critters could be the very cows off the Crossed Sabers that we shipped north a few years ago." Lightfoot just glanced in their direction once, and his sidekick didn't pay any attention at all.

There were some log cabins and out buildings alongside the creek and the road I was traveling on, and it soon became apparent that this little community had sprung up next to the old stage depot. A board with faded lettering read 'Wells Fargo Depot' on one of the principal buildings and I could see a few folks walking about minding their own business. A stray dog lay in the middle of the dusty road as I rode by and opened one eye, lifted an ear, and thumped his tail in the dust, but never moved. Lightfoot snorted him one and I could just hear him scoff, "Lazy mutt!"

I pulled up at the stage station which now doubled as a general store and saloon, and tethering my animals, went in. Inside was a gloomy interior with light streaming through a couple of tall windows illuminating a considerable amount of dust. Behind the counter was a storekeeper with sleeves rolled up and wearing a dirty apron and green sun visor cap. He turned an upside-down glass over, blew some dust out of it, and said, "What'll you have stranger?"

"You got any of that sarsaparilla?" I asked.

He gave me that look I always get whenever I ask for that drink in one of these places, then walked from behind the counter over to a shelf, found a dusty bottle and walked back, wiping it on his apron. He found an opener, popped the lid off and poured some into the glass.

"Where you headed?" he asked, eyeing my gun.

"Gold fields, I guess. What's this place called?"

"Middle Kiowa," he said. "Used to be called Wendling, after Hank Wendling who ran the stage station here back before it closed. Back then there was Upper Kiowa and Lower Kiowa on either side of us but when those settlements petered out we decided to call this Middle Kiowa. That your saddle horse out there?"

I turned and looked out the door at a couple of fellows in overalls standing around Lightfoot giving him the once over and then nodded to the storekeeper.

"Yep," I said.

"He's a mighty fine looking animal, looks to have some Tennessee Walker in 'im."

"Could be, I don't know, got him down in Texas. He's a good cowpony. How come this place was called Kiowa? Those redskins hang out in the panhandle of Texas mostly."

"Back in the day, this creek was their summer range. They used to come up here and raise hob with the Utes, Cheyenne and Arapaho. They camped out all along this creek and made attacks from here on those tribes. We call it Kiowa Creek now."

I poured some more sarsaparilla into my glass and noticed the storekeeper nodding his head to somebody behind me. Casually I turned around and looked out the door. I could see Sidekick still hitched to the rail, but Lightfoot was gone. Turning slowly back to the storekeeper I said, "If my horse isn't tied back up to the hitching post in the next ten minutes, I'm going to have to do in this town what I did in the last town this happened at." Slowly I drew my gun, took a cartridge from my belt, snapped open the gate and rolled the cylinder to where the hammer had rested on an empty chamber and loaded the sixth round. Snapping the gate closed I replaced the gun in its holster and looked up at a clock ticking on the wall back of the counter.

Two down-at-the-heel fellows who had been sitting at a table in the corner got up and hurried out and I turned to watch them go, then cocking my head at the store-keeper who was nervously wiping the dry counter with a rag, I lifted my glass and tossed the last of the sarsaparilla down my throat, then set the glass back down with a loud bang. The man behind the counter jumped and then yelled out the door, "Hurry up, you boys!"

In a few moments, I heard my horse being led back up and when I turned, Lightfoot was at the hitching rail. Reaching into my pocket, I hauled out a nickel and flipped it onto the counter, then turned to leave.

The storekeeper caught my arm and said in a sneaky voice, "Wha'd 'ya have to do in the last town that took your horse?"

I gave him a big toothy grin and said, "Why I had to walk to the next town and get another one." Chuckling, I walked out of the store, mounted up and rode on.

Nine or ten miles on up the road to Denver, I came to another small community that had sprung up around a sawmill. There were several log cabin and clap board shacks clustered around a sizable steam engine that drew water from a fast-running creek and powered a sprawling lumber mill. Dray teams and wagon loads of lumber were visible leaving on the road heading northwest towards Denver. Up and down the creek on either side of it were diggings of miners, some in operation even as I rode in, where panning, sluicing, and the operation of long toms was underway. I hauled up and hailed one of the miners. "Hey, mister, what's the name of this place?"

The fellow stood up, straightened his stiff back and wiped his forehead with a red bandana.

"This be Russellville, I guess, some folks are calling it Elizabeth Town after some politician's wife now. That's the Webber Brother's sawmill over yonder and north of here on up the creek is P.P. Gomer's sawmill. Folks are kinda building up around the two mills."

I could see that the open glade-like surroundings of ponderosa pine, and the grassland parks, were conducive to both ranching and the timber industry, with many small ranches and farms established or under development. Mining seemed to play a secondary role in the community as well, and I learned in chatting with the sourdough in the creek that even though gold had been found in Running Creek, it had never been a big bonanza and many of the miners had moved on to bigger strikes elsewhere.

"How come you are still here?" I asked.

"Well, she ain't much of a claim but she's good enough for day wages," the miner said. "A fellow can still manage a decent living without having to bust his tail in the high country, and I have the safety of the settlement here. The Indians can still be a problem, especially farther on west. You thinking about doing some prospecting?"

"Thought I might, if I can find the right spot," I said.

"You got any experience?"

"Not much, did some hard-rock mining down in Mexico a while back, but it was nothing like this here kind of operation."

"There's a fellow name of Allen who had a claim here, but he pulled out for Fairplay and the strike up there. I understand he located on Terryall Creek up near South Park City. He sent me a letter a while back and is looking for somebody to help him muck out overburden on his claim, asked me to keep an eye out for someone. Think you might be interested? It's a fair piece from here; if you do ride on up there and talk to him, tell him Orville Watson sent ya."

"Where's this Terryall Creek?" I asked.

"'Bout a hundred and fifty miles from here. You ever hear of South Park?"

"Nope."

It's west of here up in a great big grass valley off the front wall somewhere around nine to ten thousand feet up."

I thanked Watson and rode on into the settlement. Already there was a general merchandise store that offered local dairy products as well as lumber, hardware, mining supplies and feed. I stopped long enough to add some eggs and butter to my larder and then struck out west for the front wall of the Rockies.

It took me about a week to travel the distance from Elizabeth Town to Colorado Springs. I suppose I could have done it sooner, but as I traveled through the Black Forest and then the various settlements and hamlets along the way, I took my time and enjoyed the scenic beauty of the place. Some of the prairie country was a reminder of Texas except for the incredible Rocky Mountain back drop. I stayed over in Colorado Springs and upon asking where the springs were, I was told there were over eight mineral springs in the area and that a developer was currently developing the "Manitou Mineral Springs Resort." It promoted the healing properties of the carbonated, heated pools. This was something I would have to try and so finding the place, I put Lightfoot and Sidekick into the resort's corral with adjoining livery stable and asked the stable man to check the shoes on both of my horses. I had some rough mountain trails ahead and didn't want to risk either of them throwing a shoe. I found my way down to the pools and paid a dollar to rent a bathing suit and go soak in the effervescent hot water. I was given all the carbonated cold water chilled with ice that I wanted to drink, too, which wasn't much as it had a sort of funny taste that was not unlike the way things smelled in the bunkhouse after a night of beans for supper. I found out from a feller soaking near me that Manitou was supposed to be the Great Spirit of the Indians of the area, and had given them the waters for their healing properties. I came away from there with the strong sense that if it ain't broke, don't be trying to fix it.

I was paying the liveryman for shoeing both horses when he said, "Those shoes were worn down pretty bad, where you all coming from?"

I gave him an uncertain look, then said, "I'm not surprised, they haven't been checked since Abilene."

"You ride in on the Smokey Hill Trail?"

"Um hum," I said without further comment.

"Well, you're all fit as a fiddle now, where you headin'? You don't look like no prospector."

"South Park, you know how to get there?"

"Sure, just head west and follow the Middle Fork of the South Platte. That's some prime cattle country up there. You figure on cowboying?"

"Nope, prospecting."

"You could a fooled me. I figured you Texas boys wouldn't want nothing to do with anything you couldn't do from the back of a horse."

"You ever find any gold?" I asked.

"No, I've seen too many a good man get bit by the gold bug and make a mess of their lives."

"Well, if you ever pick up an egg-sized nugget you'll get acquainted with that insect mighty quick."

"I doubt it. I wish you good luck, young feller, watch out for red-sticks, the Utes are still smarting over the gov'ment breaking their word on the last treaty."

"Thanks," I said, "I'll keep my eyes peeled."

CHAPTER EIGHTEEN

A Long Trail

Kiowa Winter Camp, Sweetwater Canyon, February 1871

SONNY SABER WAS BEING HELD PRISONER
in White Bear's camp although his medicine as the Buffalo Man allowed him a certain amount of respect and awe
amongst the tribe. The women and children, in particular,
gave him a wide birth. For two weeks, he had suffered
from the head wound he had sustained when Kicking Bird
had been murdered, and was taken into Spotted Buffalo's lodge where he was slowly nursed back to health by
Seeaugway. No one else was willing to offer the Buffalo
Man aid, but Seeaugway was able to convince her father
to help this brother to Colt-on, the white-eyes who had
rescued her years before.

The summer before, Kicking Bird and Spotted Buffalo
had joined White Bear's encampment after Guikati, or
Sleeping Wolf, and Chief Lone Wolf, had sent them as
emissaries from their stronghold in the Palo Duro Canyon.
They were to urge White Bear's band to join them in the
canyons. The Kiowa shaman, Maman-ti had promised
that they would all be safe there from the white-eyes.

Even though Spotted Buffalo had been a respected
chief among the Buffalo Clan, here with this band of Kiowa,
he was merely tolerated. His relationship with Kicking Bird

had made him suspect in the eyes of the head chiefs. The profound beauty of his unmarried daughter, Seeaugway, was one saving grace in the eyes of the band, particularly Runs-With-Horses who had twice bargained for the young maiden's hand. He was refused, not on the basis of Spotted Buffalo's dissatisfaction with the offer, but out of deference to the chief's daughter's wishes. Seeaugway continued to have little interest in any of the likely suitors of the band, although since she had been wounded by Runs-With-Horses and his conciliatory attitude towards her, she had been much more receptive to the young brave's suit. She was still healing from the stab wound and it was not without misgivings that Spotted Buffalo took the Buffalo Man into his lodge. He had some concerns that his daughter's interest in the white man may be for more than just his well-being, and it might hinder Runs-With-Horses' chances for a successful marriage with her, a union he otherwise favored.

Eventually, Sonny's head quit pounding and his double vision cleared. He enjoyed the kind attention the Indian girl gave to him and spent quiet hours speaking with her, mostly learning the details of his brother's previous rescue of the girl, and learning that Seeaugway bore an undying devotion to Colt. It was easy for the tall cowboy to relate to, for his feelings for his brother ran deep as well. He had an unrelenting desire that almost amounted to need to find Colt and make him understand that what he thought was between himself and Suzanne had never ever gotten to that point. He would make him understand, even if he had to pound it into his thick skull. Beyond that he had no idea what he would do. Probably just go back to the ranch and help his dad.

Sonny was at a loss as to where to look for Colt. He tried to imagine what Colt would be thinking, where he might go, and he endeavored to put himself in Colt's boots. Would he head for Saint Louis? He had worked with some teamsters there, perhaps he would try to join up with those fellows. Sonny had a hard time seeing Colt driving a freight wagon. Maybe he would look up Kathreen, she lived there. He felt a pang in his heart at the memory of the fiery red-head and the passionate moments they'd shared. Would Colton seek her out, and if so, would the old flame she had carried for Colt be reignited? Sonny hoped not. He felt a strange resentment at the idea, a kind of possessiveness that stole over him. Maybe when this was all settled, he would go find Kathreen and marry the girl himself. In the meantime, he had to escape this Kiowa band and get on with the task of finding Colt. Perhaps he could enlist Seeaugway's help in getting away.

From the start of his captivity with the Kiowa, Sonny was kept under guard. He had the liberty to go about the encampment in the company of the Indian girl and sometimes with her father, but they were always followed by at least two braves who carried repeating rifles with them. The old Indian hag, Magpie, would sometimes follow as well and hurl insults and abuse, but Sonny mostly just laughed and ignored her. The cur dog he had befriended would tag along too, and Sonny enjoyed scratching him behind the ears, although the poor creature was riddled with lice.

One day, Sonny said to Seeaugway, "Willow, do you suppose I could get a jar full of grease?"

"Grease, what kind grease?" the maid asked.

"Doesn't matter, any kind, bear, goose, even buffalo if you got any. I need something that is oily."

"What for?"

"This poor pooch is being eaten alive by lice. I figured I could brush him down with some grease or oil and it would kill off the lice and nits, it would probably make him less ornery, too."

"I could get you some corn oil, would that work?"

"That would be perfect."

Sonny watched as the Indian girl went off to the lodge. In a few minutes, she reappeared carrying a clay jug and a hand brush that had obviously had its source from the white men. She handed them to Sonny, and the cowboy sat down and called the dog over. Thinking he was going to get another ear scratching the cur came over and sat on his haunches, his tongue lolling out and tail thumping the ground. Sonny fastened a rawhide rope around the animal's neck and began to scratch him behind the ears.

"What do you call this dog?" Sonny asked Seeaugway.

"Dog," she said.

"We need to give him a better name than that. You got any ideas?"

"The People don't name dogs, just call him dog."

"Well, he sure dug into that kettle of stew the first time I saw 'im, I think I'll call him Soupbone."

Willow grinned, her even white teeth gleaming in her dark face. "Buffalo Man funny," she said.

"Please pour some of that oil along his back and hand me that brush," Sonny said.

While Willow poured some oil, Sonny began a soothing brushing of Soupbone's back. At first, the animal tried to get away, then he turned to sniff at his coat and tried to lick up the oil while Sonny held onto the thong and kept brushing.

"What mean, please?" Seeaugway asked.

"Please? That's white-man's way of being polite," Sonny said.

"Polite?"

"Huh," Sonny chuckled. He never imagined having to explain to anyone what please and polite meant. He wondered what the Indian equivalent was.

"Let's see, it is a way of asking nicely for help or permission, to be thoughtful to another and encourage their good will."

"You mean it is nice to someone?"

"Yes, asking please and saying thank you is being nice and thoughtful."

"Uahoow—thank you, it is the same, we say uahoow."

Sonny chuckled and nodded his head, "Uahoow," he said.

"You wel-come," Seeaugway said proudly. It was plain she had learned this from Colton.

Sonny turned to the big-eyed girl who stood with a self-satisfied look, "Did you learn that from Colton?"

"Yes, Colt-on. Where—Colt-on?"

"I don't know, I must find him."

"How come him gone?"

"He thinks he killed me and Suzanne."

Alarmed, Seeaugway grabbed Sonny's arm and he stopped brushing Soupbone. "Soo-zan dead?"

"No, this medal stopped his bullet, see?" Sunny pulled the medallion from his shirt and showed the Indian girl the bullet stuck in it. Seeaugway ran an exploritory finger over the spent slug and looked at the cowboy with questioning eyes.

"Bodalk Inago?" she said with a knowing look. "Why him shoot?"

"Colt had disappeared but we thought we had found his dead body, along with his horse and saddle, and naturally we were all devastated... deeply troubled. Suzanne nearly died after he went missing and I tried to help her get over it. In the process, I fell in love with her and she finally agreed to be my wife—on the very day that Colt came back and found her in my arms. He pulled his gun and shot us and then rode away."

Seeaugway looked as if she had been struck with a club. Anxiously she asked, "Where has he gone?"

Sonny shrugged, "We don't know, he rode away before anyone could ask. I am trying to find where he is now and learn what happened to him. I need to tell him that Suzanne is still desperately in love with him too, not me."

Seeaugway said, "You know this?"

"Oh yeah, she only gave in to me after all hope of his return had passed. I knew I would never replace Colt in her heart."

"What 'bout you heart?' Willow reached out a gentle hand and touched Sonny's chest.

Sonny gave a sardonic chuckle, "It's still there I guess."

"You must go—find Colt-on, take back to Soo-zan."

"I was wondering if you could help me?"

"How Seeaugway help?" she said.

"Do you know where the Thunder Horse is kept?"

"Yes, him with other horse."

"I would need someone to catch and saddle him along with Hank, my mule. Is there anyone you could trust to do that?"

Willow looked pensive, studying on the matter and finally reluctantly nodded her head. "Runs-With-Horses do this," she said.

It was Sonny's turn to be surprised, "Runs-With-Horses would do this?"

"Yes—if me ask."

"I thought he wanted Tornado for himself, why would he give him to me?"

"Him give Thunder Horse—Tornado to Spotted Buffalo for Willow," Seeaugway's cheeks flamed red.

"Willow, you like this boy, don't you?"

"Him have good heart," she said.

"But he stabbed you with his knife."

"Him no mean, was try for you."

"Well, thanks for jumping in, why did you do that?"

"You Colt-on brother, me owe Colt heap big debt."

"So, you are willing to marry up with Runs-With-Horses to square your debt with Colt?"

"I probably share courting blanket with him anyhow, so this way me help you."

"When can we set this up? I will need my horse, mule, saddles, and all my outfit to find Colt."

"Next snow come, I talk Runs-With-Horses, him get things ready for to go," Seeaugway said.

For the next few days the captive white man saw little of the Indian maid. She evidently made good her promise to talk to the young Indian, for Sonny saw them walking out and spending more time together. Runs-With-Horses would often ride Tornado around in plain sight of the camp, but then one day he rode out on the grulla with all Sonny's rigging on and leading Hank, the mule, who was also loaded with packsaddle and paniers, albeit somewhat cockeyed. He rode to where the cowboy stood watching and without expression vaulted effortlessly from the back of the stallion and turned to indicate the lopsided pack.

"Fix!" he said.

Sonny hesitated a moment, noticing his guards watching and then stepped forward and began to rearrange the knots. He showed the youth how to tie a diamond hitch. A silent look of conspiracy passed between the two as Sonny stepped back and watched Runs-With-Horses attempt the knot.

The following week saw the Indian youth riding about the camp demonstrating his prowess with the horse and pack mule. On two separate occasions, he rode into the camp, the mule loaded down with firewood brought from afar, and this was an obvious hit with the women of the village.

Once the people got used to seeing the Thunder Horse and mule together, usually under saddle, and often left standing tethered outside Runs-With-Horses' lodge, it hardly earned any notice at all.

Although the weather remained unseasonably warm, Seeaugway let Sonny know that the horse and his things would be waiting the night of the next big snow, and for him to be ready. They were standing near the brook that ran past the camp and Sonny said, "It feels so much like spring, what if it doesn't snow?"

"Snow come," Seeaugway said.

"What will Runs-With-Horses do to trade for your hand if I take the Thunder Horse away?"

"Him glad you go—take Thunder Horse, now him have Seeaugway, you bet. He get more horse for Spotted Buffalo."

"Are you okay with this?"

"Yes, Seeaugway happy—you go find Colt-on. Me happy Runs-With-Horses come talk soon to Spotted Buffalo. Big snow come, heap cold—you go."

"Thanks Willow, you are a special friend, God bless you." Sonny held out his hand to the maid and she took it and gave it one pump.

"Uahoow," Willow said.

By the first week in March, the weather turned cold again with occasional light snow flurries. Seeaugway warned Sonny to be ready, and within a couple of weeks there came an evening when the wind was blowing snow sideways, and already a couple of inches had piled up on the ground. The camp was buttoned up tight with the Kiowa snuggled safe in their lodges in warm buffalo robes when Willow leaned over and shook Sonny.

"Buffalo Man, it time," she said.

Sonny sat up and pulled on his boots. He could see Seeaugway peering through the slit of the rawhide door as her father and mother were snoring on the far side of the tepee. The Indian girl motioned him over.

"The Thunder Horse and mulo are tied behind Runs-With-Horses' lodge and the guards have gone to their own lodges in this storm. Now is your time."

304

The cowboy pressed past the Indian maiden and passed an arm about her shoulder, giving her a quick hug, "Uahoow," he whispered and then crawled out into the cold. Seeaugway buttoned the hide door back into place and crept back to her bed.

Sonny made his way down the circle of lodges to where Tornado and Hank stood, tails against the wind. Untying them, he led them with crunching steps away from the encampment, the whistling wind covering any sound they made. Reaching the shelter of the willows and trees along the creek, he paused long enough to put on his heavy coat and a pair of gloves, then brushing snow from the saddle, he mounted and rode the grulla north, up the valley floor, keeping to the lee side of the canyon as much as possible. The gusting wind rapidly swept snow over his departing tracks.

By morning, he had reached the trail that led up out of the Sweetwater Canyon. The wind was still blowing and the snow drifting as they climbed to the trail above, and made their way back to the Goodnight-Loving trail. Once Sonny gained that route, he struck out east, putting as much distance behind himself and the Indian encampment as possible. Finally, the cold and fatigue caused him to seek out a sheltered spot along a stream and make camp.

Three days later, Sonny picked up the Brazos River Trail. He had left the cold behind and the weather had turned to a balmy mid-fifties. Sonny had escaped the vigilance of his Kiowa guards and, if they followed, he saw no more of those Indians. It was apparent the snow had covered his tracks and aided his escape. Riding east, he headed for the vicinity of Bryan, Texas. His grandfather on his mother's side lived here, although he had never met the man. Perhaps Colton had sought him out. It was also his intention to ride to Stretch and Gwen's place on the off-chance that Colt may have gone there, or that he may possibly have contacted them. He hoped to find news of his brother's whereabouts from Grandfather Fithens or his sister.

This part of Texas was new range to Sonny. He had often heard of the Brazos River country but had never been this far east. With spring in the air, there was a quiet appeal to the countryside. He saw miles of green, rolling pasturelands, well-watered, bordered by creeks and wooded breaks. Here and there were black-land plots of some farmer's cotton or corn field, and the few places he did pass showed through hard work, a slow crawl back towards prosperity as the farmers and ranchers sought to overcome the devastation the war and reconstruction had caused on the local populace. The trail led into a wagon road and it soon became apparent that he was nearing the town with the increase of farms and homes he saw. Here and there were the remains of old plantations with large sprawling houses, mostly in a state of disrepair, a reminder of an earlier time when cotton was king in the area.

Sonny rode into Bryan, a place that reminded him of a model railroad town he'd seen once in a Sears & Roebuck Christmas catalog, for here was a church, there a vine covered cottage with a white fence, a courthouse, a telegraph office, a street with various businesses, and a town square. There was a steamboat landing on the river and numerous shade trees lined pleasant wide streets. He stopped at a brick building marked Post Office and, tying his horses to the hitching rail, he went in and got directions to Rev. Elijah Fithens' place, then rode on until he located the Baptist Church with the parsonage in the back. Stepping down, he dusted himself off, and with hat in hand, walked up to knock at the front door of the house.

A tall, older version of himself with a full white beard answered the door and gave him a grave if not curious look.

"Ye-ess?" the old gentleman said in a drawn-out preacher's voice.

"Grandfather Fithens, I am your grandson, Sonny Saber of Wade's Landing, Texas. We have never met, but I am wondering if I might come in and speak with you for a moment."

"Yes, come in son, come in. How is your mother?" Sonny's grandpa moved some papers from a chair and indicated Sonny should sit down, then he took a seat in a rocking chair set next to the front room window. A big family Bible lay open on a stand next to his chair.

"Well, sir," Sonny began, "she was in good health when I left, but not doing so well otherwise. I am afraid she bears a very heavy heart right now."

"Perhaps you had best tell me all about it then. Which one are you, Sonny, or Thomas?"

"I'm Sonny. The problem began a few years ago, when Colt's body was found alongside his dead horse and we all figured he was killed from a fall off a cliff. He had been engaged to a lovely girl named Suzanne Kluesman at the time and although his death was a terrible tragedy to us all, it nearly killed Miss Kluesman."

"Yes, I remember your mother writing of the boy's death."

"For the next year or two, I cared for the girl and attempted to console her and bring her back from the brink as it were, and in the process, I became very attached to her, eventually falling in love with her myself."

"Now let me understand, you had fallen in love with your brother's sweetheart?"

"Yes, but not until after we were all thoroughly convinced that Colt was dead. All, that is, but Suzanne who just could not accept that he was gone. Finally, after much time had passed, she did accept it, too, and agreed to my suit. It was on the very day that I had asked her to be my girl and she had consented, that Colton suddenly reappeared from the brush, dressed like a gunman.

When he found Suzanne in my embrace, he cried out in anguish, drew his gun and put a bullet in my chest. My head snapped back and hit Suzanne in the face knocking her senseless and his bullet put me down as well. When I came to, he was gone."

"How come you are not dead?"

Sonny fished out the medallion from his shirt front and said, "This medal he gave me stopped the bullet."

Grampa Fithens studied the medallion for a long minute and then said, "Where is the lad now?"

"That is what I am trying to find out. Have you seen or heard of him?"

"No, son, he has not come this way. You say he looked like a gunman?"

"Yes, all dressed in black with fancy silver conchos and buckles and stuff."

"Do you know where he had been all the time he was missing?"

"No, no one knows, it's a great mystery. That is part of the reason I must find him."

"What is the rest of the reason?"

"He thinks he killed me and Suzanne and he must be wandering like a lost soul with our blood on his hands. I need to let him know we were not killed, that Suzanne is still his girl, and to bring him back home. Mother's poor heart is breaking, so is Dad's."

"So, none of you have had any word of him since all this happened, how long has it been?"

"It was last fall—October I think, just after fall roundup."

"I haven't heard from your mother for some time now, Sonny, but I sense your grief and share your burden. Let me ask you a question; do you boys believe in Jesus?"

Sonny was surprised at the question, "Why, yes sir, we do."

"Are you living a Christian life?"

Sonny paused and felt his ears grow hot. Swallowing hard he said, "I try to and I know Colt was before he went missing… in fact we all figured he had gone to heaven except for once when Suzanne had a dream and saw him fading into a dark place like a ghost."

"Is Suzanne a Christian?"

"Oh, yes sir, she loves the Lord with all her heart and plays the piano at church."

"Alright then, as believers we know that all things work together for good for them that love God. Right now, you need to get a hold of this truth and pass it on to Miss Kluesman and even remind your mother and father. God has a plan for each of your lives and is trying to work it out. I would say you have a major role in the rescue and return of your brother, but you are going to need to rely on God's guidance and leading to accomplish this task. Wouldn't you agree?"

"Yes, it's why I am here looking for him."

"Let's pray."

Grandfather Fithens stood from his chair and holding out a hand to Sonny helped him to his feet and then, indicating his grandson should kneel, knelt down at his own chair and began to pray.

> *"Our kind and loving Heavenly Father, we come to you with sad and heavy hearts for these dear loved ones on whom the enemy has wreaked such havoc. We know that you know the end from the beginning, that you know where Colton is right now, what he is doing and the things that he struggles with. Somewhere also is the tattered heart of Miss Kluesman and this poor child has been torn in her loyalties and affections. We pray that she will find the strength to sustain her for the journey that lies ahead, that she*

not lose faith and hope in you, and that in the end, she will behold the goodness of the Lord in the land of the living. We pray for our own dear daughter, that you sustain her, undergird her, lift her up, and give hope to both Jessica and Grant. May he be a rock to her. May he lead this family with wisdom and grace through these troubled times, and Father, we ask that you show Sonny where to find Colt. Help him to find his brother, and give him favor so that the truth may be made known, both to Colton and the truth surrounding his disappearance. We pray you guard them all, each one, that you will build a hedge of protection about them, that you will frustrate all the devices of the evil one and bring Colton and Suzanne and Sonny and the whole family to your desired end.

Now we serve notice on the Devil to get his hands off these young people and their families, to cease and desist all his lies and deception and that his minions be escorted by your holy angels to the borders of our domain and be cast forth, and we authorize..." here Rev. Fithens gave a chuckle before he continued, *"Huh! Huh! We authorize our guardian angels to give the Devil's demons and minions a good, solid whack with their swords as they banish them.*

We extend the covering of your precious shed blood, Lord Jesus, cover each of these young people, cover the family, and give them good success as they discover

*what is your good, and acceptable, and per-
fect will in this whole matter. In the precious,
matchless, name of Jesus we pray these
things, amen!"*

The prayer finished, the old man got slowly up from
his knees and turned to his grandson standing there.
Unexpectedly, he embraced the young man with a strong
hug. Sonny hugged him back.

"Thanks, Grampa," he said. "That sure was a
good prayer."

"Son, we put up with way too many shenanigans by
the Devil, it's time God's people reared up on their own
two feet and put that schemer to flight," the old man said.

"Can you take supper and stay the night?" he asked,
as he made his way towards the kitchen.

"I have my horses to attend to," Sonny said.

"Put them in with old Dobbins out in the corral, fork
down some hay for the bunch of them, if you don't mind."

Sonny said, "I was hoping that Gwen and Stretch
might have heard something, do you see them often?"

"No, not often. They are both busy with the ranch and
raising their young'un. We can ride over there tomorrow,
if you like."

"I would like that, I've never seen their place."

"Oh, he's got a good start on that place, Wayne has.
He's been experimenting with a short-horn breed and has
gotten some fine calves."

"I saw a telegraph office in town, I wonder if I shouldn't
send a wire to mom and dad. It's been some time since
I've heard from them. Maybe Colt's been found."

"That is a good idea," Grampa Fithens said. "We'll
send a wire tomorrow on our way out of town. You go
take care of your animals while I get supper started."

The next day a telegram was sent off to Wade's Landing for the Crossed Sabers Ranch. Grandfather Fithens said that it would probably take a few days for them to get a reply and that Sonny could stay with him while he waited. Sonny was in sore need of cash and had asked his father to withdraw some of the money he had banked from the wild-horse roundup he'd made the summer before and wire it to him in care of his grandpa in Bryan.

Wayne, or Stretch as he was called, and Gwen had taken up ranching and tenant farming on one of the large estates that had been abandoned after the war. Riding up to the place in his grandfather's buggy, Sonny could see that his sister and her husband had done a lot to fix up the place, but that there was still much to do. The buggy rolled down a long driveway lined with magnificent oaks and split-rail fences that bordered fields lying fallow, on either side. Outbuildings housed a work shop and forge, as well as chicken coop and a hog pen with farrowing sheds. There was a large barn with adjacent equipment outbuildings and what must have been a fancy stable for horses at one time. Sonny noted a number of horses in a nearby pasture and one or two in the corral next to the stable. A long, one-story bunkhouse stood idly by, the door slightly ajar and obviously unoccupied. Two long haystacks, one covered with a tarp, stood a short distance from the barn, and Sonny saw Stretch forking down hay from the other onto a large wagon while a team of matched workhorses stood stamping at flies and switching their tails.

"Looks like we're in time to help with feeding," Sonny said.

His grandfather nodded and then said, "Here comes Gwendolyn, won't she be surprised to see you?"

His sister was coming down the long flight of stairs of the big house with a little boy on her hip and was waving one hand at the approaching buggy. Grandfather Fithens stopped the buggy at the gate of a picket fence that surrounded a big yard and called, "Hello, Granddaughter."

Gwendolyn Saber Johnson looked about six months' pregnant with her second child and appeared to her brother to be the very picture of health and happiness. He grinned at the surprised look of joy on her face when she spied him sitting in the buggy, and released the squirming little boy, who was struggling to get free of her arms and hurry to the old man.

Sonny moved his lanky frame from the confines of the buggy and stood to greet his sister. He had not seen her since she had married and left home, and she gave a shout of joy as she rushed into his open arms.

"Sonny," she cried, "How wonderful to see you."

"Hey, Gwen, it's been a long time, sis," he said, giving her a bear hug and lifting her off her feet.

"Oof," she said, "put me down, you big galoot. I'm way too heavy for you to be twirling me around like a rag doll."

"Oh, 'scuse me, sis." Sonny set Gwen back on her feet under the watching eyes of her two-year-old son, then boldly patted her blossoming tummy and said, "I didn't hurt the little one in here, did I?"

Gwendolyn laughed, "Oh no, we're fine. Here's someone you haven't met yet, Nicodemus, say hello to your Uncle Sonny.

Sonny squatted on his heels and held out a hand to the little tyke. "Well hello, Nicodemus, how come they named you after a mule?"

The little boy came shyly towards the cowboy and allowed himself to be pulled into Sonny's embrace. "Not a mule," he said, "a friend of Jesus who came at night."

"That's right," Sonny laughed and stood up lifting the little feller with him. "That was his name, do you suppose they might have called him Nick sometimes?" He tickled the child who laughed and struggled in his arms.

"Yes," he giggled, "stop tickling."

At this point, Stretch hurried up and grasped Sonny's hand in an iron-like grip with a broad smile on his face, "Well I'll be dogged, Sonny Saber, who ever thought we'd see you in these parts, welcome to our spread. To what do we owe this unexpected pleasure?"

Sonny braced himself, for the whole time that Stretch was greeting him, he was pushing and pulling him back and forth, trying to out-grip him and get him off balance. It was his usual way of greeting the Saber boys, and Sonny, enduring the firm grip, matched it with his own and held his ground.

Stretch finally let go of his hand and turned to shake hands with Reverend Fithens. "Howdy Poppa, where'd you pick up this scalawag?"

"I'm afraid Sonny's visit is not one of pleasure but of dire consequences."

"We best go in the house then," Stretch said. "Hon, you got any coffee on?"

It had been two weeks since Sonny had arrived in Bryan, Texas and still no response to the telegram had come from Wade's Landing. Sonny was frustrated but knew they would be busy at the ranch with spring roundup and probably had not been able to get anyone free to go to town. He remembered how his mother had worried about the mail piling up at the post office during these times.

Sonny shared the whole story with Stretch and Gwen and learned that his sister and family had no information about Colt. Often in the evenings, they would sit around telling stories about life on the ranch when they were kids, and speculating on where Colton might have gone. Sonny busied himself helping Stretch with his spring branding, glad for the chance to be busy and get his mind, if only briefly, off his mission, but as the days piled up he grew more and more restless. Sonny had moved out to Gwen and Stretch's place to be handy to work. He had developed a close-knit relationship with little Nick and the toddler would run to clasp him about the knees anytime he came to the house.

One day, while Sonny was working calves in the corral with Stretch, Grampa Fithens came trotting up in his buggy in a cloud of dust. He hailed the men and held up a letter. The men left off what they were doing and hurried to the house. They found the old man seated at the kitchen table, a letter spread out in front of him, waiting for them.

"What's going on Poppa?" Stretch asked.

"I was in the Post Office picking up my mail, when the Post Mistress handed me this letter." Grampa Fithens held up a soiled envelope. "It is dated December 15th of last year."

"Who is it from and where has it been?" Gwen asked.

"It is from your mother. The Post Mistress said she found it behind the counter, dropped down in a crack. Let me read it to you all."

Dear Poppa, it is with guarded optimism that I write you this news. We had an unusual surprise when a young girl of twelve came riding into the ranch the other day like the wind. She was on an Indian pony that she had somehow managed to escape with from a kidnapping Comanche. Apparently it was a solitary brave and she courageously left him behind when she took his horse. She told us an amazing story. You remember the trouble we had last fall with Colton showing back up and shooting Sonny? Well we have had no word of him since and have been troubled to distraction as to what had become of him and where he was. The girl,

Pearl is her name, told us she was rescued by a cowboy she called Woody Stover, from an old man who had won her in a poker game from her drunken father. This Woody brought her to Fort Griffin. She persuaded him to send her to his folks, so he put her on a stage coach and sent her to us. We were certain this Woody Stover is Colton and Pearl confirmed it when she recognized his picture on the piano. The last she knew, Colton was renting a shack on "The Flat," and cutting wood for the army. She said he was looking for a cattle drive come spring. You can imagine the excitement this has caused here. Suzanne Kluesman, the fiancée I wrote you of, has gotten some missing person hand-bills out and is anxious to start for Fort Griffin, but her father has prevailed upon her to wait until spring when her friend from Saint Louis can join her. It is still uncertain who is to accompany them on their journey. If Sonny should show up there, please let him know of these latest developments and keep us all in your prayers. With love and fondest regards, your daughter, Jessica.

"Oh, good Lord," Sonny said. "You mean to tell me I have been wasting all of this time while Colt was at Griffin? Why do things have to get so mixed up?"

"Son," his grandpa said, *"all things…"*

"I'm packing up and heading for The Flat," Sonny said.

"You better wait for the folks to wire you money," Gwen said. Sonny reluctantly nodded.

A few days later a telegram was waiting at the Western Union office:

Colton last seen Abilene-stop: Money enclosed-stop: Suzanne, Kathreen, Hazelhurst in route-stop: Wire response-stop.

That afternoon, Sonny rode out on the Chisholm Trail for Abilene, Kansas.

CHAPTER NINETEEN

Rendezvous

Chisholm Trail, Mid-April 1871

THE HAZELHURST PARTY WAS TWO DAYS north of the Red River on the trail to Abilene when an Indian war party, a band of what Two-Bits guessed were Comanche, appeared on a ridge about a half-mile away.

"That can't be good," Two-Bits muttered. "Boss, we better hold up here and prepare for attack."

The small troop stopped and hurriedly began to make preparations. Hazelhurst quickly rode back to dismount next to the wagon. "What'll we do?" he asked anxiously.

Buddy said, "They will be after our scalps, these women, and our horses. Hobble and tie the horses to the wagon, and help us unhitch the team."

"Kathreen, you and Suzanne bring your horses over too, and then get inside the wagon. If you got any shootin' irons, make sure they're loaded." Two-Bits yelled. "Wong, dig out all the boxes of shells we got and prepare to load guns—you girls can help."

Soon the yipping and howling of the savages' war cries were heard and the travelers could see about twenty warriors bearing down on their position. With the last of the horses hobbled and tied off to the wagon, the men jumped over the high plank sides into the bed, and

318

taking up positions on both sides, levered rounds into their Winchesters and waited for the attackers to come within range.

"Hold your fire until you're sure of your shot," Buddy yelled. "You girls load for Two-Bits and me. Suzanne, keep your hand gun ready if we're over-run and save one shot for yourself, you too, Kathreen."

"Here they come," Two-Bits yelled, "let 'em have it."

A volley of shots went out from the wagon and three of the warriors fell, their horses running free. The rest of the Indians raced past firing arrows and rifle slugs at the defenders. The occupants of the wagon kept up a rapid firing as the Indians wheeled their ponies and came back, aiming for the horses. Kathreen rose up on her knees to look over the side at the oncoming Indians, and Two-Bits grabbed her roughly by the shoulder and pulled her down.

"Stay down, you crazy red-head, or your pretty mop will end up dangling from some warrior's lance."

Buddy handed Suzanne his smoking rifle and drew his six-gun to fire nearly point blank into a group of the attackers who were trying to get at the horses. A barrage of arrows and bullets thudded into the planking of the wagon or sailed overhead. The rancher and two cowboys were making inroads into the Indians' ranks while the girls feverishly reloaded their hot, smoking weapons.

The little Chinese cook was hunkered down on hands and knees in one corner, his hands covering his head while jabbering to his ancestors, and was of no use in the battle, until Gareth Hazelhurst yanked him up by his pigtail and shoved a rifle and a box of shells in his hands.

"Load this," he commanded. The terrified cook looked bewilderingly at the weapon and cartridges until he saw the girls loading guns and then with a cry of, "Ah so," he began to load Gareth's Winchester.

Their numbers severely decimated, the Comanche pulled up out of range and parlayed amongst themselves.

Everyone in the wagon filled all their weapons to capacity and waited.

"They'll be back," Buddy asserted, "keep an eye on the horses."

"And the girls," Two-Bits said.

A second charge came then, the savages riding wider apart and circling to come at the little group from all sides. Once they closed in, the Indians slid to the off side of their horses and rode furiously towards the wagon, shooting from under their ponies' necks.

"Shoot their horses," Buddy yelled and leveled a shot at a closing paint pony. The animal screamed in pain and pitched forward sending its rider tumbling into the buffalo grass. As quick as a cat, the Indian was up and darted towards the wagon to take cover underneath while the group overhead fired round after round at the rest. Two more horses went down and their riders tried to make the cover of the underside of the wagon, but were dropped by two well-placed shots from Hazelhurst and Two-Bits.

Everything was happening at once, Two-Bits was trying to keep track of the Indian underneath the wagon and defend against the attack, while watching out for the girls. Suzanne and Kathreen were concentrating on loading. Buddy was shooting yet another Indian from over the side and Gareth was handing Wong his empty pistol and leveling his rifle at the swirling attackers. Suddenly, about half of the tied-up horses lumbered clumsily away, their feet still ensnared by hobbles. The Indian brave under the wagon had managed to reach up and cut loose their tethers, and was now hanging precariously from the far side of an off-horse as the frightened animals ran. There arose an outcry of triumph among the Indians and they charged the wagon once again. Two of the Indians reached the loose horses and jumping from the backs of their own mounts, drew sharp knives and slashed through the entangling hobbles, freeing the two horses. With war-hoops, the two raced after the mounts, only to be felled by gunfire from the wagon. The other Indian dropped from the animal he was hiding behind and disappeared in the buffalo grass.

A group of five or six Indians reached the wagon at the same time, and three of them managed to leap from the backs of their ponies in an attempt to land inside with the defenders. The others were gunned down. All mayhem broke out, with the girls screaming, the men yelling, and the Chinaman jabbering about the "clazzy savrages." One of the braves raised a war club to strike Gareth when Buddy shot him and the Indian toppled over the side. As the other two warriors came over the top of the wagon, with deadly lances poised to strike, Suzanne snapped the loading gate shut on Bud's pistol and fired at the nearer one. That Indian fell on the edge of the wagon box, his lance buried into the boards of the wagon next to her, and with a blood curdling yell he dropped from the side of the wagon to land dead on the ground below. The other Indian grabbed Kathreen and was trying to toss her over the side of the wagon when Two-Bits fired his gun, killing the Indian instantly. Suzanne slumped to the floor of the wagon, but Kathreen's captor had managed to get her above the wagon board and when he fell over the side still clutching the girl, she tumbled out to land in a heap on the grass next to his body. Almost immediately, a Comanche was there to reach down and scoop her up as though she were no more than a child, and then attempted to ride off.

With a wild yell, Two-Bits Thompson vaulted from the wagon bed, his rifle in hand, and set out at a run after the departing Indian and the little gal from Saint Louis. But Kathreen was one little gal who was a force the capturing Comanche had not reckoned on. She scratched and bit and kicked at the savage, who tried vainly to ward off her surprising attack, and it was not until a cruel blow to her head from his war club silenced the girl that he was able to drape her across his knees and ride on.

Desperate, Two-Bits dropped to one knee, raised his rifle and holding a long breath, drew a bead between the Indian's shoulders and squeezed the trigger. The warrior pitched sideways and hit the ground, stone dead. Kathreen, still unconscious, toppled from the running horse and landed in a tumbling heap in the grass. Two-Bits raced towards her inert form, while at least two mounted warriors kneed their ponies in her direction. When the cowboy got to Kathreen, the lead Comanche was bearing down on him with a wicked lance leveled at his chest. Two-Bits fired his rifle one-handed, and the heavy slug knocked the attacking savage over backwards off his horse. With no time to lever in another round before the second Indian was upon him, the cowboy dropped his rifle, drew his six-gun and pumped two bullets into the second Indian, killing him outright.

Thompson scooped up Kathreen, slinging her over his shoulder while clutching his rifle, and raced back to the safety of the wagon while his trail-mates laid down covering fire.

Suddenly, a lone rider appeared on a dark horse galloping towards the travelers, a long-eared mule in tow, braying reluctantly. At once, the Indians broke off the attack, and sat their horses watching the mysterious rider.

There was something very familiar about him, and with a start, Suzanne realized that it was Sonny who was racing his pony towards them at break-neck speed. Looking back at the Indians, she saw they seemed to be giving Sonny a wide birth. At least half their number lay dead or dying all around the wagon. The defenders, once they saw the Indians had given up, allowed them to carry off those of their dead and wounded that lay in the outer perimeter of the battle area. The two saddle horses that had had their hobbles cut went with them.

Sonny pulled up in a cloud of dust and quit the saddle at a run, jerking his Winchester from the scabbard as he came.

"Lookout, here I come," he shouted and dove under the wagon to take up a shooting position.

Everything was quiet in the wagon above, the occupants staring at each other in amazement at Sonny's unexpected appearance and at the silent Indians riding away. Finally, the sound of Sonny uncocking his rifle was heard and then the rustling of the grass as the tall, dusty cowboy came crawling out from under the wagon to stand to his feet and look after the departing Comanche.

"Huh," Sonny said and scratched the back of his head, causing his hat to ride forward over his brow. "who'd a thought they'd give up that easy."

"Sonny!" exclaimed Suzanne, "where did you come from?"

Sonny turned to stare at the occupants in the wagon. They reminded him of a bunch of geese he'd seen once in a basket on their way to market. "Same place as you, Miss Kluesman, Wade's Landing by way of White Bear's Kiowa camp and Grampa Fithens in Bryan," he said.

Kathreen spoke up, "I should have known that you'd show up too late whenever there's trouble."

Sonny gave the disheveled red-head an amused look and said, "Why am I not surprised that you're in the middle of this fracas, Red, what you been doing, wrestling with a dust devil?"

"Just you never mind, at least I had a real cowboy here to rescue me from those blood-thirsty creatures." She turned and gave Two-Bits a sweet and endearing smile, her theatrics not lost on anybody.

"Two Bits, Buddy, what you boys doing here?" Sonny said, and jumped up on the wagon tongue to hold out his hand to the two range hands.

"Just helpin' the boss fetch home 'n old bull," Two-Bits mumbled, his ears still red from Kathreen's unexpected approval.

After Two-Bits let go of Sonny's hand, Buddy shook it and said, "Sonny, meet the boss of the Box 7, Mr. Gareth Hazelhurst."

Gareth shook Sonny's hand and beamed a broad smile, "Pleased to meet you, Saber, you sure put the fear of God into those Indians. What did you do to scare them away like that?"

"Aw, you boys had 'em pretty well whipped by the time I got here, guess they figured one more repeating rifle was one more than they wanted to deal with."

"Well, we're glad to have you. Would I be correct in assuming that you are in search of your brother, the same as these young ladies?"

"That I am," Sonny said. "I got word in Bryan he was last seen in Abilene and took the trail north a week or so back. When I heard the shootin', I came ridin' over to see what it was all about. I never figured it would be your party, somebody must be looking after us."

The small party had fared amazingly well given the ferocity of the attack. It was only due to Divine Providence that Hazelhurst had thought to bring the heavily-planked bull wagon, for it had provided excellent cover for the defenders. Apart from a few powder burns and some scrapes and bruises, there were no injuries other than a large goose egg on Kathreen's head. She had several scratches as well from her fall and was badly bruised, but was in amazingly good spirits after her ordeal.

"I guess I showed that red-skin not to mess with this little white girl," she grinned to her friend.

"Kathreen," Suzanne said, "you were nearly carried away to some Indian's wigwam. If Two-Bit's hadn't shot that Indian, you'd be their captive now."

"Yea, I know, and if I was they'd be sorrier than me. Ain't no wild Indian ever going to get me down."

Suzanne shook her head, "Girl, you're crazy, that was no laughing matter."

"So, who's laughing? Not me, not that Indian, not even that bow-legged cowboy over there. He packed me back here safe and sound. Who'd a figured he could run that fast?"

"You are incorrigible."

Two-Bits had just ridden up from bringing in the rest of the loose horses and heard Kathreen's latest remark. With an inscrutable look, he swung down from his saddle and strode over to where Kathreen was sitting on an upside-down bucket. He stood looking at her for a moment while Kathreen was strangely silent, then he reached out a careful hand to her chin and lifted her face to peer into her eyes.

"You alright?" he asked.

"Um-hum," Kathreen responded.

For a long moment the two of them looked at each other, then Two-Bits lifted his hand to carefully brush at her cheek and said, "Got a little dirt on you here."

"Thanks," she mumbled.

The cowboy paused just a moment longer, then nodded and turned to help his pard un-hobble the saddle horses, while Sonny stood tying Hank off to the back of the wagon. He saw it all.

Suzanne watched the whole affair through attentive eyes and smiled to herself. She wondered at her friend and just how everything was going to end up. She looked over at Sonny, curious about what he might be feeling with this turn of events. If Colt's brother was to ever realize any happiness, any true love, he might be wise to resume his suit of this Scottish lassie from Saint Louis before someone else captured her reckless heart.

The travelers hurriedly got the wagon moving and left the gruesome scene with its slain Indians. Sonny found room for his pack saddles in the wagon and relieved a grateful Hank of that burden. He joined Two-Bits and Bud driving what was left of the extra horses for the rest of the afternoon, leaving the two girls to travel by themselves.

A few days later they were camped by a small stream. Since the Comanche attack, Sonny had been taking the point, scouting about a mile ahead of the party, and travel had been without incident. Sonny had told an amazing story of being caught in a buffalo stampede and then captured by Kiowa, and that somehow he was being regarded as a powerful medicine man by the Indian tribes of the plains, at least by the Kiowa and Comanche. Suzanne wondered if that was why there was no further bother from the Indians during the attack.

That evening, Suzanne was returning from a short excursion into the bushes when Sonny looked up from where he was mending a piece of harness leather. The others were engaged in various camp chores or picketing and hobbling horses. Kathreen was by the fire chatting with Gareth Hazelhurst.

"Miss Kluesman, I wouldn't be wandering too far away from camp if I were you," Sonny said.

Suzanne had noticed that since Sonny had joined them he had been his usual, happy-go-lucky self around the others, especially Kathreen, but had treated her with unusual coolness and stiffness, bordering on awkwardness, and she didn't know what to make of it.

"Sonny, why are you being so formal?"

"Didn't know I was, ma'am," he gave her a quick look, then turned back to his work. "I wouldn't want you to fall prey to the redskins is all."

"Sonny, stop it. Surely we must remain friends."

"Must we?

"Yes! Please call me Suzanne."

"Huh, I love you too much to ever just be your friend."

"I'm sorry you feel that way," Suzanne said, "I've always counted you as my friend and I don't like this starchy way you are treating me."

Sonny put down the leather strap and looked up at the girl with penetrating eyes. "I will try to do better, Suzanne... guess I need a little time."

"I'm sorry, Sonny, you have been the best of friends to me. I know I could never have made it this far without you and I am truly grateful."

"I feel like I have been handed my head on a platter and now this... seeing you and all—being around you, has brought it all back. I am going to have to work the knots out that's all. I'll do better'n get it figured out."

"Good! Can I ask you something?"

Sonny stared at the girl, his guard up. "What?" he said slowly.

"What will you do when we find Colt?"

Sonny swallowed hard; that was the question he had been asking himself for the past six or seven months. Part of him wanted to beat his brother to within an inch of his life, and the other side of him was dying to find out what had happened to him and where he'd been. He knew the first part stemmed from jealousy and resentment at having lost out over this girl and the unjustified assault he'd suffered when shot. These were feelings he would have to rise above. The other side of the coin called to a higher and nobler part of his being, a part that went further back to their childhood and the brotherhood they'd shared. He had a deep need to find Colt and set things straight, as well as learn what all had become of him for the past two and a half years.

Sonny shrugged, "I guess I'll know when I find him," he said.

"You won't do anything foolish, will you?"

"Like what?"

"Shoot him or something like that."

Hearing it said that way, Sonny knew that no, he would never do anything like that. Colt was too near and dear to him. How could he live with such a thing, it had been hard enough when he had believed he'd lost his brother before in that terrible accident.

Sonny shook his head and gave a heavy sigh, "No, I won't shoot him."

"You don't know how much that eases my mind, thank you, Sonny, for that. How are we going to find him?"

"God knows where he is. When I was at Grandfather Fithens', he made this incredible prayer asking God to show us where to find Colt and get this whole matter straightened out. Then he gave the Devil his walking papers, so I guess all we have to do is the next thing and let God lead us to him."

"He did that?" Suzanne said.

"Yes, I never ever heard anybody pray like that. It made the hair stand up on the nape of my neck and when I got up from that chair I felt like I could whip my weight in wildcats."

"What's the next thing?" Suzanne said.

"Get to Abilene and try to find our way to Colorado, I guess."

The miles rolled away under the wagon wheels and the prairies were green with spring. The wildflowers and teeming life of the range made Suzanne feel wonderfully alive, despite the urgency of their mission. Twice, they were delayed by huge herds of buffalo and several times large bands of antelope and grazing elk herds were seen in the distance. Once they called a halt on the back side of a low hill when Sonny rode back and warned them that there was a band of Indians traveling ahead. The party ascended to the top of the low knoll on foot and watched a group of Indians about a mile off, with their women, children and tepees traveling in the direction of the last big buffalo herd that had passed the day before.

Kathreen's whole demeanor had changed towards Two-Bits since Sonny's arrival to the group. Her attentiveness and shows of affection had reduced the bow-legged cowboy to a tangle-footed mess around the camp, much to Buddy's amusement and Sonny's ire. Suzanne had no doubts as to what her friend was up to. It was obvious it was all designed to provoke Sonny, but Suzanne knew it was an uphill fight for her friend. Sonny was, as he had put it, still "unknotting" her from the strings of his heart. And he was doing better too, his attitude towards her had become more gentle, more kind and considerate, and he went about more cheerful, although Suzanne knew some of it was put on with effort. She still found him staring sad-eyed at her from time to time in unguarded moments.

Twice they passed trail herds of cattle and even spent a couple of days traveling with one. Suzanne and Kathreen were a big hit with the cowboys until finally the trail boss of the first drive complained to Hazelhurst that the hands were slacken' off in their duties, and urged their party to move on.

"I cain't get these cow-nurses to stick with the herd with you all in camp, you s'pose you could move on? It'd be less dusty for you."

Gareth said that they needed to be moving on anyway and the next morning the bull wagon and party pulled out after breakfast with the entire crew of cowboys standing around, crestfallen and hats in hand watching them go.

The second herd was an outfit of less friendly men, most of them appearing to have something to hide. They were invited to spend an evening meal with the camp, but the riders kept to themselves while watching the visitors, the girls in particular, with furtive stares and low whispers over their coffee cups and tin plates. When the meal was over, Hazelhurst thanked the trail boss and told him they'd be moving on. There was still a little daylight left and the party moved out to finally bed down along a pleasant, willow-lined stream some ten miles ahead.

"That scruffy outfit gave me the creeps," Kathreen said to her friend as the two girls crawled into their blankets under the wagon.

"They weren't very nice," Suzanne agreed.

"You got that pistol Colt gave you?" Kathreen asked.

"Right here." Suzanne patted her coat rolled up for a pillow.

"Good, if any of those creeps come crawling around, blast 'em."

"You seem a little testy tonight, Kathreen, what's bothering you?"

"Oh... I don't know. It's the same old thing, you love Colt, Sonny loves you, I like Sonny and now Two-Bits likes me. How'd this thing get so mixed up?"

"Kathreen, Sonny and I are through and he knows it, and Two-Bits would probably happily fade into the sunset if you'd quit using him to bait Sonny. You need to give Sonny some room and stop crowding poor Two-Bits."

"Hey, a girl could do a lot worse than Two-Bits, he certainly was there in the clinch for me."

"I thought you didn't want to end up barefoot and pregnant in some cowboy's shack on the prairie with flies crawling around your tea cup."

"I don't, but Two-Bits or Sonny, what's the difference?"

"You tell me, best friend."

"Well—there is a world of difference in some ways," Kathreen lapsed into silence with that remark, and Suzanne's thoughts turned to what life would be like if she were married to Colt and Kathreen to Sonny.

A few days later, they crossed the Kansas State Line. A group of thugs were known to ride the border, meeting the cattle herds coming up from Texas and demanding payment at so much a head from the drovers. They had gained a reputation as "Jayhawkers" and were supposedly under the sanction of the State House to discourage Texas cattle from coming in and spreading tick fever, but most of them were rogues and ruffians left over from Quantrill's Raiders and like groups from the War Between the States. They were largely a lawless and undisciplined lot that paid no allegiance to any but their own kind and interests. They would confront any travelers they came across, especially parties that were small and undefended, demand payment or else just rob, loot, rape, pillage, and take anything of value, and then usually murder the victims.

Sonny rode back to the wagon the third day into Kansas after having ridden out at the start of their travels for the day. He stopped to talk with Gareth Hazelhurst while the rest of them gathered around.

"We got trouble a brewing," he said.

"What's going on?" Gareth asked, "Indians?'

"No, I don't think so. It's Jayhawkers."

"What should we do?" the rancher asked.

"You want to make payment to them to pass?"

"Do you think we should?"

"No, I say we make a stand and fight."

"How many are there?" Buddy asked.

"Twenty."

"If they see these girls and the horses, they won't settle for no toll anyhow, they'll just come back and murder us in our sleep and take the girls and our stuff."

"Let's shoot 'em," Two-Bits said. "We'll hobble the horses and tie 'em off to the wagon like we did with the Indians and climb into the wagon box and blast them to kingdom-come."

"Okay," Sonny said. "You girls get into the wagon and get all the extra guns loaded. If shooting breaks out, keep your heads down and load for us. Buddy, you ride over to that plot of willows and tie your horse out of sight and get into position with your rifle. Two-Bits, you do the same on the other side by those rocks, and we'll catch them in a cross fire if they open the ball. Gareth and I will stay here with the wagon, as I am quite sure they saw me and are following my tracks back here. They won't know you boys are in hiding."

The Box 7 outfit had barely taken up position when a dust cloud was seen on the horizon and a group of rough-clad men rode up to where the wagon stood. Gareth was on the wagon seat, holding the reins of the team while the Chinaman and the girls were huddled behind the side-boards out of sight. Sonny sat Tornado to one side, his manner easy but coiled like a spring, ready to strike.

"Hold up here," a big man dressed in a dark three-piece suit said as he and the others pulled up their horses in a line, blocking the progress of the travelers. "We represent the State of Kansas and all travelers are required to pay a toll when entering the state."

Gareth Hazelhurst said, "How much is the toll?"

"Five dollars per person and two dollars for each horse. Let's see, you got nine horses and the two of you, that'll be eighteen, plus another ten dollars—we'll just round it off to thirty bucks."

"We ain't a gonna pay no toll," Sonny said.

The big man turned to look at the cowboy. "If you don't pay the toll we are authorized to impound your stuff and set you afoot."

"You can try," Sonny said, "but we have a constitutional right to shoot you dead if you do."

The leader seemed a little taken aback at Sonny's challenge, it was plain he was not used to being defied by his victims. "Young man, we are duly authorized agents of the State and you will comply with our orders."

One of the riders stood in his stirrups and peered over the side of the wagon, "Boss," he said, "there's a couple a pretty girls and a chink in the back of this wagon."

The big man nudged his horse forward and Sonny drew his pistol, cocked it and pointed it at the fellow's double-breasted vest.

"That's as far as you go, either pull iron or turn around and get," Sonny said.

The leader of the gang eyed the bore of Sonny's gun and then said, "Lets ride boys," and began to swing his horse around. At that moment, he reached for the gun at his hip and the rest of his men went for theirs. Sonny shot the leader out of his saddle, and then leaping from Tornado into the wagon, he began a rapid firing of his six-gun at the rest of the desperadoes. Gareth had piled into the protection of the wagon and was firing his pistol as well. The outlaws were firing back at the wagon when Buddy and Two-Bits opened up with their rifles, taking one after another of the Jayhawkers out of their saddles with deadly accuracy. It was over in a moment with every last one of the thieves lying dead on the ground.

Sonny climbed down from the wagon and mounted the grulla, while Two-Bits and Buddy rode back up.

"It's a good day's work done here today, ridding the border of this vermin, nice shootin' fellas," Sonny said. "We had this kind tryin' to hack a toll out of us with the Goodnight, Loving outfit in Colorado. The best way to deal with it is pay no toll and take no prisoners."

Buddy and Two-Bits nodded their heads grimly and looked at their boss who was busily writing something on a placard piece of Cardboard. Gareth held it up for all to see, it read: "*This is the only toll these Jayhawkers collected.*" It was tacked to a stout stick and stuck in the ground amidst the bodies.

The Hazelhurst party reached Abilene by the end of May after a long and tiresome journey, at least for the ladies. Suzanne and Kathreen put up in the hotel where they gladly reacquainted themselves with the comforts of a hot bath and a real bed. Gareth, Two-Bits, and Bud took a room down the hall, while Wong stayed with the outfit at the stock pens. Sonny stayed somewhere unknown to the girls. Once they were all settled in, the Box 7 men went out to finish their business down at the stockyards.

"What do we do next?" Kathreen asked.

Suzanne finished hanging up a dress in the closet and momentarily wondered why she had brought so many, given the rough country they were traveling through. "Go to the train depot and get tickets for Denver," she said.

"What'll we do once we get there?" her friend persisted.

"Look for Colton," Suzanne said simply.

"Look for Colton? My Lord, woman, have you any idea how many men we will have to sift through to locate him or anyone who might know of his whereabouts?"

"Plenty, I'm sure," the blonde girl replied, "but look at this, I have added these alterations to the wanted poster." Suzanne held up one of the posters in which she had drawn in with a dark pencil, a beard and mustache on Colton's face.

"You marked up his picture, how come?"

"His cowboy friend said he has grown a beard, I am trying to make the picture more recognizable for folks. Look at this one." She held up another doctored poster, this time with a longer beard on Colt's face.

"Well, best friend, that is a very good idea."

"Yes, I thought so. I plan to show it around this town too, perhaps someone may recognize him."

Buddy and Two-Bits had just pulled up a couple of chairs at a table in the *Bull's Head Tavern,* and were all set to enjoy a couple of beers, when a swarthy-looking character stepped up to their table and invited himself to sit down. He was ruffling a deck of Cards and introduced himself as Frenchy, late of Galveston.

Meanwhile, Suzanne Kluesman tentatively knocked on the door of the Sheriff's Office and was admitted by a deputy who studied the doctored wanted poster, and shook his head.

"Nope, sorry ma'am, but there's been so many of those Texas cow punchers through here of late it's pretty hard to keep track of 'em all. He don't look familiar to me, but maybe Marshal Hickok might a seen 'im."

"Where can I find Marshal Hickok?" Suzanne asked.

At that moment, a shadow fell across the open door and a deep voice said, "What can I do for you, Miss."

Suzanne turned to see a tall, well-dressed man with long hair, a dapper goatee and curling mustache studying her intently with searching eyes.

"Are you Mr. Hickok?" Suzanne said.

"I am, how can I help you?"

Suzanne held up the poster. "I am looking for this man, have you seen him?"

Wild Bill studied the picture for a moment and then nodding his head, said, "Yes, I think he was with a rowdy bunch of Texas cowboys that came up the trail a few weeks ago. I caught him packing his hog-leg and told him to turn in his gun until he left town. He said he was leaving then and took off for his horse. Last I saw of him he was riding west out of here. What's he wanted for?"

Suzanne was startled at the question. It had never occurred to her that in her asking, the law might have an interest in Colt's apprehension. "Oh, it's nothing really, a huge misunderstanding. He is being sought as a missing person. He's my fiancé and I must find him and explain some things."

Marshal Hickok stared intently into the blonde girl's eyes until the blue of them wavered and fell and her cheeks flamed scarlet. "So, it's more of a personal thing than a legal matter," Hickok said.

Suzanne nodded her head.

"Well, Miss, if this cowboy is dumb enough to run away from the likes of you, he is dumber than most of 'em, my sympathies lie with you. Should I see him, I'll clap him in irons and hold him for you... would that be alright?"

"Oh, no sir, he doesn't need to be arrested, just tell him I'm looking for him and need to talk to him, okay?"

"I most assuredly will," Hickok said with a smile, "and I'll see to it that he listens too. Now whom shall I say is looking for him?"

"Just tell him Suzanne is trying to find him, and thank you very much. You're certain he is not in Abilene?"

"I'm certain."

"Then I shall bid you good day," Suzanne said.

CHAPTER TWENTY

South Park City

South Park, Colorado, May 1871

WHEN I RODE INTO THE HIGH GRASS BASIN known as South Park it was easy to see how the place got its name. Before me was a broad grassland valley nearly eighty miles long and maybe half again as wide. I told Lightfoot, "Who'd ever figure on a place like this being way up here in these mountains?" The horse just looked around and acted like he wanted to run for a change. There hadn't been much chance for that coming up through Platte Canyon and the Front Range.

I kicked him into a trot and let my eyes range over the surrounding mountains that rimmed the entire basin. Rows of pines and tamarack marched down the canyons and draws like troops of soldiers only to make their last stand at the valley floor. Foothills speckled with aspen and cottonwood in the draws, indicating water and springs, were interspersed with patches of scrub oak, willow and sage. Soon, I began to see signs of cattle, evidence of ranching taking over the basin from the herds of buffalo, elk, antelope and deer which were still plentiful.

At one point, we trotted towards a large herd of elk and I expected to see the whole bunch of them flee in a cloud of dust, but to my surprise they did not, only those

337

closest paid any attention to us at all. What was the most startling was the way Lightfoot began to act. His head came up and he began to prance and dance about nervously, turning sideways toward a large bull which went on the prod and began to bugle back at him, shaking his head and massive rack while making quick starts at my horse. Lightfoot's tail came up and the hair of his coat was sticking straight out. I looked back at Sidekick and the bay was the same way. Both horses began to whistle and call back at the bull, and for a few moments I figured I was going to be caught sitting in the middle of a horse-elk fight. They carried on like that until finally my spurs got the better of Lightfoot's belligerent instincts, and the sorrel broke into a run away from the scrappy bull, with Sidekick all too willing to follow.

Riding west I began to see hay fields, some fenced in, and eventually I came to the gate posts of a ranch with the name Sam Hartsel in faded letters, swinging in the breeze. The wind was a might cold, even for this time of year at this elevation, and I could only wonder what it would be like here in the dead of winter. Riding up to a two-story house nestled among some old pines, I was met by a couple of hounds whose baying soon had a man in his mid-forties out on the porch in his shirt sleeves, hailing me. He inviting me to step down and come in for coffee.

Sam Hartsel was a rancher who had homesteaded his place ten years earlier and was running a couple hundred head on his and his wife's joint homesteads. In back of the place was a rocked-in hot spring which looked inviting and I was offered a chance to shed some trail dust, join them for supper and spend the night. I found him to be friendly and welcoming, a broad and expansive man such as was often found among men of the west. After I had soaked in the hot springs pool, I dressed in some clean clothes and went into the ranch kitchen where I met

Mrs. Hartsel who had set a place at the table and invited me to sit down and share the news. We chatted about Denver and Colorado Springs over a delicious meal of fried chicken, mashed potatoes, gravy, and all the fixings. I was put in mind of my mother's home cooking. I shared some of my cattle driving experience, and Hartsel inquired as to whether I might be interested in a riding job, but I told him about my plans to talk to Allen on Terryall Creek. He said he didn't know Allen but that there were a lot of prospectors all up and down the creek as far west as Como clear on up to South Park City and Alma. I thanked him for supper and was offered a bed for the night. After putting up my horses, we sat around visiting into the wee hours of the morning, and I learned much about the area and the burgeoning settlements springing up around South Park City. It seems that when the first diggings sprang up around the Terryall and Hamilton mining camps, unseemly large claims had been allowed to some of the greedier miners. Then, when gold was discovered at the juncture of Beaver Creek and the South Platte, fairer-size claims were staked, giving the place the name of Fairplay. It was then changed to South Park City, although there was some talk of changing it back to Fairplay. I learned that the smelter was a few miles northwest at a place called Alma, which was at the juncture of Buckskin Creek and the South Platte. Here was a wide-open town with the usual tawdry houses of ill-repute, saloons, Card and billiard houses that went along with it, its erstwhile reputation made even more-so when the small community of Dudley, just a mile up the road and owned by the Moose Mine, had established a city ordinance against such places. The manager of the mine would not allow any drinking or gambling.

We finally went to bed, but it had been so long since I had slept indoors and in a bed that I had a hard time getting to sleep. So much about the place reminded me of home, and my mind roamed freely over all that I had known back in Texas on the Crossed Sabers. My dad had a large and prosperous ranch and me shooting my brother and abandonment of my father had undoubtedly left him shorthanded and in the lurch. I felt awful for my treachery. He had not deserved my betrayal and desertion. I wondered if I could ever face him again and what he would do if I did. Finally, I took a couple of blankets and spread them out on the hard floor of the upstairs bedroom I was in and went to sleep.

It seemed I had barely closed my eyes when the rooster was crowing and sounds and smells of breakfast wended their way up the stairs. I sat up, groggily pulled on my boots and clumped downstairs to be greeted by Mrs. Hartsel and a hot cup of coffee. On the back porch, I splashed cold water in my face, and then split some wood for the stove while breakfast was finishing cooking. I then sat down with Sam and Ruth to a mammoth breakfast of hot biscuits, gravy, eggs, bacon, sausage and wild raspberry jam. I ate so much I could barely lift the saddles on my horses when it was time to leave. After thanking them for their hospitality and promising to stay in touch, I rode out and headed up for Terryall Creek to find Jimmy Allen and his placer mine.

I rode through South Park City and discovered a thriving town supplying the local ranching and mining community. A log Methodist Chapel was situated on a hillside, as was most of the town, and I also observed a Catholic Church in the town. There were many prosperous-looking businesses and I determined a man could probably buy just about anything here that he could get in Denver. I stepped down at a general store and went in as a young clerk came over and asked if he could help me.

"I need a prospector's outfit," I said.

"Step right this way," the clerk replied.

He led me to one corner where I saw an array of picks, shovels, canteens, gold pans, sieves, buckets, tubs, sluice boxes and something he called miner's moss which looked more like burlap sacking than anything. I bought a gold pan, a pick and shovel, a tub, a sieve, and a couple of buckets when the clerk said, "You need any boots?" He was looking at the boots on my feet. I looked down too and realized these would never do for working the creeks. "I better get something a little more suited to mining than riding, what you got?"

He led me to a shelf of knee-high rubber boots and I found a pair that fit me and added them to my purchases. The clerk said they had some split cow horn that was a convenient tool for sampling, and when I expressed doubt he said, "All the boys use them, you take half a cow's horn and scoop up any likely looking gravels, toss out the big stuff and pan it down just like you do with a gold pan. It's a good way to spot color." By the time he was through, I had a split cow horn, a miner's ten power magnification loupe, and a half dozen sample bottles, along with tweezers, and a small tin funnel. Sidekick wasn't too thrilled with all the extra gear, especially the wobbly washtub, but Lightfoot told him to buck up, that he looked like most of the other jackasses packing miner's stuff around and he fit right in.

I came to a fork in the road, the left one leading to Alma, and the right to Como. I was going to Como, but wanted to see Alma which was only a few miles up the road so I turned left. When I reached Alma, I could see this was a place geared more to the industry of mining with machine shops and a stamp mill banging away. I noted a stage depot here with routes to Denver and over Hoosier Pass to Breckenridge. The fare to Denver was ten dollars. A sign over a saloon on the edge of town read, *"Alma's Only Saloon,"* which was pretty funny since I saw at least a half a dozen others, and I laughed out loud when I passed the cemetery and saw a grave marker that read: *"I love you but go to sleep."* As I returned to the Como road, I met a miner leading a burro with obvious ore samples in baskets on its back and asked him for directions to Terryall Creek.

"You fixin' to do some prospectin' that-a-way?" he said.

"Actually, I am looking for a fellow named Allen who has a claim there, you know him?"

"Jimmy Allen? I should smile, son, he's got his diggings about a mile below mine. What you want 'im fer?"

"His old pard, Orville Watson, told me he was looking for help and sent me up here from down Russellville way."

"Why, I believe he is needing help. You just follow the Middle Fork on past Montgomery and Como and about four miles beyond that little burg you'll find Terryall Creek. Allen's about four miles up the creek from there."

I spent the night in Como and had breakfast in a small cafe, then after looking around I left town and took a trail that led across a valley and over a small ridge where I found what the prospector had said was Terryall Creek. The trail turned northwest and with the wind at my back I pulled up the collar of my coat as there was a bite to it, but as late morning turned into early afternoon, the air warmed and it became quite pleasant. I traveled a wagon road that followed a winding, serpentine creek which flowed through the grasslands along the base of foothills with gulches and ravines emptying into it. Numerous mining claims were being worked along the creek and most of the miners stopped from their work to give me a curious stare, some with hands resting on their gun butts.

Rounding a bend in the trail, I saw the valley open up and in the distance, at the head of a gulch, not far from the creek, was a snug log cabin with a full porch running along the front nestled in the shadows of tall ponderosa pines. Smoke of a banked fire was curling slowly into the still air from a stone chimney, and nearby was a woodshed about half full of firewood. In a corral dozed a long-eared burro, and as I rode up, I saw a husky man in his mid to late fifties manning a shovel and tossing gravel into a fifty-foot long tom sluice. The sleeves of his red flannel long johns were rolled up and he was standing with rubber knee boots in six inches of mud and water, working the claim. My guess was this was Jimmy Allen at his Terryall Creek diggings.

I pulled Lightfoot to a stop on the bank and stared down at the miner. Allen tossed a couple more shovels full of material into the long tom before he stopped and rested on the shovel handle and stared back at me with sharp, dark eyes.

"Howdy, stranger, that's some outfit you got there," he said.

"Howdy, might you be James Allen?"

"Jimmy, yeah, I'm Allen. What can I do you for?"

"A fellow by the name of Orville Watson sent me up here, said you might be looking for somebody to work for ya, is that true?"

"Orv Watson, from down in Russellville? Yeah, I sent him a letter, so he sent you, did he?"

"Yep, I go by the handle of Pecos, what's the job?"

"Pecos? You're from Texas ain't 'cha?"

"I've been there," I said.

"You look more like a cowpuncher, you sure you want to step down in this muck?"

"There's gold in there, ain't there?"

Allen looked at me guardedly, "Yep," he said cryptically.

"I can get muddy for the right reasons."

"What I need is somebody with a size twenty neck and a size eight hat to dig off the overburden of this creek bed so that I can shovel the pay streak into the sluice. You think this shovel might fit your hand?"

"Wouldn't be the first time I bandied about one of those idiot sticks," I said. "Don't know about the neck, but the hat size is about right. What's the job pay?"

"I'll give you a share in what we make, ten percent of every cleanup to start off with and if you work out, I'll raise it to twenty percent, room and board included as long as you help with the cookin' and camp chores."

"I'm good with that, where do you want me to put my gear?"

"Dump your pack on the porch and turn your horses into the corral, then come back and I'll show you what to do."

I unsaddled the animals and led them to the corral. The burro began a raucous braying when the horses entered his domain and I saw Lightfoot pin his ears back and lunge at the little feller, but the game little donkey puckered up and aimed a two-legged kick at the sorrel stopping the red horse in his tracks. I saw Lightfoot give him a wide birth after that and reminded him to mind his manners while we were here. Sidekick moseyed over and started sharing the hay with his long-eared cousin and the two of them began a long palaver about being beasts of burden.

I shucked my riding boots and pulled on the rubber knee-highs. Grabbing my new shovel, I clomped on back to the creek and climbed down next to Allen. Jimmy stuck his shovel into the muck of the creek bottom and dug away about a foot of the top soil.

"This is overburden," he said. "You see this black sand looking stuff below it?" He took the side of the shovel and scraped until a black sandy surface appeared.

"Yeah," I said.

"That's where the pay-streak will lie. You can find black sand without any gold, but you won't find gold without black sands when you're placer mining."

"Placer mining?" I said.

"Yes, gold that is washed down from its source, usually from a vein located in hard rock, will end up in the stream like this here, and it will be found in a specific area where the current locates it, in what we call the pay streak. Simply put, due to its weight, gold will drop out of the water wherever the current slows, and ends up in certain places in the stream bed. This is what we call placer gold, pronounced plasser, but spelled place-er. When you are prospecting, you look for clues as to where the current slowed, like behind a rock or around a bend, especially during high water, and that's where you find the pay streak."

"I did some hard-rock mining down in Mexico a few years back." I said.

"You did, how'd that go?"

"Not so good, I smashed a big black fella's hands when using a single jack while drilling. I don't really remember too much about it except that I did not like working underground like that."

"There are essentially three kinds of gold deposits: hard-rock where the gold has occurred in the ground or in an outcrop or ledge; alluvial, where it is tumbling down the mountainside; and placer where it ends up in the rivers and streams. Your job is to shovel as much of this top stuff off as you can, I will shovel the rest into the sluice."

"Where do I put the top stuff?" I asked.

Allen pointed to a wheel barrow, "Put it in there, wheel it over these boards and dump it along the dam."

I had noticed an earthen dam was diverting the flow of the stream through one side of the creek bed, leaving several feet of exposed ground. Water was also being channeled through a wooden trough or flume which allowed Allen to divert some of it through his longtom and sluice.

We worked until close to sunset and I was wishing I'd bought some heavier work gloves, my hands were smarting pretty good by the time Allen called a halt and

345

said, "Let's go find some supper." My back was aching and my feet were cold as I sat on the porch and pulled the rubber boots off. Limping, I carried some wood in and fixed up the fire while Jimmy Allen whistled cheerily and sliced some spuds into a pan of hot bacon grease on the stove.

"How long you been in Colorado?" he asked.

"A couple of weeks, I reckon," I said. "I came up from Texas on a cattle drive to Abilene and then rode the Smokey Hills Trail to Colorado."

"How come you quit the cattle business? Prospecting's a whole lot different than chasing cows around."

"Wanted to see these mountains and maybe get lost in 'em for a while," I said.

"Got any family?"

I hesitated and then said, "Not so's you'd notice."

"I been batchin' for nigh onto thirty years," he said. "These old mountains almost feel like family to me now."

"I'd like to look around a bit, maybe do some hunting and fishing," I said. "Are there any fish in this Terryall Creek?"

"Fishing can be good once you get away from the riled-up waters of mining. I've seen some nice eastern brook and rainbow trout in some of the holes once the water's cleared up. You'll find elk, bear, deer and antelope up most of the draws and in the higher country this time of year, and of course there is buffalo out in the basin, although they, too, are heading into the hills as more farmers and ranchers come in. You will need to keep an eye out for redskins too, most of the Ute have pulled out for west of the divide, but we still get a hunting party or bunch of renegades from off the reservations now and then. Also, the Cheyenne and Arapaho trickle through in small bunches once in a while and can play hob with isolated folk, so keep your eyes peeled, they still got a mad on."

"What about robbers?" I asked. "It seems with all the gold being mined here about, you'd have problems with thieves."

"Some," Jimmy said reflectively, "a man doesn't want to be caught out without a side-arm or at least a long gun handy, but most of the thieves hang out in the towns disguised as gamblers, card-sharps and whores. I hope you aren't a drinking man."

"Nope, never touched the stuff, don't gamble or consort either, I was never fetched up that a way."

"Good, keep your nose clean and sleep well at night, I say, 'though I don't always practice it."

Allen served me a robust supper of spuds, onions, a thick slab of ham and fresh biscuits with plenty of hot coffee to wash it all down. From my pack, I brought to the table a jar of honey that I'd picked up in town, and we enjoyed a good meal. I learned that a freight wagon came from the settlements once a week and the miners could order stuff from town to be delivered whenever it came by. It was expensive, but most of the miners figured it was worth paying the price rather than leaving their diggings to go to town since they would find more gold than what it cost to pay the freighter in the time that they would be gone. The weekends were an exception and the towns were usually a going concern when the miners came in to blow off steam and spend their gold.

The week passed quickly and soon it was Sunday. Jimmy said we would do a cleanup after breakfast and when we went down to the long tom, I watched Allen set up a large washtub at the end of the sluice, which like the long tom, was a trough-like affair with strips of lath at right angles in the box. Burlap sacking was on the bottom of the box and the lathing in the sluice was a separate lattice affair wedged into the box on top of the sacking. Jimmy explained how the strips of lattice, called riffles, created a turbulence with a quiet water area in front of each lath and this is where fine gold would settle and be trapped in the burlap. The bigger nuggets were usually lodged in the upper box of the long tom behind the first few riffles with the finer gold captured in the sluice.

The water to the long tom had been shut off the night before, and by morning most of the concentrates had dried to the point that you could brush through them and pick out any nuggets. A nugget was anything that was big enough to go clunk in the gold pan. If it didn't clunk, it wasn't considered a nugget. I watched Allen push through the material at the upper end of the longtom and pick out and drop several nuggets into his gold pan. Soon there were several pieces gleaming back from the thin covering of water in his pan. I felt a strange excitement when I saw the glistening nuggets for the first time. He had me join him and we worked through the upper riffles that were permanently nailed down to the long tom, until we could find no more.

"We'll just pan this bunch down and get rid of the tailings," Jimmy said. I followed him over to the washtub where he hunkered down and began a quick, systematic washing of the accumulated gold, floating off the lighter material until nothing was left but some black sand and the heavier nuggets. These he dumped out on a board to dry in the sun and then turned back to the long tom. Placing a screen mesh over the washtub, he now went to the headgate of the flume and lifting it, he allowed about an inch of water to flow under the gate into the long tom. He then took a stiff-bristled brush and, starting at the top he began to brush out all the lodged material that was behind each riffle. As the water flowed down, it carried this material to the end of the sluice where it discharged onto the screen, and he had me stand and watch for any nuggets that might be too large to pass through the mesh. He had me try to retrieve these, but also keep the excess gravel bushed off the screen. Once the long tom was cleaned thoroughly, Allen reduced the flow of water by half and gently tapped the wooden lattice affair from the sluice box. This allowed all the accumulated material there to tumble over the burlap and onto the screen. Setting aside these riffles, he made a quick inspection of the screen over the tub, tossed off the excess gravels and put the screen to the side. Last of all, he allowed the water to wash the burlap off into the tub, brushed the bottom of the sluice and then had me stop the flow of water altogether while he drug the tub out, rinsed the burlap up and down in the water for about five minutes before draping it over a nearby bush and carefully poured off the excess water in the tub. There was close to a bucket full of water, concentrated sand and fine gravel left in the bottom of the tub.

"Pecos, get your gold pan, I am going to show you how to pan gold."

I had been practicing all week and was slowly getting the hang of it, but was nowhere near as accomplished as Jimmy Allen. He had me fill my washtub about halfway with water and then, sitting on an upside-down bucket, I began to pan concentrates back into it from his tub, until I was down to black sand and some fine rice-sized and flour gold. This was spilled off into another bucket and the procedure continued until all the material in the first tub was processed. The final bucket of material had most of the water spilled off and the rest of the finished concentrate was poured into a heavy cast iron skillet and set on the stove to dry. Allen carefully collected the first tiny pile of nuggets and weighed them on gold scales and it came to just over three ounces.

"Looks like we're making somewhere between a half and three quarters of an ounce a day, if the rest of the pay-streak runs like it has been. That's near twice as much as what I've been doing by myself. Shoot son, I'll have to up your wages if this keeps up."

When the gold in the frying pan had dried, it was spilled out onto a clean newspaper, the black sands were blown away and we had just over four and a half ounces of gold for six days' work. I had only been there five of those days, but Allen weighed out 29.8 grams of gold on his scale and told me to put it in my poke.

"That's more than ten percent," I said.

"That's alright son, you earned it."

Gold was around eighteen dollars and ninety-three cents an ounce, and this was over seventeen dollars for the five days—a little more than three bucks a day, which was good day wages, but I could see I wasn't likely to get rich any time real soon. Still it was a good education and the gold was beautiful. I had to laugh at myself. Compared to the gold I had seen in Mexico at the Tayopa Mine with its huge vault and locked steel doors, this piddling little amount was a drop in the bucket. Even the rooms full of gold bars and coin in the dreaded caverns of Victorio Peak far out-weighed what I was getting here, but somehow this gold, the gold earned by the sweat of my brow, took on special significance. This was new wealth, wealth that the world had not previously known, wealth that had been locked in the ground and would now become useful in the mainstreams of commerce, and it was wealth that I was contributing. To me it was more valuable than any gold I might have carried away from those other places.

When the cleanup was finished, I saddled up Lightfoot and put an empty pack saddle on Sidekick. Lightfoot was looking sideways at me and wondered what business I had making him work on Sunday, but I told him, "You been getting fat and lazy standing around in this corral just switching flies, I'm taking you boys out in the cathedral of the forest for a little adventure." I led the horses out of the corral and replaced the gate so Allen's burro wouldn't get out and then rode down the creek.

A couple miles past Allen's claim, I turned up a draw that had a babbling brook draining into Terryall. A good game trail followed the stream course up into the hills, meandering through rocky cut banks and brush with scrub oak and juniper here and there. Above I could see a timber-covered bench and rode past a twenty-foot high waterfall where the stream dropped into a pool before it gurgled on towards Terryall Creek. Soon I was in the forest with ponderosa and bristlecone pine in abundance. The gully I was riding along opened up and here and there clearing edges were laced with aspen groves, while spruce, willow, and some cottonwood grew along the creek bank. In one section, a fire had burned through, clearing small brush and grasses and charring the thick bark of the trees, but it had been some years before and the place looked like a great grassy park, the trees healthy.

The little stream followed a shallow valley that widened, then narrowed and led through forested areas, then back out into open meadows, with abundant sign of wildlife. Flocks of turkey, so tame they paused in their feeding to watch us ride by with nary a worry, were everywhere. I saw bandtail pigeons, forest grouse, snowshoe rabbits, and it seemed like there was a gray or red squirrel on every tree scolding us as we rode by. I observed many species of birds with blue jays, stellar jays or camp robbers predominant, but also many song birds, even the mountain bluebird, and some that I did not even recognize.

I was riding along totally engrossed in my surroundings and found an enjoyment about the place that I hadn't experienced in a long time. It seemed in the bright sunlight and cool shadows with the pine-scented air, my troubles had all taken off to places unknown, and that was just fine with me.

I saw little sign of human encroachment other than an occasional wide spot where someone had shoveled in the creek, and it made me wonder how much gold was in the waters I was riding by. The trail continued on up from the meadows, and I could see the summit of mountain peaks ahead. Eventually, there were no more signs of prospecting, and the gully narrowed into steep rock walls with the brook racing through in whitewater rapids and tumbling short falls. At the base of a forty-foot high falls the trail I rode ended and it was necessary to back Lightfoot and the pack horse around and retrace my steps. I had to ride about a half mile back to find where the game trail diverged on an open meadow slope that led away from the stream and circled around and above the narrow canyon.

After ascending, I could look back and down to the grasslands of the basin and see the winding course of Terryall Creek. I estimated that I was already several hundred feet above the valley floor. Riding on, South Park was lost to view as I crossed over a shallow pass into a wider upland meadow where large pillow rocks of granite, some as large as a house, were piled upon each other in fascinating shapes and salted amongst the trees.

"Look at that, Lightfoot, it looks like big loaves of bread and buns were made in God's kitchen and turned to stone before He could get 'em baked."

Sidekick popped his head up and took a look, but Lightfoot just snorted me one and kept working on up the trail as though my being on him was worse than pea gravel in his oats. He probably had his doubts about God having a kitchen, too.

Off to my right stood a granite peak shaped like a buffalo and seemed to be the high point of this part of the ridge. I turned my mount in that direction. Coming to a ridge with a gradual ascent up toward the peak, I rode upwards, but noted that the trail I had been riding descended down into another mountain drainage to the north. As I climbed, I could see that a second creek ran alongside that trail through more timber and grassy parks.

"What a beautiful place," I said. It just sort of burst out of me in spontaneous admiration and it looked like Lightfoot and Sidekick agreed for there were no snide remarks coming from either one of them.

A stiff breeze was blowing as I rode on up towards the buffalo-shaped peak and it was a warm afternoon, the air pleasant and scented with pine. Suddenly I smelled smoke on the wind coming up from the valley before me, and presently I rode out onto a rock shelf near the base of the summit that supported a lightning-blasted bleached pine, half of which had fallen and stuck out over a stupendous drop-off. I could see a wide river valley below. My eyes scanned the terrain taking in a panorama of majestic forests, meadows and mountains. Suddenly I riveted on a small cluster of teepees perched at the mouth of the stream and draw I had just ridden away from.

"Boys," I said, "if we had stayed on that trail we would have busted right into that Indian encampment and that would a sure throwed the skunk into the church house."

Carefully, I worked back down off the ridge and retraced my steps back toward South Park. Once I had traveled enough distance, I relaxed and began to look for wild turkey because I figured a nice young tom would please Jimmy when I got back, and so began to keep an eye out for one. Riding back down around the falls, it wasn't long before I spied a flock of them catching grasshoppers in a meadow. Stepping out of the saddle, I tied the horses to some willows and pulled my sling from my coat pocket, then began to look for some likely-looking rocks along the stream. Something caught my eye, but then I found the perfect rock and, distracted, I forgot to check out what it was. I kept looking for a few more stones. I figured to bag one of the birds with the sling for two reasons: one, so as not to alert any lurking redskins, and two, to save lead... oh maybe for a third reason too, it had been awhile since I had used the little weapon and

I wanted to see if I could still hit my target. It took a couple of tries and fortunately my quarry wasn't spooked before I managed to leave a fat young tom flopping his feathers off under the pines. I picked up my game and went back to the horses, tied the bird off to the packsaddle, then mounted up and was headed back to the diggings when I remembered that something had caught my attention at the creek. Getting down, I walked back to where I found the stones and pulling my half-a-cow horn tester out, I scooped up some material from behind a large stone and began a careful panning of the lighter stuff away. To my surprise there were a half dozen colors in the crux of the horn. I sampled several more places up and down the creek for a distance of a hundred yards with like results.

"I wonder why no one has staked out a claim up here?" I said out loud.

When I got back, I told Jimmy Allen about my ride and the gold in the little stream.

He said, "You rode up Ute Creek, which is a seasonal stream and will probably dry up in a couple of months. I have found some gold up there, but since I already have this claim established and the safety of the other prospectors nearby, it seems better than being off by myself on the mountain."

"There's a couple of waterfalls up there, one of them pretty high," I said. "I rode on up and around it until I reached the top—lots of big pillow rock up there stacked up on each other. The top of the mountain reminded me of a buffalo."

"Yeah, that's Bison Peak, down the other side runs Willow Gulch and Indian Creek. It drains into the North Fork of the South Platte," he said.

"I saw the river and that's not all," I said. "There were five or six Indian teepees at the mouth of that gulch."

354

Jimmy Allen looked startled, "Indians you say? They've got to be a band of renegades. If they are just over the mountain from us, we best make sure we're packin' at all times."

"I was wondering about staking out a claim up there. The meadow where I got that turkey showed pretty good prospects," I said.

"You could do that," he allowed. "You'll need to go into Alma and file of course, and you should wait a few weeks to be sure those renegades have left before you set your corner posts. You know it won't be as easy as here, you'll be off the wagon road and have to pack all your stuff up to the site without a wagon."

I could tell Allen wasn't too keen about me leaving so I said, "I could still work for you some and work on my claim in my off hours."

"You'd be worn to a frazzle, son, I can get along okay without you. You need to get your diggings set up, there's not a whole lot of time before snow hits this high country, you know."

"I won't leave you in the lurch, I can do both," I said.

For the next two weeks, Allen and I worked his claim from daylight to mid-afternoon, then I would saddle up and pack Sidekick with some of the newly ordered supplies that had been dropped off by the freight wagon. I had ridden into Alma and filed a forty-acre claim that ran continuously from the lower waterfall to the upper one and encompassed a hundred yards on either side of the creek bed. Trout were plentiful in both pools at the waterfalls and often I would return to Allen's place in the evening with a mess of fish for supper. Eventually I set up a sidewall tent with a small stove and smoke stack and soon had a good pile of wood stacked up near the front. A couple of camp chairs and a collapsible army cot made for all the comforts of home and at length I began to alternate, staying with Jimmy during the week, and staying at my claim on weekends. I finished building a pole corral for the horses, and fencing in the larger meadow with poles nailed to posts and trees for their pasture.

I finally began a systematic working of the claim. Allen had told me that the stream would go dry in late summer and advised I consider building a dam and backing up some water in a reservoir to be used for sluicing once the water stopped. I had ordered a wheelbarrow and a slip scrape from the freight wagon, along with some heavy planking and lath for ripples, and with Jimmy's help built a sluice and hammered together a long tom of my own. Mine was not as long as Allen's but would have to do until such time as I could build a longer one.

Near the upper waterfall, the stream choked down through a narrow place in the rock and I found that by fashioning a sliding wooden gate and building up rock and dirt on either side, I could close the gate and practically stop the flow of water, which backed up into a large pond in the draw, clear to the base of the upper falls. From the face of the dam, I constructed a wooden flume that ran a distance of thirty feet in ten-foot sections and once the reservoir was full, I was able to direct the flow of water downstream and back into the creek bed, leaving an exposed area of creek bottom relatively water-free. Using a light buggy harness, I hitched Sidekick to the slip scrape, since Lightfoot refused, and plowed off the top layer of overburden, then using the wheelbarrow, I hauled what I hoped would be the pay gravels to the long tom and shoveled them in while water from the dam washed them down to the sluice.

By the end of June, I had my first clean up. I had worked the sluice and about thirty feet of streambed to bedrock and was at the end of my bypass flume and could go no farther without extending the flume. Jimmy came up and gave me a hand and we recovered twelve ounces of gold.

"Not too bad for your first clean up," he said. "You should take a broom now and sweep down the bedrock and work all the material out of the cracks and crevices of the rock. You will find good gold lying in there." He took a screwdriver, knelt down at a crack in the creek bed and began digging out the lodged material. Soon he had a pile which he put in his pan and then went to the dam and panned it out. There were several clunkers and rice-sized pieces gleaming in the bottom of the pan along with fine flour gold when he finished.

"This is a nice little basin here you're working. If you were to slip-scrape your leftover overburden across the front of this bowl, you could build an earth dam all the way across here and install your weir gate in the center of it. That would allow your reservoir to back up over the ground you have already worked, and you can continue to use the same bypass flume and not need to build more."

Allen encouraged me to work my own claim. "You can give me a hand whenever I need you for something more'n I can handle, and I'll do the same for you."

I finished crevicing the exposed bedrock and constructed the earth dam as Jimmy had suggested, and the result was a much larger pool of water held in reserve for the dry months ahead. Once the weir gate and flume were in place, I worked the next section of the claim, slip-scraping the overburden down to where the next dam would be. With this system in place, I worked throughout the summer on the claim and was recovering a respectable amount of color.

About once a week, I saddled Lightfoot and rode to the top of Buffalo Peak and viewed the Indians' campsite, but never saw them there again. I spent time hunting or fishing on these days, and kept Allen and myself supplied with venison and elk meat. Occasionally, on Saturday afternoon, we would go into town and enjoy a sarsaparilla, but on the last trip into Alma, I was shocked to see a wanted poster at the stage office depicting me with a beard and long hair. Allen never saw it or if he did, didn't seem to notice, but before we left town, I went into the little barber shop and had my beard shaved off and my hair cut.

When Jimmy and I rode into his claim that night, we were met by four men who held their guns on us and ordered, "Reach for the sky." From the looks of his cabin, they had ransacked it looking for his gold.

CHAPTER TWENTY-ONE

Denver and More

Abilene, Kansas, June 1871

SUZANNE STOOD ON THE LOADING PLAT-
form of the Kansas Pacific Rail Road depot and watched
as Sonny and a yardman loaded Tornado and Hank
into a stock car. Kathreen had just finished a prolonged
goodbye to Gareth Hazelhurst and his cowboys and had
stood watching them until they drove out of sight before
she turned to purchase their tickets to Denver.

"You took your time telling Two-Bits goodbye," Suzanne
teased her friend.

"Yes, he has a long way to go. I think I'm going to
miss him."

"Two-Bits and Buddy are great friends and true-blue,"
Suzanne said.

"Here's your ticket," Kathreen said, handing Suzanne
a packet of papers. "Where is Sonny? Has he loaded
his horses yet?" Kathreen was looking over Suzanne's
shoulder down the line of cars.

"The horse and mule are loaded, I imagine Sonny will
be here soon. Did you buy his ticket?"

"No, was I supposed to?"

Suzanne shrugged. "I don't know, I'll pay you back if you do. It is not real clear how our search for Colt will go from here."

Kathreen turned back to enter the depot. "I'll get him one." She entered the office and spoke to the clerk who looked up at the young lady and, when requested for a ticket to Denver for Sonny Saber, he said, "Mr. Saber has already paid for his fare, along with a horse and mule now loaded in the stock car."

"Sonny already bought his ticket," Kathreen said when she came back out. "We should go and find some good seats before they are all taken. I want to sit by a window, what side do you prefer?"

The girls were seated mid-way in the second coach on the right-hand side, facing forward when Sonny entered the car looking for them. The seat opposite the young ladies was occupied by a whiskey drummer who had just sat down and was eyeing the girls appreciatively. He opened his valise and spread several pamphlets out and then began thumbing through a notebook. Sonny stopped where they were sitting and then had to step out of the aisle and between the seats to let other passengers by. He grabbed an overhead hand rail to hold onto as the train jerked to a start.

"Here you girls are," he said while eyeing the vacant seat next to the whiskey drummer. "I thought you might have missed the train."

The whiskey drummer ignored the cowboy and went right on with his figures, making no effort to make room for the man standing. Sonny spied a seat in the back of the car and without saying anything, he began to gather up the man's literature, and stuff it into his open valise, and then to the drummer's astonishment, he picked the whole affair up and carried it to the back of the car, depositing it on the empty seat. Walking back, he said to the red-faced salesman, "I believe that seat back there was reserved for you." Then he sat down heavily bouncing the portly bald man a little as he did so.

The drummer looked from one to the other of the two ladies opposite him, annoyance plain on his face, and then turned to glare at the sober cowboy whose eyes stared steadily back at him with their warning unmistakable.

"You blasted cowboys," the drummer said as he got to his feet and made his way back to the end of the car.

"You like to throw your weight around, don't you?" Kathreen said.

"Nope, but I can't stand rude behavior either."

The train pulled out of Abilene and slowly picked up speed while the three young passengers stared out the window at the passing countryside.

Finally Suzanne spoke, "Sonny, if you are going to join us on our search for Colton, I think it only fair that we pay you."

"Sonny frowned, "Pay me—for what?"

"Your time," Suzanne said. "You would otherwise be working for your father and...."

Sonny cut her off, "No, I would be looking for Colt....I still am."

"Well, at least let us pay for your expenses," she insisted. "I am sure the fare to bring your horse and mule on this train was not cheap."

"Look, it doesn't matter, I would have had to bring them anyway, whether you were here or not," he declared. "I have taken care of it."

"How shall we travel from here on?" Suzanne asked.

"What do you mean?" Sonny said.

"Do we go our separate ways once we reach Denver, what is the best way to search for him?"

"I think we should pool our resources, check liveries, supply places, hotels, restaurants and the stage and train stations to see if anyone has seen him," Sonny replied. "Once we can establish a lead, you girls can put up in a hotel while I go track him down and drag his bullheaded hide back."

"We won't be staying in some hotel and waiting around on you," Kathreen put in, her defiance showing, "We'll be looking for him, too."

Sonny shrugged, "We'll cross that bridge when we come to it, first we got to find out where he's at."

———

Pierre LaRoush's eyes narrowed and he stepped back behind the depot when he saw Suzanne Kluesman and Kathreen McClusky standing on the loading platform. He had plied the two Texas cowboys at the Bulls Head Tavern with drinks while playing poker, and after several rounds was all ears when they spoke of having brought Miss Kluesman and Miss McClusky to Abilene. After that he managed to lose a few hands until he had gleaned all the information from them he could. He learned that the two young ladies were here in the company of Colt Saber's older brother, one Sonny Saber, and they were on the younger Saber's trail, headed for Denver. He could not believe his good fortune. Destiny had dropped this lead of his enemy into his hands and had sweetened the pot with the very two young ladies, in the whole wide world, who he most wanted to subject, ravish, and bend to his will. It was a simple matter after that of watching their hotel until he saw them head for the station with bags in tow.

Now, he watched the unsuspecting women board the train and he then quickly slipped into the depot, purchased a ticket for Denver and stepped onto the caboose just as the train left the station. Making his way through the train and carefully scanning each car before he entered, he was able to discover that his quarry was seated in the car immediately forward of the baggage car. He retraced his steps to the last car and found a seat facing the rear of the train. A newspaper would enable him to hide his face should the girls come back that way and by facing backwards, he would see them before they discovered him. Chuckling to himself, he rubbed his hands in anticipation of what was before him.

————

The miles rolled under the train's wheels with the clickety-clack of the rails providing a nice background for Suzanne and Kathreen as the two girls chatted about everything from the scenery to the fabric of the car seats they were sitting upon. When the train rolled past Fort Harker, the girls commented on the desolation and loneliness of the place and wondered at the men who were stationed there. Reaching Ellsworth, Kansas that afternoon, the train made a two-hour stopover while freight was being unloaded and loaded, and the passengers were invited to leave the train for the shops and restaurants that extended down the boardwalk from the station.

Sonny and the two girls paused at a small cafe with red checkered curtains and went in to order lunch. A pert young brunette in a starched apron that matched the checkered curtains led them to their seats and took their order. She said her name was Priscilla and she recommended the special of the day—a bacon and tomato sandwich with avocado, served with lentil soup. The trio ordered this, having never eaten avocado before. It was good, although Sonny said he didn't think the avocado had much taste. The fresh produce was a product of California, having been brought in by train, and the three of them were delighted to find it served in this quaint establishment.

Upon leaving the cafe, the girls were scandalized to see a young woman with no clothes on riding up the street on a white horse. She was being followed by a crowd of soldiers, miners and cowboys, and Kathreen threw an elbow into a surprised Sonny's stomach when she saw him straining for a second look.

"Why don't you take a picture?" she said, "it would last longer."

"Well, that do beat all," the cowboy said. "I wonder how she gets away with doing that?"

"She's a hootchy-kootchy gal from the Lady Godiva Saloon that's owned by the sheriff," a bystander offered in explanation. "He has her meet the train whenever it comes in, to advertise his business."

"What will they think of next?" Sonny said mystified.

"I think it's sad, what some girls come to." Suzanne said, and turned back towards the general store. Upon entering the business, she walked to the counter and showed the clerk one of the doctored posters of Colton. "Have you seen this man?' she asked.

"The man peered over his wire-rim glasses and said, "He looks like the fella' that tied a can to the tail of that Craig n' Johnson outfit a while back."

Suzanne's heart began to flutter, "Was he in here?" she cried.

"Yes, ma-am, bought some groceries and such and stored 'em behind my counter until he left town."

"What did he look like? Was he alright?"

"About as right as rain I guess, Miss. He sure taught that outlaw bunch a fine lesson on bee keeping."

By this time Kathreen and Sonny, seeing Suzanne engaged in earnest conversation with the clerk, came over and began to listen in.

"Outlaws?" Suzanne said. "Don't tell me he was mixed up with a bunch of outlaws."

"You should go talk to Barney, he spoke with the man the most, and no, he wasn't part of the outlaws, although he larruped them pretty good."

"Where can we find this Barney?" Sonny interjected.

"Barnaby P. Bingham is most likely sitting on the bench outside my front door," the store keeper said. "You probably near tripped over him when you came in here."

The three young people turned as one and headed for the front door, with Suzanne calling back a "Thank You," to the store man.

An old man in bib overalls sat up suddenly and then rose to his feet when addressed by Sonny and the girls. He removed a battered old hat and nodded modestly to the two ladies before acknowledging to Sonny that, "I am the one and only self-same Barnaby P. Bingham of Ellsworth, Kansas. What kin I do fer ya?"

"Do you know this man?" Suzanne held up the poster.

"Why that's Pecos, shore, Ma-am, I met 'im, and a most peculiar fellow he was, too."

"Peculiar?" Suzanne said, "In what way?"

"Well, let's see," the old man sat back down on the bench and scratched his head, his face screwed up in thought. "He seemed to have some confusing notions on spending money for one thing, said a little was a lot and kept calling a lot a little and wanted me to save the beer money I got from that Johnson thug, to buy a little lot. I tol' him there ain't no such thing as a little lot and had begun to think he was a might addled, especially when he tol' me his horse understood everything we said."

"He said his horse knew what you were saying?" Sonny put in, an amused grin on his face at this old codger's reminiscence of Colt. He could just imagine about how that conversation went.

"Yeah, and it was true too, why that hoss of his could even answer you back, and when those bullies—Craig and Johnson, bet him his horse couldn't, he stood right thar and asked that red hoss question after question, the horse nodding or shaking his head to ever'one of 'em."

"You mean to tell me this horse he has is a trick horse?" Sonny asked.

"Yep, won me ten bucks from that low-life Johnson. 'Course they were not too happy about it, Pecos came dern near shootin' Johnson before that ruffian took his hand away from his gun. Fast, say that boy was fast with a gun, sorta reminded me of Billy the Kid."

"So, Colt, er Pecos, had to draw on him," Sonny said.

"Wal, that was only after he'd punched Johnson in the gut after he started ruffin' me up. When Johnson went for him, he stepped back, neat as you please and tripped the big tub of lard and sent him sprawlin' on the deck right about where you're standin'."

"What happened then?" Suzanne asked worriedly.

"Not much," Barney said. "Craig told Johnson to let it rest and they'd go get the rest of the gang and trim the gunfighter down a few notches. They should have let it alone though."

"What do you mean?" Sonny questioned.

"Craig and Johnson are some local bullies that head a gang of owl-hoots in these parts," Barney explained. "Folks are about fed up with stuff missing and getting pushed around, but my friend Pecos took the whole bunch of 'em on when they rode up to him in the middle of the street all ready to gang up on 'im. He called their bluff and then sent 'em high-tailin' for tall cotton when he pulled a large hornets' nest from behind his back, tossed it in the air and drilled it full of holes with his six-shooter. You should of seen it, horses bucking, outlaws cussin' and pulling leather trying to stay in the saddle, until the whole bunch of 'em raced out of town with hornets—mad as hornets—on their tail."

"Huh," Sonny laughed and turned to the girls, "Sounds like Colt, don't it?"

Suzanne smiled and Kathreen laughed out loud. "It sure does," she said, "and it serves them right."

"Well Missy, the whole town would agree with you," Barney said. "They wanted to erect a statue or something for him, but by the time anyone got around to it, he had up and rode out of town. You say his name is Colt?"

"Yes, Colton Saber. He is my fiancée and we are looking for him. Do you know where he was going?"

"Funny thing, he never said, and I never asked."

"If he should show back up, could you let him know that Suzanne is looking for him and that we are on our way to Denver?"

"I'll do 'er, ma-am," Barney said with a tip of his old hat.

The three friends bade Mr. Bingham goodbye and made their way back to the train. Soon they were on their way again with much to think about.

"Do you think Colt has become a gunman?" Kathreen asked.

"I doubt it," Sonny said. "Folks can get some funny notions sometimes and Barnabas P. Bingham would certainly qualify."

"It's not like Colt... being a gunman, I mean," Suzanne said. "Where can he be?"

"It looks like we're on the right track at least," Sonny said. "Our next stop is Fort Hays, let's see what we can learn there."

That evening the train stopped at Fort Hays and the three young people quickly disembarked and hurried to the sheriff's office to view the wanted posters on display by the door. To their surprise, they found one of the posters with Colt's picture doctored to show him sporting a penciled-in beard and mustache. Curiously, the handbill showed a neatly trimmed beard and curling mustache.

"Looks like someone saw him freshly barbered," Sonny said. "Let's ask the Sheriff if he knows anything." The three of them entered the office and spoke with the sheriff who said he had not seen the man, although there had been a tin-horn bounty hunter awhile back who claimed to have seen Colt, but had been unsuccessful in apprehending him.

"Where was that?" Suzanne asked.

"Out on main street in the business district, maybe by the barber shop. The fellow said something about the barber hitting Saber with a broom or something. I checked it out, but by the time I got over there, neither party was around and nobody seemed to know where they had gone."

"We should split up," Sonny said, as they left the sheriff's office. "I'll check the barber shop and you girls check the general stores. We don't have a lot of time before the train leaves."

An hour later found the three friends back in their seats on the Kansas & Pacific Rail Road, chugging west. Suzanne and Kathreen had visited *Moses & Bloomfield's* mercantile to no avail, although a few of the clerks thought he may have been in there but there were way too many cowboys coming and going to be certain.

"Well, I had an interesting conversation with a hawk-nosed barber in Fort Hays," Sonny reported. "Seems like a fellow answering Colt's description stopped in there a few weeks ago, and claimed to have seen some 'Blue Light Lady haunt' that's supposed to be seen from time to time around a hill by the Fort. The barber said he had to throw the fella out after he claimed this specter told him we were looking for him. Said the fella was mixed up in communicating with the dead or some such thing."

"We were looking for him?" Suzanne questioned, "How'd he know that?"

"That's just the thing, the barber claimed the ghost or whatever, told this fella that Suzanne and Sonny were looking for him. You should of seen his face when I told him that I was Sonny and you were with me, and that we are looking for him."

"A ghost told him?" Suzanne and Kathreen were looking at each other in alarm.

"Some Blue Light Lady that appears from time to time walking around the Fort. They say it's the ghost of Elizabeth Polly who died helping soldiers in the cholera epidemic here in the late sixties."

"Do you believe it?" Kathreen said.

Sonny shrugged, "Who'd make up a story like that—and have our names right to boot?"

"The more important question is, did Colton believe it?" Suzanne said. "What do you think he'd do if he knew we were trying to find him?" Sonny shook his head and Kathreen shrugged.

"Maybe God directed that spirit to tell Colt," Suzanne said hopefully.

"Would God do something like that?" Kathreen seemed doubtful.

Sonny said, "God can do whatever he wants to. Grampa said He would help us find Colt. Maybe He will cause Colt to find us."

"Well, we still don't know where he is," Suzanne said. "Did that barber know where he went?"

"No," Sonny said, "just that he got mixed up in some sort of shooting scrape with a bounty hunter and then rode out of town."

"Shooting?" Suzanne was alarmed. "Did somebody shoot him?"

"No, it wasn't like that. I guess somebody was trying to take him in to collect your bounty, and had him under his gun. Colt ignored the gun, rode over and said something to the fella and rode away while counting out loud. The bounty hunter put his gun away, and Colt just rode off to the west leading a pack horse loaded with supplies."

"I wonder what he said to him," Kathreen said.

The train had no more than left the station at Fort Hays and reached full speed, when Sonny spied the comely waitress from the cafe in Ellsworth coming down the aisle. When the girl reached where they were sitting, Sonny rose to his feet and doffed his hat.

"Well, hello! Miss Priscilla, isn't it?" he said.

Looking confused, the girl stopped and then seeing Suzanne and Kathreen she recognized them and said, "Oh, hi. Yes, it is Priscilla, Priscilla Corbin. You are the folks from the restaurant back in Ellsworth?"

Sonny smiled, "You sure make a mean sandwich, that avocado was different."

"Glad you liked it. Mr. Harvey is always having us try out new things."

"Who's Mr. Harvey?" Kathreen said.

"Fred Harvey," she replied. "He is the owner and mastermind of the Harvey House Chain of Restaurants and has a tentative contract to install them along the Atchison, Topeka and the Santa Fe Rail Road line. He is planning to open a few more along the Kansas Pacific at Wallace, Hugo, and in Denver, Colorado.

"Won't you sit down?' Suzanne said. "Do you work for him?"

"Well, I hope to. He stopped into that little cafe in Ellsworth and gave the lady who owned the place some suggestions for the menu and handed me a brochure on being one of the Harvey Girls." Priscilla sat down opposite the girls, and Sonny replaced his hat and sat down beside her.

"What is a Harvey Girl?" Kathreen asked.

Priscilla dug into a bag and handed her a brochure which outlined the qualifications of a Harvey Girl. Kathreen read: *Harvey is seeking single, well-mannered, and educated American ladies, and is placing ads in newspapers throughout the East Coast and Midwest for "white, young women, 18-30 years of age, of good character, attractive* *and intelligent". The girls will be paid $17.50 a month to start, plus room, board and gratuity.* Kathreen handed the pamphlet to Suzanne who quickly scanned it and then passed it to Sonny.

"Wow, this could open doors for a lot of young women," Kathreen said.

"Oh yes," Priscilla said. "He has great plans for good service, high quality food served on fine china and Irish linen. The drafty old roadhouses near water stops with their flies, rancid meat, cold beans and weak coffee are on their way out, if Mr. Harvey has his way. He is fastidious on quality service, clean restaurants, generous portions, fair prices, and satisfied customers. He plans for a pie to be cut into fourths instead of sixths for his customers."

"What's a gratuity?" Sonny asked.

"Tips" Kathreen said.

"Tips?" Sonny was confused.

"Yes," Priscilla said, "For the girls who provide excellent service the patrons will be encouraged to leave them extra change as a way of saying thank you."

"You mean they get paid by the restaurant for doing their job and from the customers too?"

"Yes, if they do their job well."

"Huh, where I come from, if you don't do a good job you get yourself fired," Sonny said.

"It's a good thing, Sonny," Kathreen said. "Most of these girls will barely make a living wage at seventeen and a half dollars a month."

"Huh, I'm going to have to see if I can get the cows I punch to pony up a tip for me from here on out. So, what are you doing on this train?"

"Actually, I am on my way to Denver at Mr. Harvey's request, in search of both established restaurants and potential girls for the Harvey Houses," Priscilla said. "Do you think you two girls would be interested?"

Suzanne began to shake her head no, but Kathreen interrupted. "We might be," she gave her friend a cautioning look, "We may need something to do while in Denver."

"Well, should you decide to, you can meet with Mr. Harvey when we get there and he will answer any other questions you may have."

The train traveled on, reaching Cheyenne Wells where the tracks swung northwest following the river and it had not gone more than five miles when it suddenly slowed and then came to a complete stop. The engineer was blowing repeatedly on his whistle and people were jumping from their seats to stare out the windows, for the entire train had become completely engulfed in a passing herd of buffalo. There was a festive air of excitement as the passengers gazed at the magnificent wooly beasts. Some of the eastern folks had never seen the animals before, let alone being up this close. The car shook and rattled as the passing buffalo bumped and crowded it, and occasionally a woman would shriek when it seemed the car might be tipped over. Soon shooting was heard up and down the line and then some men in their coach opened the windows and began to shoot indiscriminately at the buffalo, until finally, anyone who had a rifle or even a hand gun was killing or wounding the shaggy beasts. It wasn't long before men began to congratulate each other on the number they had shot and then it soon became a contest to see who could shoot the most.

Suzanne was horrified. In their blood lust, she saw some men with a crazed look in their eye, laughing hysterically and boasting of the last shot they had made before turning feverishly to fire once again. Would nothing stop this insanity?

Kathreen leaped upon the seat and screamed into the acrid, smoke-filled room. "Stop this insanity, you brainless idiots! What is the matter with you people anyway? There is nothing honorable or noble about senselessly slaughtering these splendid beasts, to say nothing of the abominable waste. You do nothing to advance your manhood or self-respect by such stupid and cowardly actions and I am appalled to be counted among your numbers as human."

"What's the matter, lady," a fellow in a bowler hat said. "Ain't you ever killed a buffalo? I thought everybody out west killed buffalo."

"No, I have never killed a buffalo, and I never would kill one like this. This is the most despicable display of cowardice I have ever had the misfortune to witness. If I had my way, every one of you would be kicked off this train and set to butchering every animal you have shot, and you wouldn't be allowed to eat anything else again until all that is dead and dying out there is consumed."

The shooting in their car had diminished to sporadic firing and finally came to a stop altogether. "Don't worry, lady," a fellow who was wiping down a nickel-plated pistol with his handkerchief said, "The Injuns will be along pretty soon and clean up the mess, it won't go to waste."

"That is the most preposterous thing I've ever heard of," Kathreen said. "It is just such stupid, uninformed thinking and actions as this that has set the red-man against us all. The next time some poor settler or pioneer, along with his wife and family, gets murdered in their beds by the savages, they will have the likes of you to thank."

It grew quiet as a church in their car although shooting was continuing up and down the line. Kathreen stood with hands on her hips staring defiantly at anyone who might dare to lift a weapon to a window, when there sounded another set of blasts on the whistle and the train jerked, stopped, and then started to creep along again. The sudden movement unbalanced the vehement crusader and sent her toppling over backwards into Sonny's lap. The whole car erupted into loud laughter.

373

Kathreen relaxed for a moment in Sonny's arms while Suzanne and Priscilla looked on, and then she squirmed out of his embrace. Without saying a word, Sonny helped her regain her balance and offered his hand while she took her seat. Kathreen stared at him for a moment, surprised that he offered no flirtatious comment, or otherwise took the opportunity to annoy her. She turned to look at the gruesome spectacle out the window, but saw with unseeing eyes. This new Sonny was somebody she felt she hardly knew, and deep down inside of her she was a little scared.

Two weeks in Denver had netted the searching party little results. The girls had put up in a hotel near Union Station and Sonny had made an excursion up Clear Creek Canyon to the mining camps of Silver Plume, George Town and Idaho Springs, the latter which was named for some Idaho Indian Chief that had made pilgrimages every year, before the on-rush of gold seekers, to a hot springs located there. No one seemed to know of or had seen the cowboy on the poster. Inquiries along the placer claims of Cherry Creek and the South Platte returned the same results, and Sonny even booked a trip on the railroad to Central City and asked at several of the hard-rock mines and smelters for clues to Colt's whereabouts, all to no avail.

Meanwhile, Suzanne and Kathreen had been taken by Priscilla to meet with Fred Harvey and he had encouraged the girls to put up at the hotel at his expense, and engaged them to visit the nicer restaurant establishments to learn if any might be interested in joining his chain of restaurants. As with Priscilla, Suzanne and Kathreen were to be on the lookout for likely looking young ladies who met his qualifications as outlined in his handout. When at last the girls and Sonny got back together at the hotel dining room, an atmosphere of discouragement hung over the young party.

"Are you sure the telegram said he was heading for the gold fields of Colorado?" Sonny asked Suzanne.

"That is what the message read," the blonde replied.

"Well, there's gold camps booming down towards Colorado Springs and Pike's Peak, maybe I should take a ride down there."

"Let's all go," Kathreen said. "Mr. Harvey mentioned he would like to do some scouting down that way eventually and we could look for Colt at the same time."

When they reached Colorado Springs, they put up at the Manitou Mineral Springs Resort, a new establishment that was drawing crowds of people to the hot springs. Sonny figured, since Colt liked to swim so much, if he had traveled through the "Springs" area, he would undoubtedly have stopped here. Sooner or later he hoped to meet someone who may have seen him. He was basking in the hot mineral waters in one of the rented swimming costumes, when he saw Suzanne and Kathreen come from the dressing room in the latest ladies' swimming attire. The two of them made quite a picture and turned a lot of heads as they made their way down into the pool.

The trio was enjoying the water and the carbonated cold beverage that was served at pool side, when a gangly fellow in an ill-fitting swimming costume entered the pool and asked them what they thought of the place.

"I am curious why this drink is so fizzy and sparkling." Suzanne said.

The man said, "Tons of snow melts on top of the continental divide and finds its way down through the limestone mountains until it encounters hot rocks in the bowels of the earth. It then bubbles its way back up to burst out in these springs. At least that's what the geologists say. It is the limestone that carbonates the water and all we have to do is add a little raspberry or strawberry flavor to get a nice beverage for the customers."

"Do you work here?" Kathreen asked.

"Yes, actually, I'm employed as a stable hand at the hotel's livery barn, but I am allowed an hour each day to enjoy the pool. It's the best part of my job."

"You work at the stable?" Sonny asked.

"Yes, horse shoeing mostly. It's always a relief to my aching back to jump in here at the end of the day."

"Do you meet a lot of people at your job?"

"Yes, quite a few, both at the barn and here in the pool. Most folks are quite interesting and glad to tell about their lives."

"I wonder if you might have met a young cowboy traveling through here in the past month or so. He was headed for the gold fields?" Suzanne put in.

"Lady, I see a lot of cowboys coming and going, and most of them like to visit these springs. What can you tell me about him?"

"He was riding a red horse with four white socks and a white blaze," Sonny said.

"Sounds familiar, there was a Texas feller with a horse like that with whom he seemed to carry on a running conversation a while back."

"I have a picture of him," Suzanne said. "Would you be so kind as to take a look?"

"Certainly, ma-am."

Suzanne made her way from the spring and soon returned with the poster about Colt. The livery man studied it for a moment and then said, "This looks like the feller, but his beard wasn't that long. What's he wanted for?"

"I just need to find him, do you know where he was going?" Suzanne said.

"I think he was headed for South Park and the strike up in the basin," the hostler said. "We talked some about his getting a job as a cowboy on one of the ranches up there, but he seemed set on looking for gold."

"How do we get to South Park?" Sonny asked

"Well, there's a stage out of Denver that goes to Alma, but I think your friend rode up the South Platte Canyon where the Denver Rail Road is building a line into there now."

"Can we take the train to South Park?" Kathreen asked.

"No, the rails are not completed yet, they are projecting it to be done next year."

Sonny, Suzanne and Kathreen rose as one person and thanked the man and hurried from the pool.

"I'll take Tornado and Hank and ride the Canyon," Sonny said. "You girls head back to Denver and catch the stage and I will meet up with you in the basin." The friends parted at the bathhouse, excited at last to find a lead on Colt's whereabouts.

Unnoticed in the shadows, a narrow-eyed Frenchman watched them until they disappeared from sight. Then he stepped down into the pool, much like any other guest, and slowly worked his way over to where the lively man was relaxing in the warm spring water.

It took Sonny a week to ride the Front Wall and he found that Suzanne and Kathreen had already arrived by stage the day before. The girls had had an uneventful trip and were anxious to learn whether he had found any trace of his brother. Their search had thus far been unsuccessful.

"I've looked through all the gold camps on the way up here and no one seems to know of Colton," Sonny said. "I think I will look a little farther north."

"Where can he be?" Suzanne asked anxiously.

"I don't know, but we'll keep looking until we find him. You girls put up at the Fairplay House, I'm told it has a nice restaurant—maybe you can see if they want to be a part of Harvey's doings. How you all fixed for money?"

"We are getting kinda low," Kathreen said, "maybe I should wire daddy for some more."

"Let's see if we can get waitressing jobs at the hotel first," Suzanne said.

"I can make some money hunting game for the miners and selling the meat," Sonny said. "At the same time, I will try and find out where Colt's gone off to."

The following Sunday, Sonny was riding past the log church building that sat on a side hill, when he noticed a smart-looking horse with four white socks and flaxen mane and tail, tied up to a hitching rack in front of the old building. He pulled Tornado up and sat watching the animal for a few moments, then the animal lifted its head. When he saw the white blaze down its nose he said, "That looks like the horse Colton's supposed to be riding. You suppose he went to church?"

CHAPTER TWENTY-TWO

Gun Smoke in the Rockies

Terryall Creek, Colorado, July 1871

JIMMY ALLEN AND I SAT OUR HORSES
staring down the bores of four pistols pointed at us, our
hands reaching above our heads.

"You boys step down easy like and keep your hands
where I can see them," a black-bearded fellow said.

Jimmy and I slowly got down, our hands held well
away from our guns. I was beginning to feel the annoyance and peevishness that always seemed to arise in the
pit of my gut whenever some yokel pulled a gun on me.
Black beard ordered us to unbuckle our gunbelts and let
them drop. I was ready to slap iron and start shooting, but
I caught a cautionary look in Allen's eye, and so complied
with the outlaw leader's request. My gunbelt dropped
behind me but hung up on my spurs. Without moving, I
stood still and waited.

"Where's your poke?" The fellow with the black
beard asked.

Jimmy said. "We just rode into town and blew it on a
good time."

"You don't look like you been having a good time to
me," the man said. "You ain't liquored up."

"Ha, the jokes on you," I said. "You can't get liquored up on sarsaparilla." I began a loud laughter while shooting Jimmy Allen a quick wink, and then began to cackle like a chicken with hemorrhoids. I was bending over and slapping my knees as though it was the funniest thing I had ever heard, and Allen took the cue and joined in with a loud boisterous laugh of his own, causing distraction and confusion amongst the hold-up men.

"Stop that cackling," the leader said, standing angrily in his stirrups and waving his pistol threateningly.

I was bent over in laughter, my boots still entangled in the gunbelt over my spurs, which enabled me to effect losing my balance, whereupon I pitched over backward in an awkward heap, landing heavily on my rump. This sent Jimmy Allen into more fits of laughter, and further confused our adversaries who looked at him in bewilderment. Seizing the moment, I snatched my six-gun from where it lay at my heels and quicker than it takes to tell about it, fired four successive shots, sending the handguns of our would-be attackers spinning from their hands.

With angry curses and cries of pain, the outlaws set spurs to their horses and raced out of the yard and up the road towards town. I buckled on my gunbelt and stepped to Lightfoot about to give chase when Jimmy said, "Let 'em go, they'll get theirs sooner or later." The miner walked over and picked up the four smashed guns. Some had blood on them, a mute testimony that more than one of them would be nursing some very painful hands.

"Son, that was some shooting, where'd you learn to handle a hog-leg like that?"

"Practice, practice, practice," I muttered.

The cabin was a mess with flour and sugar tins spilled and stuff strewn all about, but the gold stash that Jimmy Allen kept in a butter crock under a flat hearth stone in front of the fireplace had not been disturbed.

"Well, the scoundrels never found my poke, that's good," Allen said. "You got your stuff put away safe?"

"Not really," I said. "I had my poke in a buckskin bag out in my saddle bags."

"You might want to consider somewhere safe," he said. "There's more'n one bunch of scurvy polecats around these parts. They'd as soon cut your throat as look at you."

"You know, Pecos, I was under those owlhoot's guns too. What would you have done if one of them had shot me?"

We had blown out the light and settled down for the night when Jimmy asked his question. I thought about it for a moment before answering.

"I guess I never figured on that," I said.

"Well, I was. I'm not exactly ready to visit the Pearly Gates just yet. You're kind of a loose cannon, ain't ya?"

I didn't answer him right away, pondering the question and it took me back to my previous reflections on whether or not I had a reckless death wish. Finally, I spoke.

"I'm sorry if I put you at an unwarranted risk. To me it looked like they had the drop on us and was all set to cool our heels once they found our gold. I saw the chance to take 'em by surprise and took it."

"Don't get me wrong, I am grateful for what you did and you are right, they would have snuffed out our lights for sure, but sometimes I wonder if you really are that reckless—if you just plain don't care whether you live or die."

"It makes me madder than I can get at the brash arrogance of somebody pulling a gun on me," I explained. "The blatant disregard it shows for my life is the height of insult and disrespect, and I plain don't like it. I also despise a thief. It's violation enough when someone comes along and trespasses on your property, breaks in and steals your stuff without a care for you and yours, but it is the height of audacity for them to attempt to rob

you in broad daylight as though you was no more significant than a pimple on a razorback's rump. You better
believe there is going to be hell to pay when something
like that happens."

"Pimple on a razorback's rump?"

"Yeah, something like that," I mumbled feeling a little
bit foolish.

"That's quite a picture," Allen said.

We were silent then, but the question of my not caring
still hung in the air. Finally, Allen spoke. "Pecos, what
happened to you?"

"What do you mean?" I said, fearing that I knew all too
well what he meant.

"Most young fellas at your age have the world by the
tail with a downhill drag, but I don't see any of that in you.
You're like flat beer—where'd all the fizz go?"

I made no reply but a list of what happened to my
former fizz popped up like a grasshopper on a hot rock.
The injustice of being taken from home, family, sweetheart and enslaved in Mexico, staggers the imagination.
My escape and return to find home, family and sweetheart no longer what they were, left an utter feeling of
abandonment by Suzanne, Sonny and even God. It had
sucked every bit of fizz out of me. Allen was right, I was
like flat beer... or sarsaparilla at least.

"Don't you like girls?" Jimmy asked.

"Yeah, I guess so, why do you ask?"

"Oh, I don't know, you never talk much about 'em and
when we go to town you don't pay much attention to 'em
either. You ever have a girlfriend?"

Changing the subject I said, "Have you?"

"Sure, plenty of them."

"You ever marry?"

"Yes, I had four wonderful years with my wife before
she died in childbirth."

"So, how'd you deal with her death?"

"I spent some dark days all right. I got really angry with God for taking her and it wasn't until I saw the really good of what we had, that I was finally able to get over her loss."

"What happened to the baby?" I asked.

"The child did not survive."

"That's a shame," I said. "Why do you suppose God lets things like that happen?"

"I wish I knew. I have some of it figured out, but *who has known the mind of God or who has been His councilor?* I guess that's what makes Him God. One thing I have concluded, however, is that He knows what He is doing and we can live a whole lot happier if we leave off trying to direct Him and just let Him be God."

Was I not letting God be God? What a strange idea, I wasn't stopping God from being God. If the truth be told, I was having a bigger problem with Him not being the kind of God He said He was. All this, "*God is Love*," stuff. It seemed to me that what I had been dealt at the hand of God was anything but love. There had never been a higher, or purer, or nobler love, in the history of the entire world than the love I had had for Suzanne, and now she was gone, dead at my hand. The love that had sustained me through all of those painful, dark days, lost in the mountains of the Devil's Backbone, the Sierra Madre, the love that brought me through the wilderness to El Paso and then again to my home, only to find betrayal, and that it was not love at all. I guess I really don't know what love is, if that's love, and frankly if it is, then who needs it? I could feel the bitterness of soul welling up inside of me and it was sure not something I wished to share with Jimmy Allen.

"So, do you?" Allen asked again.

"Do I what?" I said, though I knew what he was asking.

"Have a girl?"

"No!"

What happened to her?"

"She died."

"And you're mad at God?"

"Mad as hell!"

"You need to get over it," Jimmy said. "God knows what He's doing and if you want in on it you better stop your murmuring against Him and start seeking His will."

"I ain't murmuring against God."

"You should go see the Snowshoe Itinerant," Jimmy said.

"Who?

"Father Dyer."

"Who's that?"

"He's the circuit riding preacher for the Methodists over at the Log Cabin Church in South Park City," Jimmy replied, "He'd do you good."

"How come he's called the Snowshoe Itinerant?"

"When the snow gets too deep to ride a hoss on his circuit, he just keeps going on a pair of Norwegian skis and never stops. The man's got bottom."

"I don't think talking to no clergyman's going to do me any good," I said.

"You never can tell, you think about it, He preaches in town most Sundays. Now, I'm going to sleep."

I lay there a long time mulling it all over again and listening to the miner snoring. Allen reminded me of the old Mexican goat herder I had stayed with after being mauled by the mountain lion. Both men had reconciled with God from tragic lives and I wondered if I ever could. It would be a relief to hope in something again, to find a higher purpose, now that loving a wife and family and being a good person was no longer on the table. What was it old Davila had said? "God will not share His glory with another!" He had said other things as well, not the least of which was that Suzanne would not save me. Boy, that was for sure, especially now that she was gone. Could anybody? Maybe I should talk to this Father Dyer. There was that stuff about discovering who I was, and where I was going, and what I was doing here, and about finding out who I am... stuff about character and what I could be trusted with. Boy, I sure had failed the test on that one. A murderer, a fugitive on the run, who couldn't be trusted with some of the most important things of life... like, his sweetheart and brother's lives. All this and more could be said of me, and it was with a dark sense of cynicism that I finally fell into a troubled sleep.

I got to thinking about what Allen said about hiding my gold and felt a vague irritation at the necessity of it. Why couldn't people just tend to their own business. I remembered something Pop's used to say, *"Build a wall and invite a thief."* It looked to me like the thieves would come whether you built a wall or not. It was obvious from my diggings that gold was being prospected and there was no hiding that. The only advantage I had was its inaccessibility and being hard to find; still, if someone were to learn of its location, I could easily be set upon at some unguarded moment and caught unprepared. I decided to try to build some sort of fortification on my claim.

The next day, I choose a spot on the hillside above my works that gave a commanding view of my diggings and open pasture lands. The site was nestled at the base of a hundred-foot rock wall with an over-lean, and was virtually impregnable from above. Falling several large aspens, I bucked these into fifteen-foot lengths and using Sidekick, I yarded them up to the site and built a three-sided log wall, with one small opening at the end, up against the cliff. When it was completed it was an easily defended little fortification about five feet tall. I stashed a few necessary provisions behind the wall and returned to my prospecting.

The following Sunday found me in South Park City riding Lightfoot back and forth in front of the little hill where the log cabin church of Father Dyer was located. The sign said services began at eleven o'clock. I could see my horse was looking wall-eyed back at me and knew he was wishing I would make up my mind. This aimless wandering back and forth was stupid and he would be better off tied to the hitching rail in front of the church than shuffling back and forth in the dust down here.

"Wal," I drawled, "seeing you tied up in front of church on a Sunday morning is bound to improve your image in the community," then I goosed Lightfoot with my spurs and rode him on up the hill.

I stepped into the dank interior of the church which looked more like an old hotel than a house of worship, and took a seat on the back row. A lady I took to be the parson's wife was vigorously pumping an old reed organ with both feet and belting out a gospel tune to which a handful of people, mostly women, were singing lustily. I recognized the song and finding a dog-eared hymnal I located the page and joined dispiritedly in the singing. By the third song, I warmed to the task and spent the remainder of the song service enjoying singing with the rest of the congregation. I noticed that, unlike the Baptists, these Methodists sang every stanza of every song and I was amazed at the gospel content of the words. Some of the songs that I thought I knew had verses and words I had never sung before, mostly because Baptists usually only sing the first and last verse and maybe once in a while the second verse, but here was a treasure trove of wholesome religious truth passing under the watchful eye of Father Dyer that had slipped right past me in my previous worship experiences.

I found Father Dyer to be a stalwart man in a black broad-cloth coat, and of sober visage. He was tanned by long hours in the sun and wind, with striking blue eyes that I imagined penetrated with piercing directness through the pretenses of all with whom he came in contact. I misjudged him on my initial encounter as a hard, austere, even judgmental, man. That image was immediately dispelled the moment he opened his mouth to speak. With a quiet earnestness he spoke of the hope and grace of God, using as his text the parable of the *Prodigal Son*, and of the father's undying and relentless longing for the son's return. He said that while the older brother labored in the fields, and the errant brother ate with the swine, the father spent long hours looking down the lane for his lost son to come to his senses and return home.

It was the compelling way that he pictured the father that caused me to reflect on my own parents. Was it possible that my dad was waiting for me, that he would forgive me and receive me back into the family after the mess I had made of everything? I almost believed it could be true.

He said that when the son came to his senses, he made up his mind to go back to the father and make a clean breast of it and ask for forgiveness and offer himself as a servant, since he was no longer worthy to be a son. Then the preacher said something even more astounding, he said that none of us are worthy to be sons or daughters, but through the shed blood of Jesus we have all been given power to become children of God.

Father Dyer urged the people that morning to return to the father who waited patiently and longingly for our return, and just as I pictured God waiting for me to return to the heavenly family, it was a small step for me to see my dad and mom longing for me to come home. Sitting on the back seat of a rough-hewn log church, I, for the first time, began to consider going back home to Texas and face the awful things I had done.

I left the church that morning with a mixture of dread and a lightheartedness. I told Lightfoot we were going home. His only comment was that it was about time.

Riding to the Fairplay House, I had it in mind to treat myself to Sunday dinner in the dining room and mull over going back to Texas. The fried chicken sure reminded me of mom's, and the many times we had sat around the table of a Sunday. Those were wonderful memories. I thought about my father, too, what would his attitude be towards me? Dad was good, and honest, and loyal and a stickler for doing things right. Even if it broke his heart, he would require me to be accountable to the law. I made a halfhearted snort at the idea of me shuffling up to Sheriff Wiggins and turning myself in to that dense buffoon for shooting my brother. Would it mean I would face the hangman's noose? Could I stand to spend years in prison? I was thinking the noose would be better than the pen when somebody behind me threw a heavy metal object down on my table, nearly upsetting my plate.

"What the...?" I scooted back in my chair and jumped to my feet and whirled to face the intruder. "What the deuce is that, and why'd you toss it on my table?"

"Look at it!"

Something about the voice and manner of the man was strangely familiar, but his hat was pulled low over his face and I could not make him out. I turned back and picked up the heavy object. It appeared to be some kind of medal or artifact, and then I saw a heavy spent slug embedded in the center. While my mind was struggling with where I had seen something like this, the stranger spoke.

"You shot me!"

My blood froze. The voice was Sonny's and so was the appearance, but my mind was playing tricks on me. Sonny was dead, dead at my hands. I saw him go down... Suzanne with him. The torment of months and weeks and days and nights that had dogged my footsteps, and now, here was this apparition or whatever, challenging me with what looked like Sonny's medal, the very one I'd given him. Was that my .44 slug stuck in it? Was I seeing another ghost? I could not believe my eyes.

"Sonny, is that you?"

"Yes," he said with anger in his voice.

"You're not killed?" I expostulated in unbelief.

"No, you stupid, hot-headed idiot, I'm not killed."

"But I saw you go down... Suzanne too."

"I ought to knock your stupid block off," he said and pushed me back a few steps.

"H...how?" I blundered. People in the restaurant were beginning to stare at us.

"The medallion saved my life but it sure put a hell of a dent in my brisket. Why'd you shoot me?"

"I've asked myself that a thousand times... but—but you were kissing my betrothed, why were you kissing Suzanne?" I could feel the resentment building in me.

"I was in love with her," he replied. "She said she'd be mine."

"You stole her from me," I blazed in anger as the old memory rushed at me. Without thinking my hand started once more for my gun.

Like the strike of a rattler, Sonny swatted my gun from my hand and then struck me a swift blow to the chin. I saw stars flash before my eyes and felt myself falling over backwards to land on my rump on the floor. Some woman screamed and folks were leaping to their feet to get out of our way.

Sonny stood poised over me. "I didn't steal nothing. Why are you such an infernal hot-head?"

I don't know, blame it on the buttermilk biscuits or something, for I sure wasn't thinking straight. Here was the brother that I thought I'd killed, standing alive and well in front of me and all in one piece, and now I'm pulling iron on him again?

"I ain't no hot-head," I grumbled. "You had no business kissing my girl."

"Good Lord, man, you were dead and gone, and in your grave for near two years. I buried you myself," Sonny said. "You did not—God, man," I cried in desperation, "I was never dead, I got kidnapped."

"We didn't know that. I found you dead. It near killed Suzanne and it was only by the slimmest chance she pulled through," Sonny extended his hand to me. I took it and he pulled me to my feet, then he bent over and picked up my gun from where it had fallen and handed it to me. I holstered it, feeling sheepish at the spectacle we had made in front of folks. They returned to their plates at our embarrassed gestures of apology. A low murmur of the patrons resumed as the two of us righted chairs and straightened tables. Sonny took a chair and sat down while I pulled up my seat in a daze.

"Where is she?" I asked.

"Right here in South Park, looking for you," he answered.

"But I saw her go down, blood all over the place," I puzzled.

"She got her nose busted and her lights knocked out when your bullet slammed me back into her," he explained. "She's fine now and determined to find you and try to talk some sense into that thick skull of yours. Why do you always have to go off half-cocked? You've caused a whole world of hurt for everybody."

"You have no idea the things I went through—Suzanne's love was all that kept me alive," I told him. "When I saw her in your arms, the betrayal of you both was more than I could bear, reason left and Sam Colt took over."

"You're awfully glib about it."

"Glib ain't really the kind of awful I am about it," I said. "How could you just take over the minute my back was turned?"

"You knot-head, that poor girl nearly died when I packed what we were sure was your body back with your face eaten away by the coyotes and buzzards. She was the only one who said it wasn't you, even mom and dad figured it was you. It took me days, even months to get her to start eating right again and come out of the deep hole she fell into."

"Yeah, but did you have to steal her heart in the process? It still galls me."

"Colton, this has been one sad, sad, sad deal. First I find where you and Ringo go off a cliff down in the Pecos Brakes, or at least whoever it was that had all your cloths on, even down to your underwear, boots, and socks, I might add. The two of you had been laying there for more'n a week with the varmints having a heyday on your carcasses."

"Ringo's dead?" I said bewildered.

"Yeah, lost his footing in the soft shoulder on that path that crosses the slide past Mesquite Flats."

"Aw, that's a rotten shame! Who was the dirty dog that took him and my clothes?"

"I was hoping you could tell me."

"I don't know. Somebody cold-cocked me from behind and I wound up naked down in Mexico with some greaser that sold me as a slave to a mining operation in the Sierra Madrid," I said.

"We figured Suzanne would get over it," Sonny said, "but brother, let me tell you, you were so deeply embedded in that girl's heart that life lost all meaning for her. I had to leave on another drive with Goodnight and when I got back, she was skin and bones. I near had to spank her to get her to start eating again and when she finally did start gaining weight I thought maybe she had turned the corner, yet she kept insisting you were alive. She watched and waited for you for hours on end, day after day. At first I was just trying to help, I was so sorry for her, but you know better'n anybody, that you can't be around her without falling a little bit in love with her yourself, and since I was certain you were dead, I saw no harm in letting my heart go."

"Aw, Sonny, that's lame and you know it," I accused.

"No, it's not," he argued. "You know full well what Suzanne is like. By the way, that was the first kiss I ever got from her, she had just, that very day, consented to being my girl and to get on with her life, then you show up and shoot me—you stupid idiot."

"You're still in love with her, aren't you?" I demanded.

"Of course, I am, but it doesn't matter," he said. "When you showed up, it threw the last shovel full of dirt on the grave of any budding romance I hoped to have."

"She must a felt something for you if she said she'd be yours."

"Huh," Sonny gave a sardonic laugh. "Nothing like what she feels for you, bud. Believe me, I'm just your older brother who's helped her out in her time of need."

"Yeah, well you can just keep right on helping her out too, I'm gettin' out of here." I stood abruptly to my feet and saw the incredulous look on Sonny's face. I couldn't explain the anger I was feeling, not so much at Sonny, or Suzanne, but both of them together, or maybe neither; just the miserable circumstances of the whole situation. I stomped out of the Fairplay and jerked Lightfoot's reins from the hitching rack. Mounting, I sunk spurs savagely into my mount's sides and left town at a full gallop.

———

Two days later, Suzanne and Kathreen left the Fairplay House and hired a buggy to search for Colt. Both girls had been able to secure jobs as waitresses when the proprietor learned they represented Fred Harvey, and he demonstrated his interest in becoming a provider for the railroad once it reached South Park City. They had taken the day off the previous Sunday to search the nearby town of Como, today they turned at the fork and drove into the boom town of Alma. Sonny had left Sunday to talk to some miners about buying meat and told the girls he would see them in a day or two, as he intended to ride up towards Mosquito Pass and maybe on down to the camps on the North Fork of the South Platte.

Kathreen stopped the buggy in front of the post office and went in to study the wanted posters when Suzanne saw a barber shop across the street. Taking a poster, she got down and went into the little shop. A portly barber was sitting in his chair reading a paper when she came in.

"Good afternoon, miss," the barber said. "Can I help you?"

Suzanne held up the poster and said, "Have you seen this man? He may not have the facial hair now."

The barber peered at the poster a moment and said, "Oh, that's Jimmy Allen's pard. No, he had me shave his beard off. What's he wanted for?"

Suzanne's breath caught in her throat, "Do you know where he is?" she asked anxiously.

"Probably at the diggings. He and Allen are working a claim about four miles down Terryall Creek. You have to go back to the junction and then turn like you're going to Como. The

Terryall Creek Road is about four miles the other side of that town."

"Oh, thank you," Suzanne said, "You don't know how much you have helped me."

"He and Jimmy usually come into town on Saturday night," the barber called, as Suzanne rushed out the door to her buggy.

Kathreen returned to find her friend in a highly excitable state.

"I found him," Suzanne cried as her friend walked up. "Get in!"

Kathreen climbed into the buggy and sat next to Suzanne. "Where is he?" she said.

"Just a few miles from here on Terryall Creek."

Suzanne swung the buggy around and headed back the way they had come. Soon they found the junction to Como and followed that road to where it led into Terryall Creek Road. At a brisk trot, they followed the road, passing claim after claim while busy miners paused from their work to stare at the lovely ladies passing by.

"Looks like we're creating quite a stir with the local gentry," Kathreen said. "Do you know where the claim is?"

"It's supposed to be four miles down this road, somebody named Jimmy Allen's place.

The girls passed an occasional rider on the road and one of them told them the Allen place was a mile or so beyond the last group of claims. They would recognize it by the log cabin on the side of the hill at the base of a big pine tree sitting above the claim. They thanked him and drove on until, finding the place, the girls turned the buggy off the main road and up into the yard of the cabin.

Jimmy Allen saw the ladies turn their rig into his yard and came out of the cabin, wiping his hands on a towel. "Hello, ladies," he said. "What brings you to these parts?"

"We are looking for Colton Saber," Suzanne said breathlessly, "Is he here?"

"Colton Saber? Never heard of him," Allen replied. "Ain't nobody round here except me and Pecos."

"He sometimes goes by the name of Pecos," Kathreen put in. "Is he here?"

"No, he's been up to his diggings pouting for the last few days."

"Pouting?" Kathreen said.

"Yeah, got his nose out of joint when I asked him if he had a girlfriend," Jimmy laughed. "You wouldn't be the one by any chance?"

"I wouldn't, darn the luck," Kathreen said, "but she is."

"Where are his diggings?" Suzanne asked.

"Well, Miss, if you drive on up the road a mile or two and around that bend, you will see where Ute Creek comes down off the mountainside. You will have to leave your buggy, but there is a pretty good trail that will lead you on up to his claim. If you would like, I can take you up there."

Suzanne was already turning the buggy around. "No thanks, we'll find him," she said. At a brisk clip, she trotted the buggy horse down the road and out of sight. Soon they found the mouth of Ute Creek and, after tying the buggy horse, they hefted their skirts and started hiking up the trail. It was a beautiful spot on a glorious afternoon, and the girls lost no time making their way past a twenty-foot waterfall to where the trail left the trees and led out into a large open meadow. Beyond they could see a couple of horses grazing in a fenced pasture and then they spotted a walled tent nestled in a clump of pines. Farther upstream, a man with rolled up shirtsleeves was standing in muddy boots shoveling dirt into a long wooden trough. He did not see the girls.

Suzanne's heart was about to burst from her bosom. "It's Colt," she whispered.

Kathreen had to swallow her own excitement and a strange sense of apprehension. "Go on Suze," she said. "I'll wait here until you have had time to talk to him."

Slowly, her heart in her mouth, Suzanne began the long walk to where the man was working when the stillness was broken by a shrill whistle from the red horse on the hillside.

———

After Colt had bolted from the room, Sonny sat there in bewilderment as to what to do. He had found his brother and tried to talk sense into him, but never figured him to react as he did. Maybe he had been too hard on him, but thought he had held himself in check pretty well. That punch he gave him seemed justified, even if Colt didn't think so.

What did these people expect of him anyway? He was not some machine. He had feelings, too. In irritation, he got up and figured on trying to get word to Suzanne that he had found Colton, only to lose the hot-head again. Then he remembered the girls had gone off to one of the neighboring towns in search of Colt. He scribbled a quick note and left it with the desk clerk, then went out and took the trail to Alma. Perhaps he would encounter them along the way and if not, he would continue up towards Mosquito Pass. That direction was as good as any to look for Colt and he still needed to make some money hunting.

Two days later, Sonny had worked his way downstream on the North Fork of the South Platte, having left the small mining community of Webster. His search had brought him to this boom town from South Park, but no one seemed to know anything of Colt, although they were very interested in buying meat. He had orders for elk or venison with several of the miners interested in a haunch or shoulder of either. Tornado was stepping out briskly, eager to run and impatient with the mule trailing along behind. Sonny was looking for Indian Creek and the Willow Gulch drainage and wary of Indians, for he had been told by one of the locals that it was a good area to hunt but warned that Ute renegades occasionally camped at the mouth of that stream.

According to the old-timer in Webster, the upland Willow Meadow drainage was a good area with little to no hunting pressure. With eyes wide open, Sonny was intent on working his way up the gulch looking for a fat elk or mule deer. Finding no recent sign of Indians, he started up the gulch and a half hour later he spotted a five-point buck and dropped it with a long shot to the neck. He was near a buffalo-shaped peak when he made the shot, and riding to where the deer had fallen he was just finishing bleeding the kill and removing the musk glands when he thought he heard a woman scream. He paused with knife in hand and listened. A bit disconcerted, there was something vaguely familiar about that scream.

CHAPTER TWENTY-THREE

Desire or Disaster?

South Park City, July 1871

FRENCHY LEANED BACK ON THE HIND LEGS of the chair he was sitting on at the *Last Chance Saloon* in Alma and grinned at the four men seated around him.

"You mean to tell me one kid shot the guns out of all four of your hands? What kind a whiz is thees fellow?"

"He's faster 'n greased lightning and a side-winding son-of-a-bitch," the fellow with the black beard groused. He shakily picked up his glass of beer with a bandaged hand.

"We know he and his pard have dust," another of the fellows whined. His hand too, was bandaged.

"So, you were trying to relieve them of their pokes and got the tables turned on you, eh?" Frenchy said.

"We never expected the fool kid to draw on us, heck he was under all our guns," a third member nursing his right hand put in.

"Ma ami, you must work smarter with some people more than the others," the Frenchman said.

"Well, I'd like to see you do any better," the fellow with the beard challenged.

"How much gold does he and his friend have?" Frenchy asked.

"Who knows, probably plenty. They work hard and spend little, they've got to have a pretty good stash piled up and there is no one closer than a mile to the Allen diggings," the forth man said. He was rubbing the cold glass of his beer against the back of his bruised right hand.

"I might be interested in lightening his load, but first I am trying to find this man. Have any of you seen this fellow?" Frenchy removed the wanted poster from inside his frock coat and spread it out for the four outlaws to look at.

"That's him!" Blackbeard stated flatly.

"Him?" Frenchy said.

"Yeah, that's the guy that shot us all up," the man repeated. His men gathered around to stare at the poster and nodded in agreement.

"You should not tease me, monsieur, I do not take kindly to ill-advised witticisms."

"No joke, Frenchy," the man with the whiny voice said. "That's the guy who shot our guns from our hands. Why are you looking for him?"

"It ees an old score I have to settle with heem," the French man said. "Let us ride out and find this young gunman."

Frenchy rode at the head of the gang of outlaws into Jimmy Allen's yard, and when the prospector came to the door Frenchy promptly shot him. Allen dropped on the porch in front of the step. Dismounting, the five men got down and stepped over the moaning man to enter the cabin.

"Where have you searched for zee gold?" Frenchy asked.

Blackbeard said, "Pretty much everywhere. We went through all his supplies, drawers and cupboards, under his bed and in every nook and cranny."

"Well, his gold has got to be here, we must look smarter. Did you check for any hidden trap doors in the floor?"

"No," the outlaw leader said. The others looked on with curiosity.

"Check the floor," Frenchy said, "and leesten for a hollow-sounding spot."

The outlaws began a stomping on the floorboards of the cabin. Frenchy found a stout walking stick by the door and began a methodical thumping of the cabin's floor. When he thumped the stone slab in front of the hearth, he heard an empty sound echo back.

"Heer it eez," the Frenchman said with an evil grin.

Quickly the two outlaws whose hands were not bandaged dug around the edges and soon dislodged the stone slab to reveal the ceramic butter-crock. The jar was lifted out, it's weight testifying to the treasure within, and once the stopper was removed the outlaws began a combined celebration of their good fortune.

"Now that's why I don't work for a living," Blackbeard said. "Let these poor suckers wade around in the muck, I'll just come along and relieve 'em of their load and keep my feet dry."

"I wonder where hees partner eez," Frenchy said.

"Yeah, the rascal with the gun," the whiny-voiced fellow said.

"I saw fresh buggy tracks out in the yard," another of the outlaws spoke up.

The outlaws trooped out of the cabin, stepping across Jimmy Allen's body once more, and went out to where their horses were tied. Blackbeard carried the crock of gold under his arm under the watchful eye of his companions and then removed two heavy buckskin sacks from the jar and put them in his saddle bags.

"We'll divvy this up later boys, mount up."

Frenchy led the way, his eyes intent on the buggy tracks in the dust. He followed them to where they entered the road, and was surprised to see that they turned right, away from town, following the road in the opposite direction.

"They went thees way," he said and broke his horse into a trot following the easy to read tracks. Around the second bend they found an empty buggy, the horse tied to some willows. Footprints of two women or children led up a slight trail and the outlaws turned their horses to ride up it alongside a chattering brook.

Frenchy at once suspected that the buggy belonged to Suzanne Kluesman and Kathreen McClusky, for he had surreptitiously observed them previously driving about, back in South Park City. He rubbed his hands in glee, but said nothing to his companions. If the girls were here, they had undoubtedly found where Colton Saber was hiding. He would finally take his revenge on that smart-alecky Texas upstart, dispatch this outlaw riff-raff, take the gold, and then capture the women. It could not be a more ideal situation.

The trail led up past a waterfall and, reaching the top, Frenchy held up his hand. Ahead was a clearing in the forest. "Wait here," Frenchy said, "I will scout ahead on foot and see what is up there. With a little luck, we should find that scoundrel, Saber, and set upon him before he knows that we are here."

The Frenchman pulled a rifle from his saddle scabbard and, dismounting, stealthily worked his way up the trail. Rounding a bend, he came to a stop. Ahead of him was Miss McClusky, the sunlight glinting off her red hair. She was standing at the edge of a broad grassland, her eyes fixed on the figure of Suzanne Kluesman who was walking slowly across the meadow towards a lone man working a gold claim. The man was obviously unaware that he was no longer alone. Stepping from the trail to a vantage spot on the edge of the trees, opposite of where Colton worked some one hundred yards away, Frenchy chose a line of fire away from where Miss Kluesman walked. The gambler rested his rifle on the branch of an aspen and drawing a bead on the unsuspecting cowboy, held his breath. One well-placed shot and he would even the score. Slowly his finger tightened on the trigger.

———

For the next two days, I attempted to bury thoughts of Suzanne and Sonny by working myself into oblivion, and was having little success. I had ridden poor Lightfoot back from town Sunday, till he was near dead on his feet, having stopped by briefly at Jimmy's place to pick up a few things. The miner had a few questions about what was up, but was way too cheery for the mood I was in, so I just told him his opinions were about as useful as a tin-canned fart, went back outside the cabin, slammed my stuff into the saddle bags and hopped on my horse. I then ran him up the road as fast as he could go. We hardly slowed down once we took the trail at Ute Creek, and by the time I reached my diggings, the red horse was lathered up pretty good. I turned him into the pasture with barely a rubdown, and then hit my workings with a fury that was well beyond what was prudent for the kind of work I was doing.

The realization that she was alive... that they were both alive, was a relief beyond my comprehension, but darkly overshadowed by the fact that they were working closely together in this supposed search for me. What did they even come for? If they were alive then why didn't they just go ahead and have at each other and let me be? Was it guilt? Did they really care that much about my welfare, and if so, why had they even got mixed up with each other? So what if it had been two years or whatever, she should have waited. And what about God, wasn't He in control? This seemed to me to be about the dirtiest trick He could have played on all of us... On Suzanne, on

Sonny and on me. Was He so bored with his existence that He had to poke around in our lives like some brat kid poking a stick around in an ant hill? It was with a great bitterness of soul that these thoughts boiled to the surface while I worked the hours away at my claim.

But still, the wonder that Suzanne was alive. That she was here, had come looking for me and now had found me, or Sonny had at least. What would I do when I saw her? What could I do? I had made such a fool of myself with Sonny... and yet the two of them were still together, had traveled all this distance and spent the time to find me and it was this idea that seemed to rankle me the most. Why did she even have to come? Couldn't Sonny have just come and let me know that they weren't killed? I had gotten so used to the idea of them both being dead that now, to find that they were alive and still together... going through this search... this adventure together. . . well, frankly it sure tossed a wet blanket on the news.

Oh, I suppose I was glad enough she was alive, in fact I realized I was very glad of it, for both them being alive and all, and when I began to think of it in that light a smile began to spread across my face. I sat down, took out my bandana and began to mop the sweat off my brow. Looking at the whole situation in this new light I began to realize two things. Number one, like the sun coming out from behind a dark cloud, some petty jealousy, some dark evil thought or idea had held my soul with cords of envy and jealousy, so that I could not see the tremendous, miraculous deliverance and reprieve, I had been given; and that cloud had been there for a long time— ever since I shot them. And two, what kind of love must be at work here with Suzanne, and Sonny, and even God, for me to have a second chance to live my life with my love's desire?

How stupid I was. Why was I grubbing around in the mud for tiny specks of gold when the real gold was waiting for me so near at hand? "I am an idiot," I said.

I had just a few more shovels full to toss in the sluice while these thoughts swirled through my mind, when there came an unexpected scent of Suzanne on the breeze. It arrested me like hitting a stone wall. I gave a sharp cry and fell to my knees, grappling with the memory, and turned my face this way and that, trying to recover the fragrance. What was the sweet smell of Suzanne doing on this quiet summer breeze? Had it come to tantalize and torment me, to rub my nose in what had been? Was some quirk of fate sending me this soft reminder of my gentle Suzanne?

What visions stirred in my mind's eye from that essence. I envisioned her beautiful face smiling up at me from where we waited on the top of a windswept hill. In the distance, a magnificent herd of buffalo grazed slowly in our direction, as we whiled away the time stealing kisses and watching clouds. The poignancy of the memory brought tears to my eyes and I cried out, "Oh, God, please forgive me... somehow help me face her. I can't bear to lose her again.

There it was again, Suzanne's perfume, like lilac, or lavender soap, only this time stronger. What was going on? My heart beat faster and deep within me a glimmer of hope ignited. I don't know why, but just that smell seemed to bring Suzanne back to me. I was abstractly thinking I should plant some lilac bushes around the claim when I heard Lightfoot whistle. I stared up the hill to see my red horse standing with ears pointed erect and nostrils flaring, his eyes fixed on something down the trail. I turned to follow his gaze.

She was there. I don't know how, but Suzanne was there. In this place, not more than twenty yards away, Suzanne was walking towards me through the grass, the wind blowing her beautiful golden hair in wisps across her face and swirling her dress. Sonny had said she was searching for me, and here she was, the smell of her perfume real, stronger now, and I could hear the swish of her skirts through the grass. It was really she. Her face bore an indescribable look, both of fear and joy, desperation and hope, and above all the sweetest and loveliest countenance on earth. I did not know what to do. I both wanted to run to her and away from her.

"Colton, it's me," she said. "Suzanne!"

I stood stock still in disbelief. She had come, had found me after all. How did she get here? For an eternity, I stood there, my heart in my throat and then I was galvanized into action, running as hard as I could toward the girl of my dreams.

"Suzanne, it's you, you're alive. I...I... Oh, my God, can it be true, is it really you?"

Suzanne was running to my arms, her hands reaching out for me with indescribable joy shining on her face.

"Colton, oh Colton, I've found you at last," she cried as she ran into my arms.

We met and I caught her up in my embrace and whirled her about while she buried her face into the hollow of my neck. Like a drowning man, I clutched her to me, my face engulfed in the sweet scent of her hair. Suzanne squealed her delight and struggled to get her hands free and clasp them to my face. Pulling mine down to hers, she began to kiss me repeatedly while tears of joy wet her face and great sobs, interspersed with giggles, wracked her body, all the while murmuring over and over, "It's you I love, it's you, only you."

I was shuddering like an aspen leaf in a high wind. I set her on her feet and held her at arm's length to look at her, yes, it was Suzanne, my beautiful, beautiful Suzanne. She stood there the way I had pictured her so many times on the difficult trail back to her, with big eyes shining their love for me, her smile so warm and tender and inviting, her hand gently caressing my cheek.

I moved to gather her into my arms once more, but had no sooner started towards her when something hit me a shattering blow in the arm. I saw a white puff of smoke from the edge of the meadow and heard the distant report of a rifle. In shock, I crumpled to the ground. Only my sudden movement toward Suzanne had saved me from taking the bullet full in the chest. As it was, my left arm was buzzing and numb. I feared it was badly injured. Suzanne screamed and reached for me. I could hear other screams and yelling coming from the woods and looked off to see a band of men on horseback break from the cover of the trees, shouting and shooting and riding towards us.

"Suzanne, quick, we must get up the hill."

Suzanne had knelt by my side and was crying, "Oh, Colton, you've been shot."

"Yes, help me, I have a stronghold up the hill. Quick, there are shells and a rifle in the tent; get them." I rose on one knee and pulled the kerchief from around my neck and stuffed it quickly into my bloody sleeve as flames of pain bent me over, nauseous. Suzanne came to me with the rifle and two boxes of shells. I took the Winchester, levered in a round and with my right hand fired a shot at the lead rider. His horse went down and the other riders pulled up. The fellow from the downed horse clambered up behind another rider and then they came on more slowly.

"We must get up to those logs," I said pointing up the hill. We ran up to where I had built the log fortress. When the riders saw us running, they came on at a hard gallop, and we barely made it inside the structure before bullets thudded into the heavy log wall.

Taking my pistol, I handed it to Suzanne. "Can you shoot this?" I asked. She took the gun and nodded and then with a determined look on her face, she rested the butt of the pistol on the top log, and holding the gun with both hands, she cocked and fired it at one of the oncoming riders. He let out a strangled yell and went over backwards off his horse. My head swimming, I began firing the rifle after the departing riders as they raced back down the hill to my encampment. Three men went inside my tent and started rifling through my stuff. Soon, one of them discovered my buckskin pouch of gold, and when they came back out, he held it up for the others to see. With my arm throbbing, I drew a careful bead on the back of the man's head and squeezed the trigger. There was an audible pop as my bullet found its mark and the man dropped dead at the feet of the other two thieves.

"That black bearded fellow is one of the thieves who tried to rob me and Jimmy Allen a few days ago," I said huskily. "This looks like the work of the same gang."

"Oh Colt, I shot a man," Suzanne said. "Is he dead?"

"I can't tell, sweetheart, but that was a great shot. I can't believe you are here. Oh... Thank God you are. How come you are?"

"My love for you would not let me do otherwise," she said simply. Her eyes were fixed on the remaining two outlaws who were taking my gold and mounting their horses.

I smiled through my pain. Now this was the girl I remembered: short, sweet and to the point. I stared longingly at her with my vision swimming and eyes growing dim. Then all went dark.

Suzanne snapped one more shot at the fleeing outlaws and turned to find Colt slumped over unconscious. There was an awful lot of blood running from under his sleeve. Quickly she opened his shirt, tore off the sleeve and bound a tourniquet above the wound. She applied pressure until the blood flow stopped, then stretching him out as best she could, she bound the wound; his arm did not appear to be broken but was badly torn where the bullet had exited. She began to look about for a way to get Colt down the hill to his camp. A red horse was watching them from over the top rail of the pasture fence and she wondered if she could get him and bring Colt down that way, when suddenly the silence was broken by two heavy rifle shots and Kathreen's scream.

———

Kathreen stood transfixed watching the reuniting of the two lovers, a mixture of joy and sadness filling her bosom, as Suzanne rushed into Colton's arms. It was as if she had always known it would end this way. Even years ago, when Colt had so tenderly talked to her on the train, and she had felt such gratitude and thankfulness for his deliverance of her from being sold into prostitution, she had known it would end this way, known even before knowing Suzanne, that there was someone else. She had sensed with the intuitive mystic of her sex that the youth next to her in the coach, with his arm about her shoulder, loved another and could never be hers. She was glad now, glad the two of them had found each other at last. She smiled at the glorious reunion, then her reverie was shattered by the crack of a rifle near at hand and a scream from the meadow.

With a start, Kathreen whirled towards the sound and to her horror saw a dark clad man leveling a rifle at the couple in the meadow. With a loud cry, Kathreen rushed towards the shooter, and hurled a stick she had picked up, in his direction. The man straightened from his shooter's stance and turned a startled face to his would-be attacker, then his swarthy countenance broke into an evil smile.

"Ah-hah, welcome back, mon doux cherie," he said.

"LaRoush!" Kathreen gasped.

"The one and only," Frenchy said, and set his rifle against the tree. "Did you miss me?"

"Miss you? I hate your infernal guts," the red-head ground out between clinched teeth. She was eying the gun he had propped against the tree. "If I had that gun I'd blast your evil heart to smithereens."

"Aw now, mon cherie, that ess no way to greet your long lost amoureux. Do you not remember the good times we shared on the *Belle*?"

"You mean when you drugged, kidnapped, and raped me?" she said with withering scorn. "I could scratch your eyes out and stomp them into the dirt, you filthy swine."

"No, no, mon cherie," the Frenchman laughed, "I must have my eyes to behold again your nakeed glory."

At that declaration Kathreen flew into a rage at the leering face of her tormentor, scratching and tearing at him with clawed hands.

"Hey, hey! Now stop that, you hell-cat," he yelled when Kathreen clawed a deep scratch down his cheek. Stepping quickly back from the panting girl he picked up his rifle and cracked Kathreen between the eyes with the butt of it. The enraged girl gave a strangled squawk and dropped at his feet, out cold.

"That should hold you for a while," he said and turned back to gaze out in the field at the sound of gunfire. He watched in silence at the events unfolding before him. Neither Colt Saber or the girl were to be seen, but shots were coming from a barricade up on the hill, and he could only surmise when one of the outlaws suddenly toppled over backwards from his horse, that the two had somehow taken shelter behind the log wall, and were now effectively defending their position. He saw the other out-laws ride back to the camp, get down and go into a tent, to emerge with a buckskin bag held aloft by one of them. The man went down when a well-placed rifle shot split the quiet afternoon air. The other two riders hastily scooped up the gold sack from their fallen comrade and raced back for the cover of the trees. Frenchy smiled evilly and, taking his rifle, moved to intercept them.

Blackbeard and the fellow with the whiny voice pulled up their horses, once they reached the cover of the trees, and were surprised to see Frenchy standing there to meet them.

"What the hell you doing here?" Blackbeard demanded.

"Waiting for you," Frenchy said.

"Well, you ain't getting none of this," the outlaw leader said, holding up the bag of gold. "You didn't lift one finger in helping us get it and Lew and Dink are dead. You didn't even kill that clod-hopping miner; he's holed up there on the hill with some girl, and he's a dead shot."

"That's alright, I won't be going back there and neither will you." LaRoush leveled the rifle at Blackbeard's chest and pulled the trigger, blasting him out of the saddle. He turned his gun on the other outlaw, who began an immediate whining for his life, and shot him as well. Calmly he walked over, picked up the buckskin sack and lifted it to his saddle bags. He then recovered Jimmy Allen's gold from the outlaw leader's saddle and added it to the rest. With a satisfied smile, he turned back to where he had left the red-head, intent on getting his hands on her. To his surprise, she was not there.

———

Kathreen came to with a start. For a moment, she did not know where she was. She sat up, her hand going to a swelling bruise on her forehead, and a low moan escaped from her lips. Then she remembered her plight. She saw LaRoush confronting two men on horseback, and quickly she sprang to her feet, then ran up alongside the stream, following a well-trodden game trail; she must get away, and find Suzanne and Colt. Had LaRoush killed them?

She did not know, but for now, she feared for her own life. She must lose the diabolical Frenchman in these hills, and then make her way back to her friends; if they were hurt she must get help. Suddenly two shots rang out back in the glade where she had last seen LaRoush.

The trail broke out of the woods into the meadow and went winding past the mud dams of Colt's diggings, then led to the base of a forty-foot high waterfall. She was trapped, LaRoush would be coming. Desperately she retraced her steps, and found where the trail went up and around the falls. Out of breath she scrambled to a vantage point, and looked back to see the Frenchman following her back trail. He was riding his horse at a slow trot, his eyes alternating from the ground to the trail ahead. In panic, Kathreen plunged on up through an open grassy park filled with house-sized blocks of pillow rock, the likes of which she had never seen before. Ahead was a sharply defined granite peak, shaped like a buffalo. Her heart pounding and her breath coming in sobs, Kathreen pressed on. Oh, how she wished she had a gun or a weapon of any kind, she would stop this evil man once and for all. She had nearly reached the top when the click of iron shoe on granite rock hauled her up short to look back. There was LaRoush, slowly riding up with a wicked grin revealing yellow, uneven teeth.

"Here you are, mon cheri, you've led moi a merry chase, all that much sweeter shall be the ravishment of you." He stepped from his saddle and Kathreen screamed. It was a wild, desperate, frightened scream that echoed back mockingly from the granite promontories of this wild, lonely place.

LaRoush made a sudden rush toward the girl and Kathreen scrambled to get away. From a rocky bench, the broken and bleached remains of a lightning-struck pine tree had split, with half toppled over and extending out over a deep canyon, but the other half was still standing, its roots clinging to the shelf as though it was reluctant to let go and plunge the whole affair over the precipice. The troubled girl took refuge behind the sharp, bleached branches of this downed giant. Behind her, a rock wall blocked any further escape. While she tried to elude the cruel grasping hands of the impassioned Frenchman, he managed to catch the back of her blouse, tearing a piece of it from her shoulders, leaving it in his hands.

"Ah, thees est better, cheri, I shall strip you bit by bit, come heer."

"Let me go, you fiend," Kathreen cried, screaming in terror once more. Avoiding his grasp, she climbed onto the broken spar of the downed pine, holding onto the denuded branches for balance, and then backed away from her attacker. Looking down, she found to her horror, that she was standing over an abyss that dropped hundreds of feet below to a rock-strewn bottom.

LaRoush climbed to the base of the split snag, his hand resting against the upright portion of the dead tree. "Come here, you foolish girl, before you fall to your death."

There was a note of concern in his voice, and Kathreen said, "Take one more step and I'll jump."

"No, mon cherie, give moi your hand—I will help you back."

"Why, so you can rape me again?"

"No, no, mi amour, so we can know the sweet romance we knew in Saint Louis."

"Sweet romance, bah, you lied, drugged, kidnapped and raped me."

"No, no, this is all some misunderstanding, give moi your hand and I will pull you to safety." The Frenchman extended his hand toward the girl and edged closer.

Kathreen screamed again as the ancient snag shifted beneath their weight and gravel rattled off over the ledge. Losing her balance, the girl teetered over the chasm, while desperately clinging to two spindly dead branches trying to right herself, when the twigs snapped and upset her balance again. She started falling from the precarious perch to a certain death, when LaRoush shot out a hand and caught the back of her dress once more, pulling her back into his arms. The two of them stumbled back against the trunk of the dead snag. The girl was trembling with shock and panic, while the gambler smiled into her hair and held her close. He began to run greedy, questing hands up and down her body.

Presently Kathreen regained her equilibrium, and as her rescuer's fingers became bolder, taking more liberties with her person, she pried her arms between his and pushed him away. When his hands grasped and squeezed her bottom and pulled her up against him tight she cried out, "Stop you depraved monster."

"I am not depraved, but I will have you." LaRoush said with heated voice. "There is no one to stop moi now." His back against the old snag, he grappled with the girl, seeking to lift her skirts and reach within her clothing, when a stentorian voice broke through the protests of the assaulted woman.

"Unhand my girl, you low-down snake!"

Kathreen and LaRoush stopped their struggles and looked up as one to see Sonny Saber standing before them, a long, bloody Bowie knife in his hand, and fire in his eyes.

Quick as a cat, LaRoush thrust Kathreen in front of him and, drawing her tight against him, he pulled a knife from his belt and held it to the struggling girl's throat.

"Drop your knife, monsieur, or I will slit her throat."

"Sonny!" Kathreen cried. "It's Pierre LaRoush—the one who kidnapped me and sold me into prostitution."

"Has he harmed you?" Sonny asked.

"No, not yet, but he said he was going to violate me, that no one could stop him."

"Did you say that?" Sonny's voice cracked like a whip and the Frenchman jumped as though stung.

"Oui, Monsieur, I shall have moi way with the mademoiselle. Drop your knife."

"You harm one hair of my girl's head and I'll drop your sorry carcass off this mountain."

"Ah, so you want mademoiselle for yourself, eh? You can have what's left of her when I am done, now throw down the knife."

"Sonny, don't trust him," Kathreen cried. "I think he shot Suzanne and Colt."

"I did not shoot the blonde cheri, only that *batarde* Colt," Pierre let out an evil laugh. "Suzanne goes back with me, along with thees leetle one."

"You shot my brother?" Sonny said in alarm.

"So, the irritating cowboy is your brother—then you may as well join him." LaRoush stabbed his knife into the trunk of the snag and made a grab for a pistol concealed in his sash.

"Look out, Sonny, he's got a gun!" Kathreen thrust her arms up, spoiling her captor's aim as the small pocket derringer stabbed an orange dart of flame. The bullet whined off into space.

A malevolent look of unmitigated hatred came into the Frenchman's eyes. Dropping the empty derringer, he yanked his knife from the tree and jerked Kathreen back in a death grip, his blade raised to slash across her throat.

"If you so much as scratch her, you are a dead man," Sonny warned. "Have you no fear of God?"

"I will kill her and God be damned," the Frenchman snarled.

"You are cursing God?" Sonny was incredulous.

"I have no fear of God, what has He ever done for moi? Everything I have, I got by myself, including this girl. Drop your knife, monsieur!"

Sonny remembered Colton telling him of the time some desperadoes had held up the stage coach he was on. He had frustrated their mischief by telling them God was observing what they were doing. Taking a page from his brother's book he said, "God is watching what you are doing now, you rebel, use your head, your very life is in danger, His anger is about to explode, you're doomed."

"Doomed, eh? Who's going to doom me? Not thees little one." Kathreen screamed as Pierre jerked her up tighter against him and brandished his knife. "And certainly not you, if you care anything about her; and you can forget about God 'cause He does not exist."

"Oh, yes, He does. God is angry with the wicked every day."

"I don't care if He is, in fact I defy Him to do anything. If He is so powerful let Him come down and face me, man to man. I will carve out His heart."

"Mark well that God doesn't miss a move you make; He's aware of every step you take. The shadow of your sin will overtake you," Sonny said.

"Ha!" LaRoush said. "I dare Him." Then turning his eyes heavenward, the enraged Frenchman began to rant and yell, waving his knife skyward and screaming for God to come down and fight him. "God, where are you? Come down and fight like a man, I will draw and quarter you, then we shall see who is the greatest."

Kathreen was looking back fearfully at her crazed captor when Sonny yelled, "Kathreen, jump!"

Wrenching free, the frightened red-head broke from LaRoush's grasp and leaped from the dead snag to run to Sonny.

The raving Frenchman barely noticed her departure. It was as though he had become consumed with a ravening hatred of the Almighty, for he continued to rant and revile God, while challenging Him to come down and fight.

Suddenly, out of the clear blue sky, a thunderbolt shot down and struck his raised knife sending thousands of volts of electricity through the convulsing, incinerating body of the luckless brigand. The smell of burning hair and flesh was strong on the air as well as that of sulfur and ozone, while the charred corpse of Pierre LaRoush tumbled from his perch to land in a smoking pile of rubble and refuse on the ground.

"Oh, Sonny," Kathreen said with a desperate cry, throwing her arms up around his neck and clinging tightly. "What an awful man." Her eyes fell upon the gruesome spectacle of what was left of LaRoush smoldering on the rocky table, and she shuddered, "You saved me."

"I'm sorry you had to go through all that, Kathreen, I only wish I could have got here sooner."

"My gracious," Kathreen cried, "what happened?"

"Lightning struck him," Sonny said.

"Just like that—he's gone? I wouldn't have believed it if I hadn't seen it." The relief in Kathreen's voice was obvious.

"The man was a fool."

"Where did you come from?"

"I was dressing a deer down the backside of this mountain when I heard you scream. I rushed up here as quick as I could. Is that LaRoush's horse?"

"Yes. Sonny did you mean that?"

"What?" Sonny's face turned red.

"That I was your girl?" Kathreen still had her arms locked around the cowboy's neck clinging to him while he looked down at her. Her red hair framed her lovely face and her penetrating green eyes stared up at Sonny with an unfathomable light. This time, on a mountain top somewhere in the Rockies, the lanky range rider from Texas physically felt his heart slip away, to be lost in the depths of this beautiful girl's gaze.

Bending to kiss her he said, "Yes, sweetheart, you've been my girl for a long, long time."

"What about Suzanne?"

"Well, I never had a snowball's chance with her anyway, and was just too stupid to know it. I have always loved you—just not always well. Can you forgive me?"

"Yes!"

"Yes? That's it, just yes?"

"Yes, I think you may find these waters are deeper than you think they are," and she pulled Sonny's face down until his lips met hers.

They kissed long and deep then until finally Sonny broke from their embrace, "I'm sorry I was ever so arrogant as all that."

"I guess we've both been a bit full of ourselves, haven't we?"

"I can do better."

"Me too," she said.

"Where is your horse and how did you end up here anyway?" he asked.

"I have no horse, oh, it was terrible. Suzanne and I had discovered that Colton was working a mining claim right down this mountain, and we drove to the trail head in a buggy. After we had found the place, I stayed behind to give Suzanne a chance to talk to Colt alone, and I saw them finally meet out in the meadow. That's when LaRoush showed up. Somehow, he had followed us. He ambushed Colt from the woods, and when I confronted him, he knocked me down with his rifle. I was out for a while, and when I came to, he was talking to two ruffians, so I snuck away and took to a trail that led me up here. I heard two shots and then he followed me, chasing me until I wound up here, and I ran out on that dead tree after he tore my blouse. I threatened to jump off the cliff but he caught me and pulled me back. He was tearing at my clothes when you showed up. Oh, thank God you did, you saved me from a fate worse than death."

Sonny lowered Kathreen to her feet. "We best get off this mountain and see what's become of Colt and Suzanne. Can you ride?"

Kathreen was trying to arrange her torn blouse over her shoulders. "Yes, that blackguard has ruined this dress."

"My jacket is on my saddle, let's ride"

Kathreen nodded and walked to the waiting saddle horse.

"Follow me down to where I left my horse."

The cowboy and the girl found where Tornado and Hank were tied and quickly Sonny mounted up. He had Kathreen direct him to the trail down the south side of the mountain, and they were riding single file when he called to the girl.

"Kath, does it strike you funny that I should be on this mountain at precisely the right time and place that I needed to be in order to help you out?"

"What did you call me?"

Sonny smiled sheepishly at the back of the girl's head as she led the way down the trail.

"Kath—is that all right?"

Kathreen turned to smile back at him. "It is for you, but nobody else. What do you mean by funny?"

"Well, not funny ha, ha, but funny—strange or peculiar. What are the chances that I would be here at your moment of distress?"

"If you think that's funny, what about the fact that Colton's mining claim is here on the other side of this mountain?"

"Yeah, the very one I'm hunting deer on. Do you think that's a coincidence?"

"Well, didn't you tell me that your Grandpa prayed we'd find Colton and everything would work out alright?"

"That's right, he did. It was the most powerful prayer I think I ever heard."

"Well, there you go, don't you folks say, *'Praise the Lord,'* or something like that?"

"Yeah," Sonny mused, "I guess with God there is no such thing as coincidence. Thanks Lord, please let Suzanne and Colt be okay."

With cruel curved talons, sharp hooked beak, and a grizzled red-neck, a vulture watched the departing humans with beady unblinking eyes until they passed from sight down the trail. Then with a clicking sound and a foul flapping of wings, it lifted off its perch and made a long slow glide to the lightning-blasted pine and the ghastly remains below it.

CHAPTER TWENTY-FOUR

Through it All

Ute Creek Claim, July 1871

SUZANNE FOUND A HALTER ON THE FENCE post, and keeping the pistol handy, she struggled to bridle and saddle the sorrel. The horse was unusually nervous and kept snorting and whistling, his ears pricked towards where Colt lay. Finally, she had the saddle secured and attempted to mount, but the red horse would not stand for her. In frustration, she led him up the hill to where Colt was. The outlaw she had shot lay where he had fallen and, as she passed, a quick glance assured her he was dead.

Puzzling as to how to get Colt onto the horse, she watched the cowpony snorting and sniffing his master's body. Two feeble attempts to lift Colt up were met only with a groan from the unconscious man, and she was near the point of giving up and going for help when she saw the rope coiled to the saddle. Retrieving it, she fastened a loop about Colt's body under his arms, then tied the end off to the saddle horn. Leading the horse, she carefully brought him back down the hill, skidding Colt along on his back over the grass.

Colt's horse was reluctant to leave the camp and even stuck his head inside the tent while Suzanne huffed and puffed and finally managed to lift and roll Colt onto the low camp cot that served for his bed. It was as if the horse knew something was wrong with his master and was doing his best to help the girl. For the next several minutes, Suzanne worked to remove Colt's shirt and boots, while alternating the pressure on the tourniquet. She was surprised to see several scars on his back, stomach, arms and legs. What must have happened to him? With a makeshift bandage torn from her petticoat, she made a fresh dressing for his arm, making the cowboy as comfortable as she knew how, and then turned to lead the red horse back to the pasture. She left the animal saddled in the event she would need to go for help; perhaps Colt's mining partner back at the little cabin would come to her aid.

Suzanne was busy kindling a fire in the little stove to heat some water, intent on bathing Colt's wound and securing a better bandage, when she heard horses approaching. Frightened, she caught up the pistol and checked the loads. Five of the six cartridges were spent and she was fumbling to replace the bullets with those in Colt's gunbelt when she heard Kathreen call out.

"Suzanne, are you here?"

"In here," Suzanne cried. "I need help."

Sonny and Kathreen appeared at the door of the tent. Her friend was disheveled and the top of her dress was torn. Sonny appeared grim, gazing back over his shoulder at the dead thief slumped over the woodpile.

"Looks like the body count is piling up," he said.

"There's one more lying dead up on the hill," Suzanne replied.

"And two more over at the edge of the woods," Sonny added. "It looks like you folks were fighting some kind of war. Who are these guys?"

"Thieves and outlaws." Suzanne replied. "Colt said they tried to rob him and his partner earlier."

"How bad is Colt hurt?" Kathreen asked.

"He's been hit high in the arm; I bandaged him up as best I could, but we need to get him to town to a doctor as soon as possible. He's lost a lot of blood. Can we get him back down to the road where we left the buggy?" Suzanne asked.

Sonny felt his brother's forehead and shook his head. "He's feverish, I don't think we should move him just now. I'll go for the doctor. You girls stay here."

"Maybe I should go with you and show you the way. Colt's partner would be able to help us get Colt down to his place at least." Kathreen said.

Suzanne looked at her friend. She seemed reluctant to leave Sonny's side. "Kate, you wouldn't leave me here alone?"

"You seem to be doing just fine," Kathreen said quickly. "The sooner we go, the sooner help will come."

"Kathreen! What happened? How did you find Sonny?"

Sonny put in on behalf of the frightened red-head, "Suzanne, I was on the other side of this mountain hunting meat when I heard Kathreen screaming and came upon her standing out over a ledge with that fellow LaRoush attempting to molest her."

"LaRoush!" Suzanne said in alarm. "How did he get here and—where is he?"

Kathreen said, "He rode up with those outlaws just after you left me. He said he'd been trailing Colt from Galveston, and we found one of your wanted posters rolled up in his saddle bags. He's the one who shot Colt, and then he tried to abduct me. He intended to come for you, too, and kidnap us both."

"Both of us? Oh, that fiend, where is he?" Suzanne was looking nervously past her friends out the door of the tent.

"After knocking me out, he waylaid and killed the last two outlaws—the two who escaped from you and Colt and took the gold. I came to in the meantime, and ran off

422

up the trail, but he saw me and followed. Once I made my way to the top of the mountain, he caught up to me, and backed me out on an old dead tree that hung over a cliff. I was scared to death, and screaming for my life, but then he turned all conciliatory and tried to help me back to safety. When I almost fell, he pulled me back in his clutches and began to take indecent liberties with me. I would have killed him if I'd had a gun." Kathreen seemed quite shaken in the telling of the tale.

"Well, what happened?" Suzanne said.

"Sonny appeared like an avenging angel and shouted, '*Unhand my girl!*'" Kathreen said as she fixed a worshipful gaze on the tall cowboy.

Sonny smiled boyishly and wrapped his arms around Kathreen, pulling her back against him. "I'd never let him harm you, the miserable coyote."

The surprise on Suzanne's face was overwhelmingly obvious as she stared at the two of them, for a bond had certainly been forged between them.

"God killed him," Kathreen said, a look of awe on her face. She looked up at Sonny, her head leaning back against his chest.

"Killed him? How? Where is he?" Suzanne stared at her two friends.

"He was going to cut Kath's throat with his knife. I tried to talk sense to him, told him God was watching him, and he went into a rage, blaspheming God, and threatening to cut His heart out. When I told him that kind of talk would doom him he just grew angrier and began to wave his knife in the air like some insane maniac and threatened God more loudly."

"Oh, Suze, it was terrible. When he removed his knife from my throat to threaten God, I twisted out of his grasp and jumped from the log to run to Sonny. His hatred toward God was indescribable."

"Good gracious," Suzanne said. "Then what happened?"

"It was the most amazing thing I ever saw," Sonny said. "Out of a clear blue sky, a thunderbolt struck the knife he was waving about and LaRoush was burned up right before our eyes."

"Incredible, God did that?" Suzanne's eyes were opened wide.

"I reckon so," Sonny said. "He's buzzard bait now."

Suzanne turned wondering eyes on Kathreen. "You say he was after you and me? How come?"

"You—me—the gold. He double-crossed the others, shot Colt, and said he was going to take you and me away with him and—and—have his way with us. But he never counted on Sonny." Kathreen flashed Sonny another proud smile, then turned and kissed the sober-faced cowboy.

"Looks like I was rescued again and didn't even know it." Suzanne said. "Thank you, Sonny, for being there again for me—for both of us."

Sonny nodded and squeezed Kathreen closer, "I think it was the Lord."

"What do you mean?" Suzanne was puzzled.

"Well, ask yourself this question, how did I happen to be on the opposite side of the very mountain you girls were on? And how about this: lightning flashes around in these mountains all the time in the summer, so LaRoush stands on a lightning-struck snag, waves his knife about like a lightning rod and cusses out God—talk about tempting fate."

"I see what you mean. Do you think the Lord led us all to this place and time?" Suzanne asked.

Slowly nodding, there was little doubt Sonny was convinced, and Kathreen looked back at her friend with lowered brow, a knowing look, and slowly nodded.

"Thank you, Lord," Suzanne said reverently, "you were there all the time. I can't wait to tell Colt."

"Yeah," Kathreen said. "Suzanne, do you remember that prayer I made for you down by the river the day we tied knots in Two-Bits and Buddy's clothes?"

"I'll never forget it—that prayer was so sweet."

"Looks like He answered it," she said.

"And it looks like you two found more than that evil Frenchman up on the mountain, too."

The couple smiled back at Suzanne and nodded. Further words were not necessary.

A low moan came from the cot and Colton weakly raised a hand to his head.

"We'll go for help," Sonny said. "Will you be alright?"

Suzanne nodded.

"Try to keep his fever down, we'll be back soon."

———

It was like I was being hauled across a hot desert on my belly. My mouth was so dry I could scarcely swallow and my tongue was two sizes too big. At first I didn't know where I was and was having difficulty seeing. The room, or wherever it was, was swimming before my eyes and it felt like a red-hot running iron was stuck in my arm. I moaned and tried to sit up when soft, gentle hands pushed me back and a sweet voice told me to lie still.

"Water," I whispered and there was a rustling about, then a tin cup of cool water was pressed to my lips, while a strong arm lifted my head to drink.

"Where am I?" I croaked.

The same gentle voice said, "You've been shot and have lost a lot of blood. Please lie still."

What was it about the voice? I knew this voice but couldn't quite place it. I needed to go to the toilet, and tried to get up, but the movement set up a terrible throbbing in my arm again.

"You must lie still," the voice said.

I asked for another drink of water, then emptied the cup that was offered me and let my head drop back. I was just slipping back to sleep when the voice asked me if I was awake.

"No," I said.

"Oh, Colton, you had me so worried, you've been raving out of your head. Please Lord, help him."

I was wondering who this was... where I was. I thought I must be on my cot, and knew it was at my gold claim. I lay there with my eyes closed and tried to puzzle it out, but my thirst was unbelievable. A cool, wet rag was put against my forehead and someone was softly wiping my face. I raised a feeble hand and caught the wrist of my helper and opened my eyes. It was a woman, a beautiful woman... like an angel, but my vision was blurred and my eyes had trouble focusing, she smelled so good too, like lilacs—then I remembered.

"Suzanne, is that you?"

"Yes, Colton, I am here."

"Where did you come from? How did you find me?"

"I came all the way from Texas and prayed and prayed and prayed, and finally I found you."

"What happened—ugh! I need another drink."

A cup of water was again held to my lips and after that I could talk better.

Suzanne said, "You and I had just met when someone shot you, don't you remember any of that?"

"I think so," I was beginning to remember. First I had smelled her perfume, and then there she was. I could smell her now. My heart began to beat faster and by dint of sheer will, I cleared my vision and focused on Suzanne's lovely face.

"Oh Suzy, it's really you, I'm not dreaming? Where did you come from?"

"Colt, don't you remember me finding you here and the gunfight in the meadow? We were set upon by thieves."

426

"Ahh!...Yeah, now I do. What happened to 'em?"

"We killed two of them and the others rode off. They are dead now as well."

"Oh—well never mind that. How are you here? I—saw you—dead."

"You never shot me, the bullet hit Sonny's medal and his head knocked me out."

"That's what Sonny said... I never wanted to hurt you."

Suzanne studied my face for the longest moment while my eyes looked beseechingly up at her. Finally, she said, "I know you didn't. When did you see Sonny?"

"A couple of days ago in town. He threw his bent-up medallion at me, all mad about the shooting."

"I haven't seen Sonny in the past few days. I wonder why he never came and told us he had found you."

"I don't know, we had words and he hit me, and then... well, I took off and came back up here to try'n figure things out. It's hit me pretty hard, believing all this time I had killed you and him, and—now to find you okay. You are okay, aren't you?"

"Yes—Colt, did you fight with Sonny again?"

A slight color tinged the pallor of my face and my eyes wavered a moment before they stopped and looked steadily back into the amazing blue of hers. "I did," I said slowly, "even went for my gun, which was stupider than I can get, that's when he hit me."

"Colt, can you actually believe anything could ever displace you from my heart? Even after all this time, and finally reconciling to your death. You are as much in my heart as that night on the hill above your folk's place when you came back from Yuma, even more."

I took a deep quavering breath and let it out. "Then can you tell me what you were doing in his arms?"

"Missing you... wishing it was you. Lost and so alone and so undone. Honestly, if Sonny had not been there for me, I would not even be here today. You owe a lot to your brother and I doubt you can even appreciate the sacrifice he has made to bring me here to find you."

"Some sacrifice," I said bitterly.

"Colt, that is unworthy of you. Sonny loves you, he was wrung out like a dishrag when he thought you had been killed in that terrible accident down in the breaks. He went back to that place time and time again to see if he could find out anything more about what had happened, and he rescued me when no one else could."

"But why did he fall in love with you?"

"I don't know, I never wanted him to, I didn't ask him to, but he was the one there for me when you weren't, or couldn't be, or whatever. Where were you? What happened that you would stay away for more than two and a half years, while I waited and waited and waited?"

I grimaced and felt the old resentment rise in my throat like bile. Why God had let that happen to us was still a huge bone of contention stuck in my craw, but I needed to gain satisfaction on this other question first.

"Do you love Sonny?" I asked.

Suzanne stared silently and steadily back at me with a slight smile playing at the corners of her pretty mouth. Patiently she slowly shook her head and said, "Listen Colton, do you remember that cold winter's night some years ago when we stood on papa's porch saying good night? It was after we'd had a wonderful evening with a barn dance and sleigh ride. You tried to kiss me and I stopped you. Do you remember what I said?

Heh! It was one moment I would never forget. I gave her a flat smile and nodded my head. Slowly I repeated the words: *"When I fall in love, it will be completely for I'll never fall in love 'til then."*

Suzanne said, "I believe that when you came into my life—the very first time we met, that we were destined to be together. I didn't know it at the time, it took going through some delightful, and yes, some terrible, experiences to learn it, but once you won my heart, became so embedded at the very center of it, I became yours... I was then... I am now... and I will forever be. I care for Sonny, love him like a brother, but he was going to have to live with the knowledge that my heart was full of you, with your memory, and the marvelous loving you had left me with. He knew that and was struggling to come to terms with it, but make no mistake, Sonny loved me in his own way as much as you. He was honorable, a gentleman and patient with me, and he laid that all aside to come and find you—for me. Knowing that in the finding of you, all his hopes for me would be dashed forever. If that isn't love, then I don't know what is."

I sank back on the cot, my mind a whirl and my arm burning. It sounded at last like Suzanne wasn't conflicted about Sonny's affections, but right now I was just too tired and sick to figure it out. I lapsed into silence and she must have let me doze, for when I woke again, the sun was going down in the west with its last rays shining in through the door of the tent. Suzanne was sitting back against my saddle bags, her hands clasped about her knees and her chin resting on them. With the resplendence of the sunlight behind her, she was gazing at me with such a fixed, dreamy look that for the moment I forgot all else and gloried in her angelic appearance.

I smiled at her, "What are you looking at?"

"You," she said simply, but the smile that broke out over her features and the totally absorbed look she fixed on me called to the deepest place in my soul. Once again, it found and brought out to the light of day all the beauty, and longing, and surrender that had been ours in that long-ago journey to the Sweetgrass. It had been so lost that I was startled to find it back, filling the little tent with its wonder and delight.

"I thought I would never gaze upon your face again," she said soberly. "Now, here you are, back where you belong."

"Suzanne, I can't live if living is without you. What of my brother?"

"I feel the very depths of gratitude for Sonny, and you will too. If he hadn't been there to remind me of you I'd have despaired of life. I would have never survived the hurt your loss was to me."

"You are so pretty. I love you."

"I love you."

She said it with such tenderness and devotion that even a dunderhead like me got it. "Will you still marry me?" I asked hopefully.

"Yes." She held up her hand with my ring still on her finger and the sun's last rays dazzled blue lights from its surface. "We are still engaged, aren't we?"

"Sure we are," I said, feeling the wonder of that long dead idea, now resurrecting.

"Pearl didn't think we would be," Suzanne said.

"What? Pearl? So, you met that little pixie, why'd she say that?"

"She had some idea that the engagement period had expired with you being gone so long."

I laughed softly, "Why, that little scallywag. I suppose she was maneuvering to edge you out and edge herself in." I was chuckling at my young protégé and the bemused look on Suzanne's face.

"She certainly was," Suzanne said. "It's a good thing she's not older, she informed me that she was going to marry you. That girl is a force to be reckoned with."

"She did have a heap of strange notions. I gather she got to the folks alright."

"Yes, she fell from a run-away Indian pony that she somehow mysteriously acquired, and landed on Tommy, and the two of them have been fighting ever since."

As weak as I was, I asked Suzanne to explain what she was talking about, and she told me of Pearl's arrival at the ranch. Apparently, nothing has been the same around there since. I laughed in spite of my arm, knowing altogether too well the tempest that swirled around that little lady.

"When?" I said.

Suzanne had paused in her narrative and was looking at my obvious recollection of Pearl with an amused expression. My question took her by surprise.

"When what?" she said.

"When will you marry me?"

"Right now—as soon as we can find a preacher."

"There's a circuit riding Methodist preacher in South Park City. I went there last Sunday and listened to him. He's pretty good."

"Let's go find him," Suzanne said. With that she leaned forward on her knees to carefully embrace me on the cot. She began to shower my face with kisses from her sweet, soft lips. The fire of her kisses finally relented and I fell back into a restless sleep.

I do not know how long I slept, but my dreams were filled with disturbing thoughts of God sending blue-light ladies to find me, and Sonny and Suzanne playing hide-n-seek in the hay, while all the time I needed to get up and go find a bush. Sometime in the dark, I half remembered getting off the cot and stumbling out of the tent. When I returned, Suzanne woke from her place on the floor and helped me to lie back down, covering me with a blanket. She said something about Sonny and Kathreen not being back before morning.

"Kathreen?" I mumbled, "Is she here?" then I drifted back to sleep.

I awoke late the next morning, feverish and thirsty, Suzanne had made coffee and was boiling a couple of eggs when we heard riders approaching, and Sonny's call.

"Hello the camp, Suzanne, Colt, are you in there?"

"In here," Suzanne called.

Sonny's head poked through the door of the tent, then he stepped in with a package in his arm. Kathreen was behind him. "Here's some medicine I got from the doctor," he said. "He wanted to know if the bullet is still in his arm."

"I don't think so," Suzanne replied. "I probed for it a little bit but didn't find anything."

Sonny stared down at his brother, then reached a hand to feel his forehead. "How ya doin', pard?"

"Been better," I mumbled. "I need some water."

Sonny took a cup from Suzanne and handed it to me. "I'm afraid I have some bad news for you, Colt. Those outlaws gunned down your mining partner, Jimmy Allen."

"Allen's dead?" I said.

"No, not quite. Kate and I found him lying on his porch with a bad bullet hole in his side. He was unconscious and near bled out—probably would have if he hadn't staunched the flow of blood with a gunnysack that was lying there. We managed to get him to Como and were lucky enough to find the doctor in town. He's resting in some widow's home, and the doc doesn't know if he'll pull through or not. The doc says to get you in there as soon as we can so he can look at your wound."

"We would've been here a lot sooner if we hadn't had to take Mr. Allen in," Kathreen said. "How you doing, Colt?"

I looked at the red-head and noticed something different about her. She still seemed the spit-fire I remembered but somehow older, wiser and maybe more settled.

"Hello, Kathreen, it's been awhile."

"I should say it has," Kathreen said. She pushed Suzanne and Sonny aside and sat down on the edge of my cot and grasped my hand. "Where the heck have you been?"

432

Maybe she wasn't so different after all. This was more like what I remembered. "It's a long story," I said. "better told when I can see and think straight."

"Huh," she laughed, "whenever was that?"

I chuckled at her frankness, "Somewhere back before I met the likes of you two," I said, my gaze going to Suzanne.

"Really, Colton," Suzanne said, "we'd like to know, it's been so terribly long."

"Here's the short of it," I said. "I got hit in the head by someone I never saw, was found by some half-breed Comanche that I don't remember, was sold to a fat Comanchero across the Rio, who in turn sold me to some mining operation down in Mexico that bought up kidnapped people to enslave in their mines. I worked in a mine for a short while, then was assigned range duties to manage a herd of cattle they kept up on a mesa, and was given a little cabin and a housekeeper named Penny. All this time I had amnesia and did not know who I was, or remember anything of my past, until one night I had a dream of you, Suzanne, and then it all came flooding back. Penny had been kidnapped from San Antonio and we made plans to escape, but the place was closely guarded by a strong man named Hutchinson, who had Indians working for him. One night we pulled it off, and made our way down the river, and nearly escaped, but were caught after we chose a wrong trail in the dark and had to back-track. Hutch and his henchman came upon us and we were drug back to the mining camp where Penny was thrown into the common house for women and I was locked up with the men in the cave where they kept the slave labor. I discovered that the cave had a secret passageway that led eventually through a net-work of underground caves and tunnels to an old Pueblo cliff dwelling some distance from the mining camp, but overlooking it. I had visited it once before from the camp.

From there I was able to stage another escape plan, was eventually able to sneak Penelope out of the women's barracks, and was all set to leave when Hutchinson discovered us. I had a big fight with him and would have been killed if Penny had not leaped on him from behind and sent the both of them over the cliff to their deaths. I retraced my way through the tunnels to climb out through a snake-infested den, upon a promontory that served as an Apache signaling site, and was just in time to witness the attack and burning of the gold camp by the Apache. For the next several days, I back-tracked the supply caravan's route in northern Mexico until I was attacked by a cougar whose neck, I somehow managed to miraculously break."

"Wait a minute," Sonny said. "A cougar attacked you?"

"Yeah, it was dark and I'd left my gunbelt by the fire when it jumped me. I thought I was a goner, but was fighting it for all my worth when we fell over backwards and the headlock I had it in snapped its neck after I landed on my elbow. There was a loud crack and the dang thing went limp in my arms. I was pretty badly clawed up and unconscious from loss of blood, when the next day this old Mexican goat herder found me—or his dog did. He got me back to his shack and nursed me back to health. You know, the way he fixed goat meat wasn't half bad. Anyway, I finally made my way to the Rio and El Paso, caught the stage to Saint Gaul, bought a horse and rode home. I guess you know what happened after that."

Sonny said coldly. "No, we don't know what happened after that. Why'd you take off?"

I swallowed hard, "Didn't figure there was anything left after you two were gone," I said lamely. "I could just see that tin-horn Sheriff Wiggins stringing me up for your murders, although at that point I really could not have cared less."

"We have been looking all over for you," Suzanne said. "Wiggins is no longer sheriff, Clay Anderson is."

"Anderson?" I was surprised. "That big galoot from the Box 7?"

"That's a whole other story in itself," Sonny said. "Where'd you go?"

"Wandered around the Llano Estacado and found this shave-tail kid, barely dry behind the ears, that some drunken bum had won from her pa in a poker game; and ended up rescuing her from his clutches. We made our way through the Palo Duro and a whole passel of Indians until I was finally able to get her to Fort Griffin and put her on the stage to Wade's Landing."

"Pearl said you were going on a cattle drive." Suzanne said.

"Yeah, I signed on with a herd headed up by, of all people, John Wesley Hardin, and managed to keep from killing him or being killed by him until we reached Abilene. I then took the Smokey Hill trail to here. And that's the short version."

Sonny said, "You rode for Hardin, what was that like?"

"Well, picture the most puffed up, obnoxious, over-bearing, ignorant, spoiled brat with a fast gun, and let your imagination run wild," I replied.

"So, what was the story about some ghost talking to you?" Kathreen put in.

"I have no idea on how to figure that," I said. "Apparently, there was some woman who died in a cholera epidemic at Fort Hayes a few years back, and the locals see her ghost every now and then; they figure she is waiting to be buried where the army promised to bury her."

"Did you see her?" Kathreen asked.

The three of them waited expectantly for my answer, so, feeling a little foolish I said, "Yeah, I was minding my own business, had just finished supper and was sitting by my campfire when I see this funny blue light gliding along up on the hill across the river. It came down towards me and disappeared in the brush on the other side. Pretty soon I forgot about it and went to bed. I had this same tent pitched and was awakened sometime later by the sounds of someone putting wood on my fire. I sat up and looked out and here was this pretty lady in a white bonnet and blue dress sitting and staring into the flames. I was dumbfounded, then she looked up at me and said, 'Suzanne and Sonny are looking for you.' You can imagine how shocked I was, it like to bowled me over, and when I looked again, she was gliding off across the river without even touching the water. What clinched it for me was that both my horses saw her too. I still don't know what to make of it."

"How do you think she knew?" Sonny said.

"God told her to do that," Suzanne replied.

We all cast curious and doubtful eyes on my sweetheart.

"God?" I said. "Would He do something like that?"

"I think He would," she replied. "He loves you Colton."

"You're saying that God used a haunt to tell me you were alive?" I was still having difficulty with the concept.

"Why not, or an 'angel unaware'," Suzanne said. "Didn't he use some demon-possessed slave girl to testify to the truth of who Paul and Silas were?[1] He can do anything He wants."

"By the way," Kathreen said, "What did you say to that bounty hunter back in Fort Hayes that made him put his gun away?"

I gave her a sheepish grin, "Told him if he didn't holster it by the time I counted to three, I'd plug 'im between the eyes."

"Would you have?" Kathreen said.

"Probably not, thank God he took my bluff and put it away."

"That's not all, Colt," Sonny said. "Did you know I was on the other side of this very mountain when I heard

Kathreen screaming and was able to rush to her aid in time to rescue her from the clutches of that deranged Frenchman?"

"What deranged Frenchman?" I said.

"Oh, Colt," Suzanne cried. "You don't know that Pierre LaRoush was with that outlaw gang. He's the one who shot you and then he chased Kathreen up to the top of the mountain and had her trapped out on a dead tree hanging over a cliff. He was going to kidnap her, then come for me, when Sonny showed up."

Kathreen said, "The scoundrel was assaulting me when Sonny ordered him to stop. I jumped away when Pierre began to rave and blaspheme God while waving his knife about."

I was mystified. What would Pierre LaRoush be doing here? Turning to Sonny I said, "I think I know the place, wha'd you do?"

"That's just it, I didn't have to do anything," he replied. "I was about to pull my gun and plug him when a bolt of lightning struck his uplifted knife and he was electrocuted instantly. It looks like God accepted his challenge and took him out."

For the first time, I was starting to have second thoughts about God having it in for me. If what they were telling me was true, it began to look like the Lord had orchestrated this whole adventure to bring us all back together. And if that was the case, then I was indeed indebted to Him, for not only did I have my beloved Suzanne and my brother back, I no longer had their blood on my hands.

Later, I was resting in the sun with Suzanne, as Sonny and Kathreen broke down my camp and brought in my horses to pack things up. I noticed Sonny's horse Tornado and Lightfoot not getting along too well, when a thought came to mind.

"Suzanne, do you trust me?"

"Why yes—I guess I do. Certainly, I do. Why do you ask?"

"I tried to shoot Sonny and ran out on you after I thought I'd killed you that horrible day. It was nothing but foul jealousy, and I've been struggling with that ever since. Can you trust me?"

"Yes—Colt, I love you."

"Even after I ran out on you?"

"You didn't run out on me."

"I did the second time."

"Not really, you thought I was dead. Would you have left if you knew I wasn't?"

"Probably, I was so hurt and mad at you and Sonny and God, and everybody. I quit trusting God after I thought I couldn't trust you and it wound me up here instead of at home where I should'a been, discovering the truth. Can you ever forgive me?"

"Yes! Things are not always like they seem, are they—do you trust me?" she asked.

I looked at her and hesitated a moment. "I know I love you, and can't live without you. I was wrong to lose faith in you, I should have known there was a good reason why you…" I never finished the sentence. "But yes, I do trust you and love you with all my heart. Do you think it's possible to obey God if you don't trust God?"

"No, although there's a lot of people who try," she said. "The scripture is clear on that, *'He that hath my commandments, and keepeth them, he it is that loveth me…'"*[1].

"I heard a preacher say once, 'You can't obey God if you don't trust Him'."

"Precisely!"

"I thought at the time, it sure explains why no one hardly does what God says… most of them don't even know if He exists, let alone that He's trustworthy."

I knew right then what this was really all about, me trusting God again, and doing what He wanted me to do, and that was to go back home and face the music.

"Lord," I prayed, "I'm sorry for not trusting you, for getting mad, and taking off like I did, and blaming you for all the bad stuff, when it was our enemy who caused it. I'm sorry for every bitter and mean thought I had about you, and for my jealousy too. I confess this as sin, and all the rest of my sins along with it, and ask you to forgive me."

Suzanne and I sat in silence for a moment and then she said a quiet, "Amen," and reached to squeeze my hand. "He does, you know?" she said.

I smiled and nodded at my sweetheart. It was abundantly clear that a great weight had lifted from my shoulders. Now all I had to do was go home and face mom and dad.

CHAPTER TWENTY-FIVE

I Will Arise And Go To My Father

New Mexico Territory, late summer 1871

"COLT, TELL ME ABOUT PENNY," SUZANNE said. The two of us were sitting beside the campfire one evening about two weeks later, on the trail south into New Mexico Territory. We had decided to take the Goodnight-Loving cattle route back, as Sonny was familiar with it, and it was a far more direct way than what we'd previously traveled coming to Colorado. I had found a couple of clean-limbed geldings with tack, and paid top prices in the gold camps, but needed animals for the girls to ride since their saddle horses had gone back to Texas with Hazelhurst. We'd returned Jimmy Allen's gold to him, and saw him recovering under the watchful eye of the Widow Douglas, then took our leave with a promise to write when we had reached Texas. Sonny and Kathreen had gone off spooning somewhere down towards the headwaters of the Pecos, which we had reached the day before. My arm was still stiff and sore, but I had taken the sling off and was attempting to exercise it a little while we relaxed, when she asked the question.

"Penny? Penelope Stauffer, probably seventeen or eighteen, and kidnapped by Comancheros from near her home in San Antone. She was given to me as a house-keeper after I bested one of the mine bosses in a boxing match in which she was the grand prize."

"You had to fight for her?"

"Yeah, I was not myself then and had no idea I was fighting for her, I was just fighting to keep that big goon from hitting me in the head. I didn't even know I had won her or why I had won her."

"So, what was she there for?" Suzanne seemed uneasy. "Why did they give her to you?"

"At first, I had no clue and we just stayed together. Once I remembered everything, I made certain she kept her distance."

"Kept her distance, were the two of you close then, before that?"

I felt my ears burn and was glad for the darkness. The line of questioning was uncomfortable, not because I had not acted honorably, but because I knew it was troubling to Suzanne. "Sweetheart, no, we were not close like you mean, we shared a one-room shack and a bed, but once I knew who I was, I slept on the floor after that. Nothing improper ever happened between us."

Suzanne was silent for a long moment, then she said, "What did she look like?"

"Okay, I guess, turned up nose, freckles, big eyes, brown hair—nice smile—nothing like you though."

"How about her figure?"

"That was okay, too, I guess."

"What did you do for privacy, surely you must have seen her...?" the question trailed off.

"Once, when we visited the pueblo, she took her clothes off to swim in a cistern that was up there and I saw her like that, but that was before I had recovered my memory. Otherwise, I always gave her plenty of space to dress and stuff."

"What happened when you saw her like that?"

"Nothing, I don't remember it too well, I seem to recall it provoked memories of you somehow although I didn't know it was you. It was sad and lonely, with a lost kind of feeling and sorta spooky too, like spirits or something were haunting the place. I remember wondering why I felt so sad, something seemed to be telling me I should not be looking at her like that. I told her to put her dress back on and she did. I felt that a couple of other times, too, when I had amnesia."

"Tell me," Suzanne urged.

"I don't remember it well at all, but there was a girl in the river once and then Mrs. Jones. I saw both of them without their clothes, and I remember how forbidden it all seemed."

"Who were they?"

For the next few minutes I explained what I could remember about Sarah's rescue from the Rio Grande and Mrs. Jones' attempted seduction. I was surprised to learn that Suzanne and Sonny had actually talked to Sarah.

"When I finally remembered who I was—who you were, it came at night with a troubling dream of those times. I had called out your name in my sleep and it woke Penny up. She shook me awake, and asked me, 'Who is Suzanne?' When I heard your name, I remembered everything and jumped out of that bed. That dream disturbed me—them being naked like that."

"You mean like the unveiling was taking place when it wasn't supposed to be?"

I looked at her with surprise. Suzanne had this mysterious, intent look on her face as she fixed those incredible blue eyes on me.

"Exactly," I said. "I couldn't quite figure why that all reminded me of you, but that's it. I was—am still—waiting for your unveiling."

"Too bad that Snowshoe Preacher was gone," Suzanne said wistfully.

"Yeah—probably just as well though."

Suzanne gave me a surprised look, "What do you mean? Didn't you just say you..." She didn't finish.

"Looks like we're going to have to wait and do this thing proper," I said. "Otherwise, your pop will probably think I stole you."

"Papa gave you his permission to marry me."

I swallowed hard, "Well, that was a long time ago and permission can be withdrawn. I think it best I face him after what I've done and tread softly with your heart. We want our folks' blessing, don't we?"

"Indeed we do," Suzanne said, "but you may be interested to know that papa told me to come and find you—to follow my heart and our story."

"He said that?"

"He did, he said, *'I don't know what adventures, pleasures, unhappiness or peril wait for you on this trip, but I know you have to go, that you will not be complete until you do.'*"

"Wow!" I said, "Your pop's a smart man. I'm glad you took his advice. I was one lost cowpoke until you showed up." I reached over and pulled her from her seat onto my lap and held her close while staring into her eyes. I could see the firelight dancing in their blue depths, then I bent and kissed her full red lips. She responded, kissing me back, at first properly, modest, and chaste, like the lady she was—then with more intensity until I felt a tentative probing of her tongue against my lips. Startled I broke from the embrace, and pulled back. *There it was again.*

"What's wrong?" Suzanne started to sit up. "Was that too forward of me?"

I grinned at the frown furrowing her pretty brow.

"No honey—apples."

"Apples? I don't understand."

"That mysterious scent of apples—on your breath—I had completely forgotten about that.

"What a happy discovery again!"

Suzanne lay back into my arms and smiled shyly, a finger between her lips and a fingernail tapping against her pretty white teeth. "You like that?"

"I love it," I said. "You look so good in love. I may not be privileged to your unveiling yet, but I can surely explore all those other delicious delicacies we shared. Do you remember our kissing in the teepee up on the Sweetgrass?"

Smiling she said, "I do, we nearly got into trouble."

"How about at our cabin site on the perfect little hill— Suzanne's hill?"

"Oh, Colt," Suzanne suddenly sat up. "You don't know! The Indians burned our little cabin down."

"You're not serious," I said.

"Yes, it's true. Sonny, Rusty, and Lance withstood an Indian attack up there, and said the whole place had been destroyed, burnt to the ground. Sonny figured it was a good thing we weren't there, that we may not have survived."

I was dumbfounded, all that hard work gone up in smoke. "You say they were attacked, what happened?"

"Sonny could tell you better. Some Comanche were trying to take some horses they had and they took a position on top of our little hill and made a stand for it."

"Let me guess," I said. "Sonny threw a rattlesnake and it caught their chief around the throat and bit him to death."

Suzanne's face registered surprise. "How did you know that?"

"I heard a cowboy relating that escapade to us boys one night while sitting around the campfire. It's taken on gendary proportions."

"Sonny seems to have something of a reputation as a great medicine man with the Indians too," she laughed. "They call him the Buffalo Man, did you know he survived a buffalo stampede?"

"I did not," I said. It seemed to me that my older brother had a lot more to tell me than what I had been told. I sat staring into the fire then with Suzanne sitting quietly beside me.

"Don't you have to break your engagement with Sonny?" I asked quietly.

"Engagement with Sonny? He and I are not engaged." Suzanne seemed surprised at the question.

"You're not?"

"No—well, I guess it was more or less implied, but we never actually got officially engaged."

"What did you get?"

Suzanne was quiet for a moment and then drew a deep breath. "I told him I would be his girl," she said.

"Oh." I was needing to go get private and got to my feet. "Think I'll take a little walk," I said.

"You want me to come with you?" Suzanne asked uneasily.

"Naw, I won't be gone long. Give a holler if you need me."

I wasn't really having a problem with my older brother and Suzanne any longer, but thinking it through, it seemed like it would be best to close the chapter in that book. I would make it a point when next I saw him.

A short cry from Suzanne riveted me in mid-stride and sent me racing back to our campfire. We were still in Comanche country and although we had seen nothing of the Indians, I was berating myself for having left Suzanne alone. I had rescued her once from the Kiowa, I may not be so fortunate a second time. When I arrived back at camp, I found Suzanne sitting quietly by the fire.

"What's wrong, why did you holler?"

Suzanne slowly looked up at me with big sad eyes. "You said if I needed you to holler."

"Yeah—what do you need?"

"You."

A wave of tenderness and love swept over me. I dropped to my knees, gathered her into my arms and held her close. "You have me, all of me, I am forever yours, and I love you so." I squeezed her tightly.

"Can I sleep in your tent with you?" she said.

"What'll we do with Sonny?"

"He can take my place in Kate's tent."

"We can ask them," I said. "Do you think that's a good idea?"

"Yeah—no, I don't know, all I know is that I don't want to be apart from you anymore. The most horrid time of my life was when you were missing. I saw you one time, I don't know if it was a vision or a dream or what, but at one very low point of that whole time, I saw you in a dark place, like a cave or tunnel. You were calling to me and reaching out and then you began to fade away like a ghost until you disappeared. It was horrible, like you were in your grave."

I immediately was reminded of the time I had been beaten and brought back to the mines after Penny and my attempted escape. They had thrown me into the cave that served as the men's quarters and slammed and locked those big steel doors shut.

"I was in a place like that," I said.

Suzanne looked at me in wonder and I told her of that day and of my ultimately finding the escape tunnel.

"I think it a wonder that when one gets to the place where you think there is no hope, no way out, God always has a way." Suzanne said. "He certainly heard my prayers for you and brought you back. Maybe not in my good time, but most assuredly in His."

I was nodding assent and silently thanking the Lord when Sonny and Kathreen came walking up.

"Sonny," Suzanne said. "I can no longer be your girl."

Her declaration left the three of us with our mouths hanging open. I was a little embarrassed, Sonny fidgeted like a kid in church having drunk too much sweet tea, and Kathreen said, "Talk about stating the obvious, Suze, you have a way of clearing a room—or even a whole prairie."

I wrapped an arm around my girl and pulled her close. "Thanks," I said. "That ought to settle that."

"Glad you brought that up, Suzanne," Sonny said awkwardly. "We just came back to tell you two that Kathreen has consented to be my wife."

————

The Goodnight-Loving Trail followed the Pecos River south through New Mexico Territory and we pressed on for Texas. The girls had prevailed on us to fashion together a teepee that would accommodate all four of us, and it enabled us to enjoy the relative safety of close quarters, to say nothing of good companionship, and sharing our various stories in detail. Sonny and I could keep a close eye out for danger from external forces as well as the internal ones at play with our sweethearts. There were definitely times in our love-making that... well let's just say it's a good thing the other couple was there— for all of us.

I awoke with a start to find Suzanne had climbed from her bedroll and was kissing my face.

"Wake up, sleepy head, Sonny's already up and getting set to break camp."

I sat up in bed, yawned, rubbed sleep from my eyes, and then blinked at the lovely image of Suzanne perched on her knees. The sunlight streamed in through the open door of the teepee and silhouetted her lovely form in all its glory through her night clothes.

"Come here," I said, and pulled her suddenly to me with my good arm and began smothering her face with kisses.

"Oh, Colt, your beard is scratching me, you need to not kiss me so hard before you shave."

"I'm sorry darlin', stay right here and I'll go scrape my face."

"Oh you... one more kiss then, gently please," she said, and pulled back to close her eyes, purse her lips, and hold her face up for the requested buss.

I quelled the ravenous beast within me and gave her a soft gentle kiss. "How's that?" I said.

"Just right, now get your britches on and get out of here so I can get dressed."

Sonny rapped on the side of the teepee. "Hurry up, you two, I want to make fifty miles today. I think we can get to Horse Head Crossing if we hit the trail soon."

I crawled out into the bright sunlight of what was already promising to be a hot day and got up to wander over to the fire and the waiting coffee pot. Kathreen poured a cup and handed it to me.

"Wish I had some tea," she said.

"Better get used to roughen it if you're going to get in harness with that lanky son-of-a-gun," I said nodding to where Sonny was saddling up Hank.

"Oh, I am, but I expect we'll still be able to find ways to set the doilies out. Your mom does."

"Yeah, she does," and I gulped hard at the reminder that I would soon be facing mom and dad and the things I'd done. I was dreading it, but I had to do it. I would sure be glad when it was over, even if I had to face jail time, anything would be better than the way I had disappointed mom and dad. Just one more reason why it was best to hold off on Suzanne and me tying the knot. Could I expect her to wait if I ended up a jailbird? "Lord, I hope she will."

It's funny how we always expect the worse. We had been on the trail for over an hour and moving down a draw to where the river flowed along cut-banks of clay with higher canyon walls on either side. We were riding in single file with Sonny in the lead, followed by the pack mule Hank, Kathreen, Suzanne, and me bringing up the rear, leading Sidekick. My packhorse didn't seem to mind dragging the teepee poles we were bringing along, but I could tell Lightfoot was thoroughly disgusted with the whole procession. My mind was so preoccupied with what was waiting for me back at the ranch, that I had failed entirely to see that my cowpony was upsetted off. I could just imagine what he was thinking.

"Never mind, old hoss," I said to his twitching ears. "You'll get to be your own freestyle broomtail soon's we get back. I'm sure there'll be plenty chance for you to run away from the horseflies once I face the music at home and get back to range-riding unless, of course, I end up in the hoosegow." Lightfoot just snorted me one and looked wall-eyed back at my right boot toe. I thought for a moment he was asking me to spur him one so's we could bust out past those two female equestrians and take the lead.

"Equestrians?" I said. "Those girls are Baptist... at least Suzanne is. I don't know if Kathreen's anything yet."

Lightfoot rolled his eyes like I was a hopeless cause, and then let me know he also took a dim view of that smart-alecky dark stallion; he was about the ugliest jug-head he'd ever seen, prancing around up front and playing the big stud like that... it wasn't like it was his fault some jackassed, two-legged numbskull gelded him when he was just a baby. 'Course he did allow as how he didn't have to act like some infernal idgit whenever some silly mare came dancing around winking at everybody. He informed me that somebody should have a talk with the grulla regarding his manners; he was plumb rude, always nippin', and bitin', whenever civilized horses came around. He had half a notion to have a show-down with the big fella.

"You don't have the equipment for it," I kidded him. He told me to shut up, but then wanted to know if I would lend him my shootin' iron, and I outright laughed at him. That's when he broke wind, locked his jaw, and shut up for awhile.

Suzanne had turned in her saddle and called back. "What you laughing about?"

"Nothin', darlin'," I drawled, "just this fool horse."

"What's he doing?" she called.

I chuckled and jerked up on the reins. "He wants to shoot Tornado."

"Shoot Tornado?" Suzanne was puzzled. "How do you know that?"

"I just do," I said.

"Colt, do you talk to your horse?"

"Certainly, darlin', doesn't everyone?"

My sweetheart looked skeptical. "Does he talk back?"

"Well, not in so many words, but I can tell what he's thinkin'."

"So, what's he thinking right now?"

"Probably a cross between dumping my sorry carcass in that patch of prickly pear over there, and a long cool drink in the river."

"What's that got to do with shooting Sonny's horse?"

"Shh!" I said, "He's already forgot about that, don't remind him." Lightfoot just chuffed and pulled at the bit.

I leaned back in the saddle, pulled my hat off and wiped my brow with the sleeve of my arm, then stretched my neck and let my eyes trail up into the blue of the sky. It sure was hot, too bad we couldn't hole up under the cottonwoods and take a dip to cool off. I settled my hat back on my head, and dropped my gaze, when something on the ridge above us caught my attention. Silhouetted against the blue of the sky was an Indian warrior in full war paint and regalia, riding along parallel to us and keeping pace.

Uneasy, I wanted to signal Sonny, but feared scaring the girls, so I kept my peace and watched the brave. My eyes wandered to the ridge across the river, and I was surprised to see not one, but several Indians riding in single file on that side of us as well. They seemed to be in no hurry, just rode along with an occasional glance in our direction. Soon, the rider on our side was joined by another and then another. It was plain to me that a war-like bunch of Comanche had us bottled up between them and were probably waiting for a good place to swoop down and end all of our matrimonial plans, as well as any others.

"Suzanne," I called. "You got all your guns loaded?"

"I think so, Colt, why do you ask?"

"Just wondering, holler up at Kathreen and see if her's are."

"Kathreen, Colt wants to know if your guns are full."

"You bet," she said. "Sonny just told me this was where Buffalo Hump had his camp on that first trip with Mr. Loving and Mr. Goodnight."

"Good," I called. "You girls hot?"

"Yes," Kathreen hollered back, "can we stop?"

"Keep ridin'," Sonny called gruffly.

I knew then Sonny was aware of our escort, and it was a queer deal. The Indians seemed to take no hostile action towards us, even when we crossed several places where they could easily have raced down and caught us out in the open. It was almost as if they were escorting us out of their country... without bothering us. I thought about what Suzanne had said of Sonny, how he was regarded as some Medicine, Buffalo Man with super powers. Could it be that he was held in reverence by these primitive people, and was being given safe passage through their country? Stranger things had happened. My trust in God ratcheted up another notch or two. Once again, I felt a deep gratitude for the Lord's care and watch over us.

The Indians accompanied us for another hour or more and then they were gone as suddenly as they had appeared. If the girls had seen them, they had had enough sense to not show it, and we continued on for awhile longer before Sonny led us down to a low spot along the river to water our horses and cool off. Kathreen was the first one to speak.

"Didn't you two see those damn Indians?"

"Kathreen," Suzanne said, "you shouldn't swear, after all, the Lord just delivered us out of their clutches."

"Yeah, well, He did, but these two just rode on like they weren't even there."

"Wha'd you expect us to do, Kate, open up on 'em with four guns?" Sonny said.

"Well, I don't know, they scared the pea-waddin' out of me, how about you Sue?"

"Scared I was, best friend—scared half to death."

"Why didn't you tell us of the danger?" Kathreen demanded.

"I was hoping we wouldn't have to." I said.

"Wouldn't have to? How long were they following us?" Suzanne asked.

"Most of the morning," Sonny said.

"Well, what else are you not telling us?" Kathreen asked.

I shrugged, "That's about it."

"Can we get down and cool off—maybe have some lunch?" Suzanne said.

Sonny nodded and we all swung down and started digging in our saddle bags for lunch.

———

We arrived at Wade's Landing two days later and rode through town amidst curious stares of the few folks that were about. I stood by the picket fence gate, my hat in hand, as Suzanne and Kathreen ran up the walk to the Kluesmans' house. I saw her mother come to the door and then cry in delight as she embraced her daughter. For a moment they held each other, and then her mother's penetrating gaze looked back at where I was standing. She pushed her daughter back giving her a kiss on the cheek, and then held out a hand to Kathreen, welcoming her back. Sonny had removed a couple of the girls' grips and muttered, "You coming?" to me as he squeezed past and walked up to the porch. Mrs. Kluesman stepped back and greeted him as he carried the bags into the parlor, then she turned to face me and beckoned me to come up the walk.

With feet like lead I walked towards Suzanne's mom, my eyes concentrating on the path before me.

"Hello, Colt," she said, "it's been a long, long time."

I nodded, "Yes, Ma'am… I—I've come to realize how dreadfully wrong I was in shooting Sonny and Suzanne and then taking off. I am here to beg your forgiveness. Can you forgive me?"

Suzanne and Kathreen stood silently waiting on the porch, their eyes fixed on Mrs. Kluesman; Sonny had stopped his rustling around in the parlor. All of us held our breath waiting for her response.

Mable Kluesman took a step towards me, closing the distance between us, and wrapped her arms around me, holding me close. "Oh, yes, dear boy. I forgive you, although I do not feel I have anything to forgive you for. All the dreadful circumstances of what you must have gone through—I can only wonder and thank God that you are safely back with us."

I tried to swallow past a lump in my throat, "Thanks," I managed to mutter. "I need to talk to Mr. Kluesman, where is he?"

Suzanne's mother nodded over my shoulder and I turned around to see Gunner Kluesman standing in the walk, his firm gaze fixed on my face.

"Mr. Kluesman, I've come home to face the consequences of my actions. What I did in the shooting of my brother, and the unintended results to Suzanne and your family are inexcusable and have caused you all unwarranted grief. I am here to accept whatever charges you deem proper for my outbreak against you, Mrs. Kluesman and Suzanne."

Gunner rocked back on his heels, his jaw clenched once and fire flashed in his eyes for a moment. "Do you have any idea what you put her mother and me through, to say nothing of our daughter?"

"Yes, sir, I was wrong, very wrong, to go off like that... I'm sorry, very sorry. Can you please forgive me?"

"Oh, Colt... come here, son." The big blacksmith held out a burly arm to me and I stumbled towards him, tears welling in my eyes. We embraced and slapped each other on the back while I mumbled, "I am truly sorry, pop—do you forgive me?"

"Of course, son, I have no charges against you—other than stupid," and he gave a gentle laugh.

Suzanne, her mother and Kathreen stood watching us with tears streaming down their faces, then broke out in nervous laughter as Gunner pummeled me on the back and near squished the life out of me.

"Welcome back, son, welcome back... all of you. God certainly has answered our prayers."

———

"Well, that went better than I thought it would," I said to Lightfoot. I was pushing the red horse up the road from town to the ranch ahead of Sonny, who was following on Tornado with Hank and Sidekick in tow. Fear and trepidation mixed with an eagerness to get this over with had my horse in a fast trot. My brother was hanging back, giving me space to meet the folks on my own. It suddenly occurred to me that I had never really asked Sonny to forgive me. After all, he was the one who I had transgressed against the greatest. I pulled my horse in so hard that the pony nearly sat on his tail in the dust of the road. He may have even said a bad word, but I was too busy pondering my glaring oversight to pay any attention. Sonny came trotting up to stop and look at me questioningly.

"What's up?" he said.

"Sonny, I've got to be the biggest nincompoop ever. I just realized in all that's happened that I never apologized to you for shooting you."

Sonny looked a little sheepish. "Yeah, I know."

"Brother, I am sorry. Of all the dumb things I have ever done, that was the most senseless, asinine, downright idiotic, foolish thing I've ever done."

Sonny just sat there looking at me and nodding his head, his mouth turned down at the corners. "You could say that," he said objectively. "You'll get no argument from me."

"Sonny, you're the best friend I've ever had and far and away the best pard and brother a feller could ever want. You got to know I never ever wanted to shoot you. I have regretted it ever since."

"Yeah, I know," Sonny nodded his head again.

"I should have kept trust in you—so do you forgive me?"

"I will if you ask."

"Sonny will you please forgive me for not trusting you and tryin' to plug you?" I said.

"Yep."

"Thanks, and thanks for what you did for Suzanne too, I'm eternally in your debt."

"S'all right, you better ride on and let Mom and Dad see you're okay."

I nodded and goosed Lightfoot on up the road towards home.

When the ranch came into view, I felt a pang at the old familiar scene. It was near three years since I'd seen the place but little had changed. There was smoke from the kitchen chimney, the two long windows on the upstairs gable end that always looked like sad old eyes, and the Chinaberry tree in the front yard with a rope swing hanging from a branch. Dust rose from a corral where one of the cowboys was working a horse on a length of rope, and it looked like mom was hanging some wash on the clothesline. My father was working on a piece of machinery at the tool shed, and as I drew closer, a girl that turned out to be Pearl, banged the front door open and ran out to leap off the porch, followed closely by Tommy, who threw an apple-core at her. I almost didn't recognize him, he had grown so tall. He yelled at Pearl, calling her a "dumb nut!" and then the two kids stopped in their tracks and stared after me with mouths agape. I trotted on past them touching the brim of my hat, and rode to where mom, her back to me, was stretching a sheet on the line. I stopped and slid to the ground. Upon hearing the horse, she turned with a surprised look on her face at the unexpected visitor.

"Hi, Mom!"

Mother's face registered confusion, and then shock, as she stared intently at me, then with a scream she dropped her laundry and rushed to embrace me.

"Oh, Colton—my son, my son," she cried brokenly, then held me tightly and sobbed and sobbed as if her heart was broken.

I held her close and tenderly patted her on the back. "I'm alright, Mom, I'm alright. Sonny and Suzanne, they found me, I've come home."

"Oh, thank God you have," Mom said. "I have prayed and prayed for you to come back. It has been so long. Let me look at you." She pushed me back at arms' length and stared into my face, then burst into more weeping and buried her face into the front of my shirt, her arms clutching me tight. I looked past her as my father walked up to stop just beyond where we were standing, a grave look on his face.

"Dad, I..."

"You've come back," he said.

"Yes, Dad. I am not worthy to be here, I have done some terrible things and nearly tore this family apart. I know I probably can't be one of the family again, but I'd gladly live as one of the hands in the bunkhouse and work for nothing... maybe just my keep... if you'll let me. If I have to go to jail, I will."

Dad just stood there slowly nodding, a knowing look on his face. His eyes seemed to glisten, and his expression changed, as a slight smile seemed to play about tremulous lips. It was then that I noticed he was silently crying, or chuckling, or maybe both at the same time. He reached out both arms, not trusting himself to speak, and I broke from my mother's embrace and ran to dad's.

Sonny rode up and found us that way, then sat his horse with a big cheese-eating grin, enjoying the sight of our reunion.

Grant called to Tommy, "Go tell Pops to kill that corn-fed steer, we're having us a barbeque."

FINIS'

EPILOG

DAD, MOM AND EVERYBODY FORGAVE ME
and I was restored to my place in the family. We had a
great feast and I spent long hours telling all that had happened to me. The Kluesmans came out, and at one point
I went to Suzanne's father and asked him again for his
daughter's hand. He held up both hands in front of me
and backing away, said, "There is no way I am inserting
myself back in between you two, if there is one thing
for certain, it is that God intends for you to be together.
My only regret is that I didn't pay better attention and
encourage my daughter to follow her heart instead of our
collective heads. You marry her and the sooner the better."

It took a couple of weeks to make all the arrangements and finally on a Saturday in September, Preacher
Cummings performed the ceremony at our little church;
with practically the whole community in attendance.
Suzanne, looking so good in love and the wedding dress
she'd sewn, was beautiful beyond telling. Sonny stood
up for me along with Tommy, and of course Kathreen
was Suzanne's maid of honor. Becky and Pearl, Rusty
and Lance were all part of the wedding party as well.
Pearl had a long talk with me and informed me that the
only reason she was bowing out gracefully and letting
Suzanne marry me instead of her, was because she
couldn't play the piano. I allowed as how that was reason
enough, and she said that Tommy looked like me, and
was more her own age anyhow, and then she walked off

as if that was the end of that. I chuckled and smiled at her resolute departure.

I am taking my bride by coach on an extended honeymoon to Saint Louis, and it is our intention to look up Ben Martin and give him the reward monies from the poster, once we reach San Antone. I will pay him out of my gold stash, and Kathreen will return her father's cash once she goes home, if she doesn't spend it all first. We stopped the first night at the fine new hotel in Saint Gaul, after a long, but too short a stage ride, which we had all to ourselves. Suzanne seemed to be preoccupied with my hands, holding them up to her face; rubbing, squeezing and kneading them, as if she'd just discovered I had hands for the first time. It was funny and a little weird... but nice. We have just enjoyed a fine wedding dinner in the hotel's dining room, and now I am sitting savoring a cup of coffee and looking across the table into the most beautiful eyes in the whole world.

Unbidden, a flood of memories assails my thoughts and I recall the long and twisted trail that finally landed me here. I am filled with both gratitude and wonder. I'm still not sure about everything: all that stuff about who I am, what I am doing here, and where I am going, but I know part of it. First, I'm one of the luckiest men in the world, now that I am Suzanne's husband. I am also one of God's kids, and part of a great family here as well. Second, not everything is what it seems to be. There is an unseen world at war, an enemy that seeks to rob, kill, and destroy, and that he was arrayed against Suzanne and me. But this only serves to remind me to step up into the adventure, while practicing justice with an eye to mercy, and—the hard part—walking humbly before God. I long to bring my strength to Suzanne... to fight for her as she fought for me, and to fight for the good life the Lord has promised us, while remembering to keep an eye on my motives. They can be so sneaky. Finally, I know this is not the end of the story, in fact this is only the beginning, the dress-rehearsal for the real things of forever. A fact I haven't thought enough about, but as I do, it's always a new astonishment... that we are going to live forever... where everything is the way it's supposed to be, and that Suzanne and I, joined together by God, will enjoy Him forever. That once there, we will be whole, real people, our true selves, and all our glory will be in knowing Him as we are known. Speaking of that, I look intently at Suzanne. Right now I know where else I'm going, and some veils will be stripped away. There's a heaven of another kind right up those stairs over there.

"Colton, what are you thinking about?" Suzanne said, a pretty blush suffusing her cheeks.

I smiled my delight, "You," I said, "about heaven in your arms, and having, and holding you."

"You think it's like that?" she blushed.

"It will be. Don't you remember our trip to the Sweetgrass?"

"How could I forget? But that was so long ago, do you still want me like that—all the apples and honey and wine?"

"More than ever. Do you still want me like that?"

"Oh yes! Much, much more than ever."

"To be like Eve with me?"

Suzanne blushed and lowered her head, looking shyly up through sparkling eyes and my heart lurched into my throat.

"Yes," she whispered.

I arose from the table, my heart thudding in my chest, and reached to pull back her chair, while she stood to her feet. Taking her arm, I led her up the stairs to the door of our room and then opened it. As Suzanne made to step into the room I suddenly swept her up into my arms and, kicking the door open wider, I carried her over the threshold and gently set her on the bed. Turning, I closed the door and locked it, my senses swirling in pure joy. At last our time had arrived, paper-work done, no one to say don't, none to disapprove, no green snakes to mar the sacredness and privacy of this moment. Just this sweet girl, me, and the Lord's blessing.

Thus, new life began.

THE END

END NOTES:

Chapter Four—Page 44,

1 The first United States patent for a reel lawn mower was granted to Amariah Hills on January 12, 1868. In 1870, Elwood McGuire of Richmond, Indiana designed a human-pushed lawn mower, which was very lightweight and a commercial success.

Chapter Six—Page 63,

1 Sherlock Holmes smoked a Churchwarden pipe.

Chapter Fifteen—Page 115,

1 Crowleytown's Atlantic Glass Works in Crowleytown, New Jersey, is often credited with producing the first Mason jars, which were embossed with the words "Mason's Patent **Nov. 30th. 1858**." But only a year later, Mason sold that patent and others to The Sheet Metal Screw Company, which was run by Lewis. R. Boyd.

Chapter Seventeen—Page 167,

1 *Sentinel Hill Haunting*—When a cholera epidemic hit Fort Hays, Kansas in 1867, a young woman named Elizabeth Polly was among those who attended to and comforted the ill and dying. Some say she was a trained nurse, while others maintain she had no medical training. When she wasn't working tirelessly with the sick soldiers, she was said to take a moment to stroll upon

nearby Sentinel Hill. Eventually she too, contracted the disease and her dying wish was to be buried upon the hill. In the fall of 1867, she was given a full military funeral but alas, the soldiers were unable to grant her last wish as the hill is composed of bedrock, so she was buried at its base. The first recorded report of her sighting was made by a man named John Schmidt in 1917, who reported seeing a woman dressed in blue walking across his farm towards Sentinel Hill. Following her, he saw the apparition walk into one of his sheds, but when he arrived no one was there and nothing had been disturbed. In the 1950s a patrolman claimed to have hit a woman dressed in a long blue dress with a white bonnet with his patrol car. However, when the officer got out of the car, there was no woman and no damage to the vehicle. Elizabeth's ghost continues to roam the hill in her long blue dress and white bonnet. Purportedly, her ghostly spirit emits a blue light and the locals began to call her the Blue Light Lady. The ghost of Elizabeth Polly has been seen many times over the years haunting the lonely hilltop that she had frequented so often in life. http://www.legendsofamerica.com/ks-forthays.html

Chapter Twenty Four—Page 255
1 Acts 16:16-18

Page 256,
1 John 14:21

CPSIA information can be obtained
at www.ICGtesting.com
Printed in the USA
FSOW01n2011171117
41367FS

9 781545 600191